ANNIE RUSSO

Tenacity Born

J.L. Baumann

POST MORTEM PUBLICATIONS

ISBN: 978-1-941880-30-2

PUBLISHER'S NOTE:

This is a work of fiction. Names, characters, places, business establishments, educational institutions, locales, and incidents are either the product of the author's imagination or are used fictitiously. Any resemblance to actual persons (living or dead) or real events is entirely coincidental. Where trademarked products appear in this book and Postmortem Publications was aware of a trademark claim, the designations have been printed in initial capital letters. Any titles of literature, news events, music titles, or lyrics printed herein are to be considered solely a reflection of the reality of the times and not to be construed as original content by the author.

Chapter One

What kind of a person would wear a cowboy hat in this neighborhood? I thought as I studied him, unseen from the bay window in the living room. It was the afternoon paperboy delivering the newspaper and I just couldn't take my eyes off him as he plodded on from house to house.

Then, as my grandmother walked into the room from the foyer, interrupting my side show, she casually mentioned, "You know son, he looks to be a very nice boy and he's probably your age as well," she added, shuffling on to the kitchen and not expecting a reply.

And so, I went back to study my new discovery, the world's only cowboy newspaper delivery boy, and decided him to be of average height, average build, and was quite notably going about his business at an average speed. *How weird*, I thought to myself. In addition to the larger than life Stetson which he wore, as I downwardly observed, there was a very expensive, fringe covered suede coat that was followed by a pair of camel hair trousers. Naturally, he also had on a pair of pointed-toed cowboy boots to match.

It was a grey and nasty day outside, with three days of old snow on the ground. The wind had made it bitter, but not so cold as to keep the mounds of snow piled up against the sides of the road from melting. I could literally feel the freezing air as it relentlessly blew against the window panes before me and, because of this chill, had directly gotten a new appreciation for the relatively ugly sweater that I had been wearing.

Now, all these conditions had made it perfect for slipping, sliding, and otherwise losing your footing to thereupon fall directly upon your butt, especially when wearing cowboy boots, or so I thought, but this did not happen. Slowly instead, the buckaroo just seemed to dissolve away, back into the bitter cold from whence he had come, but not before my mind had gotten emblazoned with one of the most bizarre fashion statements ever to have appeared in the small suburban town of Lenape.

It was not the authenticity, nor the ostentatious cost of the garments which he wore that had generated his distinct individualism, -it was where he wore them. For you see, the Native Americans who were the original inhabitants of this area were long gone due to the British, not the cowboys.

The real fact was, that instead of risking their inevitable and utter annihilation by the relentless invasion of their lands, which they had come to realize was not preventable, these native inhabitants simply took the pittance offered them to leave, and without further bloodshed on either side, simply abdicated their homelands and went west. This of course, was much to the delight of the English, so much so, that they hence did the honorable thing by naming the town after them. Thus, until this very day, there was a never a need for a cowboy, let alone for a cowboy hat, because by now the Lenape Indians had long since become a myth.

Lenape was a small town. In fact, it was only a borough of three miles square and quite proudly boasted that it had no industry. The few blue-collar residents which resided there all worked in the outlying industrial centers, while the majority of its inhabitants, who considered themselves to be professionals by trade, worked in the big city. There was a merchant class who owned the small retail establishments located in the center of the town that never made the merchants wealthy, but still gave them a great sense of perceived pride, and a goodly measure self-respect to boot.

Lenape was the quintessential Early American town. It was replete with all its downtown street names manifesting themselves in fact, such as Church Street, Elm Street, Park

Avenue, and most patiently, Main Street, which did proudly showplace its quaint, yet efficient, railroad station precisely adjacent to the First Presbyterian Church. With the church's spire standing as the tallest and most majestic structure in the entire hamlet, its prominence did not go unnoticed by anyone. Besides its inherent obligation to reach out unto the heavens above, its function was to also respectfully lord over the town's oldest graveyard, which existed directly beneath its shadow, as did everyone else in the hamlet.

The town had not one school bus, for it was small enough that the entirety of its student population was deemed to live within walking distance of the school. This did not mean that Lenape had no early morning traffic though, for there was indeed a flourish of activity. On any given workday, there was always a prodigious amount of professional men to be routinely and systematically deposited at the train station by the non-working housewives of the community. Intrepidly thereafter, the majority of these women would then drive on, predominantly by station wagon, to one of the various town schools in order to relieve themselves of their children, some still attired in their bathrobes.

The "new" Lenape High School was graced with the architectural imprint of Frank Lloyd Wright, befitting and affirming the town's commitment to reflect a progressive atmosphere. The "Old" Lenape High School, built in the style of an antebellum courthouse, thereafter became the Jr. High School from whence graduation from it not only signified that a greater degree of personal responsibility had been learned, but certified as well that all of its graduates were ready indeed for the next level of indoctrination.

I walked to school alone. The distance was only four blocks long, and so far, it had never been an eventful experience for me whatsoever. All the other students, however, who also walked this daily journey, usually traveled along in a multitude of small defined groups, clustered together, which seemed to me more a function of their family's status than anything else. My family, being residents of the town for less than a year, had achieved no status at all and so I had thus determined that I was just as uneventful to them as they were to me. Of course, this did not matter to me in the slightest, since the end conclusion was always the same, rain or shine, with or without the snow.

Once I had arrived at my locker, I would always reassemble my garments, rearrange my books and papers, and then proceeded on as scheduled. This path, supposedly to enlightenment, accomplished by classroom to classroom reconnoitering and habitual repetition, always seemed to me wholly uninspiring. Even the other inmates who surrounded me never changed much either, for we were always seated in the same alphabetical order. *Oh, my poor nugatory plight,* I thought on many a day.

And so, it was, that on precisely one of these great moments of uninspiration that the school's announcement speaker unexpectedly came on, demanding everyone's attention to then shockingly blurt out, "At 12:30 central standard time the President of the United States, John F. Kennedy, has been shot in Dallas, Texas!"

Immediately thereafter, as an utter and complete silence filled the room, Eugene Kavanagh cried out in horror, "Oh my God!" only to have the dead silence promptly return.

For about a five-minute period, a temper of apprehension and anxiety had pervaded the entire school until eventually the deafening silence was broken once again by the audio system now announcing, "Due to the solemn events of today, the school will be canceling *all* classes for the rest of the afternoon. All students are hereby released from the school grounds and expected to go home."

Everyone collected their possessions from inside their desks, and with almost no sound to be heard, stood up and proceeded to the classroom door. Then, once I had arrived at my locker and had deposited into it all of the academic materials which I currently had in my possession, there to be entombed until after the crisis was under control, I, like everyone else, promptly left for the day.

I tried to remember the last time I was let out of school early, but I could not. Also, in having to tread home with no possessions to carry simply seemed strange to me, and consequently my thoughts began to wander. The benign grey day had seemed to rob all color from the well-kept Elizabethan homes which presented themselves to the uneven, cracked, and equally grey sidewalk upon which I traveled. The anticipated winter season had arrived early. There was no sound of grass cutting, hedge clipping, pool splashing, or music playing to be heard anywhere. Humanity had locked themselves tightly inside their homes now, resolutely waiting for the spring to reappear and bring back the Kodachrome of life to all who anticipated surviving the oncoming winter.

Being in no hurry to go home, I stopped for a moment to examine the residence of the town's only orthodontist and found out that my intuition was confirmed: it was indeed exactly as rumored—a very large and extravagant manor, complete with a long wrap around black iron veranda which had most flamboyantly vaunted itself over the home's pure white exterior in an obvious attempt to artistically excogitate the worth of his fees.

Then, curiously, I noticed that another student was now approaching me from my left as I still stood facing the doctor's not-so-humble abode. Unconcerned, I did not move, leaving the choice to pass by, confrontationally or not, to him. Eventually, upon reaching the boundary of my domain, he stopped, looked at me directly and then formally stated, "Hi, I'm Eugene Kavanagh. I live down the street from you. You're in my history class."

"Yeah, you sit in the middle of the room," I acknowledged.

He wore no hat, nor I, for John F. Kennedy was the first president of the United States not to have worn one in public and had still been hailed as one of the most handsome and fashionable young men in the country without one, despite the hat lobbyists. There did exist at that time, however, a second compelling argument that perhaps Sean Connery, a.k.a. James Bond, was even more handsome and fashionable than Kennedy, and certainly more exciting, but he wore no hat either, so the argument became moot. Socially it was just "not cool" to go to school with a hat on, even if your hair froze. The burden of men's fashion had now presidentially come into being. It was now the common man's duty to bear his own share of suffering in order to be socially presentable without complaint, just as women have been doing with their feet for centuries.

Eugene's hair had an auburn tint to it and was curly, short, and neat, with no perceptible part. The tight curling of his hair had also kept it looking smart and orderly, even when it obviously wasn't frozen. His attire appeared new and expensive, right down to his wingtip shoes. He had a pale and undistinguished complexion in contrast to his emerald green eyes which, regardless of his ostentatious regalia, were not quite remarkable enough to have qualified him as having a salient appearance.

Neither of us removed our hands from our coat pockets, which were sheltering them from the cold.

"So, which house do you live in?" I asked.

"I live in the big white colonial with the forest green trim, you know, the one with the swimming pool," he replied.

"Well, I've had enough of just standing here gawking at Dr. Gelt's house. I need to move on," I stated indifferently, ignoring his intentionally imperious remark, while turning to resume my familiar trek home. Then, seeming now to have collected a "new friend" from my brief sojourn as he tagged along, I just decided to ask him off-handedly, "How long have you lived here in Lenape, Eugene?"

"About a year," he answered flatly.

Unbelievable! I have finally met someone in the same situation that I'm in, I thought. *I guess his arrival in town was just as equally uneventful as mine, and the proof of this is, that until he had shouted out, 'Oh my God!' in class today, I had hardly ever noticed him at all before.*

"So, what do you think about today?" I then asked him candidly.

"I don't know," he shrugged underneath his three-quarter length herringbone overcoat. "I guess I'll just have to watch the Walter Cronkite news tonight like everyone else," he replied to the situation in a considerably more sedate manner than he did when he was in the classroom.

Now, mildly curious as to what he did with his leisure time, I asked as we still plodded along lackadaisically, "So, what do you do in the afternoon when you get home from school?"

"I deliver the afternoon newspaper," he answered matter-of-factly. "It gives me some spending money of my own," he then also qualified after a short pause.

"You've got to be kidding me," I commented satirically. "Don't tell me that you wear a cowboy hat when you deliver the paper, do you?" I expressly questioned him, stopping to hear his answer clearly.

"So you've seen me," Eugene surmised as he paused for a moment before adding, "You know, your grandmother is very nice to me."

"Yeah, she said that you were a nice boy and that I should make friends with you," I casually responded in turn. "And, by the way," I prodded further, again beginning to trudge on, "how come I've never seen you walking this way from school before?"

"Because my mother usually takes me and picks me up from school every day in her Cadillac," he said evenly.

"And then you deliver the papers," I interjected.

"Right," he affirmed definitively, unexpectedly stopping in his tracks. "Well, this is it," he added, dramatically out stretching his arms in front of the "big white colonial with the forest green trim."

"Well, I guess I'll see you in class tomorrow," I told him plainly, stopping a moment to witness his display.

"Yeah, I guess so," he replied in resignation, returning his hands to his pockets.

"No point in delivering your papers now," I appended, "They'll only want the morning edition after what happened today."

"No, I still have to deliver them," he responded, "or else I won't get paid."

"Well, let me get going then," I said in turning to go on my way, "Catch you tomorrow," I added fatalistically.

"Everyone just calls me Gene!" he shouted back, still standing from the edge of his driveway.

"Okay!" I yelled back over my shoulder as I kept on walking.

Eugene Kavanagh was the third child of Patrick and Kassandra Kavanagh. He had two older sisters, and all three siblings were spaced two years apart by birth. The oldest child, Kathleen, was the brightest scholastically and additionally had the most aggressive nature of the three children. Having experienced more than her share of public ridicule by her classmates for having to wear glasses since attending grade school, 'Kathy' had resolutely resigned herself to being unattractively intelligent.

The middle child was anointed Christina in the sanctification of the mother's heritage and was an exact duplicate physically, albeit in miniature form, of the mother. Christina was a heavenly little thing, who ostensibly had no need for any intellect what so ever.

The matron of the family personified the prototypical Greek Goddess of a woman. Long, luxurious dark hair in ringlets prosceniumed her translucently light complexion of Hellenistic beauty while accentuating her rich and seductive lips. Buxom, curvaceous, and all displayed in fact, she reportedly retaliated once in the defense of her beauty that she "had more than most girls had," and according to the Kavanagh family folklore, when the mother was just a girl of sixteen, her father had refused a substantial financial offer for the right of an import company to use her image on their jars of grape leaves and tomato products that were sold throughout the United States. So, it had been determined, as the tale had been passed down, that were it not for her father's poor decision, her beauty would have unquestionably become, to this very day, a commonly recognized national treasure.

As the chatelaine of the Kavanagh demesne, Mrs. Kavanagh had administered it as distinctively as she had kept her appearance. An unpretentious "smart look" was the image she endeavored to obtain in order to present to the public the family's self-aggrandized esteem. A considerable effort was expended to achieve this goal, and because of her extreme diligence to this task, she was quite successful. She was the bulwark of the estate in all its glory, and it was no less one of her cardinal goals to have her efforts be embodied in the manner and bearing of her son. Eugene, the one and only name that she ever had uttered for him, denoted to all concerned that he was her "little man"—and was decidedly hers and hers alone to mold.

Fortune, endemically a manifestation of the family's wealth, remained mindfully a prerogative of hers to auspiciously command in the foundation of her son's anticipated success in life. Fame, as she had experienced, had a fallacious quality about it, which she had readily accepted was not within her sovereignty and therefore had given it no weight of importance in her son's refinement, considering such an endeavor to be a frivolous waste of time. Thereupon, Eugene's education began with his introduction to Aesop's Fables.

Eugene's eldest sister, Kathy, was amused by her younger brother. She constantly contributed to his melioration as well. Experimenting recreationally with his natural trust and confidence, she whimsically instilled within him her own brand of influence whenever she had felt she was bored. The natural trait of a young male to be more rambunctious than his female counterpart was not something that she cared to acknowledge, and so she tried her best to purge any of this annoying behavior from ever taking hold within him in the first place.

Outward aggression and the broadcasting of one's own ambitions and intentions were considered an unadvisable trait for a young man to have, she proposed, and she had made her very best effort to install this concept within him. Politeness and understatement was the more desirable behavior to publicly display, she would advise him, and volunteer nothing was her mantle.

When Kathy was admitted to college and Eugene had approached his first year in high school, her experiments upon her younger brother were discontinued, but not before an effeminate demeanor had been appropriately ingrained within him.

Eugene's second sister, Christina, lived in a temporal world of her own and felt that her younger brother's only purpose was to take from her an undeserved portion of the attention pie that was to be dished out by her mother. The one and only commonality that she shared with her older sister about Eugene was that they both referred to him as "their little brother" ad infinitum. It was Patrick Kavanagh alone to whom *she* answered, for he was the omnipotent father, and she understood that unequivocally. She also knew that she was his favorite pet and played the part for all that it was worth.

Patrick Kavanagh, president and CEO of Kavanagh Construction Inc., personified 'to a T' the position to which he had achieved. Standing six foot two and weighing a formidable two hundred and sixty-two pounds, he commanded a respectful audience. A World War II veteran, having served under the command of George S. Patton Jr., he did not escape the indoctrination of the value of 'winning.' The intrinsic value of the concept that a person's discipline is the primary underpinning their success in life had never diminished one iota from his character. After the war, he had retained a position as a project manager for a large military contractor.

It was a personal matter to have his contracts completed under the scheduled time allotted. It was also an equally personal matter to receive a financial bonus for doing so as well. Often, he would point to the wall in his office, which was in full display of his numerous plaques and awards for outstanding performance, and blatantly make the comment to his visitors, "I put those awards and trophies up for the benefit of all those who believe they have no self-worth, not for me, and I am unashamedly paid well for this act."

Patrick and Kassandra Kavanagh were children of the greatest war machine ever built. The Great Depression had hammered into their souls a definitive impression of frugality upon all those who had survived the New Deal's integral psychology that perpetual poverty was a natural way of life. The disassembled immigrant families from the late eighteen hundreds who had come over during a somewhat better economic period had now banded back together again, simply to survive. This reestablishment of personal intimacy had thus generated a redoubtable standardization of values over which everyone seemed to universally agree upon, even if its purpose was simply to just 'get along with each other.'

Now perhaps one the most notably shared principles of all was the benefit of having chickens, for although poverty was indeed still a fact of life throughout the country, regardless of their race, creed, color, or national origin, everyone just seemed to love them for a variety of reasons.

Then in 1932, as the depression had gotten in full swing, Herbert Hoover, campaigning to be elected, had promised that he would have the government provide every family a free chicken in a pot so that the entirety of the voting electorate could have a nice Sunday dinner. Strangely enough, however, even after not winning the election, the very society who had rejected him still expected that the new administration should honor this proposal. Nonetheless, by 1943, eleven years later, still poorer than ever, no one could ever remember Franklin Roosevelt ever giving anyone a free chicken, or a pot to cook it in, unless they were employed by the federal government. Clearly, this inequality was a problem, but more importantly, how to fix it was the question.

The current administration's new deal to solve this malingering debacle, to them, now seemed easy. It would simply try to contravene the public's very concept of eating chickens in the first place. This they attempted to do by fabricating a totally new socially progressive program touting shared austerity to be a 'good thing' in which the general population was simply expected to haplessly accept their chickenless lives without complaint.

This strategy, however, changed nothing in the realm of reality and thus, regardless of how much the administration attempted to convince the public that a chicken was now a luxury commodity which needed to be reserved solely for the politically elite, they could not. "Where did all the chickens go anyway? Did they just fly away?" some of the people now began to ask. "I'm just not going to swallow this anymore," said others, now reflecting the obvious. "We need answers!" then came the cry in solidarity.

Finally, at wits end, the government now proposed that it was the Germans and Japanese who had diabolically and heinously cornered the entire chicken market and therefore, *they* were the ones to be blamed for everyone's misery. Naturally, this completely fabricated story was not liked by the Japanese in the slightest, and hence with 'complete surprise' declared war upon the chicken starving people of the United States.

Subsequently, after hellfire and brimstone had rained down on the entire world for over the next three years, the truth had finally become exposed: these two countries in fact had no more chickens to eat than any other at the outset of the war, and by now had practically none whatsoever. Subsequently, once this revelation had been certifiably confirmed by conquest, we accepted their surrender and the war had become officially over.

Patrick and Kassandra Kavanagh were the embodiment of this free and victorious society, and in light of having personally experienced the horrors of war first hand, they both had come away with a profound sense of exactly what the right thing, or wrong thing, was to do. And as the gracious nobility of the victors did in fact prevail, the "right thing," was thence honorably employed.

America was to send tons of chickens to the vanquished in exchange for the complete and unconditional absolution of 'any and all' transgressions, real or imagined, by the triumphant. This agreement was also to include a 'small' transactional profit to the actual purveyors of the chickens for extolling the benefits of capitalism. Everyone, except for the Russians, was happy, for although they were out of chickens, too, they still refused to embrace Capitalism to get them.

Fortitude, Fraternity, Freedom, and Fortune were the four fundamental principles that the Kavanaghs sought to instill their son Eugene. But their war time experiences, however, the element of their economic suffering, and the exultation felt in the self-satisfaction of achieving their own goals, no matter how well they tried, could not be simply transfused into their son by osmosis. These historical realities to Eugene had no more significance to him than his readings of *The Adventures of Hercules* or the escapades of *Jason and the Argonauts*. Nonetheless, armed with these fantasies and his family's good intentions, he felt that he was now fully prepared to enter high school.

Chapter Two

It was precisely at nine o'clock in the morning, when after the school bell had rung, that all its students were required to be present, each in their own assigned 'homerooms.' First, the attendance was taken, and then immediately thereafter, the wall speaker would begin with the daily announcements. These announcements, however, were not just informative messages. In place of starting with a passage from the old testament of the bible, which had been the accepted practice just a few years earlier, an inspirational quote was now read in its place by the Vice Principal in an intentional, albeit feeble, attempt to alleviate the unpleasantness associated with the whole affair. Unintentionally, nonetheless, the only inspirational result that it produced was the prodigious amount of levity that the students had expressed over the Vice Principal himself.

To Eugene, other than the school having installed this annoyingly bombastic public-address system, he did not see much of a change, if at all, from the last school which he had just come from. Even the exact same students were there, *"corralled exactly as before,"* he thought.

In the second year of his high school studies, however, there was a slight distinctive change in that Eugene had been allowed to select an elective class of his own choosing. This to him made all the difference in the world as he eagerly signed up for an ancient history class which had been scheduled on the very first period of the day. He outwardly relished the subject to such a degree that his history teacher openly institutionalized Eugene as his favorite disciple.

So with his mother's portfolio of Greek fables, which he had never forgotten, Eugene's fantasies found an applicable reality that he felt could only be recognized by his pedagogue, Mr. Ganz, the high school's very own esteemed history professor.

Their mutual admiration over the subject had provided the impetus that would then begin to define the basic thoughts of Eugene Kavanagh in his perception of applying these historical parables unto reality. Without first obtaining the understanding of this conscious process, Eugene feared that his future would only become an ectoplasmic clone of Walter Mitty, in having no definitive personal existence at all, doomed to exist in the fantasies of the past. But now, he felt he was on the road to true enlightenment. The shared approbations of the relative lessons to be gleaned from the study of history, allegorically or true, as they related to the present, gave the two colleagues a great sense of common purpose.

Mr. Ganz was a fastidious German philosopher. Always adduced in a well-pressed grey suit, it was his reputation to have never been seen in public without so much as his jacket off. A slight, balding, soft spoken man with a faint accent, he pedantically wore a distinct pair of round silver framed eye glasses which, in the right angle and light, would sparkle against his pale and indistinct pallor. He was the classic visual depiction of a professor of some variety or another and consequently, in tandem with his erudite manner, was respectfully treated as one by all.

One day, not having any assignments due, Mr. Ganz opened his class with a direct question.

"Mr. Kavanagh, have you read the Adventures of Hercules?"

"Yes sir, I have," Eugene declared proudly.

"Have you read them all, Mr. Kavanagh?" the professor qualified.

"Well, I'm not sure I have read them all, Mr. Ganz," replied Eugene dolefully, recanting his blatant display of pride.

"Well, on Hercules' quest to Hell he had stayed for the winter at a farmer's house to rest, weary from his travels and tribulations," Mr. Ganz began. "Have you read of this exploit, Mr. Kavanagh?" the professor then addressed Eugene again.

"I don't believe so, Sir," Eugene answered in a rueful manner.

"Is anyone in this class familiar with this tale?" the professor queried in general, perusing the room while imperiously standing behind his desk for a reply which he knew would not come. Then, after a sufficient silence had confirmed that no one had read the piece, he continued.

"First, if anyone here wants to find out specifically what Hercules experienced while at the farmer's house, I suggest that you read it for yourself," he prefaced. "However, I will give you this for your reflection," he offered gratuitously.

"After being befriended at a farmer's house for the night," he began again, "and following a harrowing day's journey, Hercules stopped to rest on a nearby rock to think back pensively about his good fortune. He amused himself in the recollection of the many battles which he had won and over the many 'good deeds' that he had performed, recalling with great self-satisfaction how he had particularly benefited the farmer with whom he had just stayed. Hercules then looked up to the sky and openly announced to the gods proudly, 'Imagine, I have given this poor farmer's daughter a child of Hercules. What greater gift could be given to another man?'" Mr. Ganz concluded, momentarily pausing. "Now, does anyone have a comment to make?" he ensued, as Eugene was the only student to raise his hand.

"Yes, sir, I do," stated Eugene with a renewed spirit.

"Would you please enlighten us with your observations, Mr. Kavanagh?" Mr. Ganz solicited politely.

"Well, the story reveals Hercules' narcissistic conceit," Eugene offered succinctly, making no other comments.

"Is that all, Mr. Kavanagh?" the instructor questioned, raising his eyebrows.

"Well, that's just what I was thinking, Sir," Eugene replied in a diffident manner.

"Mr. Kavanagh, I give you an 'A' for your class participation, but I would like you to also consider this," Mr. Ganz began to elaborate further, "On a higher plain, if, in reality, Hercules, the demigod of all demigods, *was* the most beautiful man, and actually *was* the most capable man of all the known world, I put to you that he would not be narcissistic at all. He would be merely stating the truth and consequently be just in his revelations. Would it also not follow then, that hubris can only be a mortal sin?" Mr. Ganz rhetorically proposed.

"Now, of course, this is easily proved," the professor continued with a thin smile of ascendancy, surveilling the entire class for a second, "because, this I know for a fact—that none of you here are Hercules," he deftly concluded.

Eugene righteously deserved his status in the world of Mr. Ganz and continually endeavored to enhance his position of notoriety within it. He kept ahead of all the class assignments and had volunteered to participate in every supplementary project that was offered. Tardiness was never considered an option to Eugene in Mr. Ganz's first period class. It was just unthinkable. However, this could not be said for his homeroom attendance record. It was the worst in the entire school.

This total disregard of punctuality when convenient to Eugene was not all together his fault, however, for it was a trait he had learned from his parents. His mother felt that the family's financial position had all but exonerated them from having to be concerned with any of the town's plebeian ordinances, and that included the school's dictates as well.

Since she and her husband were both seen to drive about the small borough in their own separate Cadillacs, it did not take long for everyone to acknowledge their pertinacious presence. Thus Kassandra, the matron of the family, saw no reason at all to be in a hurry to simply justify someone else's schedule. To be seen speeding in a Cadillac might possibly be construed as a weakness, she had determined. Other people were required to adhere to *her* schedule, and to be viewed as driving about in haste would simply denote otherwise.

Desperation, she contemplated as well, was not a quality that a dignified person was to openly display either. Why, simply to be associated with that word would have made her nauseous beyond belief. No, Eugene was considered to be 'present' whenever she had arrived with him at the school, and that was that.

Patrick Kavanagh in turn, the patriarch of the clan, declared the family motto to be, "You just can't fight success," and in reinforcement supplemented, "and if you try it, I can guarantee you, it will cost you more than you will gain."

Together, these two philosophies had permeated the entire family's demeanor and was openly evidenced on many occasion by Eugene going directly to Mr. Ganz's class in the morning and apathetically skipping the homeroom experience altogether. Now, although this behavior had been dutifully reported by the homeroom teacher, it went no further, as it had only become regarded by the school's administration as a victimless tort which seemed to affect no one else, and thus ignored as a tolerable infraction.

English, Eugene's secondary appetence, had also become a favored subject of his, and as such was also treated by him with the same relishment. Thus, respectively, the entire humanities department reciprocated in finding him to be a most pleasant and well-mannered young man.

Mr. Kreski, the high school football coach and Eugene's assigned gym teacher, had a totally different perspective of the boy. He was a large, brutish, brick house of a man simply called the "Coach," and was a force that Eugene had to reckon with, whether he liked it or not, for physical education was compulsory. He had a beet red complexion with the shadow of small veins about his neck and temples which bulged to the surface of his skin whenever he had become aggravated, which was often. In the age of fashionably long hair, Mr. Kreski exhibited the crew cut of a marine and drew the silhouette of a Mac truck. He also had the temper of a Hun on steroids and was decidedly *not* a humorous man. He detested the effeminate boy.

It was just a matter of time before Eugene's self-concerns caused him to be late to his scheduled gym class and was thereupon most starkly introduced to the concept of military authority.

"I do not see Mr. Kavanagh on the line, and I do not see his name on the absent sheet!" Coach Kreski bellowed out at large one afternoon when Eugene was nowhere to be seen.

Instantaneously, Eugene came running from the locker room and abruptly stopped when he had reached his assigned position on the basketball court's out of bounds line with the rest of the class already there.

"Present!" Eugene blurted out.

"Do you have some kind of medical problem that I am not aware of Mr. Kavanagh?" the instructor vociferated in the manor of an army drill instructor. "Or perhaps you have some kind of mental problem as well, like you are too stupid to tell time, even with those two gold watches you wear?"

"One of them is an I.D. bracelet," Eugene meekly responded, but unafraid.

"Well, apparently, since you know the difference between an identification bracelet and a watch, you can help me out," the coach continued to abuse him in a loud tone. "In no less than five hundred words, I need from you a paper explaining the time differential between normal people who have to live in reality, and those who live inside a Ping-Pong ball. I want that paper in my office by your next gym class, or you *will* fail this grade period. Do you understand me, Mr. Kavanagh?" he obstreperously emphasized in no uncertain terms.

"Yes, sir," Eugene sedately responded.

After school that evening, the unrepentant student wrote down "time does not exist in a Ping-Pong ball" fifty times and remanded his work the next day to the secretary of the athletic department. Eugene received a "D" for that period, but was never late for his gym class again.

In his third year of high school Eugene joined the golf team. The entire class of sixty-seven had less than two hundred students, and when the golf team tryouts were held only five students had showed up in attendance. The school's problem was that to qualify as entrants in the inter-county golf tournament, they were required to have a six-man team.

The obvious remedy to this problem, as the school's administration felt, was that since "the boy with two watches" was known to have a father who could afford the goodly cost of the sport, Eugene would be thus the perfect candidate to solicit. It was also thus determined that a direct visit to Mr. Patrick Kavanagh himself by Mr. Hart, the certified head of the athletic department, would be necessary to achieve the school's best results, and so he was dispatched.

Thereupon, a fortuitous agreement was forged by both parties. For accepting the position of the sixth man on the team and thereby enhancing the school's prestige, Eugene was thereafter to be "awarded" the minimum grade of "B" for his athletic contributions, along with receiving a school letter for his so-called sports achievement. He was also never again to be assigned to one of Coach Kreski's classes. Ironically, however, the gentlemanly conduct of the sport, along with the financial exclusivity of its participants, fit Eugene's self-image to a tee, and the sport remained with him as a personal enjoyment for the rest of his life.

The science and math departments were also not of any interest to Eugene. Consequently, those teachers who had taught those subjects simply processed him as best they could, along with as little concern for him as he had held for them. Math in particular was viewed to be solely an academic annoyance to Eugene. He could not, did not, and would not even try to understand its use or its concepts at all. The conundrum of obtaining a satisfactory scholastic point average in this area was this time assigned to Kassandra who, upon hiring Eugene's math teacher to be his personal tutor at a most generous stipend, miraculously engineered for her son a most equally generous grade.

Katie Jameson sat directly in front of Eugene in at least two of his classes every year since he had come to Lenape. Her family was not new in any manner to the community. The Jamesons had immigrated directly to the town from Ireland in the mid-eighteen hundreds. Being one of the more fortunate immigrants, Katie's great-grandfather had a valued trade as a bookbinder and had found employment straightaway by which he could easily provide for his family, ever since becoming a complacent component of the town's society in keeping up with its respectful and peaceful continuity.

Barely five feet two, Katie, a comely and agreeable girl, had such a quiet disposition and gentle manner that her presence went virtually unnoticed unless she had the occasion to speak, which was not too often. Her short chestnut brown hair and matching eyes pervaded an unpretentious countenance which allowed her to blend in with most any convivial activity. Her ambition was to simply have a happy family life.

Katie's father was an affable insurance agent who earned an income sufficient enough as to not have his wife work. Her mother was a serene woman who bore six children pleasantly. The entire Jameson clan had embodied the innocuous white collar, middle class American family which sustained itself by vapidly servicing the general public in methodically executing a non-physical task which is so tedious or legally restrictive that most would pay someone else a premium to perform.

Having been raised since birth in Lenape, Katie had attended practically every one of the town's scheduled cotillions, holiday parties, and church socials that were available to her. Outwardly, Katie's actions had always understated her motives. Passivity was a major tool in her social arsenal and she could wield it quite adroitly, especially when Eugene became a target of her desires.

Attaining seventeen years of age, in his junior year, Eugene had now obtained his driver's license. He also had obtained a brand-new Ford Mustang from his father, and as soon as he was given its keys to have and to hold, it had become unmistakably showcased in the student parking lot on a daily basis.

Not that anyone could have missed the candy apple red convertible as it rolled onto the school grounds every morning, Katie's reaction in seeing it was no different than any other girl's, for she too, was a product of the muscle car times. Then, fanaticizing that it could actually be *her* showcased in the world's most popular sports car, she set her cap for Eugene.

And so, on one particularly drab and innocuous day, barely after a week had gone by since Eugene had first brought his new car to school, as fate would have it, the teacher was late to class. Katie, who had now positioned herself sideways in her chair, and after having thoughtfully resolved that this was the exact providential moment to which she had dreamed about, as unassumingly possible then asked, "Gene, are you going to the Junior Prom?

"I haven't thought about it," Eugene replied in a disinterested manner. And although he maintained his position with no further comment, he still did not look away.

Katie continued to look at him steadily, also without saying another word, while offering him her best rendition of a Mona Lisa smile. Nonetheless, she did not retreat from her indominable stance a single inch. Finally, giving in to her unwavering omnipresence, and full well realizing the latent consequences of his actions, Eugene said to himself, *'Damn the torpedoes,'* as he fatefully responded, "Are *you* going?"

"I don't have a date, if that's what you're asking," Katie reflected sadly.

"Did you want to go?" Eugene asked her in return, still feigning a hint of unconcern in trying to gage the degree of wanton desire that she was willing to display.

"Of course I want to go, Gene," she said coyly.

"Well, I guess I could take you, that is, if you want to go and no one else asks you," Eugene offered, as if reluctantly assigned to an arduous task.

"Would you really take *me*?" asked Katie.

"Sure," was his one-word answer.

"Well, then, we have a date," Katie smiled acceptingly, abruptly ending the conversation.

Katie knew that she had gotten exactly what she had desired and did not want to overly complicate the contract, so she said no more. She did, nevertheless, add to it a small gratuitous gesture, for now turning back around in her chair for his benefit, and his benefit alone, she softly sighed, "Oh my," as if she had been emotionally and uncontrollably compelled to do so. *I know he's not deaf,* she then mused to herself contentedly.

The titillation which Eugene began to feel on the way home from school that afternoon unfortunately would not last for very long, as he just couldn't help from thinking the closer he got to home, *Oh, my God, what is my mother going to say?*

With great trepidation, Eugene waited all afternoon until the evening meal had been finished and his mother was all alone in the kitchen putting away the dishes before making his next move. Dreadfully fretting the inevitable, he had decided that the direct approach was the simplest, as well as the least agonizing, method of solving his problem. So, in trying to best alleviate any further torment, he boldly commenced to engage his mother with the de facto statement, "Mom, I have invited a girl to the Junior Prom next month."

"I hope you know how to dance," his mother needled him amusingly, not deferring her attention away from wiping down the counter next to the sink. Distressed, in having immediately taken the comment to heart, Eugene said nothing in return. Kassandra, in sensing that her remark had only added to his obvious anxiety, summarily stopped what she was doing, and in turning around to face him directly, affectionately assured him, "Don't worry, I'll have your sister help you. She'll do it if I ask her."

No point of etiquette was overlooked. An invitation to dine at the Kavanagh estate was thus propitiously dispatched to be personally delivered by Eugene to Katie on the very next Monday at school. Proper introductions had to be made.

"So, how long has your family lived here?" asked Kassandra, initiating the meal's conversation.

"Oh, I was born here," Katie answered simply.

"I understand you share a class with Eugene?" Kassandra questioned.

"We have the same English teacher," Katie confirmed with a light smile.

"Oh, that's nice," the matron of the house commented while she paused for a moment for a reply. But Katie did not elaborate any further. "So, since Eugene has told me that you have lived here all of your life, I guess your father must have a pretty good job," she proposed.

"Oh, he has his own insurance agency downtown next to the hardware store," Katie imparted, glancing over to Eugene warmly for a second in the hope that he would give her some sort of support. Passively, however, he said nothing, only to return the same smile.

"So, he's in that little office building right next the gas station too, then," Kassandra continued.

"Yes, ma'am," Katie confirmed.

"And your mother, does she work anywhere?" Kassandra continued to question as if she was a passport inspector.

"Oh, my mother has never worked anywhere outside of the house," Katie responded in total unconcern, consciously denoting that her family had no financial issues of importance.

"It's nice to have your mother at home, isn't it?" Kassandra responded, now with a small approving smile.

"Yes, ma'am, it is. It's a lot of work to keep up a house," Katie politely remarked, obviously in full support of the country's professional home makers.

And so, after Katie's blithe congeniality had eventually all but absorbed the officious tone to which she had been subjected, and finding pointless to continue her barrage, Kassandra relented. Patrick and Kathy each had nothing to ask, while Christina could care less. The conversation was then finally and harmlessly turned over to the current events of the day. Katie had now officially passed the Kassandra test with flying colors, to the sheer delight of Eugene. Kathy, though, to her chagrin was not pleased at all, for it was she who was assigned to give her brother his dance lessons.

For the next few weeks, while Eugene was self-absorbed with becoming a Beau Brummell, Katie felt herself to be the consummate social engineer. To her, sex was a function of the family unit which, out of educational curiosity, she had already experienced, but how to best take advantage of this situation without having to surrender her publicly chaste reputation was now at the top of her thoughts, and so an unspoken pact was made. Eugene was to provide the invitation, the corsage, and the chariot of Cinderella, while Katie only had to provide him with an elusive promise.

On that following Monday afternoon, after Eugene had kept up his end of the bargain, the elusive promise became not so elusive after all when, in the solitude of the Jamesons' cellar, Katie allowed the gift of carnal knowledge to be most gratefully acquired by Eugene. To this day, it has always remained a complete mystery as to who took advantage of whom that afternoon but, henceforth, they then presented themselves to the world at large as a couple.

This new arrangement had also spawned another change in Eugene's past attitudes. He now pitied his single friends and began to shift his alliances toward the other fellas who also had a dedicated "steady." Consequently, it was on one of those totally mundane Wednesday afternoons that he had decided to completely forsake the last of his lone buddies.

Mrs. Marcelia Hall, the advanced English teacher, was two things. One was a dramatic thespian of grandiose magnitude, and the other was a lover of her young male students. She was a large, pulchritudinous woman with jet black hair that she wore at shoulder's length. Her light pancake complexion was offset by her cherry red lipstick and very large and opulent pair of black horn-rimmed glasses. A hug from her turned any young boy's complexion as red as her lipstick, which was done quite often, right in front the entire class.

These privileged few, sardonically referred to as "the teacher's pets," were subsequently rewarded by being given "special assignments" for extra credit. Participation in this humiliating tradition, as was legendary in the high school's folklore, invariably assured that all the players involved would receive an A for their final grade.

And, so it was in this particular class, that Eugene and his best pal Bill O'Donnell had always been neck and neck in the race to obtain the coveted position of Chief Brownnoser in the all-over hierarchy of Mrs. Hall's literary minions. Eugene and Bill had been seen as buddies by everyone, both intellectually and socially, until Eugene and Katie had become viewed as a single item. This, Eugene had hence determined, had completely changed his entire social dynamic and consequently, on one otherwise innocuous afternoon, having already known that Bill would not be showing up for class, Eugene decided to settle, once and for all, the issue of exactly just who was going to end up with the coveted title of Suck up Supreme for the year.

"Does anyone know where that nice Bill O'Donnell is?" Mrs. Hall broadcasted out to the class when she first had noticed that his name was not on her absentee sheet after everyone had taken their places.

Then, having gotten no response, the teacher got up from her desk and walked around from behind it, confronting the entire class directly.

"Are you all sure that *no one* in this class can tell me where Bill O'Donnell is?" Mrs. Hall dramatically repeated once more.

Again, there was no response. Dejectedly, Mrs. Hall started to turn away in total resignation but, out of the corner of her eye, she had caught the shadow of a hand rising slowly to her right. It was the hand of Eugene Kavanagh, and the die was cast.

Immediately, Mrs. Hall went right over to where Eugene was seated and once she had arrived, standing squarely next to his desk, she focused her entire persona down upon him to the exclusion of all else.

"So, do *you* know the whereabouts of Bill O'Donnell, Eugene?" Mrs. Hall now asked a third time, as her vexation had become even more obvious.

"Yes, I do, Mrs. Hall," Eugene spoke slowly, feigning to be totally distraught with his head hung down and offering no more.

"Well, can you be so kind as to inform me of what in God's name could ever have happened to him?" Mrs. Hall asked, placing her right hand against the top of her chest in an open exhibition of fretful apprehension.

"Bill was—suspended this morning," Eugene said in complete mortification while he kept on staring down upon his desktop.

Now, upon hearing his reply, Mrs. Hall suddenly reeled back in surprise and producing a small gasping noise from her breast impulsively clutched onto the large button center of her blouse. Then, pausing briefly to compose herself, she further elicited, "For whatever reason could he have been suspended for, Eugene?"

"Smoking, Mrs. Hall, smoking," divulged Eugene with a heavy sigh, looking away in disgust to the outside window adjacent his desk. Then, in trying to distance the messenger from the message, he finally turned to face her directly as he looked up and clearly blurted out specifically, "Yes, Mrs. Hall, he was caught smoking outside behind the gym by Mr. Kreski, and got suspended."

"Oh, my goodness, I can't believe it," she impulsively inhaled, her eyes filling the rims of her glasses in total surprise.

Then, in complete and utter shock, she slowly turned, and without saying another word, she began to slowly shuffle her way back to the organized familiarity of her desk. And no sooner had she taken her seat, still in shaken vulnerability, Eugene adroitly seized the opportunity to play the role of Brutus and deliver final coup de grace to his now lone and former buddy, Bill.

"And he was my friend too!" Eugene called out in total commiseration with her angst, as if their fallen compatriot had now become a shared cross to bear.

While most of the class had just rolled their eyes up at this treacherous performance, others, who were safely sheltered behind the backs of the students sitting directly in front of them, comically pretended to gag themselves with their fingers. Eugene was victorious! Thrilled with his magnificent performance and the masterful application of his Machiavellian tactics, he now proudly accepted the mantle of being the school's biggest schmoozer, just as if he had received an Olympic medal.

Eugene Kavanagh's senior year could not have been a better time for him. Crammed with all sorts of amusement, he drove Katie everywhere and anywhere they both had the inclination to go. Nonetheless, his last year in high school was still not perfect, for he had still one distressing thought that refused go away. His father demanded that he apply for admission to at least two of the most prestigious military academies in the country, and that was set in stone.

He was happy enough with the draft deferment that he would be granted for attending *any* college, but regardless, he did not in any manner look forward to being physically, or especially mentally, regimented into the Armed Services' way of life. He was content with his peaceful composure and considered himself to be a free thinker. Just how long he would last in a military academy he shuddered to think, but all the same, he was obligated to make the best of it.

Chapter Three

Perhaps it had been because of the "D" that Eugene had received from Mr. Kreski, or perhaps it was because of the nefarious "C" that he had gotten in math, it was not specifically determined, but both of the military academies to which he applied had sent him notices of rejection. Unsurprisingly, this news did not upset Eugene in any manner, but his father had a completely different reaction. When Patrick Kavanagh was told the news, he immediately and most vociferously registered his disgust by stating, "Well, I guess that's what you get when your kid grows up playing with dolls instead of trucks."

It was then that Eugene's parents had secured him an apartment on the edge of the State's college campus, where he *was* accepted. With his college being only an hour's drive from home, it made easy for Eugene to come back and visit so that he could replenish his lavish support on a regular basis, and yet retain his privacy.

He was also given a company gas card, as well as the use of his mother's personal credit card. The money was certainly welcomed, but he vehemently rebelled against being monitored. In his first step of independence, Eugene took a part time evening job as a manager at a local ice cream shop so as to earn some spending money which would be unaccountable to anyone but himself. *I am away from her clutches and I don't need for my friends to be approved, my habits arranged, or my amusements to be chosen. I can do what I want to do now, and without her monitoring everything little thing that I spend my money on either,* he declared to himself upon receiving his first paycheck.

Now, besides Eugene's financial condition at hand, there were other important matters that had to be reckoned with as well. The entire country was now fast becoming completely divided into two basic factions which were uncontrollably drifting farther and farther apart to such a point that everyone had become forced to take a side.

On one hand, there was the first faction that called themselves The Government, and on the other, there was the second faction that called themselves The People. Normally they got along, but the problem now was that each side was refusing to listen to each other's point of view while both of them were acting as if they could operate independently.

The government's self-image was that its purpose was to induce the expansion of capitalism and free enterprise to the rest of the world by its military might. Many others did not see it that way. Although the intellectual expansionism of a free market had been heartedly supported by most everyone, a growing number of the people began to vehemently disagree over the government's methods on just how do it.

To love thy neighbor to accomplish the same goal was now fast becoming a more favored method to be considered, but no one on either side was willing to compromise. So, while one half of the country spent its time with righteous body counts, the other half of the country spent its time counting how many righteous bodies one could love. Then, with all things considered, Eugene decided to align himself with the love faction.

~

It was no surprise one day that during Eugene's first Thanksgiving recess he had received a letter from Katie. She had gone off to attend a university in the Midwest and he had only received one short letter from her previously. Now, with her second letter in hand, Eugene went over to his stereo set, put on Arlo Guthrie's *Alice's Restaurant,* and sat down to read her letter.

First, after she had inquired as to Eugene's general contentment, Katie stated that she now become interested in socializing with another "very nice guy," but that she still coveted a marriage to him. Her letter also requested a marriage time frame and a definite commitment to which she could rely upon. Consequently, after surmising that Katie had already "socialized" her new guy in the same fashion to which she had socialized him, Eugene took it upon himself to relinquish her from this great obligatory expectation to which she had thought existed.

After all, I already read that book, Eugene now thought, purging any guilt from his consciousness while drafting the "Dear John" letter. And immediately thereafter crafting the letter, containing the standard well-wishing release clause, it was off to the ice cream store for Eugene, fraught with the best of intentions in bestowing upon one of girls who also worked there a most spirited experience in his notorious vehicle.

As far as his college studies were concerned, for the most part, they seemed to him somewhat banal, particularly since the special attention which he had receiving from Mr. Ganz was missing. His campus social life, still in all, was not boring at all. Eugene had joined a fraternity which, according to its charter, existed in theory to enhance the scholastic development of its members. The actual truth was that it existed mostly for its member's social development, and that was precisely why Eugene had joined.

It was here that he met Scott Campbell, a psychology major with a minor in English. Scott was a thin, tallish fellow that wore his sandy colored hair straight down to his shoulders. With portentously long facial features, thin lips, and a set of beady brown eyes, Scott had projected the face of gravity incarnate. Whenever Scott was confronted directly, he often gave the deliberate impression that his presence was one of a serious nature which always seemed to require a specific answer, regardless of how trivial the situation might seem to be. In many cases he used this practiced performance for intimidation purposes. At other times, he was simply amused by the reactions elicited by his imperious deportment. Eugene had recognized this distinguishing characteristic in Scott and classified it as a skill, rather than a talent.

Scott Campbell's father was a successful doctor, as was his father before him. His family was well respected throughout their local community and the accumulation of greater financial wealth was never deemed a concern that was needed to be addressed. Scott had normally dressed himself unpretentiously in a pair of crisp blue jeans along with the ubiquitous college sweat shirt, and completed his ensemble with a pair of white converse sneakers. The two socially equal young men became fast friends. Eugene would expound about the historical truths about life, while Scott applied them to their immediate condition.

On one of the nastiest days of the year, with the rain being driven intermittently by a most frigidly cold northeastern wind, the two comrades left the sanctity of Eugene's apartment in search of some "action." This time they had decided to take Scott's Buick Electra. It was sumptuous in size and had all the creature comforts imaginable, yet was imperial to the average blue-collar worker. It was also agreed that because of its size and comfort, Scott's car was by far more utilitarian than Eugene's, should they have to entreat a convocation of females for their pleasure.

Although engineered with a humongous gas tank, Scott's Buick still needed to be replenished from time to time as it only got twelve miles to the gallon, and right now his gas gauge was on the verge of empty. Certainly, neither of them wanted to go outside, for both were dressed to the nines and the weather outside was completely brutal, but how to accomplish this noxious task was not their problem. It would be the gas station attendant's headache, for it was the attendant's job to pump the gas. All they had to do was pay him from the sheltered comfort of the car.

Scott had pulled the vehicle up to the pump and watched as the worker had bellicosely come out of his service cubicle to battle the frigid wind and sporadic rain to eventually arrive at the driver's window. He was a squat man who had bundled himself up in some grey and rumpled clothes as he sloshed about in a pair of unsnapped rubber goulashes, and in recognition of this man's feat, Scott had lowered the window about three inches and said, "Fill it up, please," as politely as possible, empathizing with the attendant's condition.

Outwardly aggravated, the employee then caustically muttered under his breath as he turned to commence performing his function, "You ought to come out here and pump it yourself."

Hearing the station man's lament and not liking that it was directed at him, Scott turned to Eugene after raising the window back up and said, "You know, this guy pumping the gas is a wretched human being."

"How do you know that? Maybe he is just having a hard day," Eugene suggested alternatively.

"Oh no, he is definitely a scurrilous bastard who doesn't give a damn about anyone but himself, and I can prove it," Scott propounded vehemently.

"How can you possibly prove that?" Eugene questioned as Scott had piqued his interest.

"It's very simple," Scott said flatly, "When he comes back, I will only lower the window a crack to find out how much I owe him. When he tells me, I will take my time and count out the money in one-dollar bills, which of course will piss him off even further, and then after I stack them together and fold them over I will merely poke them through the crack in the window for him to take so *I* obviously won't get wet. I will also put in the stack an extra five-dollar bill, and I will bet you that he won't say a damn word. He will just keep it," he adamantly proposed.

"Well, how will you know that he deliberately kept it?" Eugene again queried as if to test Scott's resolve that the man was indeed a "scurrilous bastard."

"I will take my time, you'll see," Scott told him. "First, I will adjust my seatbelt, then I will play with the mirror, start the engine back up, sit for a second, slowly reach over to turn the lights back on, and then, if I have to, I'll even go through the glove compartment and just pretend to fadoodle around for something. Mark my word, you will have plenty of time to observe him to your satisfaction," he guaranteed. "And then, if he does not offer to give me the money back, you owe me the five bucks, okay?" he proposed straightforwardly.

"That's a deal," Eugene confirmed as he then proposed in turn, "And if he does return it, then I get the five dollars, right?"

"Right," committed Scott.

Now, after pumping the gas, the disgruntled attendant again approached Scott's window, held up his greasy right hand and said, as if he was the world's rudest cab driver, "You owe me twelve bucks, Buddy."

Scott then lowered his window once again and gave the man the money exactly as planned and then began to fidget with his car, as was the strategy. It didn't take long, however, for the two sociologists to notice that the attendant, now plodding back to his base while continuing to count the money, for one brief second, had suddenly stopped dead in his tracks and looked up. Then he looked back down again at the money in his hand and, as quickly as humanly possible, stuffed the now 'rain soaked wad of cash' into the left pocket of his coat and scurried like startled pudgy rat across the slick pavement to once again be sheltered in the safe asylum of his cubical.

Once out of the driveway of the station and back on to the main highway, Eugene admitted, "Yup, I guess you were right, Scott. When he saw the five, he definitely stopped in his tracks before going back to his booth, just waiting there until after we left so he could cash in at your expense. I guess it's just like you said, he *is* a scurrilous bastard," he stipulated conclusively.

"Told you so," said Scott clinically.

Then, as a silence pervaded the air for a moment while Scott was trying to negotiate the big Buick through the inclement weather, Eugene taunted, "Well, are you going to let him get away with it?"

"He didn't get away with anything. You are the one that lost the five bucks, Ole Buddy," Scott replied as he laughed out loud.

"Well, if I can teach him a lesson, would it be worth the five bucks you won?" Eugene entreated Scott provocatively.

Scott smiled, but did not respond as he just continued to give the road his full attention.

"I can't believe that you of all people would let this bastard go without receiving his just desserts," Eugene continued to chide.

"Okay, Gene, exactly what do you think you can do?" Scott finally acquiesced.

"First of all, let's turn around and go back and *I* will confront him. Go on, turn around before we've gone too far," Eugene prompted.

"Okay," replied Scott compliantly, turning around at the next traffic light.

Then, there was nothing but silence for a moment while Eugene tried to hatch a plan. Since they had only gotten about five miles away from the station, he knew that he did not have much time to concoct one and, therefore, had to think fast.

"You know, what I think I'll do is, be you," Eugene suddenly declared, looking directly over to Scott.

"What do you mean by that?" Scott asked suspiciously.

"Well, I'll be a reporter, you know, a gorilla journalist, or maybe like a guy from the national inquirer, or maybe even better, a state investigator. Yeah, that's it, a state investigator for fraud," he decisively concluded. "Do you have a pad or something to write on, and a pen?" he asked eagerly.

"Yeah, there should be a note pad and pen in the glove compartment," Scott answered, while thinking to himself in amusement, *Oh, this ought to be a good one alright.*

Eugene now began to grapple about the glove box for a minute until he had retrieved the exact theatrical props which he had felt were necessary for his ruse.

"Now, you need to pull over and let me drive," he instructed in trying to take over full command. "He knows you, but he never had the chance to get a look at me," he stated practically. "And besides, I'm wearing my full-length Lord and Taylor coat, and that will make me look important, so that should put him off guard, too," he hypothesized further.

And no sooner had Eugene finished his sentence, and just before Scott began to tactfully pull the car over to the side of the road to exchange their seats, Scott commented, "You know, he will probably recognize the car."

"No, he won't," argued Eugene, "I will park it about fifty feet away by the front corner of the lot by the phone booth and then walk up to the pumps. It's too dark and crappy out for him to see anything. When I get out, you just slide back over into the driver's seat again and leave the door open just enough to pretend that you have a camera, okay?"

"Sure, this is your operation," Scott replied in a sporting manner.

After pulling the big black Buick slowly into the station, Eugene proceeded to park it exactly where he had said, just as if he was going to make a phone call. He then deftly flung the car door open, got out and directly walked towards the attendant's cubicle with the gait of a person on a serious mission.

Upon approaching his target, who was now standing idle outside of his compartment with a cigarette in his hand, Eugene reached into his left overcoat pocket and took out the small spiral note pad. Then, halting directly before the man, he retrieved the pen from his left inside coat pocket with his right hand, clicked it dramatically in the air, and in the most solemn manner, squarely looked the half-frozen fellow directly in the face and said, "I am officer Krupke from the State Investigator's Office, and I want to know if you have been working here all evening?"

"Yeah, eh, Yes, sir," he nervously answered, tossing his half-finished cigarette onto the wet tarmac.

"Well, we just received a complaint that a gas station in this area was conning the folks out of their money, just like George C. Scott did in *The Flim-Flam Man*. One guy just claimed he lost five bucks this evening," Eugene stated in a most suspicious tone as he pointed the pen directly towards the man while dramatically raising his eyebrows.

"Oh no, dat can't happen here, officer," he instantly responded. "You see, we got da drop box over here, and when dey gives me da money, I just stick it in da drop box. It's not my bizniss what day gives me, and I never count it," he claimed in fit of anxiety.

"Then what happens when they don't give you enough money to pay for the gas? Wouldn't you be fired for that?" Eugene asked him bluntly.

Stunned, the man just stood there before Eugene with a completely blank look on his face. Suddenly, however, as if the attendant had just gotten a dose of electrical shock therapy, he convulsively snapped right back to life, only to repeat the same explanation. "Oh no, you see officer, we got da drop box over here, and when da people gives me da money…"

"Just hold it a minute, pal," Eugene authoritatively interrupted. "We have been filming you for the last hour from *that car over there*," he testified, gesturing to the opened front door of the car. "Well, we have all we need anyway," he then declared, "I'm just going to have Danno book you," he told him flatly. "You just stay right here, and you don't move," he ordered the obviously panic-stricken man with another shake of his pen.

The attendant just stood there, frozen in such fear that he had lost all thought of getting frostbitten, while Eugene had abruptly turned and hastened back to the vehicle. Still caught off guard, the man stood motionless by his station as he began to slowly fixate more intently upon the car. Eugene then opened the Buick's back door, got inside, and with the thud of finality, slammed it closed. Scott, now fully opening the front door to face the man directly, laughed loudly, sarcastically calling out, "Smile, you jerkaloe, you're on candid camera!" Thereupon, he also slammed his car door closed and quite expeditiously sped off from the station.

Next, as the man's surprise had immediately turned to outrage, he fanatically ran after the exiting vehicle while shaking his fist in the air and uncontrollably screaming out, "You damn hippies, you damn hippies!"

Finally, after all the laughing had subsided, Scott awarded Eugene, "The five-dollar performance of the year," as the two of them were now in total concurrence over the man's true character by agreeing, "That guy was really pissed off!"

~

The whole college experience had become a happening for the entire country. The emergence of the community college had now extended the opportunity of receiving a draft deferment to even the lower economic classes. Thus, scholastic achievement en masse took a back seat to the politics of social engineering. The restructuring of the lower economic class's access to an "equal opportunity college education" was now beginning to show its effect, specifically in that the peace and love faction was obviously gaining ground.

The sensationalistic media was having a field day, now both in color and profit, as it perniciously and relentlessly contributed heavily to the already divided politisphere in stereotyping both its sides into a gargantuan melodrama that seemed to have no bounds of decency.

"Read all about it! How the military secretly encouraged the Mei Li massacre to increase their body count."

"Read all about it! How Charles Manson rules all the hippies and the SDS from jail."

"Read all about it! How Eldritch Cleaver will be anointed the Supreme Black Leader over all his people!"

All the inferences were there.

The television networks weighed in, as well. Promoting man's inhumanity to man, it graphically depicted the entire society in the sole terms of debauchery, mayhem, and belligerence. This tactic manifested huge returns for the medium, while the public's "right to know" was being clandestinely edited for a greater market share.

The American "free press" was not free. Everyone was paying for it. In fact, many were still paying for it with their lives.

Then, on May the fourth, nineteen hundred and seventy, the unthinkable happened: two of these uncompromising factions clashed together on a Midwest college campus, resulting in the deaths of four of their students, armed moreover with only a contentiously different point of view. The media was in heaven. The other nine students, who were only wounded, were reported to be grateful they got to live, while the government touted they were morally righteous in killing the ones they did. It was further printed that the government was completely just in their actions because a court had issued them writ to legally do so.

The entire nation was in shock. This one unbelievable and abominable incident had brought about such inherent sorrow throughout the land that it had devastatingly affected everyone. Greed, want of power, and intellectual bigotry had concertedly railed against the true peace lovers in a wanton attempt to silence them through threat of death. Sheer force now appeared to be sanctioned omnipotent and thereafter became employed by both sides in their quest to definitively win their cause. A social sickness had set in and it took the slaughter of the country's own children, by its own hand, to poignantly and shamefully remind everyone of what constitutes a sin.

The end of the 'Vietnam Conflict' was now seen as inevitable, and as the draft had become redundant, so too did the real reason why so many students had signed up for college. Then, when it had become altogether apparent that not every prospective graduate would be employed within the up and coming field of plastics, many of them simply quit their studies and traveled around the country with their brothers who were returning from the foreign battlefield.

Everything was now up in the air, but the one specific thing that did become manifestly clear to everyone was that marijuana had become the most popular drug of choice to be taken when being directly and inescapably confronted with the horrors of life. Valium came in at a respectful second.

And so, as the entirety of mankind had watched itself from the solitude of the moon, and the legacies of Woodstock, the Kennedys, and Martin Luther King could not be erased, the entire country turned a new page in history.

Chapter Four

"And a good time was had by all," stated the secretary at the close of each meeting in the fraternity to which Scott and Eugene had become members, while their last two years in college did echo this same sentiment as well. Once their core requirements had been finished, leaving them with only the subjects of their own choosing, life became a piece of cake, which they intended to slice in manner they so desired.

Their weekends were now filled with rock concerts, trips to the beach, the mountains, or anything else they had the passion to experience. Regardless, on Wednesday nights, like clockwork, they always hosted a poker game at "The Cincinnati Kid's Hole in the Wall Hideout," which at any other time sufficed to be known as Gene's Apartment. They were up tight, outta' sight, and in the groove.

Eugene's considerable sized apartment had been meticulously decorated. Upon entering the apartment, once the light switch directly to the right of the door was turned on, it automatically illuminated a collection of railroad lights and torchiere lamps that had been strategically appointed around the room, subsequently producing a multi-colored psychedelic sheen upon the black Naugahyde furniture positioned to the right side of the living area. Then, directly against the wall and amidst this setting, was an eight-track console stereo which also had been set to automatically come on with the lights. Prepositioned, once the record flatly hit the turntable, the sound of *Satisfaction* by the Rolling Stones was immediately heard to be woefully denied.

In the center of this grouping, with its four-seater couch, matching love seat, and easy chair, sat a dark wood coffee table displaying a large pair of glass ashtrays, while at the sides of the furniture sat the end tables supporting the various lava lamps which, when turned on, would colorfully entertain the curiosities of most anyone. The new color TV was also cornered there, so that all seated could have an unobstructed view when watching it, but in fact, it was almost never turned on.

However, there was a good reason for this, for the cadre of souls that regularly occupied this area believed that the thought police had complete control over the television media and if they watched its commercials, it would make their minds rot. With certitude, they were all in total agreement that the advertisements being broadcasted were used to surreptitiously brainwash them by employing subliminal messaging. Secretly transmitted in the style of a "Big Brother" campaign, the purpose of these embedded messages, as they truly believed, was to induce them to unconsciously conform to the evil government's own secretive agenda, whatever that might be.

It also was universally agreed upon that the proof of this mind controlling technique existed in the de facto citing of the many unanswered questions that no one could ever seem to explain, such as: Did the government make me eat those fourteen tacos against my will, or did the God of Cannabis command me to do it? Another popular mystery was: Exactly how much would your psyche be tainted if you only watched the *Doby Gillis* re-runs, then followed by *Gilligan's Island*? Suspiciously again, there was no empirical evidence to doubt otherwise. Perhaps the greatest cryptogram of all was: "Will Sherman the pet boy ever gain enlightenment from the historical lessons experienced from trekking through time with his dogmeister Mister Peabody in the Wayback Machine?" Once more, they were only met with, "Who knows?" and "Only time will tell." In any case, this was the general thinking of all who gathered here.

Opposite this formal seating area, and to the left side of the room, was a four stool, apartment sized bar for the drinkers, and behind its far corner stood an old white porcelain Frigidaire adorned with a multitude of brightly flowered decals. Directly centered behind the bar hung a velveteen painting of four dogs engaged in playing poker, while on the floor underneath it was situated two plastic insulated coolers, one for ice, and the other for left over drinks, for there was no sink. Also kept under the bar on its one and only shelf, conveniently placed next to a dozen or so mismatched drinking glasses, was a woven bread basket stocked with a variety of cigarette rolling papers, half-used match books, and a various selection of alligator roach clips.

The hard liquor of choice, when the "Juice Heads" chipped in, was Seagram's Seven, which naturally was the primary ingredient in the ever popular Seven and Seven cocktail. The bar area also doubled as a convenient place for the pot heads to roll their joints.

Now as far as party bartender was concerned, it was generally known that anyone acting as such could prepare a Seven and Seven, but it took a true artist to double as a pot tender. By hand, he was required to not only roll pin joints, boats, party numbers, shot gun doubles, and camel clones, but a proficiency in the preparation of bongs, and the skill needed to properly pack a pipe was also a talent that was greatly appreciated. The satisfaction achieved from the assisted consummation of the patron's high endeavors was always in direct proportion to the recognized fame of the pot tender, and the efficacy of his endeavors. It was this fame that determined the pot tender's worth.

To the back of the main room was the entrance to the kitchen. This is where the poker game took place. A set of hanging colored beads had been nailed over the archway to separate the solemnity of the gamblers from the more festive party goers, but it did little to stop the actual noise from bleeding through.

In the long and narrow kitchen, there was no cooking paraphernalia to be seen at all. A large white porcelain sink sat directly upon a silver toned Formica counter at the far end of the room and both above and below it was a row of white enameled cabinets which stretched across from the windowed side of the room to end directly next a round-shouldered Kelvinator standing flat against the right-hand wall.

The center of the room was dominated by an oblong shoddy wooden dining table, surrounded by six matching, maroon colored chairs, their seats being obviously tattered with wear. The overhead light fixture had been removed and replaced by green shaded lamp, having been chained to hang about three feet above the table.

At the table's left was the outside wall with two double sashed windows that overlooked the parking lot, while directly underneath them was an old cast iron radiator, painted white with enamel. A large galvanized outside garbage can, never known to be empty, had been functionally stationed in the corner opposite the kitchen's entrance. Finally, just past the beads and before one got to the garbage can, was the apartment's hallway that led to the bathroom and the apartment's two bedrooms.

The first of the two bedrooms to come upon was stylized in the "traditional look." A complete walnut bedroom suite, queen sized, with side stands and tufted sitting chair were functionally placed to pronounce the country living effect. On the far side of the bed, a component stereo record player sat atop a lowboy chest of drawers at the ready to listen to Carole King declare herself to feel like a natural woman.

Twenty-five-watt light bulbs were intentionally placed into the shaded lamps atop the stands on both sides of the bed. This produced a soft lighting effect that was designed to project a serene and secure environment. It was in this room that Eugene displayed his valued treasures. The walls were decorated with a half-dozen pastoral paintings of various sizes and his high school athletic letter, which he had framed in gold. Finally, atop a low bookshelf coming into the room, Eugene exhibited his pewter chess set. He was at best an average player, but the purpose of the highly polished set was not for playing, it was only on display to subconsciously illustrate his intellectual proclivities.

The second bedroom had a diametrically opposed ambiance. Sporting a king-sized water bed, there was little room for any other furnishings. An electric blanket was placed on the floor under the mattress for heating the water to the desired temperature. The rails enclosing the mattress were built out of two-by-twelve planks which all had been joined together at its corners with four large brass door hinges. A two-by-eight plank was placed on the top of four upright cinder blocks at the head of the bed that served as a utility shelf.

Upon this make-shift headboard were placed two lava lamps, one at each end, along with two matching six-inch stereo box speakers. In the center was placed a bright orange oblong ceramic ashtray with a small perforation in each of its ends, into which a pair of sandalwood incense sticks had been inserted. Finally, and most noteworthy, on the wall directly above this entire ensemble, there hung a poster of Jimi Hendrix, who was unquestionably challenging your level of experience.

The far side of the bed was only about a foot from its bare wall and the near side had only a lone coffee table adjacent to its rail where an end table would normally be. A component turn table, with its controls facing the bed for convenient accessibility, sat atop the right end of the table and was wired up to not only to the set of speakers on the headboard, but additionally to a set of boxed impulse lights sitting on the floor at the foot of the bed. The overhead light was replaced by a black light which, when turned on, most colorfully and vibrantly illuminated the psychedelic Jimi Hendrix poster.

Additionally, on the top of coffee table and directly next to the changer was methodically placed a box of matches, a candle, a Bic lighter, and a black Melmac ashtray for the expected festivities. A folded terrycloth towel had been placed under the table for any unexpected consequences as well. Still, with all the fastidious planning and diabolical engineering that went into this production, Eugene's dramatic orchestration was yet incomplete until one was introduced to the sound of Jim Morrison singing *"Come on Baby Light My Fire"* in full concert with the impulse lights. Then, indeed, it was an experience of the times.

Such was the physical world of Eugene Kavanagh, as designed and synthesized by himself. He was the master of his own domain. Championed by Scott, the two Wednesday night card sharks parlayed the invited players and spirited partiers into a veritable writhing menagerie of unwitting volunteers whose purpose was to provide them with a variety of entertainingly profitable social experiments. It was their zoo, and the park did not open until nine o'clock in the evening.

The local girls were usually the first to show up in twosomes and threesomes, followed by the party dudes. Thereafter, came the gamesters to be followed by the sorority girls. Business was usual most of the time, but acknowledging that the next day was a still Thursday, it was requisite that a semblance of sobriety be kept. This was an emanate reality that could not be ignored. Conversely, the special Friday Night Soiree, thrown immediately after the midterm finals, was also an emanate reality, but this one blew caution to the wind like a snow blower in February.

Once the last of the examinations were final, the dreadful feelings that had been shared by all who took them needed to be exorcised from their souls. This was when the cathartic ritual to cleanse them from their lingering angst would begin. While all had been part of the same ordeal as one, it nonetheless created a chasm by its very nature between the continuing committed and the scholastically condemned. They both would move on of course, but now in different directions. In the final analysis, however, it was the angst of separation that first needed to be addressed, for it had infected everyone. Therefore, it was universally accepted by all, that as soon as the mid-terms were in the history books, the only way to only cure this affliction would be to party their pants off.

Preparation was already underway when the secret knock was detected at the door. It was only about eight o'clock, and while Eugene was intently focused on counting the decks of cards and attending to the projected needs of the intended marks, Scott proceeded to answer the front door.

"Hurry up, for God's sake, this stuff is heavy!" a voice yelled out from behind the door.

"Just how heavy is your load, Brother?" Scott answered tauntingly, pausing momentarily from the other side.

"I feel like a midget assigned to carry the fat lady in the circus, Brother. Now just open the damn door!" the voice behind it demanded.

"Now that's a heavy load," greeted Scott with a smile, finally letting them in.

And thus entered two of Scott and Eugene's most revered and esteemed fraternity members, "Big Dick" and "Little Peter." The duo, also known as the "Festive Facilitators," now struggled past Scott with their load of beer in six-packs, cigarettes in cartons, and prodigious amounts of pogybate, all stuffed chaotically into a half-dozen of the largest brown paper bags available at the local A&P. Acrobatically, they pushed on, attempting not to lose control of their bounty. Nonetheless, once they had gotten about six steps inside the door, and precisely front of the bar, they discharged their entire burden loudly onto the floor.

"Well, we made it. And I think we've collected all the essential components that are necessary to produce a most stupendous soiree," Dick emphatically stated in his deep baritone voice.

"Oh, we intend to party down, Brother," Pete added enthusiastically.

"Big Dick," as his nom de plume implied, was the large and hefty one of the twosome. Displaying a most pleasant countenance conjoined with a notably affable demeanor, Dick was the party coordinator and a one-man security team. As far as anyone could remember, no one had ever caused a raucous altercation while Dick was present, for at six-foot-six he was a "pretty big guy."

His partner-in-crime, "Little Peter," having only achieved a height of five foot four and thinly framed, was completely the opposite of Big Dick in every way. Curly headed and colorful, he was always a walking fashion statement. Peter was the technical doctor behind the bar and a veritable cornucopia of stories, jokes and witticisms. His gregarious and pertinacious behavior was an essential quality obligatory to his craft and consequently was the impetus of his title, "The Potentate of Pot Tenders."

The concept of the "Professional Partier Enterprise" had embraced both Dick and Pete with the same irresistible motivation that manifested itself within Eugene and Scott as to their gambling activities. The inducement of having an unrestricted good time, and also to profit by it as well, was a theory that was just too compelling for any of them to resist. Consequently, all together, the young entrepreneurs sought to conquer one of the world's greatest puzzles, how to mix business with pleasure, become successful, *and* maintain your dignity—and all at the same time.

"At what time are you going to start the card game, Gene?" Peter inquired loudly toward the kitchen, where he figured Eugene was potting about.

"I figure about ten thirty or so. I want to give them enough time to get into a good mood. What do you think, Scott?" Eugene called back loudly.

"I think shrewd is the mood, that's what I think," Scott stated shortly, while placing a stack of ashtrays about the living room.

"I think there will be a lot of people coming tonight," Dick prognosticated smoothly.

"Yeah, and we're going to get high, high, high, till the mornin' come," Peter vocalized, while arranging his parlor for the flies, confident that over this realm, *he* was the Lord.

"Did you bring the munchies, Peter?" Eugene called out from the kitchen.

"Does the Pope crap in the woods?" Peter called back. "I got some Fritos, Twizzlers, Tootsie rolls, and Twinkies. And I collected five bucks from about a dozen jamokes to help pay for all this stuff, too," he informed everyone out loud. "If we run out later, I'll collect again for pizza, some more liquid refreshment, or whatever they want, but as always, I need to collect cash for my stash, 'cause there ain't no freebies, baby!" he stated flatly. "Finally, just so you know, I believe I have a more than sufficient quantity to achieve enlightenment for all," he added in an upscale tone.

"I invited a couple of sisters from the I Ata Thi Sorority, or whatever sorority they actually said they were from," Scott casually remarked. "I'll tell you who they are Pete, so you can prep them for me, —but I most definitely *do not* want them blown away," he resolutely commanded. "I simply want them, let's say, gratefully receptive. I'll take either one and split the cost of their ah, indoctrination, with anyone else who wants the other."

"I'd like to see them first," Dick replied, casually arranging the albums on the music stand by the stereo.

"Not to worry, Big Dick, Scott does not consort with skanks," he dramatically responded in the third person.

"Well, I think we have everything set," Eugene said with an air of finality upon entering the room. "When they come in, I guess the party will start all by itself. I put some ashtrays on the poker table in the kitchen. Do we need any more of them out here?" Eugene asked openly from across the room.

"I put one on every table, I gave two to Pete for the bar, and I put the giant one on the coffee table over here by the couch," Scott confirmed.

"So, we're all set then," Eugene declared. "You got a cold brewski over there for me, Mr. Barkeep?" he asked, addressing Pete specifically.

"Does a one-legged chicken have lips?" Pete retorted. Fatefully, however, no sooner than the beer had been popped open came the first knock at the door, signifying that the evening's adventure was about to begin. Discontinuing his perusal over the music selection, Dick slowly sauntered towards the front door to admit the first of the revelers who were hoping to indulge themselves as soon as was permitted.

Some of the revelers came early so they could get a good seat that was comfortable. Others came early to position themselves to where they thought the 'action' was going to be. Still, there were more who simply arrived at the beginning because they did not want to miss anything.

Regardless, once situated, many of these guests tried to convince themselves that they were only there as a spectator, solely as an observer of a social experiment. The reality was, nonetheless, that they themselves were also being observed by everyone else as part of the same experiment, and ironically showing up early could never really changed this fact, for only leaving early could. Substantially, all the same, once the party was in full swing, no one ever really cared.

Then the regulars filed in, singles, doubles, threesomes, and more, all to mill about in search of their familiars. The lava lamps were lit, and the stereo was playing Joplin. And while Hendrix and Dylan were assigned as their dedicated backups, the philosophical couch radicals began to debate the existence of the purple haze, the ultimate goals of the SDS, and the Kent State Massacre.

The bar area's cultural preferences were of a more convivial nature. "High times" had been declared while the mellow yellow fellows discussed the concept of free love with the earth mothers. All was copacetic. The music style, as referenced by its clientele, was that of The Mommas and the Poppas, Donavan, Morrison, Crosby, Stills, Nash, and Young, and every other musician that had embodied the popular mantle, *"If you can't be with the one you love, love the one you're with."*

Then, after Sgt. Pepper's Lonely Hearts Club Band had encapsulated the entire room, and the conventional seating had all been filled, it was now up to the beanbag chairs to take the next hit. But this this was to no avail either, for the folks kept on arriving. Soon, even the floor had become overtaken, turning itself into a virtual homogeneous carpet of compassion. It now had become official: "the party was on."

Chapter Five

"For all of you who wish to partake in the noble pastime of poker, the 'Hole in the Wall' is now open!" called out Eugene over the stereo's best attempt to eulogize *The Night They Drove Old Dixie Down*. "And, if you will all be quiet for a second, Peter the Pot Tender also has an announcement to make," he expounded, standing in front of the entrance to the kitchen. "Dick, can you turn down the music for a second?" he formally requested.

"I got it," responded Dick, rising from his chair to lend his assistance.

Then, as soon as the stereo had been lowered and everyone's full attention had been garnered, Eugene resumed his introduction in pronouncing, "Pete, you have the floor."

"Well, fellow stoners and juice heads, the world of Planet Peter is offering either two ice cold Budweiser beers, the brew that cannot be matched by any other beer, at any price, or two Millers, which, as you know, stands clear among beers, to the first one who can solve this riddle. Now, for you space cadets ready to graduate to the next level, instead of your beer of choice you may opt to receive not one, but two primo, hand rolled, single paper dubies," he eminently declared. "Now, I will recite this one time," he paused for a second, while holding up his index finger dramatically to get everyone's attention while looking around the room, "and the first one to correctly come up with the answer can claim their prize. Now, listen carefully," he again began.

"Peter Packer, The Pot Packer, packed a peck of pot. And if Peter Packer, The Pot Packer, packed a peck of pot, just how many packs of pot did Peter Packer pack?" he propositioned, momentarily waiting for someone to reply.

"Can anyone tell me?" he asked further, still not receiving a response. "Well, then I have to assume that no one has the answer and so, since I have no takers, I'll just have to tell you," he pretentiously submitted with the grin of an unchallenged expert. "The answer is thirty-six," he revealed flatly. "It takes four kilos of brick packed Columbian Gold to equal one bushel, and there are four pecks to a bushel. Each peck should produce thirty-six packs of twenty "grade a" camel clone cigarettes to a pack, so therefore, the standard number is thirty-six packs," he explained authoritatively. "Now, if you feel you are being ripped off by your current supplier, then contact me, Peter Packer, The Potentate of Pot Packers, for I will do you right," he advertised in finality. "And now, I am going to turn you back over to the host with the most, Eugene Kavanagh, the Cincinnati Kid of the Cards!" he enthusiastically declared in conclusion.

"We have five chairs available to those of you who have a twenty dollar buy in," Eugene denoted in a business-like manner. "And everyone with the funds to play is invited."

Eugene then summarily turned and disappeared through the hanging beads behind him to take his place at the far end of the table with his back to the sink, while Scott took his customary position in front of the beaded curtain.

"Just step right up, one at a time," Scott barked out with a smile, as if soliciting for a carnival attraction.

"How's it goin', Scott?" pleasantly greeted Tom, while his fraternity brother shook his hand before passing through the hanging beads. Tom was a hefty six-foot gregarious fellow with jet black curly hair that was offset by an eggshell white complexion. Slovenly dressed but constantly jovial, he emanated an affable nature that was enjoyed by all.

The next fellow to enter the room was George. Physically slim and sporting a goatee, George had straight, shoulder length medium brown hair and had on a faded Rolling Stones tee shirt, threadbare jeans, and an equally worn out pair of sneakers. The epitome of an industrial arts major, George had always looked as if he had just tuned up someone's car. He spoke little but, whenever he did, he was simple and direct.

Billy James Lee was the next in line and was nothing like George. He had a stocky build, short blond hair, and a medium complexion with light blue eyes. He possessed an easy-going pleasant smile that gave him the image of the all-American boy. He wore a brown plaid dress shirt, a pair of kaki dress pants, and a set of well shined oxford penny loafers. Billy also had the propensity to comment unabashedly on everything from politics and religion, and even if coma babies are in fact possessed by extraterrestrial aliens. There was no subject that he did not have a comment on.

Following directly behind Billy was Roy. Tall and lanky, Roy had a proportionately long face with a pleasantly inviting visage. Wearing a white alligator Banlon, black pleated cuffed trousers, and tasseled shoes, he typified the golfing industry right down to his smooth Bing Crosby voice and congenial demeanor.

"You know, I think *I'll* take the last spot at the table," Scott informed Eugene, following Roy into the kitchen.

"Are you going to play, too?" Eugene asked, looking like he was surprised.

"Yeah, I think I'll play this time," Scott answered him matter-of-factly.

"Well, if all of you sit down and give me your twenty dollars, I can give you your chips. Then, maybe we can get this game started," Eugene charged.

After collecting the money and putting it in a Corona cigar box to his right on the table, Eugene began distributing the chips.

"First, I think that we all should state our names," Eugene suggested as soon as his task was finished. "And so, for the record, I'm Gene," he announced to all, to then glance over to his right.

"Tom is my name, and winning is my game," the light-hearted fraternity secretary announced with a smile.

"I'm George," the player to Tom's right said with no expression at all.

Next, came the co-host, who presumptuously articulated, "I believe everyone here knows me as Scott."

"Well, I believe that everyone here knows me as The Winner, but I'll play along and let everyone just call me BJ," Billy James mocked provocatively.

"Well, I'm Roy," the last player said mildly, "and I am here to play poker."

"The green chips are a nickel, the blues are a dime, and red ones are a quarter," Eugene stated clinically, after everyone's buy-in had been collected. "Now, you all should have twenty dollars' worth," he officiated at large. "There is a quarter ante, and you are allowed two raises each turn with a maximum of a dollar raise each time. I will deal first, and then after that, the deal will go to the next player to the dealer's right. We are playing straight poker, and five or seven card stud, dealer's choice. There will be no wild cards or any other such ridiculous rules. So, what do you say?" he solicited and waited for a reply.

"Okay by me," said Tom, followed by "Sure" from George, and "just, deal the cards" from Scott.

"Just deal the cards," mimicked BJ as Roy simply replied "Ditto."

"The name of the game is straight, five-card poker, boys," Eugene announced as the lyrics *"Sunshine came softly through my window today,"* bled over and into the kitchen's otherwise serious nature. "I am still one ante short, fellas," he ascertained, after dealing out the initial cards and checking the pot in the center of the table.

"Oh, I forgot," said Scott, throwing a chip into the middle of the table.

"Just forget to deal him a card," BJ directed to Gene sarcastically, while Scott responded to his remark by simply peering at him in silence.

"If I put up another ante, can I play with six cards?" laughed Tom out loud, making light of BJ's comment.

"Tom, do you have a bet?" Eugene asked in a serious tone, trying to get down to the actual business of playing the game.

"Nope," was his one-word answer.

"George?"

"I'll bet a nickel."

"Scott?"

"I think I will make that a quarter."

"BJ?"

"I'm in for a quarter."

"Roy?"

"I fold."

"The dealer is in for a quarter, and Tom, are you in or out?" Eugene specifically asked.

"I'm in for the two bits," he responded, throwing a quarter chip into the center of the table.

"And it's another twenty cents to you, George," Eugene prompted.

"I'm in," said George, tossing in four more chips onto the mounting pile.

"Now, how many cards do you want, Tom?" Eugene continued.

"I'll take three," Tom replied.

"How many, George?"

"Just two," George answered shortly.

"And how many does Scott require?" asked Eugene with pomposity.

"I shall take one, thank you," replied Scott in turn.

"I have an ace," stated BJ, turning it over for all to see, "so I will take four cards please, Gene."

"Okay, BJ, here you are, and good luck," Eugene offered in a tongue-in-cheek manner, thereafter announcing, "and the dealer takes two."

Pausing a moment to look at his draw, Eugene then turned to Tom and resumed.

"It's your bet,"

"I'll pass."

"And you, George?"

"Pass."

"And you, Scott?" Eugene asked again.

Leaning back in his chair and putting his hand to his chin, Scott paused for a second before responding, "I think it's worth fifty cents to me," and threw in two chips.

"I'll see that," said BJ, and did the same.

Eugene picked up his cards, studying them for a moment before replying, "I will see your bet, Scott, and raise it another half-a-buck," adding four more chips to the pile. "And now it's a buck to you, Tom," he continued.

"I think I can handle that," responded Tom, throwing in four more chips.

"Too rich for me," stated George, laying down his hand.

"I'll see your raise, punk," Scott retorted efficaciously, smiling directly at Eugene and putting in another two bits.

"It's another half-a-rock to you, BJ," Eugene continued.

"You mean I gotta' pay to see this crap?" BJ answered with a smile.

"Yup, it's called, 'pay to play' BJ. You oughta know that by now," interjected tom.

"Okay Gene, so, wadja' got that's worth a buck and a half?" asked BJ, calling to see the raise.

"A pair of kings," Eugene flatly displayed, turning to his right to solicit, "Tom?"

"I guess a pair of tens won't cut it then," commented Tom, before surrendering them to the table.

"Okay, Scott, let's see what you got," Eugene challenged.

"Read 'em and weep," Scott gloated, "I have The Three Musketeers: Jack, Jack, and the other brother Jack too," he presented. "So, what say you, Mr. BJ?" he prompted.

"Well, I did pick up another ace," responded BJ, which he showed in turning it over, "but it just wasn't enough," he confessed resolutely. "It's all yours, Scott," he acquiesced.

And the game continued, replete with every single one of the standard bantering and degrading innuendos perceived to be necessary and customary in projecting their images to the world as adult gamblers. Both rooms were now filled to capacity while the whispering smoke of inebriation had insidiously infiltrated the senses of all, and the sublime had now moved into the realm of the bizarre. The latest political philosophy concerning the war and how it affected everyone had now become a faded shade of pale against the livelier and more colorful debate over whether or not a woman ought to be wearing a bra in public. There was even some calling for a demonstration to be held right then and there, for it seemed that the "No Bra" faction was clearly gaining the upper hand, but yet the argument went on.

Dick had chosen, as usual, one of the more comfortable Naugahyde easy chairs to sit in. It was next to the main coffee table in the lounge area. Ensconced here, it was now easy for him to conduct his surveillance activities. He, of all the hosts and guests as well, was naturally the mellowest fellow there, and whether it was because of his size, his serenity, or his attractive appearance, he was never in want of a beautiful girl.

It was then, while Dick had been seated in his throne while discussing the merits of communal living with a most unpretentious and opinionated long-haired Aphrodite who had summarily and righteously commandeered his lap, that two even more strikingly beautiful girls had abruptly appeared directly in front of him. Clearly, they were at mission's end and wished to be recognized as being present and fully accounted for.

Unlike the girl in the brightly flowered Mumu before them, both these debutants were wearing professionally made tie-dyed, skin-tight jeans along with a pair of matching sorority sweatshirts. The taller one stood about five-foot ten, and had long curling red hair that hung down just past shoulder length, chestnut colored eyes, and the tiniest waist imaginable in proportion to her hips. She also had a set of the most the generous breasts to be seen anywhere in the room, everwhich to Dick's amusement, suddenly got him thinking, "*I do believe in cantaloupes. I do, I do, —I do believe in cantaloupes.*"

Her indisputable "sister" was nothing like her at all. She had short, curly, light blond hair and a petite figure that went unnoticed against the backdrop of her large and sparkling green eyes.

"The little guy whose rolling pot over at the bar said you would know where Scott is," the red headed girl proposed in a stilted manner.

"Well, first of all, it would be nice to know your names," Dick replied mildly, turning to the girl atop him and saying clearly, "You need to get up for a second, babe."

Slowly, the girl did what was asked, while Dick rose up from the chair as well. Then, once realizing the formidable size and bearing of the party's gatekeeper, the redhead instantly adjusted her aggressive tone to respond in an alluring fashion.

"Well, big boy. I'm Rose, and this is Annette, my little sister, and we are supposed to be the guests of Scott."

"Well, in that case, I guess I'll just have to take you to him, won't I?" Dick responded evenly, turning his attention back to the displaced girl for a moment to add, "Be back in a second, this won't take long."

Next, after strolling over to the entrance of the kitchen, Dick reached out and held the beads aside for the two girls to pass by, following on from behind.

"I'm calling your bluff," George was saying to Roy, putting four chips in the pot.

"Okay, George, you're in for a treat," said Roy. "You see, this is called a straight, so if you have not seen one before, here it is," he began to reveal, turning up hold cards.

Finally, after the last card had been turned over, which had evoked a muttered "Damn!" by George, Dick stealthily leaned over to Scott to personally informed him, "Here are the guests you ordered. Pete sent them to me, and so here they are," he affirmed, nodding slightly and shifting his eyes in the girls' direction.

"Did Pete provide them with anything?" Scott asked of him in a low tone.

"I don't know. You'll have to ask them, but I'm going back out front now," Dick dismissively replied, standing back up to address the entire room. "And by the way, everyone, the big one here is Rose and the little one is called

Annette," he courteously announced before leaving them behind, promptly leaving the room.

"If you want to get high or have something to drink, just tell Pete at the bar you're with me," Scott informed them dispassionately from over his shoulder, not getting up from the table. "Oh, and by the way, there is also some Boone's Farm Strawberry Hill in the refrigerator over there, if you want some," he additionally offered, nodding over to the far back corner of the room in not putting down his cards.

"No thanks, I think I'll just go out and get me a couple of hits and come back later," declared Rose. "Are you coming?" she asked, addressing her partner directly.

"No, I think I'm going to stay and have some of the Boone's Farm right here," she replied casually.

"Well, I'll catch you on the return, then," Rose accepted, summarily exiting through the beads.

"Okie dokie" Annette responded, turning directly to Scott to verify, "So, you say it's the strawberry one, Scott?"

"Yeah, I think so," answered Scott apathetically.

"It's behind me on the top shelf of the fridge, next to the Lancers. There are also some glasses in the cupboard over the sink," Eugene helpfully offered.

"Hi, I'm Roy," he announced.

"I'm George," he added.

"I'm Tom," came next.

"And I'm BJ, —I guess you already know Scott and Gene," he outspokenly assumed, believing he was the last one to be introduced.

"Not really, BJ, I just met Scott the other day in the library when he invited Rose and me to the party," Annette clarified. "I know a few people in the other room from around the campus, too, but that's about all," she edified, while ambulating behind George and Tom to get at the refrigerator at the back of the room.

"Well, I'm Eugene, and this is my place, but everyone calls me Gene," he formally stated, moving his chair further into the table so Annette could pass behind him. "And as long as you are going to open the wine, would you also pour me a glass?" he courteously added.

"Sure," Annette replied, taking the bottle from the refrigerator and placing it on the counter. She then reached up into the cupboard above the sink to take out two water glasses, and after placing them on the counter, she closed the cupboard, unscrewed the cap from the bottle, and filled each of the tall glasses half way up. Recapping the bottle, she placed it back into the refrigerator, put one of the glasses on the table next to where Eugene was seated, and then casually walked around behind him again. Finally, once she had gotten over by the side window, which was kitty-corner from where Eugene was seated, and right before where Tom was seated, she punctiliously sat herself down, right atop the radiator.

"Thank you," Gene then said to her considerately.

"You're welcome," she replied. "It's okay if I sit here, isn't it?" she asked.

"Yeah, it's okay, I guess," Eugene answered before turning to his left to say, "Well, it's still your deal, Roy."

"It's seven card stud, gentlemen," Roy now announced, resuming the game.

Eugene's mind, however, was no longer on the game. The instant she had entered the room, he had taken notice of her. She was like a little doll, he thought, still in her play clothes. Her large green eyes that seemed to overwhelm her small upturned nose and her pursed pink lips had, to him, given her the image of a small defenseless bird, *and a rare blond one at that,* he thought. He even fantasized briefly that he was Jason on a quest for the Golden Fleece, albeit a small fleece, but a true golden one nonetheless. For the first time in his young life, he was utterly amused in being able to apply his Greek fables into allegorically including himself.

Annette had gotten quite comfortable on the radiator with her glass of strawberry flavored wine, deciding she would simply relax and patiently watch the show until her sorority sister returned. The first thing she noticed, beginning to make her observations, was that the tumbler she had taken from the cabinet was real crystal, and that Eugene's clothes were equally as expensive. Eugene was also well-mannered in addressing the others at the table and appeared to be altogether pleasant, even tempered, and sometimes witty.

Critically, Annette had deduced that even though his mild intellectual disposition would not make him the most exciting, dashing man of physical pleasure, he still might have some other important mitigating features to take into consideration, should she decide to possess him. *Certainly, his authoritative manner is worth something,* she figured. *After all, he is the ultimate person in charge of this whole shebang,* she concluded.

"We're playing five card stud," Roy declared, restarting the game. "Two down, two up, and the last one down, and that's my choice," he ruled.

After the two first cards were dealt down to everyone at the table, he tossed a card upright to Eugene, revealing the two of clubs, and enunciating in his renowned low-pitched voice, he began to narrate,

"And a low blow to the host," he noted as he tossed Eugene a deuce.

"The queen of desire to needy Tom," he continued.

"I'm wantee, not needy" interjected Tom.

"A lucky seven to Georgie Porgie."

"Then it's ten little Indians to big Scott."

"And now it's a crazy eight, right where it belongs," he kiddingly remarked with a thin smile.

"Hey, I resemble that remark," BJ quipped."

"And a king to a king, which I deserve, and I'll bet a buck 'cause I'm in luck," he rhymed while he reached down forthwith with his right hand and tossed in his chips. "It is up to you, 'Mr. Low as you go,'" Roy asserted to Eugene.

Picking up his hold cards off the table, Eugene glanced at them for a second, threw them back down abruptly, picked up four quarter chips, and after pitching them into the pot, remarked in a frivolous manner, "Oh, what the hell."

"The queen will stick around just to keep the king honest," followed Tom, adding to the growing pile in the center of the table.

"I'm in," said George.

"I'm in," declared Scott, following suit.

"So, I'm crazy, —but I'm in, too," confirmed BJ, not be excluded.

And with that said, Roy returned to dealing the cards.

"A five to the deuce, how pathetic. An ace to the queen, the high guy on the block. A pair of sevens takes the lead. A nine to the ten with a possible straight. An ace to the eight, a possible dead man, and the king gets a jack," he judiciously ordained.

Then, after pausing a moment to look again at his own cards showing, Roy declared, "It's the pair of sevens' bet."

"The pair of sevens bets another buck," said George.

"I'm in," said Scott without hesitation.

"You know, I might be crazy, but I'm not stupid. I'm outta this hand," said BJ, definitively casting down his cards and leaning back in his chair.

"And the dealer remains in," Roy coolly announced in the drawl of Howard Cosell.

"'Hope springs eternal in the hearts and minds of men,'" Eugene then recited. "And that being said, I will put a dollar in too, just to save my soul."

"Huh, if Gene's in with that load of boloney, I guess I got to stay in too," reasoned Tom, tossing in his wager as well.

"Well, it's down and dirty time folks," Roy ominously noted, dealing out the final cards. "And it's still the pair of sevens' bet," he declared, once he had finished.

"Another buck," George answered, tossing in another four chips.

After turning up the corner of his last card dealt, Scott slowly and apocalyptically tapped on the top of his cards. Then, after individually glaring at everyone at the table, he defiantly announced, "Well, gentlemen, I'm bumping it up another buck. So, now, it's going to cost you two bucks to stay in," he smugly challenged, reaching over and picking up a stack of chips. "Here's mine," he self-assuredly added, demonstratively placing them down with a pronounced thump, explicitly next to the largest pot of the evening.

"Not me, boys," declared BJ with a most contented grin.

"The king believes his treasury can afford the additional simoleons," Roy decreed, thus making his contribution to the cause.

Folding his right hand up and resting it on his chin, as if he was Rodin's Thinker, Eugene now looked up and away in disengagement and began to muse out loud, "Let's see, Confucius said, 'It is more shameful to distrust our friends than to be deceived by them,' and since I trust that everyone here is trying to deceive me, I can only conclude that this lesson should cost everyone at least *three* dollars. Yes, I shall now raise the stakes to three dollars," he definitively advanced, "for I do believe there is deception afoot," he pronounced in taking a line from Sherlock Homes.

"It's now three bucks to you, Tom," Roy officiated in a more serious tone.

"You know, I feel the same way that Gene does, heh, heh," responded Tom light heartedly. So, I guess I have no choice but to call," he justified, adding his wager to the cache.

"And here's my two bucks. I'm also calling," said George flatly.

"I'm out," Scott declared unexpectedly, tossing down his cards.

"You're out? Gee, if I'da known you were fakin' it, I would have stayed in," BJ chided pretentiously.

"That was the whole point, BJ," Scott addressed him snidely.

"Well, I believe the king has no choice but to call either, after all, the king is still the king, and it's the kingly thing to do," Roy genially underscored. "You shall now reveal the truth, Sir Gene, for it is to call now," was his final dictate.

"Though they be little, they be fierce," Eugene paraphrased as he turned over his cards. "Let's see, I had a two showing, and look here," he exclaimed, "I have two more of the little guys, now that makes three and that's triplets, but what about my lonely five?" he pondered out loud again to his fictional friends in the air. "Oh my, he has a brother, too, another five," he presented like a grinning Cheshire Cat. "Now, boys, this is what you call a full house," he pretentiously stated, tossing down the final card. "And I am so happy that all of you got a chance to help me pay the rent," he gloated unpretentiously.

"Beats my two pair," said Tom.

"And mine," said George.

"And so, the kingdom has fallen. And as for the three kings, it shall be written, —they were more greedy than wise," dramatized Roy, continuing on with his tale. "The treasury now belongs to you, Sir Gene," Roy ruled, reaching over and pushing the hoard of chips in Eugene's direction.

Call after raise went by uninterruptedly for about another hour, until Annette's companion abruptly returned through the beaded curtain to unabashedly announce, "Well, Mr. Scott, I am having a good time without you, and I just wanted you to know it."

"This was my last hand, anyway," Scot responded decisively, tossing his cards over to Roy as George was collecting the chips. "Just let me finish up here and then I'm all yours, Big Red, okay?" he proffered.

"Suurrre," Rose drew out slowly with obvious disbelief. "Well, anyway, I'll be out by the bar," she declared with a flip of her wrist, leaving just as abruptly as she had entered.

"So, how are you doing, Annette?" Eugene asked in trying to take advantage of the interruption.

"Oh, I am doing just fine," Annette said innocuously. "But I was just wondering, what is that bottle of Lancers you have in the refrigerator?"

"It's a Portuguese rosé wine. It's not as sweet as what you are drinking, but it is a lot lighter," Eugene explained provocatively.

"Can I try some?" Annette asked demurely.

"Sure, in a minute Annette, but let me take care of this first, okay?" Eugene respectfully qualified, for it was his turn to deal and a look of impatience was clearly written upon Scott's face.

Thus, without waiting for a reply, Eugene immediately announced, "Gentlemen, this will be the last hand dealt, as we have come to the close of the evening. So, if you want to play in a final two-dollar high card draw, I will shuffle the deck, Tom on my right will cut it, and I will place it in the center of the table. We will begin with George to cut first for the highest card, and the winner will take all. Also, in case of a tie, the highest card holders will split the pot, okay?" he offered rhetorically. "Now, who is going to be in?" he solicited in finality.

"I say cut the cards," answered Scott as he threw in his chips.

"Me, too," said George solidly as he did the same.

"Sounds like a great idea to me, I only got two bucks left, anyway," stated Tom amiably, adding to the pot.

"It's okay by me," said BJ, "After all, who wants to play without Scott," he quipped in following suit.

"Here's mine," said Roy, also putting in his chips.

"Just shuffle the cards, Gene," Scott said impatiently.

Then, after Eugene had put in his chips and gave the deck a thorough shuffle, he squarely placed the deck in the center of the table and Tom reached over and cut it.

"Well, let's just get this over with," George vented, in drawing a ten. "Not bad, but not good," he uttered flatly, replacing his cards back on the top of the deck.

Scott, standing up, reached over to only draw a six, put back down his cards and said, "Gene, count my chips for me, would you? Scotty has someone to beam up." And without waiting for a reply, or even offering a final remark to anyone else, he bluntly left the room.

"You see that," BJ commented after drawing a jack, "The one time I had him beat hands down, he up and leaves the room."

"It's your cut, Roy," Eugene pointed out in a business-like fashion.

Again, returning to his imitation of Howard Cosell, Roy began, "And the question is, will Roy experience the thrill of victory, or the agony of defeat? He cuts the cards, but now hesitates to turn them over, and then suddenly, with a flip of the hand, he turns them over, and it's all over! Oh, the humiliation! A measly three! And so, the question is: Does Gene have what it takes to become the next champion? Well, we're about to find out," Roy ended, placing his draw cards back on top of the deck.

Eugene then reached over, cut the deck, looked at Roy, turned up a king and responded, "I believe he does." However, returning his cards to the deck, he then quoted Yogi Berra in saying, "But, it ain't over till it's over," Tom," raising his eyebrows, while directly looking to his right.

Tom, remaining silent, stretched out his arm, ascended his hand to the top of the deck, and then promptly turned over a six.

"Lucky dog, lucky dog, I'm a lucky dog!" Eugene laughed. "Well, boys, if you cash in your chips, I will give you your money," he announced victoriously.

"What chips are you talking about, Eugene?" asked Tom, pretending to be surprised. "Don't you mean, turn in your chip?" he chuckled in good sport. "I think you owe me a dime now," he said, tossing in the last of his stake.

"Here you go, Tom, and now we're square," Eugene cordially responded, tossing over a dime over to where Tom was standing.

Finally, after Eugene had finished settling up all of the other player's accounts and the cigar box was officially closed for business, he finally leaned back in his chair with a sigh of relief, quite contented to have no more deals to be concerned with. Annette, on the other hand, had her own deal she was about to begin.

Chapter Six

"So, what do you think of my den of iniquity, Fair Maiden?" Eugene asked of the ever-patient Annette, still enthroned upon the radiator.

"I think that I will give you that answer after you give me what you promised me, Sir Knight," Annette responded in kind.

"Oh, the Lancer's, of course. How forgetful of me," said Eugene, a little rattled as he got up from his chair. Going over to the refrigerator, he retrieved the earth toned, crock styled bottle and placed it on the table. Turning around, he subsequently reached over to the cabinet above the counter, and taking out another two crystal glasses, put them also on the table next to the wine.

One more time, Eugene went back to the counter and upon opening the flatware drawer underneath it, he removed a fancy silver contraption and also placed it on the table. Finally, putting his right index finger up to his temple to scratch it, he tried to think if he had forgotten anything else, and satisfied that he had not, set out to begin his mini demonstration.

"Would you care to join me and take a more comfortable seat over here, Miss Annette?" Eugene offered politely, motioning to the chair where Tom had been seated.

"I think I will do just that, Mr. Gene," Annette accepted graciously.

Suddenly, however, as if Eugene had been hit by a bolt of lightning, he had become acutely reminded that there was still a thriving amount of people in his living room, for the volume of Led Zeppelin's *Stairway to Heaven* had just gotten abruptly turned up. Immediately, he couldn't help but think, *God, how do I get rid of them without being insulting and tainting my reputation of being cool? I don't want to just throw them out, after all, they are my guests. But still, if I don't say something, how will I ever get rid of them? I know I'll never be able to get her alone with them in there,* He concluded. *Anyway,* He dismissed to himself, *I think I should pay attention to just wooing her with the wine in the first place. That's the smart thing. And, if that goes well enough—then I'll throw them out,* he decided.

Meanwhile, as these thoughts were racing inside Eugene's head, Annette had abandoned her former position atop the radiator and took her place, as proposed, at the table.

"My glass is still empty," Annette said in a tone more impatient than informative, instantly recapturing Eugene's direct attention.

"Well, you just can't unscrew the bottle and pour it out, you know, not like the cheap stuff that Scott buys," Eugene said in a not so disguised attempt to disparage his perceived competitor. "I have to remove the cork first. That's what this thing is for. It's a cork remover," he plainly said as he held out the silver apparatus which he had formally placed on the table.

"So, make it work, then," Annette coyly directed.

"You see, first you have to peel off the seal," Eugene explained, scoring the lead foil on the bottle's neck with the sharp end of the corkscrew. Then, after momentarily laying the devise back down and having removed the foil, he proceeded. "Now, you take the corkscrew part and screw it into the cork like this, and as you do—can you see the handles on the sides rise?" he questioned, briefly looking up to check on the degree of Annette's attentiveness.

"Yeah, I see it," Annette replied.

"Well, now you just push them down and presto, the cork is out," Eugene demonstrated to the resounding "pop" of success.

"I've never seen one of those before. That's pretty neat," she candidly remarked.

"Now, you just fill up the glasses half-way, like this, and there you are, a nice glass of rosé," Eugene concluded, condescendingly believing that she knew nothing about wine at all. "Go ahead, try it and tell me what you think," he entreated.

"Wow, this stuff sure is different. It's not sweet at all," Annette said, after taking her first sip.

"No. It's called dry. That stuff you have been drinking is considered sweet. This stuff you kind of have to get used to. They serve it in fancy restaurants. It's more expensive, but it doesn't give you near the headache the next day if you drink too much," he advised her as he now retook his seat next to her at the table.

"I didn't say it was bad, I just said it was different," Annette corrected. "I think it tastes pretty good, just as it is," she said, taking another sip. "So, this is your place?" she questioned, now returning her glass to the table.

"Yeah, I'm here until this spring when I graduate," Eugene replied, taking a drink a drink from his glass."

"So, what is your major?" Annette then asked.

But before Eugene could reply, in through the rattling of the colored beads a hand poked through, brashly and heedlessly casting them aside to announce the return of Scott.

"Listen, good buddy, I'm going to take Big Red over to my place. Can you take care of Annette here? Because I'm leaving, *right now*," he emphasized. "I talked to Dick, and he is going to start closing it down in a couple of minutes, anyway," he both stated and asked, in the same breath.

"Sure, I can," Eugene affirmed obligingly, only to recover his manners by instantaneously responding directly to Annette, "Well, what I mean is, if you need a ride home, Annette, I will be happy to give you one, because like you heard, Scott's now going to be leaving with your friend."

"It's okay by me," Annette answered without concern. "I'm the one who's driving anyway. I'm parked across the street," she informed him. "Listen, Rose goes wherever she wants to go, and does whatever *she* wants. I'm not her keeper," she proclaimed resolutely.

"Then I'm off," said Scott curtly, disappearing as inconsiderately as he had come in.

"Well, would you care for a refill?" Eugene considerately asked, deliberately attempting to show the stark difference between his demeanor and Scott's.

"Sure," Annette responded, moving her glass closer to him on the table. "The only thing is, before you do, I have one small request I'd like to make, if you don't mind," she petitioned.

"What's that?" Eugene asked.

"Well, you know how you are called Gene instead of Eugene?" Annette referenced.

"Yeah?" Eugene acknowledged.

"Well, my actual name *is* Annette, but no one really calls me that. It's Annie, okay?" she clarified affably.

"Sure, I got it, Annie, no problem," Eugene smiled acceptingly, while refilling her glass. "Now, I really don't want to leave you sitting here all by yourself, but if I don't go out there right now, they'll all be crashing on the floor, and if that happens, they will never leave," he explained in a vexing tone. "So, if you like, you can either wait here, or come along if you prefer, but I *have* to do this," he stressed.

"Oh, I'd rather just wait here for you," Annie replied in a nonchalant manner.

"Okay then, I'll be right back," Eugene answered, promptly leaving through the beads while thinking, *Oh, may God have mercy on my soul.*

Never before was Eugene so motivated in accomplishing a task, and thus, once he had actually got past the kitchen area, he bee-lined it over to the bar where Pete was performing a 'shotgun,' and in trying to not interrupt Pete's performance, he personally placed his hand on Pete's shoulder and spoke directly into his ear.

"Pete, I need you to close this thing down *right now*, if you could. I have Annie in the kitchen waiting to be alone with me and I really need you to get everyone in here to split, if you catch my drift. Could you help me out, pal?" Eugene implored anxiously.

"Does a hobby horse have a wooden wang?" Pete kidded, "You got it, Gene," he told him unreservedly, only to look up immediately and announce, "Folks, this show is goin' on the road! You have five minutes to make your final purchase and take home a souvenir, and this time, all sales are really final," he stressed.

"Thanks a lot," proffered Eugene, releasing his grip on Pete's shoulder and promptly leaving to inform Dick of his plans. *Oh man, that Pete is a real piece of work, but what a pal, what a pal, what a pal,* he gratefully thought.

Once he had reached Dick, who was still stationed regally in his throne with his newly acquired goddess of peace and love back atop his lap again, sans sandals, and now with her legs dangling across the arm of his chair, his main problem again took center stage as he still dreaded to himself, *Now, how in the hell long is it really going to take to get all of these lethargic layabouts out of this place?*

"I heard him," announced Dick, before Eugene could utter a word, in referring to Pete's announcement. "I guess you've reached your outer limits with that little blond you have cooped up in the kitchen," he casually stated with a broad smile. "Personally, I don't think you can handle that little firecracker all by yourself, but I'll help you out, anyway," he ribbed amusingly. "So, just go back into the kitchen and do not adjust your set in any way, for in about fifteen minutes, complete control of your humble abode will be returned to you," he instructed. paraphrasing the introduction to *The Outer Limits*. "You do realize, of course, that your new reality will be to clean up this crap zone all by yourself, don't you?" he specifically brought up.

"Not to worry, Big Dick. That's cool, and thanks a lot," Eugene acknowledged. "Well, I'll be hanging out in the kitchen, so let me know when their gone" he established. "Oh, and by the by," he further proposed in a more secretive tone, "I believe that tonight I am going to be more lucky than just at cards," he predicted before braggadociously hot-dogging away.

"I hear ya," called out Dick in acknowledgement, just before Eugene had the chance to completely disappear between the hanging beads.

Although Annie had not moved since Eugene had left, she had not remained in the same place either. She was in Monaco, editing manuscripts on her husband's yacht. Perhaps Grace Kelly would invite her to an elegant party. Oh, the shopping! The gowns! The food and champagne! And all provided to her by a troupe of neatly trained and courteously reverent servants. Then, with no warning at all, her European tour had gotten instantly canceled when she heard the unempathetic voice of reality declare, "Well that's done," as Eugene came back into the kitchen.

"They should all be gone in a few minutes," Eugene additionally proclaimed, again taking his seat at the table. "So, how are you doing?" he considerately asked.

"First, you can give me another refill, and then I will tell you," Annie conditioned evasively.

"Okay," Eugene responded, picking up the wine bottle off the table to begin the task he was assigned.

"Well, to answer your question, I'm doing just fine, now that I don't have an empty glass," Annie qualified with a playful smile.

"Oh good," Eugene commented amiably. "You know, I forgot. Didn't you ask me something before I left?" he questioned searchingly.

"Yeah, I asked you what you're majoring in, that's what," Annie reminded him.

"Oh yeah, I'm sorry. It's history. I'm a history major," he replied simply, taking a sip from his glass.

Annie had consciously concluded that this situation was all about control. Could she control him or not? And if she could, what was in it for her? So, just to test the waters, she had determined that for every subject brought up, or opinion solicited by him, she would respond to it in a contrary manner, *just to see how far he would go to please me,* she entertainingly calculated to herself. *Now, if I can get him to behave as I please, and I find him interesting enough to play with, what reward should I give him in order to reinforce his conditioning?* She additionally continued to ponder.

Eugene, however, had only one thought, and one thought only: *What do I have to do to win this trophy?*

"What is *your* major?" Eugene asked return in turn.

"Are you *really* interested in what my major is, Gene?" Annie replied in challenging the dubious motivation of his questioning.

"Sure, I am," Eugene nimbly replied in his best attempt to appear sincere.

"Well, I'm an English major, with a minor in art," Annie said compliantly. "I didn't want to take any of those structurally controlled courses like chemistry or biology, not to even mention the school of business," she reinforced. "I like the abstract subjects much better, like art and literature," she answered candidly.

"I know what you mean," responded Eugene, offering to relate to her world. "My father is a businessman and has to deal with the government all the time, and I don't want to do that. I like history, and that is why I'm a history major. I like to read about it, write about it, and I will probably teach it. I don't want to have to fight with people every day just to make a living like my father does," he explained as comparatively as he could.

"Sometimes, it's just not worth it," Annie commented supportively, taking another sip from her glass.

"Oh, and by the way, I didn't ask you, when do you graduate?" he questioned in trying to date her age.

"Same as you, in June, and then I'm taking off for a year before I do anything," Annie informed him, suggesting she had no sense of financial urgency.

"Yeah, I need a break too," Eugene agreed without elaborating any further.

He hoped that Annie would voluntarily reveal more about herself without him having to ask any more questions, so it wouldn't seem that he was prying, but she gave him no further response. She simply sat there with a pleasant look on her face, not responding at all.

It was a stand-off, Annie with all the cards, and Eugene trying to get her to reveal them. Still, he was in absolute mortal fear of asking the wrong question, so he also just sat there in silence too, hoping upon hope, that *she* would break the silence. He had never felt so full of apprehension. Then, as if rescued by an act of God, Big Dick and Little Peter both unexpectedly broke in through the colored beads to give Eugene their report.

"All is secure on the western front," said Dick.

"Yeah, and like the shepherd said, we're all done, and we got the flock outta there," Peter announced with a grin.

"We'll lock the door behind us, Gene, but like I said, you got a lot of crap to clean up," Dick reminded him.

"Don't worry, I got it. And again, Dick, thanks a lot," Eugene said appreciatively, "and you too, Pete," he added.

"Well, we'll catch you tomorrow," said Dick as he left the room.

"Yeah, we'll catch you on the flip side Gene," echoed Pete as he followed suit behind Dick.

Leaning back in his chair for a moment, Eugene now paused quietly so that he could hear the outside door to the hallway close when Pete, to no surprise, called out in his final exit, "That's if you don't catch anything tonight, ha-ha-ha!" And then, as the prayed for resounding "thud" was heard from the solid wood door resolutely slamming behind them, Eugene could never have been more thankful.

"Where exactly did you find those two?" Annie inquired.

"They are my fraternity brothers. They are in charge of The Good and Welfare Committee," Eugene lightly snickered. "They're a little wild, but they do keep things in line. And they usually do help clean up, but I told them that they could go, since they did all the kicking out this time," he clarified.

"So, you're going to have clean this place up all by yourself, after *they* left that mess out there?" Annie asked skeptically.

"I don't mind, and besides, I made some pretty good money tonight," Eugene emphasized cheerfully, trying to enhance his image as a winner.

"Well, I'll help you. I don't mind," she offered obligingly.

"Okay, if you don't mind, sure," Eugene said, rising from his chair, still holding his glass. "Come on, let's go, and tell me, what do you want me to play on the stereo?" he asked as he held the beaded curtain aside.

"Do you have The Carpenters?" Annie asked, entering the living room, also with her glass in hand.

"Yeah, I think I have it in my bedroom. If you wait here a minute, I'll go and get it," Eugene replied, putting his glass down on the top of the bar.

"The last time I had to wait for you, it took forever for you to return," Annie blatantly called out while Eugene left down the hallway, thinking *I'm going to be the one in control here, buddy.* Then, putting her glass down on the bar top next to Eugene's, she began to collect the filled ashtrays that were left about the room.

After returning quite punctually this time, and without responding to her last comment, Eugene walked directly over to where Annie was standing, illustratively held out the Carpenter's *Close To You* album, and dutifully asked, "Is this what you want?"

"Yeah, that's good. I haven't heard the whole album yet," Annie told him without any discernible emotion, placing a stack of ashtrays on the far end of the bar and taking a seat by her glass, task completed.

Eugene, meanwhile, had walked over to the lounge area and put the record on the spindle, moved the arm over, and clicked the selection on. After closing the lid to the console, he now only needed a second or two for Karen Carpenter to start suggesting that the evening had indeed, only just begun.

"So, how are you feeling now?" Eugene attentively asked, taking the seat next to her.

"Oh, I'm feeling just fine. That Lancers has given me a pretty good buzz. Yup, I'm feeling pretty good all right," Annie recertified. "Oh, and by the way, I have a couple of numbers here that the little funny guy must have left on the bar," she playfully displayed in her hand. "Do you get high, or do you just smoke straights?" she asked bluntly, referring to the Marlboros he openly smoked.

How good does it get? Eugene instantaneously thought before answering, "Sure, I get high. Pete left them for me."

"Well? Do you want to?" Annie proposed, fantasizing that she was Charlotte about to save Wilber from his inevitable capture by some other web spinning creature, musing, *Really, he should already know, there is no escape!*

"Yeah, I'll get high with you," Eugene affirmed, reaching out to take the joints from her hand. "So, how long have *you* been smoking?" he asked directly.

"I've been smoking since I was fifteen," Annie admitted. "Of course, they were only the cigarettes that I stole from my father. And I never really did smoke that much," she qualified. "I didn't start smoking pot until I came here to State," she confessed even further.

"My parents let me smoke at sixteen," Eugene informed her flatly, lighting one of the joints, taking a hit, and then offering it over to her. "They said they would rather have me smoke in front of them, then to have me sneak around behind their backs and do it dishonestly.

"And you know, that reminds me," he continued, while Annie took a drag on the doobie, "I almost got suspended for smoking in high school once," he began to reminisce. "I didn't want to miss my history class on the other side of the building, so I left my old buddy, Bill O'Donnell, out by himself in the back of the shop area where we used to sneak a smoke. And I have to tell you, I wasn't gone two minutes when Bill got caught by the gym teacher and got suspended. Boy, that was a close one," he reflected pridefully, likening himself to be the envied survivor of a latent catastrophe.

"I never got caught, either," Annie shared, offering Eugene back the number. "They always seemed to be raiding the boy's bathroom, but they never did the girls," she expounded observationally, while Eugene took back the doobie and took another hit.

"Wow, am I ever stoned—wesheech," Annie uttered euphorically. "So, where is the bathroom here anyway, Gene?" she asked, slowly getting up from the bar stool.

"It's down the hall, the second door to the right," Eugene told her. "You know, this bone is about done for," he noted out loud, as Annie all but disappeared down the dimly lit hallway.

Pressing out the last of the joint with his thumb and forefinger, Eugene carefully put the roach down on the edge of the wide ceramic ashtray in front of him and reaching over with his left hand he retrieved the bread basket of paraphernalia that still remained atop the bar top where Peter had placed it. Next, taking out a small electrical clip, he placed the roach between its jaws and sat, waiting for Annie's return.

After nearly four minutes had passed by, which seemed to him like an eternity, Eugene began to think, *how long is it going to take her?* Then, after a few more minutes had passed by, his patience had turned into concern and consequently, as politely as possible, he spoke out just loud enough to be audible from the living room, "Are you okay, Annie?"

"Sure I am. Why don't you come on in here?" Annie called back.

Having no idea of what she was doing, Eugene got up from the bar, abandoned The Carpenters, and proceeded to find out what exactly it was that she wanted. As he got to the entrance of the hallway, he noticed that the door to his main bedroom was half open, whereas he always had kept it closed. More curious than concerned, Eugene then slowly walked in through the bedroom door, and with only the light from the hallway behind him, it appeared that Annie had taken up residence—right in the middle of his bed.

He could not believe his eyes. After turning on the light switch by the door, which then softly illuminated the room and engaged the stereo, it was revealed that she had indeed gotten herself under the comforter atop his bed. Verily stunned, Eugene hesitated at the door until he definitely realized that he was not "looking out on the morning rain" as Carole King was now proclaiming, he was looking directly at Annie. Instantly jarred into reality, he knew that he must do something, but nothing specifically came into his mind. Consequently, he simply crept slowly over to the edge of his bed and gingerly sat down on its side.

"What took you so long?" she questioned imperiously.

"Well, I was waiting for you to come back to the living room," he replied sheepishly, feeling a loss to say anything else.

For almost a full minute he sat there, motionless and mute, when suddenly, she turned on her side, propped herself up on her right arm, and with one smooth motion, deftly flipped over the top of the comforter with her left hand and exposed herself to be totally naked. She had his full attention.

Stupefied, Eugene's soul was transfixed while his entire psychological being had been summarily focused in awe upon that one single wonder that lay explicitly before him, Annie Russo.

"Nice, isn't it?" she rhetorically declared, staring engagingly into his eyes with the wryest of smiles.

Eugene reached over slowly with his right hand, and starting at her shoulder, began to smoothly run his hand down along her side to her waist and then up and over her hip to the outside of her thigh, finally ending at her knee.

"It damn sure is. You are so beautiful," Eugene calmly declared with the conviction of a martyr who felt that he was about to give up his life for the cause. She had complete control over him now, and she knew it. Utterly and unequivocally, *he* knew it, too, gladly surrendering his mortal soul, for he had full well accepted that Annie was indeed, *"to die for."*

Chapter Seven

Enrico Russo was a stout, hardworking, earthy, and plain-spoken paving contractor. Generally good natured, his success was born out of the simple philosophy that if you worked hard, saved your money, and got along with everyone, you would be rewarded. He was raised a strict Roman Catholic and believed that all people suffered in one form or another. This great intellectual pathos had given him a most valued insight into the problems of others, and thus he was understandingly receptive to their struggles. Work, nonetheless, was a finite fact of life to be accepted, and a contract was a contract, for whether it was a job to be done or a promise to be kept, it was still to be honored above all else, regardless of the circumstances.

Compassion, on the other hand, was considered to be a totally separate issue. On a personal basis, he was always known to be quite empathetic and had the capability of commiserating with others without its associative judgment. He had the rare of gift of healing. He understood the insidious and pernicious nature of self-pity and had the innate ability to graciously exorcise it from their souls. This was a talent of his which was appreciated by all, he was well liked man.

"Ricky," as he was called by his wife Jolanda, had especially done his best over the years to prevent any such feelings of self-pity to ever exist in his own home. Self-reliance was his philosophy, and he practiced what he preached.

The few simple rules of respect for your mother, your family, and God were all that he demanded from his children. He tried not to judge them for their passions and felt that, since both of his offspring were girls, it was the mother's purview to contend with their day-to-day personal development, not his. And in this, he did not interfere.

In return for her acceptance of this responsibility, he went to church every Sunday and prayed that his wife would be at peace with the results of her obligations. This underlying moral and social agreement, in which Jolanda was a willing participant, had given her the exclusive responsibility to attend to the girls' health, happiness, and overall good fortune. This was her life's purpose, as was her understanding, and took it to be a God given covenant, even beyond her commitment to her husband.

Jolanda Balestera's parents were from Verona. They were one of the few immigrants that had come to the United States from the northern and more prosperous region of Italy. Her parents came over with enough money to open a small produce market, but were also part of the minority of Italians who came with the specific purpose of becoming Americans. They had given birth to two sons, Aldo and Carlo, and a single daughter Jolanda, who the mother had named after her favorite flower, the violet. The market provided a good living for the industrious family, who all worked it diligently together.

The Russo family had come over from the southern and almost completely destitute part of Italy in virtually the same time frame as the Balesteras had. They had immigrated after it had been universally determined that the imminent starvation which they had been facing was by far more unpalatable than just going America. Their ultimate goal, like most other Italians from their region at that time, was to come over temporarily and simply save up enough money to return home and retire in comfort. Unintentionally however, most all of these folks were fated never to see their Italian homeland again, but nonetheless, thanks to the Second

World War, the three Russo progenies, Enrico, Marco, and Anthony, were all appreciatively given that very opportunity in Nineteen Forty-Two, courtesy of the United States Army.

Enrico's parents had known all along that Italy had no chickens left to eat before the war, for that was the primary reason they had left, and having already been unpleasantly displaced once before, ostensibly over the same problem, they wisely chose to say nothing when the war did break out. However, this did not mean that nothing was done, because even though the starvation conditions in Italy were still certainly high on their list of concerns, the actual thought of the Germans being in sovereign control over their country was simply intolerable. Consequently, the newly Americanized Italians were proud to encourage their sons to enlist in the war effort. Jolanda's parents felt no differently and were proud to have their daughter marry one of their very own Italian liberators, duly dubbed a "hero" for his services.

Before the war, Enrico had worked beside his father in the city road department since the age of sixteen. He could lay brick and block like a mechanic, as well as pour and finish concrete like an expert.

Although he worked hard and liked what he did for a living, it was not his original thinking to go into business. It was Jolanda's parents who encouraged him to do it, and with a little financial support, he purchased a used asphalt paver and a six-ton roller. Instantly, he was no longer considered a member of the working class, for now he was viewed as a "Boss" in the community.

Initially, his business consisted of laying down driveways for local homebuilders and parking lots for small businesses. He worked by himself in the beginning until he could afford a helper and then, after a few years, he had two good, solid workers. It wasn't until nearly five years later that his business had become an enterprise for him to run, instead of one that he still had to labor in as well. This specifically happened on the day in which he was awarded his first city road contract, as thereafter it was only a matter of maintaining his company's good reputation and public esteem to retain this ascendency.

Jolanda was grateful for having a good husband, a good home, and never having to want for food. Even though she was thoroughly content with her temporal possessions, it was her belief that she was only half-blessed after the birth of her second child, Capricia. Because of the complications with Capricia's birth, she had been told that she would never have any more children and felt that it was her sorrowful fate that she could not provide her husband with the sons that she had promised. She consequently confessed to her priest that she believed it was her punishment for being "prideful."

"Pride is certainly a sin," Father Bernardino confirmed to her as he asserted his fundamental spiritual dominion over his penance seeking parishioner. Upon the acceptance of her confession, the priest thereupon decreed that Jolanda attest to and confirm her commitment to the church once more by subsequently reciting three "Hail Marys" in an act of contrition and contribute as generously as possible to the Poor Box. Conclusively thereafter, once performing the assigned obligation, it was thus forever declared that Jolanda was spiritually forgiven and that her sin of pride had been absolutely reconciled.

Regardless of the church's procedural pardon, Jolanda nevertheless personally rationalized that because she was being punished physically for the rest of her mortal life, her absolution was only granted to her in part. The salvation of her soul was one thing, but still to suffer God's punishment for the rest of her corporeal existence was another. Sadly, she would never recover completely from losing the daily joy of living which she had so profusely embraced before she had given birth to Capricia. Still, she was a very pleasant soul, and certainly a pleasure to be with, but never again would her former natural effervescence return, as it simply vanished into the world of lost balloons.

Accordingly, having no sons to carry out the family name, the responsibility of this tradition had all but fallen directly upon Annie's head, now designated the family torchbearer by fiat. Annie was two years older than her sister and looked nothing like her in the least. Nor did anyone else in the family either.

"A long, long time ago, a great German Barbarian army had invaded the land where our family had lived," the story went, "and one day, when one of the fiercest Barbarians of all had cast his eyes down upon your great, great, grandmother, when she was just a young girl of sixteen, she had stopped him in his tracks," Annie was told.

"She had such a beautiful smile that it had turned the raging warrior away from his life of plundering, pillaging, and generally all over dishonorable behavior, into being a respected and admired successful country farmer. And that is where your beautiful smile and blond hair comes from, your great, great, grandmother, Tesorina," Jolanda had told her, "So you are quite special, like a little angel with golden hair."

The Russo family lived in a post-war three-bedroom house, complete with an attic and cellar. The attic had two dormers atop the front of the house denoting its Cape Cod style. Sets of decorative shutters were hung about the windows and were painted an emerald green to match the trim encasing the soffits. The rest of the house was painted white.

There was a flagstone walkway connecting the sidewalk directly to the front door. A colonial lantern was mounted atop a six- foot post which had been planted to the right of the path approximately half way to the portico, guarding the main entrance to the home. Enrico had constructed a wide brick driveway about ten feet to the left side of the house which ran directly up to a large free-standing garage toward the back of the house.

An enclosed covered breezeway connected the garage to the back porch of the home, which served as a terrarium in the summertime, replete with exotic plants, hanging and otherwise, acrobatic hamsters, and chirping parakeets. It also provided a sheltered way to get to the garage in the wintertime. A matching brick walkway had also availed itself from half way up driveway to lead straightforwardly over to the side entrance of the kitchen. The landscaping was kept simple and neat.

Annie had always been the more rambunctious and adventurous of the two girls. In the summer, she would organize "camp outs" in the back yard with her grade school girlfriends using an old canvas army tent which her father had bought from a surplus store. Her sister was always "too scared" to attend.

Annie had achieved leadership status throughout her class when it was leaked out by her girlfriends that she had actually hit her father in the head with a flying flashlight one night when he was outside the tent pretending to be a ghost. She built not only snowmen and snow angels in the wintertime, but had constructed a snow fort as well, to guard her creations. She became her father's daughter, and he loved her for it.

Emboldened by her father's support, Annie did not differentiate her friends based on their gender, and until her mother bought her a training bra, the matter was of little concern. This is not to infer that she did not know of the basic differences of the two sexes, for her four uncles had provided her with a more than ample supply of male cousins to play with, as well as the neighborhood begetting its own.

While Enrico's practical nature had pervaded her basic motives, it was still her mother's influence that prevailed in the development of her general demeanor as a female in a man's world. Jolanda had imparted within her daughter the effectiveness of using her femininity as a naturally accepted means of obtaining her objectives, and as a result, Annie had become aggressively adept in wielding its effectiveness. The magnitude of her considerable desires and ambitions evoked a constitutional vigor within her that engendered a vivacious quality about her that was beguiling to almost everyone. Naughty or nice, she became a force to be reckoned with.

In her fifteenth year, Annie had found out by way of the daily chatter in the girl's bathroom that Bobby Taylor, one of her schoolmates, had acquired a homemade go-cart for his birthday. This news had so fascinated her that she had become fully determined she was going to take it for a ride, and that was that.

Bobby's father was a welder and had built the cart out of spare lawnmower parts in their garage. Its carriage had been constructed out of a flat piece of aluminum plate and was reinforced with an angle iron frame. There were no enclosed sides or body covering of any kind.

A Briggs and Stratton engine was mounted above the rear axle and directly in front of it sat a high-backed seat from an old bar stool that had been bolted onto the floor. A small steering wheel and modified turning mechanism from an old John Deere lawn tractor had been mounted onto a silver tubular frame that had been constructed midway in the craft which bridged both sides of the cart.

There was a single foot pedal mounted on the floor of the right side of the nose of the vehicle which was connected by a cable to the engines throttle for it to regulate the power in the rear wheels. Mounted on the floor of the left side of the driver's seat was a hinged lever that acted as a break when pulled up. Once employed, an old rubber motor mount was engineered to apply pressure directly upon the rear axle in the hopeful task of halting the enterprise before arriving at an unpleasant conclusion. A modified hand break assembly from an old Volkswagen was affixed to the right side of the driver's seat that, when raised, engaged a clutch belt apparatus which remained locked into place until the button at the top of the handle was pressed.

Reaching a top speed of perhaps only twenty miles an hour, the undercarriage, having the driver positioned only six inches from the ground, gave the operator the physical illusion of traveling at supersonic speeds. Painted black and silver, the contraption was anointed the "Whirling Dervish" by Bobby and his buddy John, personifying their self-images as the town's mystical dare devils.

Bobby lived only a block away from' the town's elementary school, which made it a relatively short and easy task to push the machine along the side walk for them to reach their approved destination of operation. The two boys were allowed by their parents to race the machine around the school's parking lot and recreational field on those Saturdays in which there were no public events scheduled. It didn't take long for their activities to go unnoticed before they began to unintentionally acquire the interests of some of the local school girls their age who had occasionally come to witness their show, and thus was how Annie had learned of their location.

When grouped together with the other boys his age, Bobby appeared to be no more significantly different than any of the others. He was the quintessential product of the times. He attended the neighborhood junior high school along with all of the other students his age who were determined to live within its walking distance.

Being a little shorter than most of the other children, he actively worked at developing his athletic stature. He attended the community YMCA at least twice a week in the evenings with his best friend John, where they lifted the free weights used for body building before they went swimming.

His dark and curly brown hair was worn down past his ears so that the sides could be combed back into the popular style referred to as a "DA," while a single lock was positioned to curl down, Elvis style, across his forehead. Bedecked in the wintertime with an old leather bomber jacket from World War Two that his uncle James had given him, Bobby felt qualified to consider himself "cool." Cognitive of his social surroundings, Bobby was always neat, clean, and orderly in his appearance. His light blue eyes and congenial smile enhanced an outgoing deportment which managed to engage nearly everyone's attention.

However, Bobby Taylor's extraverted and sometimes questioning behavior was not necessarily seen as a good thing by many of his teachers. Transmuting his challenging demeanor into unfairly classifying him as a disruptive and instigating element, who only annoyingly complicated their environment, was a constant irritation to Bobby, but it did little to quench his indomitable spirit. To his credit, nonetheless, he neither outright defied, nor disrespectfully confronted, their authority.

When his point of view could not be refuted to his satisfaction, he simply dismissed them as irrelevant to his entire existence. The more it was tried to bend him into accepting such rationalizations as, "Because that's the way it is," or "Well, when you learn to do it my way first, *then* I'll explain it to you," or, "That is how the School Board has determined it should be taught," the more he found those who used these phrases to be an altogether insignificant inconvenience to his schooling.

Not that he had particularly provoked the teachers over whom he had no interest in, but his outwardly independent nature at times was still taken as an affront to their self-perceived importance. It was his passive unconcern of their whole existence that was the problem, for they full well knew, that to have a challenge ignored, especially in public, is tantamount to an unmitigated rebuke of their dignity, from which no recourse can be quartered.

The minority of the teachers who had embraced Bobby's outward individualism as being philosophically refreshing, nonetheless, thoroughly enjoyed him. Transcending their own self-recognition, they often interfaced with, and even encouraged, his originality. It was not by coincidence that these particular teachers who had supported his curiosities were also the very same ones who had embodied within their souls the time proven concepts of Aristotle, Plato, and Socrates. They were those who chose to honor their profession of teaching for its own altruistic goals, rather than seeking to enhance their own diminutive power, fortune, or self-aggrandizement from their endeavors.

Conversely, the majority of those "educators" who felt challenged by Bobby's independent thoughts and behavior, in an act of self-deprecation, and in rank-and-file, voted to disregard any honorable notions of self-respect by endorsing a most lucrative engineered employment contract whose superlative purpose for its very existence had become no more than a mirrored reflection of their own greed, sloth, and virulent mediocrity.

Independence to them, whether in the soul of another colleague or that of a student, was considered as a matter of direct conflict, and abhorrently a bad trait to possess; it should only exist philosophically, like their own integrity, they deemed.

When Bobby first attended junior high school, it seemed to him that nothing much was different, notwithstanding the walk to get there was a tad longer. After school, he still worked on his bike, tended to his coin collection, or experimented with an old ham radio set, which he had gotten at Christmas. Saturday mornings hadn't changed, either, for racing his go-cart with his best friend John whenever the weather permitted was still his most passionate venture.

John Ramsey usually kept to himself. He was of average height and had developed a noted muscular physique from working out not only at the YMCA with Bobby, but at home with his own set of weights as well. John had light gray eyes and a quiet bearing. He wore his light blond hair long and had one large circular curl that hung down across his forehead. Practiced in the deportment of James Dean, John had fashioned himself a real rebel without a cause whose favorite song was *The Wanderer* by Dion.

John was the first one of the school walkers to officially have a girlfriend to "go steady" with. This development had demanded that John would no longer be occasionally riding his bike to school anymore. It was now his social obligation to walk with his girl Barbara to and from the school every single day. Additionally, no longer were John's pals welcome to come by his house after school either, for this time now was to be spent with his girlfriend alone. Regardless, this new situation had nothing to do with John's Saturday morning ritual to race the cart with Bobby.

From the moment Annie had first heard about the Saturday morning cart racing at the elementary school and had observed it from afar, she decided that if she was ever to get a ride on it, she had to go there. She additionally determined that the best thing to do was to make friends with Barbra, for then her chances to get what she wanted would be even better. This, she figured, was easy enough, for both she and Barbara were in the same gym class together.

"So, what is it like to go steady with just one boy?" Annie asked Barbara in the shower of the girl's locker room on the first day the opportunity became available.

"Well, he walks me home every day," Barbara stated, then pausing for a second to assemble her thoughts, she added, "And even though he won't hold my hand in public, he lets me hold on to his arm when we walk together," she said proudly. "He also takes me to the school dances, so I don't have to sit on beggar's bench, you know, looking all desperate and everything. Sometimes I can even get him to slow dance with me, once or twice anyway, and that's nice. Then, once in a while, he'll even buy me a soda on the way home," she boasted, stopping to adjust her shower cap.

"His mother drives, you know, and when she goes to the store in that old Ford they have, we make out at his house," Barbara continued. "And, oh yeah, I don't get teased by the shop boys anymore, 'cause John'd punch 'em out," Barbara then imperiously declared in a tone of finality.

"Yeah, he does look pretty tough," Annie conceded. "So how did you get him to go steady, anyway?" she questioned further, turning off the shower she was under.

"A few months ago, when it was really freezing out, I went over to his house this one afternoon when his mother had gone to the store," Barbara began again, turning off her shower as well to follow Annie over to the towel hooks on the tiled wall behind them. "I wanted to know if he was going to be at the grammar school on Saturday with Bobby, racing his go-kart, but he told me no, because it was too cold outside for his hands. Then he told me that he got 'em all frostbit a couple of days before, and they still hurt from it—you know he's got a mornin' paper route," she asided.

"No, I didn't know that," Annie responded, now unlatching her locker.

"Well, anyway, so I just said to him, 'Let me see your hands,' and when he held 'em out, I took them and put them under my sweater blouse and told him, 'This should warm them up.' Then, after that, I told him straight out, if he wanted any more, we had to go steady first, and that was that," Barbara declared in a factual tone before adding, "Now, all I had to do after that is hold out for about a month until he finally caved in," she gloated with the smile of a satisfied minx.

~

It was on the second Thursday evening of May, while practicing with the barbells in the weight room next to the gym at the YMCA, that John had asked Bobby directly, "What do you think of Annie Russo, Bob?"

"Why, what do you think?" Bobby responded as he added some more weights to the barbells.

"Oh, I think she's as good looking as Barb," John said casually, sitting on a side bench as he waited for his turn on the padded safety mat. "You know, Barb told me Annie likes you," he casually mentioned.

"Oh yeah?" Bobby replied mechanically, "Well, just be quiet for a minute, will you? I'm going to try to press this," he seriously declared.

Bobby stood for a moment with his knees slightly bent and his hands on the knurled part of the barbell, which he had adjusted to weigh a total one hundred and forty pounds. He paused for about five seconds, then snatched up the bar and cleaned it past his chest into a brief holding position that was level with his shoulders. Then, from his position under the weights, he rose up, and in one swift motion pushed up his entire upper carriage until he had finally gotten the object of his conquest straight-armed above his head, stood there motionless for about three seconds, and then jumped back to let the load fall independently to the floor.

"Pheeew, man, it took everything I had, but I got it up there," Bobby announced with the utmost degree of self-satisfaction as he grinned from ear to ear.

"Yeah, you got it up, all right. I'm a witness," stated John.

"Well, it's your turn. I'm taking a break," announced Bobby while he went over to the bench where John was sitting.

"You know, Barb says Annie wants to meet you," John apprised him, resuming his previous conversation, while getting up to take his turn on the mat.

"Oh yeah, what for?" Bobby asked. "I ain't gonna take her to those stupid school dances you take Barbara to," he said with perfect clarity.

"I don't know what she wants," postured John. "Look, all I'm tellin' you is, Barb said that Annie told her that she likes you and she wants to meet you. I don't know, maybe she wants you to feel her up," he laughed, while reaching down to adjust the weights. "Barb says Annie doesn't stuff her bra with toilet paper like Dianne Peterson does," he tattled, still chuckling away.

"Yeah, you really think so?" responded Bobby, beginning to show some interest.

"I don't know, but Barb says Annie's are really hers, and she's in her gym class, so she oughta know," John testified.

"No, I mean, do you really think she does want to meet me?" Bobby corrected.

"Barb said Annie is coming with her on Saturday to watch us race the cart, —if it doesn't rain. So, when they get here, and it's my turn to drive the cart, you walk her around to the back of the school and make out with her, —and then you feel her up," John taunted again with the slyest of smirks.

Chapter Eight

It was around nine thirty in the morning when a light knock was heard on the back door to the kitchen of the Russo home. Jolanda did not have a hard time recognizing through its window that it was Barbara Petreski who was interrupting her morning chores. Dressed to the nines for an expected spring day, Barbara had displayed herself in a bright multi-colored blouse tucked into a pair of pink stretch pants with foot stirrups that were secured by a pair of cherry red low-heeled sandals along with a matching red leather belt, which, as the saying goes, had been cinched around her waist as tight as dick's hat band. Her signature teased bouffant hairdo, which had perfected her presence, was only upstaged by her incessant gum chewing. She knew she was a noted piece of merchandise, and fully enjoyed it.

"Good morning, Barbara," Jolanda greeted, pleasantly opening the kitchen door. "Do you and Annie have something planned?"

"Yeah, Mrs. Russo," Barbara answered. "Me and Annie are going up to the school park and watch the guys race their go-cart. Is she ready?"

"I don't know, but you can go up to her room and see, if you want," Jolanda said, holding open the door with her right hand while moving aside to let the teenager pass.

"Thanks a lot, Mrs. Russo," answered Barbara, traipsing off to Annie's room with the sound of her gum snapping.

Annie's room was to the right from the top of the stairs and was cracked open when Barbara walked up to it.

"Knockie, knockie," announced Barbara, opening the door a little wider in order to evidence that her most colorful presence had indeed arrived.

"Come on in," replied Annie, sitting pat at her mirrored white wood vanity without looking over.

"Is that what you're wearing?" Barbara questioned in disbelief, going over to Annie's four poster French provincial bed to plop herself down upon its edge.

"Uh huh," responded Annie, acknowledging Barbara while at the same time finishing up the last touches of applying her eye makeup. "One second while I curl my lashes," she said, reaching down to pick up the tong-like silver device of mutilation and beautification that was required to complete her task. "There, now I am ready," she proclaimed, standing up to squarely face her comrade in arms.

"Like I said honey, is that what you're gonna wear?" Barbara repeated in a tone that was delivered with both ridicule and disbelief.

"What's wrong with a rib tickler? I think it looks great," Annie defended.

"It's not the blouse, silly, it's the jeans. Don't you have any white shorts?" Barbara asked, insinuating Annie knew nothing of proper spring attire.

"Of course I do," Annie retorted, "But I want to ride the cart," she cantankerously stated.

"Bobby's dad told him that he could only let the boys ride it," Barbara declared in fact, clutching on to her matching red shoulder bag, which had been cast aside on the bed, and standing back up. Then, not waiting for a response, she simply threw the bag back over her shoulder and headed straight to the door, stopping briefly to turn her head and say, "You coming?"

"Yeah, let me get my wallet first," said Annie, opening the top drawer to her white and gold Louis the Fourteenth dresser. "Well, I don't plan on asking his dad's permission, anyway, I only need his," she expostulated. "That is why I am also wearing my hushpuppies instead of those things on your feet," she added, closing her bedroom door behind them.

~

It was about ten thirty on that bright spring morning by the time the girls had gotten to the playground, noticing the boys were already racing the cart. About fifty feet from where the parking macadam began and about another fifty yards from the north side of the brick school, stood the last of the indigenous majestic oak trees that been left on the grounds after the town had finished erecting its new so-called bastion of education. It was here the two girls thought to wait until the cart had come to a rest.

Under this tree of learning and quiet contemplation was situated a large weathered picnic table with a set of permanently attached benches for ostensibly reposing in intellectual reflection. Ironically, however, anyone with any intelligence at all when sitting under this magnificent green umbrella, even for an instant, invariably came to the same conclusive epiphany, "Exactly what moronic person of higher learning callously chopped down the rest of trees?"

Regardless, after arriving at the table, Annie and Barbara immediately proceeded to sit themselves down atop the battle-scarred table with their feet resting directly upon the bench that faced the parking lot. This in turn provided them with an unfettered view of the parking area where the two boys were going about their business.

It was an archetypical clear and sunny day. The area trees surrounding the schoolyard had just sprouted into a light green sea of activity as the chattering robins and sparrows flitted about in a desperate attempt to keep the omnivorous bushy tailed squirrels from invading their territory. It was a magnificent day to be alive.

Once situated, Barbara took out a hand-held transistor radio from her bag, turned it on, and began to adjust it so that she could find a station which was currently playing a Beatles tune. After a few minutes of successfully fidgeting with the gadget in trying to accomplish her goal, she carefully put the radio on the bench, positioned the antenna for its optimum reception, and looked over to see that her boyfriend was now standing by an old, round, one-gallon metal gas can at the edge of the lot.

"I'm over here, Johnnie!" Barbara shouted over the noise of the engine, while frantically waving her right hand over her head.

John, hearing the disturbance behind him, turned halfway around, looked in the direction of the tree, and upon seeing the girls, put up his right hand in the air to acknowledge their presence, but said nothing. He then returned his attention back to maintaining his function as the track pitman, directly in time to observe Bobby slowing down from his final lap.

The finish position was designated the same as the starting position, which in turn was denoted by the placement of an old wooden fruit crate filled with the pit crew's "essential supplies." They consisted of two cans of Ritz sodas, two Devil Dogs, a church key, a hammer, a screwdriver, a pair of vise grips, and an old grease stained towel. Having disengaged the clutch and taken his foot off the gas pedal, Bobby subsequently forced the cart into a slow roll before applying the final pressure from the hand break. Finally, after the cart had come to a complete stop, John expeditiously went over to the back of the machine with a screwdriver and shorted out the spark plug against the engine block. Precisely as intended, this action conclusively shut the mechanical wonder down, instantaneously returning the omnipresent tranquility of the day.

Happy with his performance, Bobby got out of the car smiling, and standing up, said, "Well, it's your turn, John," unaware of the girl's arrival.

"If you hold on for a second, I'll get Barbara and Annie to come on over here," John responded, pointing over to where the aptly named "Mohegan" tree stood.

Quite curious now, in looking over to where John was pointing, Bobby's interest in Annie unambiguously began stir.

"Sure, go and get them," Bobby said.

John went over to the two girls, and upon nearing his destination, he did not greet them together, but instead spoke directly to Barbara.

"If you want Annie to meet Bobby, you need to come over to where the go-cart is," John told her in absolute terms. Then, without waiting for any reply, he turned to walk back to where Bobby was still standing by the old fruit crate.

"Sure, Johnnie, sure," Barbara responded obediently.

Annie had already gotten off the table and was waiting impatiently as Barbara gingerly turned off her transistor radio, punctiliously removed herself off the table, stealthily took the gum from her mouth, and then pressed it firmly underneath the picnic table. Putting the radio into her bag, Barbara then slung the strap from it over her shoulder, pivoted around toward the boys, glanced over to Annie once again, and remarked cheerfully, "Well, let's go and meet Bobby."

"Hey Bobby, how's it runnin' today?" asked Barbara as soon as she and Annie had gotten close to where the go-cart was situated.

"It's running just great," Bobby replied congenially.

118

"Here, I brought you my friend, Annie. She wants ta meet ya," Barbara declared unabashedly.

There was complete silence for a moment as Annie shifted her eyes in Barbra's direction while evidencing a wholly annoyed look upon her face.

"So, you're friends with Barb," Bobby replied affably, directing his conclusion expressly to Annie.

"Yeah, I'm in her gym class," Annie confirmed, saying nothing more.

"Well, this is the Whirling Dervish, my go-cart, and I guess you already know John over here," said Bobby, demonstratively pointing over to his buddy with his thumb. "It's John's turn now, so, if you stand back a little, we'll get it going again and you can watch," he proposed.

"Okay," Annie said, stepping back a foot or so, "I can do that," she amiably remarked.

John was already getting himself positioned in the cart as Bobby went over to the rear of the vehicle, stretched down, wound a knotted length of rope around the notched pulley at the top of the engine, put his left foot onto the back of the cart and ripped the rope from the device as it revolutionized the apparatus into initializing the combustion process that metamorphosed the dormant device into the one and only, awesome and dynamic, "Whirling Dervish, —The Go-cart Extraordinaire." Next, once engaging the clutch, John began to slowly move away from the starting position, and upon clearing the first curve in the pavement, he summarily took off, full throttle. Consequently, John now being fully occupied, Bobby returned his attention to Annie.

"So, what do you think of the Whirling Dervish? That's what we named it," Bobby emphasized in a more heightened tone over the sound of the engine.

"That's what you said," Annie reminded him, "but that's okay," she dismissed casually. "Did you build it yourself?" she asked as a point of interest.

"Yeah, me and my dad. We built it out of old lawnmower parts," Bobby told her unpretentiously.

"Yeah, it looks like it," she proffered realistically. "So, where did you get that name for it, anyway?" Annie questioned him further.

"I got it from my mother. When my room was so messy one day, she said it looked like a whirling dervish had hit it. She said it's what you call a small tornado. So, that's where I got the name," Bobby pleasantly explained.

"I think it's really cool," interjected Barbara, replenishing her chewing gum.

"You got a girlfriend?" Annie asked Bobby point blank, to his surprise.

"No," answered the young mechanic.

"How come?" Annie asked bluntly.

"Cause he ain't got the time, that's why, you know. It's cause he's always messin' around with the cart," Barbara interposed, grinning and chewing her gum at the same time.

"Not all the time, Barbara," Bobby reprimanded, looking a bit perturbed.

"Well, then, when you're not working on the cart, exactly what *do* you do?" inquired Annie in a softer tone.

"Other stuff," Bobby blandly answered, changing his position to better observe John racing the cart. "Excuse me, but I got to pay attention to John," he then said as politely as possible, in trying to avoid any further questioning while at the same time looking away.

"Well, just how long are you going to pay attention to him?" Annie persisted.

"Until he's done," Bobby replied resolutely, "We'll probably be about five minutes more, and then we'll be done for the day," he added in a more gracious tone.

"Well, I guess I can wait that long," Annie remarked, as she turned again and moved away.

"It ain't so bad Annie, am waitin' with ya," encouraged Barbara as the two of them now retreated back to the tree.

"Oh boy, isn't that a relief," Annie mentally noted.

Bobby now began to pick up the tools that were left about the pavement while John was winding down his last lap around the lot. Finally, after coming to a complete stop, John removed himself from the cart, and after standing up put his hand on Bobby's shoulder and said to him in a low voice, "Listen, I'll finish cleaning up here and you go over and to talk to Annie. And tell Barbara I said to come over here too, okay, pal?"

"Sure, I can do that," Bobby validated.

And even though Bobby outwardly appeared to be calm, he still could not help himself from thinking *Just what am I supposed to say to her?* as he casually moseyed along.

"Barb, John says he wants to see you," he said plainly, having first delivered John's imperative directly to Barbara.

"Okay, okay, I'm on my way," Barbara muttered out loud, getting up to trot back over to where her Johnnie was cleaning up the cart.

"So, are you guys all done for the day?" Annie asked.

"I'm done with the cart, if that's what you mean. I still have to take it back home and check in with my mom. After that I don't have any plans," Bobby answered with a slight shrug from his shoulders.

"I don't have any, either. I could meet you back here about three, if you want," advanced Annie, trying to perfect her planned entrapment of Bobby, and specifically his cart.

"That's cool," Bobby agreed. "Well, I've got to go over and help John now," he noted in a practical tone. "So, I'll see you back here under the tree about three, then, okay?" he asked in conformation.

"Sure, I'll be here," Annie replied as Bobby left to help John wind down their operation. "And tell Barbara I've got to go too, and I *will* see you later!" Annie called out to him in final affirmation.

"No problem!" Bobby hollered back over his shoulder.

Bobby was well aware that an overt display of jubilation would be perceived by his peers as "un-cool," and so he deliberately walked in a nonchalant manner until he finally got back to where the cart was.

"Annie says she's gotta go now," Bobby relayed to Barbara as soon as he had reached the tarmac.

"Okay, Johnnie, I gotta go with Annie now. I'll call you when I get home," Barbara said dutifully, leaning over to kissed him on the cheek and squeezing his arm. "See you later, Bobby," she announced after turning to go on her way.

Then, as the two of them watched her leave and thought that her show was completely over, Barbara all of a sudden stopped, turned about, and loudly twittered, "Byeie!" while jubilantly waving with one hand and chewing her gum like a contented cow.

"Okay, let's go. I got other stuff to do too. I'll push first, and you steer," John volunteered, walking over to pick up the box of supplies.

"Sure, no problem," Bobby said as he got into the cart while John put the crate into his lap.

"So, how'd it go?" John questioned, huffing and puffing the cart along.

"I'm gonna see her at about three o'clock this afternoon back here at the school," Bobby informed him as he steered the cart onto the sidewalk.

"That's cool, man," John struggled to respond.

It only took ten minutes for the boys to get the cart back to Bobby's house, and in having to intently concentrate on their task, they had said no more, even while rounding the corner into Bobby's driveway.

Bobby's house was developmentally the same as all the others in the subdivision; a three-bedroom, one bath, Cape Cod with a cellar, attic, and free-standing garage. Regardless, once the machine had gotten rolled into its corner parking space at the rear of the garage and the brake had been secured, John now commenced to give Bobby some of his expert advice.

"You should wash up and change your clothes before you go back and see her," John counseled.

"Yeah, sure, I intend to," said Bobby, who inquired in turn after getting out of the cart, "So, what are *you* going to do for the rest of the afternoon?"

"I'm gonna go back home, clean up, and then meet Barbara over at Beaver Pond. Then I gotta be home for dinner, but after that, we could go over to the bowlin' alley, hang around a while and see what's goin' on, if you want," John suggested.

"That's cool, see ya later, man," Bobby responded while putting the box of tools back under a work bench.

"Yeah, keep it cool, man," John maundered back from the driveway.

Bobby now began to contemplate the ramifications of his actions, and since it was a Saturday afternoon, and the one bathroom in the house was free for him to use at his leisure, he figured that he had plenty of prep time. After taking off his clothes and throwing them in the hamper across from the sink, he stepped into the tub where he remained for a good five minutes in trying to imitate The Beatles singing "She loves you, yeah, yeah, yeah."

Once finished with his shower and having put on his jockeys, Bobby began the ritual of arranging his hairstyle. After combing his hair straight back, he then put down his comb, reached into the medicine cabinet over the sink, took out a tube of Brylcreem, and once taking off the cap, as to apply the pomade to his hair, he began to tunefully sing, "Brylcreem, a little dab'l do ya, Brylcreem, you look so debonair, Brylcreem, a little dab'l do ya, they love to get their fingers in your hair." Then, no sooner than he was finished with his self-anointed prognostication, and was still laughing in amusement, there came that interruptive knock on the bathroom door.

"Come on in there, son, give someone else a chance!" his father called out in levity.

"I'm almost done!" Bobby called back.

Feeling that his hair was almost perfect, Bobby now put down the comb, obliquely positioned himself in front of the mirror of Snow White, held out his hands palms up, as if presenting himself to his doting audience, and declared out loud, "Man, you are one cool guy!" only to pause for a second at his own reflection. "Now, just to put on a little b.o.derant, —and then add a splash of my killer Brute cologne, —and all is complete. So, once again, I am, as usual, The Irresistible Man about Town," he smirked unto himself in conclusion.

Next, once this initial stage had been completed, he sauntered off to his bedroom to further perfect his official presentation. He first selected his blue-on-blue Ricky Ricardo two tone casual shirt with its vertical black pin stripes and matching collar. His second preference was a pair of sharkskin trousers that he had saved up for by working part time at the corner garage. Finally, once he had added his shiny black Guido shoes to his ensemble, he felt quite comfortable that he could easily pass as a member of the Four Seasons.

You know, that Annie is certainly pretty enough to complement me. That is, if I were to be seen with her in public, he thought, once finally leaving to meet her. Yet, as confident as he outwardly presented himself to be, he still could not keep himself from trepidatiously cogitating, *well, I just hope I don't blow it!*

~

Annie and Barbara never did make it to Barbara's house. Instead, they walked across the town's main highway and over to the new mall, figuring it was the easiest way to kill a couple of hours.

"So, wada ya think of Bobby?" asked Barbara as they looked through a shoe store window.

"I think he's cute," said Annie.

"Yeah, I think so too, but I like Johnnie better. He's the quiet type," Barbara qualified, continuing to snap her gum. "So, what do ya think of those pumps? Ain't they so old lady like? And look at the price! You'd need a rich old man to buy them too! ha, ha, ha!" she laughed.

"Yeah, and who wants one of those, either," agreed Annie, chucking as well.

"Exactly! Old guys and old lady shoes, who would want either of them?" Barbara reiterated, suddenly going silent and expectantly glancing over to Annie.

"Only old ladies!" burst out Annie laughing, as Barbara joined in.

Finally, after abandoning their window shopping at the shoe store, the two girls began to meander over to the Orange Julius kiosk in the center of the mall.

"So why is the quiet type better?" questioned Annie, in review of one of her unanswered thoughts.

"Cause there's more time for makin' out, that's why," Barbara answered matter-of-factly. "You see, he tells me that he loves me, and that's good enough for me. And as long as he goes with me to the dances and takes me to the movies, or bowlin' once in a while, I don't care what other stuff he thinks about, I only care what he thinks about me. And besides, I'm the best girl for him, anyway, and everybody knows it. So, there's nothin' to talk about," she explicated.

"But what about me and Bobby, then?" Annie asked comparatively.

"Well, you see, he's just like you, always asking questions and talking to people, you know, like you got to know everything. I'm tellin' ya, you guys'll get along just great, if'n you ever get to first base, you know, with that talkin' an all, —ha, ha, ha!" Barbara chided. "Like the song says, 'You got to hug him, and squeeze him, and love him, and show him that you care.' Cause you ain'ta be gonna be ridin' that cart just a wishin' and a hopin', Annie," Barbara counseled in paraphrasing Dusty Springfield.

"No, I didn't figure that," Annie confessed. "But what if he doesn't like me?" she anxiously proposed.

"What's not to like? You got all the equipment. And am damn sure he won't turn it down, unless he's a homo of course, but I don't think so, ha, ha, ha!" Barbara laughed. "Listen," she began to explain in a more serious tone, "He wouldn't be meetin' ya if he didn't want ya. So, just go with him where he wants to go and then let him cop a little feel, and then you get what *you* want, or he don't get no more. You got it? You get the picture, honey?" she questioned intensively.

"Yeah, I guess so," answered Annie, trying to mentally determine the wisdom of Barbara's suggestions. "Oh my God! I've got to go!" she then gasped, suddenly breaking off the conversation after looking up at the clock in the center of the mall. "I don't want to be late!" she exclaimed as she immediately abandoned her friend.

"I'll see you in gym class, Annie!" Barbara hollered out just before Annie had vanished into the nearest department store that led to the outside of the mall.

Once Annie had become free of the mall's artificial environment, the conscious recognition of such a beautiful spring day had now begun to overwhelm her. She felt as young and alive as Miss Jean Brodie did in her prime. She was practically skipping when she had crossed the highway that lead to the short-cut path that exited at the school's playground. But once the school itself had come within sight, and after looking down at her wristwatch, and realizing in fact that she would not be late, she accordingly slowed down her gait.

Although Annie was quite relieved to know that she was on time, it did not in any way alleviate her anxiety, for now she began to worry, *Is Bobby really going to be there?* as her initial desire of riding in the cart had inexplicitly fallen into second place.

Chapter Nine

And there he is, leaning against the tree, *waiting there, just for me,* Annie thought to herself as she was filled with an excitement that she had never felt before. *He is so handsome, and oh my God, look how he's dressed, and I still got my jeans on.* Nervous as a cat on a hot tin roof, Annie now slowly approached the object of her newly acquired desires, and being almost completely stunned by her own inability to control them, she simply walked up to Bobby and stood before him with nothing to say.

"Well, I see you made it," greeted Bobby, imagining himself to be James Bond.

"Yeah, I'm here," Annie responded in fact, trying not to reveal the emotional rollercoaster ride within her.

"So, how well do you know Barbara?" Bobby asked, trying to find some common ground.

"Well, like I mentioned before, we share the same gym class. And sometimes she comes over to the house and we just mess around awhile, that's all" Annie elaborated.

"So, how do you know about me?" Bobby continued to interrogate with a congenial smile.

"I saw you racing the go-cart from the pathway a couple of times before, when I took the shortcut home," Annie confessed, pausing for a second before compulsively adding, "Gee, it must be pretty cool to ride that thing, huh?"

"Yeah, it's pretty cool, although it seems to go a lot faster when you're really riding in it," Bobby remarked with his best professional face on.

"So, how come you're all dressed up?" Annie asked in a more natural tone as the butterflies in her stomach began to settle down.

Bobby, now occupying the seat of interrogation as to *his* motivations being scrutinized, was clearly uncomfortable in not having a prepared response.

"What?" Bobby questioned aloofly, pretending he did not understand the significance of answering her question, while deliberately using the extra time to gather his thoughts.

"I said, how come you're all dressed up?" Annie repeated, slowly and clearly.

"I thought it was so beautiful out today, I just felt like it, that's all," Bobby casually explained.

Good answer, Annie thought.

"I got some money on me, would you walk me over to the soda shop?" Annie requested.

"Sure, that's cool, Annie, but I can buy my own. I'm not poor. I work part time at Barilla's garage in the afternoon sometimes," Bobby proudly said. "Come on, let's go," he added.

"Okay," Annie replied, as together they began to stroll away from the tree.

"So where exactly do you live?" Bobby questioned.

"Actually, I live only a few houses away from John over on Hillcrest Drive. We're gonna pass it on our way to the soda shop," Annie annotated.

"I know where Hillcrest is," acknowledged Bobby.

"Well, what do you think of the Beatles?" redirected Annie on a more aesthetic plane.

"I like some of their stuff. I like the Stones and the Four Seasons a little better though," Bobby agreeably noted.

"I like the Supremes," offered Annie, "I think they're really boss. My dad bought me a transistor radio for my birthday and I usually take it with me, but Barbara had hers along today, so I left mine at the house," she explained.

"Your dad has the paving company, doesn't he?" Bobby interjected, deliberately changing the subject.

"Yeah, how'd you know that?" Annie asked in surprise.

"He gets your car fixed at the garage sometimes," Bobby informed her candidly. "Your old man's okay. He never complains like most guys do, having to pay to get their car fixed and all. Actually, he's pretty funny sometimes, especially when he talks about trying to get the tar off of everything he touches," he said in a complimentary tone.

Now approaching the thoroughfare across from their destination, the pair fell silent for a second as they looked for an abatement in the flow of traffic. After a brief moment or two, when the opportunity had all of a sudden presented itself, Bobby exclaimed instructively, "Come on, let's go!" reaching over and grabbing onto Annie's arm while stepping off the curb and onto the street.

Oh, wow, he's trying to protect me, Annie emotionalized while hurrying to keep up with him.

Once across the street safely, Bobby hesitated briefly to release Annie before inquiring in concern, "You okay?"

"Yeah, I'm fine," stated Annie to the release of Bobby's grasp, pulling down on her blouse to regain her composure.

"Well, we made it here without getting creamed," Bobby pronounced. "Are you ready now?" he asked invitingly with his hand out in the direction of the small strip shopping center which housed the local laundromat, pet store, music store, and the object of their efforts, The Sundry Soda Fountain Shoppe.

"All ready, I'm gonna get a cherry Coke," Annie announced cheerfully, as onward they proceeded.

Once inside, Annie expressly went over and planted herself down on one of the red swiveling cushions that were fixed atop a dozen silver stools which had been bolted to the floor directly in front of the soda counter. Dr. Fizz, as the local kids in the neighborhood called him, was the owner of the shop. He was of moderate height and build, and most notably always presented himself in a starched white shirt, matching apron, and bright red bow tie. His hair was dark and curly, and matched his bushy eyebrows perfectly. His eyes were equally dark, and his face was knarred with character, which came alive with the widest of smiles whenever he approached his patrons. Immediately upon seeing his two new customers come in, he came down from the opposite end of the counter to where Annie had seated herself and arrived there precisely as Bobby sat down as well.

"Do you have any idea what you want this time, young lady, or do I have to play twenty questions again?" the proprietor petitioned Annie straightforwardly.

"Well, I thought I would get a cherry Coke this time, that is, if you have any cherry syrup left back there, Dr. Fizz," Annie playfully teased.

"Well, I know I got some new coffee syrup in the other day," the now animated man proposed alternatively, turning around to reach up and retrieve a tall glass from a shelf behind the counter. "And I could probably make *it* taste like cherry, just for you, that shouldn't be hard, —after all, I am a doctor," he chuckled, filling up her glass with seltzer as Annie only rolled up her eyes and said nothing. "Humm, now, let me see, just how much syrup should I use?" He said to himself out loud, pushing down slowly on a silver pump handle and glancing sideways at Annie.

"Don't forget, I just brought you a customer," Annie minded him.

"Well, I guess I will just have to see what he wants right now, then, won't I?" Dr. Fizz replied with a small wink from his right eye, putting the soda directly in front of Annie and smiling like a Cheshire cat.

"So, you are going to be having a...?" Dr. Fizz paused, soliciting Bobby with a "come on" gesture from his right hand in waiting patiently to have his looming interrogative answered.

"Oh, I would like to have a coffee soda, please. It sounded pretty good," Bobby politely requested.

Visually taken aback from Bobby's respectful demeanor, the shopkeeper paused in cartoonish surprise, put his hands to his face, looked up into the air and questioned, "What's up, Doc, with all this politeness I am a party to? I must have taken a wrong turn at Albuquerque."

Next, after having finished his Bugs Bunny imitation, the Doctor abruptly returned to his task at hand as he took another glass off the shelf, flipped it in the air, caught it, and then smoothly placed it precisely under the fountain head. Filling it with seltzer, he subsequently whisked it over to the syrup pumps and deftly drew a most generous supply of the sugary flavoring directly into the dedicated soda water.

Taking out a long silver spoon from a recessed container with his right hand, while holding the glass in his left, the fountaineer then slowly stirred the mixture together. Whereupon officiating its completion to his satisfaction, Dr. Fizz then glanced over to where Bobby was seated, and with the libation still in hand, he reached over with his other, flicked open the lid to another recessed container, reached in, took out a cherry, tossed it into the air, and waited a second until it landed precisely into the soda.

Skillfully, the Doctor then smoothly slid the concoction along the surface of the counter where it appeared to magically come to a stop, squarely in front of the lad. Now to Bobby, this moment had signified to him that the performance was complete, but as all great performances need a finale, the impersonate prestidigitator was not quite finished yet, for with a wave of his right hand and the declaration, "I suppose you will need one of these," a straw then appeared from out of nowhere and landed exactly where it was intended to be, right beside the soda.

"Well, the show is over, —and that's all folks! Let me know if you two need anything else," Dr. Fizz declared, dismissing them with a smile and promptly retreating to the opposite end of the counter.

"That guy just weirded me out," Bobby whispered over to Annie as soon as the Doctor had left.

"Yeah, he's pretty cool, isn't he?" Annie spoke up secretively after sampling her drink. "I'll bet your soda's killer, though."

"Whoa, you're right, this stuff is killer. Is it always this good?" Bobby responded after taking a taste.

"For me it is. I don't know about everybody else, but mine is always fantastic. He likes me to call him Dr. Fizz. He's a nice guy. And, since you were polite and not a smart ass like some of the others, maybe he likes you too. Maybe you can get him to like you enough to tell us where he kept that straw he just gave you," Annie giggled.

"I wondered about that already," Bobby confessed with a slight amount of consternation as he cut his eyes askance at her.

"So, what tunes do you really like?" Annie asked, hoping to discover Bobby's secret wanton desires by intuitive comparison, sipping some more of her soda.

"Oh, 'Big Girls Don't Cry' is one of them, along with 'Walk Like a Man,' by the Four Seasons. They're probably my favorites," Bobby enumerated as he was conspicuously enjoying his soda, along with his crafted response.

"What are you smirking about?" Annie responded, impishly poking him in the side over his obvious innuendo.

"Hey, look out, you might make me spill my soda!" Bobby exclaimed, wincing back from her prodding.

"Well, you deserved it, and besides, I'm all finished and I gotta go," Annie declared, grinning while she dismounted from her pedestal to stand impatiently akimbo.

"Just hold on a second, I gotta pay the man," Bobby replied, rushing to finish his soda. "Excuse me, sir, we're finished, how much do I owe you?" he asked the shopkeeper, who was now straightening out the comic book rack towards the back of the shop.

"It's on the house this time, pal," Dr. Fizz announced.

"Well, how much is hers, then?" Bobby asked, denoting his assumed responsibility.

"Just make sure that little Annie Banannie don't get squashed out on the highway," the Doctor dictated.

"Sure, okay, I can do that, and thank you, sir," Bobby courteously replied, getting off his stool and putting his change back into his front pocket.

"Come back again when you're thirsty, kid," Dr. Fizz called out as the two of them had passed the juke box on their way out the door.

"So, are you going to walk me home safely?" asked Annie as soon as they had gotten outside, deliberately prompting him to honor his newly acquired moral imperative to not let her get run over.

"Well, I got a free soda out of the deal, so I guess I should," Bobby acceded with a smile. "We could cross at the light this time and go down Summerland. It crosses Hillcrest," he noted.

"That's good. I only live a half a block down from there," Annie accepted.

"I know, you already said you were only a couple of houses down from John," Bobby reminded her.

So, on perhaps one of the most beautiful spring days of the year, the couple meandered on, aimlessly dallying away to the exclusion of any worldly purpose whatsoever. And while Bobby remained in a silent mode, Annie chattered on unabatedly, passionately relating how she felt about, and was affected by, every currently known rock and roll tune that she could think of. Eventually, after Annie had gotten down to over half of what would be considered as Casey Kasem's American Top Forty hits, Bobby had finally mustered the resolve to ask her, "How come we didn't have to pay for the sodas?"

"Ha, ha, ha," Annie laughed. "I never have to pay for my soda," she flaunted. "My dad put his driveway in, and he gave him a good deal. He's one of my dad's friends. It was me who named him Dr. Fizz, and he *loves* his little friend Annie, that's all," she brazenly touted.

"So, you got a pretty good racket goin'," Bobby declared wryly.

"What do you mean? Mr. Finelli is a really nice guy, and that is his real name, too, if you want to know," Annie told him explicitly. "And I can pay for my own soda, too, any time I feel like it!" she scolded. "I stop by because he's a lot of fun and I like him, that's all. I play the juke box with my own money, and I always have a good time when I go there, and it is the *only* reason why I go there. You understand?" she chastised.

Then, reaching over and tugging onto his arm, Annie forced him to stop and face her directly. Saying nothing, she just stood there to study the obvious guilt which she had decisively wrought upon his face for his tawdry accusation. And there he stood, motionless, with nothing to say at all, until at long last Annie began to grin.

"Are you kidding me?" Annie then blurted out. "It's a great racket!" she admitted, now grinning from ear to ear.

"Why, you little tease!" Bobby cried out in retaliation, playfully pushing her on the shoulder.

By the time the two young hearts had arrived at the corner of Hillcrest and Summerland, they each had discovered within them a new feeling of compatibility, which neither of them had anticipated. The reality of reaching the destination from which the hopeful dreamers would part had now brought upon them an awkward silence as each of them awaited to be asked the most dreadful and inevitable question to ever be uttered, "When am I going to see you again?"

Smiling, it took only a moment for Annie's boldness to override any such fear of rejection, as she then quite clearly and deftly delivered those exact words of intimidation right into the soul of her intended conquest.

Thereupon, Bobby sheepishly replied, "Well, I don't know. I have to go to church tomorrow."

"I get out of school the same time you do. You could meet me by the bike rack on Monday, then, over by where the school buses leave," Annie suggested.

"Yeah, sure, I could meet you there," Bobby elatedly replied.

"Well, then, I will be there," Annie told him in certitude. "So, now, aren't you going to kiss me? After all, this *was* our first date," she declared, directly challenging his "cool" reputation.

"Out here on the corner?" Bobby squirmed.

"Okay, you can take me under that weeping willow tree over there, and do it then," Annie said, pointing to the more secluded lot across the street. "Nobody will see us," she assured him firmly.

"Okay, I'll go over there with you," Bobby consented, providently accepting his fate.

Once under the massive willow and encased by its ribbons of spring green branches that hung pendulously low onto the carpet of moss beneath them, they found themselves completely and utterly sheltered from the outside world. Then, once Annie had looked about once more, making sure that their privacy was sufficient, she wasted no time in throwing her arms about Bobby's neck.

"Isn't it beautiful under here? Isn't it just beautiful?" Annie repeated, looked directly into his eyes.

Without saying a word, Bobby then pulled her closer by her waist, leaned forward, and kissed her, —for how long he did not know, but he did. And then it was all over; he was now "cool" indeed, while Annie had now become his very own story book princess.

Impassioned as neither of them had ever been before, both left the sanctity of their secret garden in a daze of euphoria. Each within the sanctity of their own thoughts, they now traveled together into the unchartered realm of their very own version of love.

Once Annie had gotten home, she immediately began to recall the entire day's events from the knock at her bedroom door by Barbara to the exact moment of embrace that had encompassed her soul's desires. To her, it was the most complete day of her life. *Mother Nature was in her most glorious state today,* she mused to herself. She felt in her heart that it was she, and she alone, who was the explicit object of Mother Nature's serendipitous generosity that day, and that her fortune was unquestionably real, as real could be.

All of the day's affairs, without any exceptions, were examined and perused, over and over again, to the smallest of details. Viewed in the most precious and joyful terms of endearment that could possibly be conceived, Annie had become enamored with life itself, for Bobby was now her very dream come true.

Bobby was simply overwhelmed; thus, *his* thoughts only came to him in bits and pieces. *What's going to happen now?* was his main concern, followed by *What do I tell John?* and conversely, *Exactly, what is Annie going to tell Barbara?*

His psyche seemed to have gone wild, for he could not help from vacillating between the feelings of exhilaration and those of distressful apprehensiveness. Finally, in an attempt alleviate this condition, he consciously tried to gain some relief by mentally concentrating upon his formally scheduled duties. Distressfully, however, all attempts at this procedure had only ended up in total failure, for Annie had utterly destroyed his entire will to concentrate on anything but her.

The passing minutes were now viewed as the enemy, evoking an unbearable suffering, while both of the lovers wished in vein that the seconds which make them up would instantaneously surrender. From moments, to minutes, to hours, they had both become entrapped in a strobe light effect of pure surrealism, and although they felt this new-found love could be the greatest odyssey to which they would ever embark upon, they also knew full well that their adventure would go no further until they were once again united under the providence of Father Time himself.

Bobby, come Monday morning, like a leprechaun who had dreamt that he had found a pot of gold, was so enamored with his good fortune that he just had to go back to where the alleged fable had all begun. He had to witness with his own eyes, once again, the magnificent splendor and grandeur of the magical and mystical weeping willow tree that had granted him his treasure. Existentially vindicated, once his destination had come into view, his passion soared. *How will I get through the day? How will I get through the day?* he kept repeating to himself all the way to the front door of the school.

Annie, come Monday morning, like a fairy in *A mid-summer's night dream,* felt that she was at one with the willow. Flitting about, she nimbly prepared herself for the day's anticipated emotional feast. *The first and foremost requirement of seduction was predicated upon one's own physical appearance,* she thought. *Everyone knows that. And it's not vanity, because I am a girl. It's mandatory that I must look my best,"* she rationalized, while taking an unusually long time in primping herself for the day's most bountiful harvest. *I want to be Bobby's girl. I want to be Bobby's girl*, she kept humming to herself, all the way to the front door of the school.

Chapter Ten

The population of the town in which Annie lived, like many others at that time, had verily exploded after World War Two by prodigiously propagating over twenty thousand new young residents in its exuberance to celebrate its victory. This naturally caused a problem with the overall school system in that it had not been designed to handle such a multitude of new students. New schools had to be built, but how to fund them was the question. Hence, it was decided by the school board that because of the economic necessity a "more centralized school system," was the only way to go.

The "neighborhood system of individual attention," as previously afforded to the students and heretofore touted as an educational tenant, was now clandestinely condemned by the supposed guardians of the students' welfare under an advertised masquerade that was termed to be "a better and more affordable education."

The old system of one-on-one teaching, had now become totally discarded in favor of the new mechanized union approach, which emphasized that the teacher's welfare was paramount to the students' in declaring that the previously personalized symbiotic system of respect and learning was simply to inefficient and obsolete.

It had therefore become subsequently acknowledged and accepted by most all that by invoking a carefully drawn and conclusively regulated job description that a "legally binding" contract for employment, could in fact, publicly regulate, and therefore define, the very basis of a student's matriculation. This new manner of providing a "quality education" had now been applied throughout the country by edict, de facto proclaiming that the very task of teaching was to hereafter be defined as a regimental function of the government, and no longer considered an art.

The physical aftermath of these actions precipitated that the school itself, at the end of the day's classes, would quite furiously and most expeditiously expel the hordes of young students, who had been indiscriminately entrapped within it bowels for the entire day, summarily out the front door, there to be vehemently thrust upon a seemingly impregnable barricade of awaiting school busses. Eventually, after all the bussed students had been collectively re-entombed in their big yellow caskets, the object became to whisk them away as efficiently as possible in an ending testament to the day's antagonizing conflicts between the recalcitrant and the inculcators.

It was only because of this ritual that Annie had reached her appointed destination ahead of Bobby on that sunny Monday afternoon. She had even risked detention not to be late for the encounter by exiting out of one of the school's emergency side doors.

Bobby, in all his passion, had also risked receiving detention by engaging in direct combat with the mob at the front door as soon as the three o'clock bell had gone off.

In classic Pavlovian fashion, this daily occurrence never appeared to change, and to alleviate the consequences of having to place the blame of this chaotic behavior on anyone in particular, —especially on one of the members of the staff, it was widely accepted by all that it was indeed the bell who was the guilty culprit that was responsible for this ugly occurrence. Fittingly, its punishment was to receive a sentence of solitary detention, even on the weekends when no one was there to hear it ring.

Intensely incognizant to all these surroundings, the purgatorious pair of lovers were much more than just physically entrapped. They were also caught in an emotional limbo from which neither of them could escape until they were both again united. Each of them fought valiantly and courageously on that next Monday, not be denied their little slice of heaven as they dauntlessly pushed on.

And there she is, confirmed Bobby to himself, *only a short way to go now,* he thought to himself as Annie first came into his sight while rounding the last of the school busses in line. Although it wasn't particularly cold out, he nevertheless had worn his prize leather jacket along with his best Hi-Roll shirt. *I wonder if my hair is still as perfect as it was the last time I combed it?* he pondered further as he came closer to Annie, who was leaning against the end of the bike rack while facing the sun in the opposite direction.

Annie knew in her heart that he would honor his commitment to her, and because it was her duty to look good for him, she dressed to the max. She had on her above the knee, albeit mini, olive green skirt and matching short heeled pumps. Her white pressed and pleated blouse was open to the second button, revealing a crucifix of gold upon a chain around her neck. Atop her blouse she wore a tan jacket whose olive-green leather trim had also matched the rest of her wardrobe.

Fretting about in open anxiety would simply ruin her contrived pose, and that would not do, she calculated, even if her books did get heavier by the minute. *No! I must wait here as exactly as I am. He'll be here, he'll be here,* she kept reciting to herself as she began to get tired of standing there like a statue in a fixed position. *And it will be a glorious rescue too!* she fanaticized, *even if it is only from this stupid bike rack.*

"Annie, it's me, over here!" Bobby called out while fleeting up the sidewalk about ten feet away. Turning to face him, she now stood straight up from her position of leaning against the rack and adjusted her books and purse. Then, by the time she had finished correcting her stance, Bobby had finally arrived by her side.

"You ready to walk me home?" Annie smiled flirtatiously.

"Sure, come on, I'm ready to go," replied Bobby, leading her onto the sidewalk with his right hand at the small of her back.

"So, where is your locker?" Bobby asked, removing his hand once they had gotten to the main walkway.

"I'm down by the chemistry lab on the bottom floor," Annie answered plainly before asking in response, "Where is yours?

"Heck, mine's almost to the vice principal's office on the way out the door. I've got to fight to get to it every day. It's a real pain," Bobby certified.

The approximate mile Annie had to walk home every day had always seemed to be a boring chore of drudgery, but in the mental solitude of this simple task, she used the time to re-evaluate the childhood dreams of her past. The new physical reality of her life was challenging her younger fantasies with every step that she made. *Death to my Chatty Cathy,* she thought as she walked along, *and death to Barbie, too. This is the real thing,* she told herself as she decided to take no prisoners.

From the moment that she had heard Bobby's voice call out to her at the bike rack, Annie was keenly aware that everything that she was about to say or do at this very moment could have some unforeseen bearing upon her intended storybook life. But, naturally sanctioned by God, and mankind as well, she felt it was ordained to have her life turn out this way. It was her love of adventure that compelled her to advance into this new and passionate land called love, and she felt quite confident that she was wholly ready.

It was a princess' obligation to surrender her innocence unto a tender and loving knight of the realm, she surmised, while at the same time, wondering exactly how to go about this mandate and yet retain her poise and dignity. Although she was readily prepared to throw all caution to the wind, she had decided to not be in a hurry either, electing to let the eventual "fait accompli" happen whenever it was destined to be.

After a nonstop conversation concerning their shared opinions of their individual teachers, the school itself, and the trials and tribulations of having to attend it, they finally arrived at the corner of Summerland and Hillcrest and the Shrine of the Enchanted Willow Tree once again. Then, as Annie was still instructing Bobby on how she had planned to attain an "A" for her art project, Bobby, emboldened by his new sense of self-confidence, suddenly stopped, put his hand out, gently clasped on to Annie's arm as he interrupted her esoteric confabulations, and inquired, "Isn't this where we go under the tree?"

"Only if you want to," Annie demurely responded as best she could.

"Well, what do you think?" Bobby pressed further as he gently tugged on her arm, attempting to cajole her off the walkway and onto the spring grass. And so, once more united, the two infatuates again became one under their own personalized canopy of desire, as no longer would each be wondering how they'd face the world alone, for now they had each other.

On Wednesday afternoon, it had been determined they would again experience the exceptional antics of the amazing Dr. Fizz. And no sooner than they had gotten past the front door of the shop, instantaneously they heard the shopkeeper explicitly call out in an admonishing tone, "Well, I see that you failed again, Miss Annie!"

"What do you mean? I don't fail at anything," Annie flung at him impertinently, while she and Bobby took a seat at the counter where they had seated themselves before.

"Oh, no. You failed, all right," Dr. Fizz repeated doggedly. "But granted, it was not your fault, it was his," he stated sternly, now pointing his finger directly at Bobby.

"What'd I do? I'm innocent. I didn't do anything," Bobby rebutted.

"No, no, you two don't seem to understand," Dr. Fizz edified. "She failed to get run over, and it was all *your* fault," he emphatically declared. "So, just take it like a man, son," he then paternally advised, pausing for a second while Bobby had no response. "Well... good job young man, good job!" he then surprisingly congratulated with a broad smile. "So, now that that's settled, what's it going to be?" he inquired, now turning his attention to Annie.

"Well, since it was all *his* fault, like you said, I deserve a hot fudge sundae, and I want all the stuff on it too," Annie pronounced indignantly.

"Okay, you got it, Annie Banannie," validated the doctor.

Turning around to face the back counter once more, he then picked up an ice cream scoop with his right hand, spun it in midair and caught it, synchronously flipping open the cover to the freezer with his left.

"And make it snappy!" demanded Annie, grinning behind his back.

Taking a sundae glass from the shelf on the wall, the doctor scooped out two large portions of strawberry ice cream, tossed them into the glass, and cast the scoop directly back into the stainless, water filled catch basin affixed to the counter below. Then, flipping open the hot fudge container, took hold of a long protruding, stainless-steel handle and stirred the contents within. And as if the ladle would hold more, simply because of his labors, he protractedly removed it from the container and dramatically poured the fudge on top of the ice cream. Replacing the ladle, he thereupon turned about to the front counter and placed the glass down.

Continuing unabatedly, he mechanically reached over, and flipping up the lid of a recessed container, removed an aerosol can of whip cream, and after applying an ample mountain of snow to the top of the sundae, he carefully addressed his creation with a shower of crushed nuts which he had retrieved from a recessed container on his left.

Finally, after garnishing the apex of his artistic fabrication with his classic meteoric cherry, Dr. Fizz gingerly placed it directly on the counter in front of his "peppery petunia" and asked assumptively, "I believe it was strawberry that was your desire, young lady, was it not?"

"I guess it will just have to do," Annie offered in feigned circumspect, auspiciously smiling nonetheless.

"And just for your information young lady, when you mix chocolate and strawberry together, the name for it is called a 'Hoboken,'" counseled the doctor, while putting a long silver spoon alongside his latest creation. And then, not waiting for a reply, he turned his attention directly over to Bobby and said, "You got a name, son?"

"Yes sir, its Bobby," he responded courteously.

"No, no. I mean a real name, not your given name," the doctor clarified. "One that everybody calls you. One that's only yours. Now you see, you can't use Dr. Fizz, because that's my name," he emphasized, putting his finger into the air. "You could use maybe somethin' like "The Kid" or "Mr. Cool" or maybe even "That guy with the leather bomber jacket," you know, somethin' like that," he figuratively explained. "You get the picture, but not, I repeat, *not Dr. Fizz,* you can't have that, 'cause, like I said, that's my name," he pridefully re-enforced with a wide smile, while pointing to himself with his thumb.

"No, sir, I could never be a 'Dr. Fizz,' I believe you are an original," Bobby respectfully testified. "I just go by Bobby, that's all," he said plainly.

"Well, young man, I mean Bobby, I believe it was a coffee soda the last time, was it not?" Dr. Fizz asked, cordially accepting Bobby's decision to remain innocuous.

"Yes, sir, it was," answered Bobby, impressed with the shop keeper's recall.

"Well, is that what you want now, or are you going to just sit there?" the Doctor questioned, still awaiting an order from the young man.

"Oh, yeah, it was great, and I'd like another one, please," Bobby requested.

"Okay, Bobby, I got it," Dr. Fizz responded, proceeding to prepare the concoction.

This time there was little fanfare afoot when the Doctor prepared the drink. Instead, once he had placed it on the counter, he just pretentiously put his hand up to the side of his face, and pretending to shield his next comment from Annie's ears, he proceeded to conspiratorially leaned over and not-so-secretively, whisper to Bobby, "I'll just leave you two alone now."

Then, after tossing down his magically appearing straw, Dr. Fizz once again left to walk back to the far end of the counter to attend to some of the other students who were fervently attempting to conquer the high-score on the pin ball machine.

"Are you going to be racing the go-cart again on Saturday?" Annie casually queried, not looking up from her sundae.

"Probably," Bobby answered. "I haven't talked to John since last Saturday. I need to go to the 'Y' and work out tonight. I'll see him then, and then I'll know," Bobby answered informatively as he took a drink from his soda.

"Can I ride it?" Annie asked bluntly without any expression at all.

Caught by surprise, Bobby stopped drinking and paused for a moment before carefully replying.

"I don't know, can you?" Bobby artfully dodged, just to see what she would say.

"Well, you would have to teach me how, of course, but that's not the reason I asked," Annie told him specifically. "I was told that your father told you, not to let any girls ride it. But, anyway, I'm not asking your father, I'm asking you. Can I ride it?" she again asked flatly.

"My father never said that," Bobby corrected with a small smirk across his face.

"That's what John told Barbara," Annie testified with certitude.

"Yeah, I know that. That's because we don't want to be pestered by everybody, but my father never really said that. That's just what we told Barbara. You see, we knew that she would tell everyone else, so we didn't have to. And besides, she doesn't want to ride it, anyway. She told John that," Bobby dismissively added with a chuckle, —but still, he avoided answering her question.

Turning sideways on her stool, Annie grabbed onto Bobby's arm, and turning him sideways as well, forced him to face her directly. Now she commanded his full attention; and with her eyebrows raised, and a determined little purse of her lips, she said as distinctly as possible, "Well, I am not Barbara, and I want to ride the cart. Now, do I have to ask your father?"

Suddenly, as if Bobby had just been given a dose of electro-shock therapy, he had a horrible picture in his mind of her walking right up to his front door and asking to speak directly to his dad. *Oh my god! How embarrassing! She just might do it,* he thought as he weighed his response. Annie, meanwhile, had said no more. She simply sat there, silently and unflinchingly, looking straight into his eyes, still wondering yet if her approach was really going to be effective.

"No, you don't have to ask him," Bobby positively assured her. "I can show you how to drive it," he asserted with authority, trying to respond in a manly fashion. "Let me talk to John. I'd have to get the cart over to the school early then, like around nine," he explained in a practical tone. "That would give me about an extra hour or so to teach you. Is that okay with you?" he offered considerately.

"Yeah, I can be there at nine alright," Annie confirmed, adding gratuitously, "You know, I think you are so cool."

"Yup, I guess I am that all right," Bobby smiled smugly, turning back to finish his soda in a new state of relief.

Equally content with herself, Annie also turned away to finish her confection, and not another sound was heard between the two of them until the finality of her clinking spoon discardedly chimed *all done* in the bottom of her glass.

"Is that all, folks?" the prestidigitating proprietor asked as he virtually popped out of nowhere once more.

"Yes, sir, Dr. Fizz. Now, how much do I owe you?" Bobby asked amiably.

"So, let's see. Buying or being?" Dr. Fizz pondered out loud. "Which is it? Being or buying? Humm, I can see this could be a problem," he dramatically stated, looking up for some heavenly inspiration while scratching his chin. "Eureka! I got it!" he then exclaimed with his finger pointing upward in denoting his moment of enlightenment. "Being you are buying today, Bobby," he emphasized, "it will cost you one half of one simoleon. Yes, just one half of a Georgie Porgy. In other words, that will be, I believe in your terms, a half-a-rock. You know, fifty cents, my good man, and that will cover you, and your little accomplice, as well," he verbosely established.

"Thank you, Dr. Fizz." Bobby said politely, placing two quarters on the counter as he stood up from his stool.

"Goodbye, Dr. Fizz, see you in the funny papers!" Annie cried out with a small wave, waiting by the juke box where she had wandered while Bobby was negotiating the fare.

"Oh, by the way, one thing," Bobby said confidentially, leaning back over the counter to Dr. Fizz, "I think I'll take you up on that 'Mr. Cool' thing, okay?"

"A wise decision," Dr. Fizz professed in thoughtful recognition, while Bobby left to attend to Annie.

"Yeah, like Annie said, see you in the funny papers," Bobby called back before exiting.

"You got it, Mr. Cool!" Dr. Fizz endorsed loudly, just before the door had closed.

As the springtime's sun was passing into the summer time's domain and the days grew increasingly longer, it only postponed the inevitable lament that the lovers would feel each day when the darkness of separation was to be ultimately cast upon them. And as their love grew, so did its notoriety.

And even though Mother Nature had been thoroughly aware of their secretive activities, considering it a private matter, they were still fully aware that those pesky humans would never treat their privacy the same. They knew all too well that they would eventually have to face a public reckoning as to their union, —the only question was, when?

~

"Annie's got a boyfriend," Capricia blurted out at the dinner table only a few days later at the end of the evening meal. "She's been walking home with him from school," she added.

"I'm sure he's a nice boy," said Jolanda, placidly downplaying the revelation.

"So, just who is this guy that's walkin' my daughter home?" Enrico subsequently questioned.

"Oh, you already know him, Daddy, he works sometimes in the afternoon at Barilla's gas station. His name is Bobby Taylor," Annie responded brightly.

"You mean that kid that wears that brown leather jacket? The one that built that go-cart, that he and his pal race over at the elementary school on Saturdays?" questioned Enrico, demonstrating his cognitive awareness.

"Yup, that's him. Bobby says he knows you from the station," Annie confirmed unreservedly.

"I guess he's okay, —at least he's not a punk like a lot of them out there," Enrico stated plainly. "He does pretty good work at the station, when he's there," he asided. "But then again, he don't complain about getting a little tar on himself either," he further offered in a more accepting tone. "Well, as long as he treats you with respect, I guess that's all what's important," he subsequently decreed with a wave of his hand. "Now, if that's all there is, I'm going over to your uncle Tony's," he announced, getting up from the table in not wanting to hear any more from the "peanut gallery," as he would often remark.

"Is he a Catholic?" Jolanda openly inquired while she and Annie had then gotten up to clear the table.

"I don't know, mom, I didn't ask him," Annie answered in a pained tone. "I know he goes to church on Sundays, and that's about it," she clarified a little further in trying to satisfy he mother's curiosity.

"Annie and Bobby, sittin' in a tree, k-i-s-s-i-n-g," taunted Capricia from the chair while she dawdled with the last of the food on her plate.

"That's enough, Caprice, leave your sister alone," Jolanda reprimanded.

Oh god! How close could she have come? Annie thought, propitiously ignoring her sister's comments.

"Annie, maybe you can bring him by the house sometime, so I can meet him?" her mother requested, both pleasantly and insidiously.

"I only just met him mom, it's no big deal," Annie understatedly dismissed, replacing the flowered centerpiece back on the table. "Well, anyway, I have some homework to do now," she declared, promptly leaving the room.

"So do I," Capricia likewise announced, instantly getting up from her chair in full pursuit of her sister.

"You've got to tell me all about him," Capricia called out, half way up the stairs.

"Never. You're just a little squeal bag!" Annie retorted, resolutely slamming her bedroom door behind her.

"I promise I won't say anything to anyone, anymore," Capricia submitted in a soft voice from outside the closed door, holding her hand up to the side of her mouth in trying to accentuate her offer of a secret pact.

"Bug off, Squeal Bag! And get away from my door, or I'll tell Dad some things about you, —and I guarantee, you ain't gonna like it, fink," Annie threatened.

And so, finally, after having the gauntlet of ultimate fear thrown at her, Capricia wisely retreated to her bedroom, still undeterred in saying to herself with a small grin, *I'll just ask her tomorrow.*

157

Chapter Eleven

It was exactly at a quarter after eight on that following
Saturday morning when John showed up, early as promised.
Walking around the side of the house to the garage at the
back of the property, John could see that its door was
already open for business, while Bobby was fastidiously
wiping down the cart with an old hand rag for the day's
adventure.

"Hey, man, you owe me for this, you know that?" greeted
John, causing Bobby to look up from his work.

"Yeah, I know, I owe you one. I'll pay you back," Bobby
acknowledged as he returned to meticulously detailing his
machine.

"That's cool. So, what do you need?" John proffered in
assistance.

"I think I got everything except the soda. It's in that little
refrigerator over in the corner, next to my Dad's beer,"
Bobby informed him.

"Your dad keeps his beer in the garage?" asked John in
surprise.

"Yeah, he buys it by the case to save money and then he
keeps the extra out here. That way, if he runs out of it in the
house, he's still got some that's cold," Bobby explained.

"Your old man is pretty cool, you know?" complemented
John.

"Yeah, he's okay. He doesn't give me any crap," Bobby
told him openly. "I do my chores like I'm supposed to, and
he leaves me alone unless I need something. He's the one
who really built this. I only helped him. So, I guess you
could say he's pretty cool all right, as far as dads go,
anyway," he qualified. "Now, you want to put a couple extra

sodas in the crate and see if I missed anything else?" he directed in a more officious tone.

"Yeah, sure," replied John, going about his task.

"Oh, and by the way, is Barbara coming? Bobby asked.

"Probably not until about ten, I guess," answered John, putting the four sodas in with the tools and checking the box's contents. "As far as I can tell, everything's in here now," he reported, looking up to ask, "You ready?

"Yup. Well, what do you think?" solicited Bobby, while standing back to survey the machine.

"I think it's cleaner than it's been in a long time, Bob," answered John. "Anyway, let's blow this joint," he said declaratively.

And so, pushing the cart out of the driveway and onto the sidewalk, the two best friends intently began their journey down the shortest path to the elementary school.

"So, where did you go with Annie last Saturday afternoon?" asked John, steering the cart down the tree lined sidewalk.

"We went over to the soda shop on Plainfield Avenue," Bobby informed him, pushing from behind the cart.

"You mean you didn't take her behind the school and cop a feel?" John called back to him over his shoulder.

"No, I did not," Bobby replied indignantly.

"You gonna try to cop a feel today?" John continued to goad him.

Immediately upon hearing this second remark, Bobby subsequently stopped pushing the cart, causing it to slowly come to a stop. He then walked around to the side of it to formally face John and straightforwardly explain the seriousness of his quest.

"John, I don't want to scare her away," Bobby said in earnest. "And besides, I know her father from the gas station. I could get into a lot of trouble here, —who knows what she'll tell Barbara, and there you go, it's all over the place. I don't want to screw this up. She's a stone fox, and you know it. So, just please help me out with this, will you, pal?" he requested sincerely.

"I was just giving you the razz, Bob," John recanted, "The only reason that I'm here today is to help you out. Don't worry, I'm not going to mess it up for you. I give you my word," he promised. "Now, of course, I can't help it if she falls for me instead, you know," he smirked in a friendly gesture in trying to "out-cool" his buddy.

"Oh, gimme a break," Bobby mocked, stretching out his hands with a returning smirk.

It wasn't until they had gotten in sight of their goal that Bobby had begun to feel some sort of relief from his angst, noticing that Annie was nowhere to be seen. To appear unprofessional and inept was one of his greatest fears, as he realized that a bad overture is an instant death to the best of shows. Nevertheless, now having the extra time to get ready both physically and mentally, he had become even more anxious than ever.

After having rolled the cart over into its exact starting position, the two young lads then proceeded to set up the appointed recharge area. A brisk breeze was intermittently blowing about the air which rustled the leaves from gust to gust throughout the giant oak tree while the chattering birds fluttered about, attempting to build their nests. It was a perfect day for kite flying, roller skating, and go-cart racing, while the indominable rays from the sun were so intense that they would virtually blind anyone who had the misfortune to look up and face them directly. *This is going to be a great day, I can feel it,* Bobby said to himself as he and his compadre went about their business.

"Well, it's nine o'clock," then came out of nowhere while Bobby was squatting down, attentively adjusting the engine's carburetor.

Is that Annie? Bobby thought as he looked up, putting his hand to his brow in an attempt to shield the brightness from the sun behind her.

"Oh, Annie, you're here," Bobby said, after determining that the silhouette which was standing directly between him and the sun was indeed her.

Thereupon, after this fact had been confirmed, Bobby stood up, adjusted his eyes accordingly, and beamed such a smile that it warmed Annie to the core of her existence, and feeling that she was truly the object of his happiness, only made her affection for him even greater.

"Who'd you expect? Casper the Friendly Ghost?" Annie impishly smiled.

"No, I expected my first student driver," Bobby replied as professionally as he could muster.

"Well, I put on my new blue jeans just for you," Annie modeled coquettishly before him.

Not to mention one of those rib tickler blouses like she had on last week," Bobby thought, but made no comment at all.

"That's nice," Bobby responded, trying not to think any more about it. "Now, if you just get into this thing, I'll show you how to get started," he instructed in the simplest of terms, attempting as best he could to solely keep his mind on her safety.

"Hi, John," Annie eventually acknowledged, beginning to crawl into the vehicle.

"I see you're lookin' good, Annie," replied John with a grin, "Barbara should be here about in about an hour, just so you know," he reported.

"Is she going to ride this thing too?" Annie questioned.

"Are you kiddin'? Wrinkle her clothes and mess up her perm? It ain't gonna happen. It just ain't her bag," said John, clearly amused by Annie's question.

"Are you ready now?" interceded Bobby, making sure he had Annie's full attention.

"As far as I know," responded Annie.

"Well, once John pulls the cord back, it will turn on and you won't be able to hear me, okay? So, pay attention," Bobby adamantly stressed.

"Okay," Annie answered in a serious tone.

"Now, if you slowly pull up on the lever to your right, it's the clutch," Bobby pointed out, "it will make the cart start to go. Then, once you pull it up all the way, you will hear a couple of clicks, and it will lock the lever in place. Now, to release it, you just pull back up on it again and the press the black button on the end, see, right there," he instructed graphically, "and it will unlock so you can lower it and cut back off the power. The lever on your left is the break. All you have to do is pull up on it, and the harder you do, the faster the cart will stop," he explained attentively. "So, now really pay attention," he emphasized sternly, "the cart *will not stop* while the clutch is still on. Do you understand that?" he reinforced, looking intently into her eyes.

"Yes, I understand that," Annie expressly answered.

"Now, one more time," Bobby emphasized. "Once you have engaged the clutch, the cart will start moving, and then if you want to go faster, you just step on the gas pedal down there," he pointed out, "and it will go faster. Okay? Are you sure got all that?" he asked her with the firmness of a parachute inspector.

"Yeah, I got it," Annie affirmed.

"Are you positively sure?" Bobby sought to verify further.

"I believe so," answered Annie, adjusting her previous response.

"Well, just keep it going in a circle around the lot, then," Bobby capitulated fatefully, "Oh, and by the way, that thing in the middle is the steering wheel," he jokingly smiled.

"I figured that out for myself," Annie irascibly answered him back. "So, is that all? Can I go now?" she petulantly requested.

"John, you want to start the engine?" requested Bobby.

"No sweat. Got it under control," John categorically replied, pulling the rip cord and thus causing the entire enterprise to vociferously come alive.

Still standing next to the cart, Bobby again pointed to the right side of Annie's seat and yelled over the sound of the engine, "Now just pull up on that lever!" and then mindfully stepped back so she wouldn't run over his feet.

Finally, after following Bobby's direction, the cart now proceeded to slowly move away. Then, while beginning to weave from side to side as it gradually approached the end of the lot, both Bobby and John started to yell out, "Turn it! Turn it!" And turn it Annie did, just enough to stay on the pavement. Dauntlessly, she moved on, even if only at a snail's pace, to where she had finally encircled the machine back across the starting line.

"Step on the gas, Annie! Step on the gas!" the two boys now encouraged, as she passed them by. And when she did, "Holy Mother of God!" she screamed out compulsively as the spirited machine spontaneously lurched forward with such a shocking speed that it made it feel like her big toe had gotten stuck in a light socket. Impulsively, she jerked her foot back from the gas pedal, but this did not seem to slow the machine down one iota. In panic, thinking that the contraption was going turn over, her hands froze to the wheel as the cart drove straight off the pavement and onto the ball field area, where it finally began to slow down about fifty yards straight out from the parking lot.

Eventually, after the cart had gotten back to the pace of a crawl, Annie, now even more determined than ever not to lose her imperturbability, cautiously began to turn it around, while Bobby and John came yelling after in hot pursuit, "Release the clutch! Release the clutch!"

Ultimately, however, after Annie did successfully, albeit slowly, turn the cart about, her spunkiness returned to her in full force. Most decisively and quite absolutely, she had no further intentions whatsoever of surrendering unto the machine's cantankerous nature. *So, that's how this thing works. Well, it's not going to get the best of me!* she thought, obstinately "putting the pedal to the metal."

And once again, the cart unreservedly lurched ahead, but this time it was the two boys who were now in a panic, suddenly being forced to quickly scramble aside. Then, as the unexpected tempest whooshed past them in a cloud of dust, briefly causing them to lose their composure, they now began to blare out in unison, "Just take it easy! Just take it easy!" as once more they tried their best to catch her.

Annie now let the cart slow down a little, only to again speed it up so she could get a better understanding of its responsiveness. *Ha! I'm the one who's in control now!* she rhetorically projected to the cart, and none too soon, for she was fast approaching the edge of the tarmac.

Now all I have to do is get this darn thing back to the finish line, Annie thought, promptly and completely removing her foot from the gas pedal. For the first time, she reached down to pull up on the hand break and, to her surprise, it actually did begin to slow the vehicle down. *Oh, wow! This gives me more time to steer,* she discovered elatedly, while curving it around to slowly address the finish line.

164

The only apparent problem now, however, was that the cart was reticently refusing slow down any further, even as she kept pulling up on the break as hard as possible. But then, at that precise moment where aggravation surrenders unto prayer, the little light bulb in her head began to blink, "Release the clutch! Release the clutch!" And thus, in dutifully following her instructions, the wild ride of Miss Annie Russo was officially over.

"I see you made it back all right," loudly declared Bobby, the instant he and John had caught up to her, panting from the labors of their charge.

"Yeah! You tried to run me over like the Leader of the Laundromat," castigated John, while shutting the engine down with the screwdriver.

"Oh, you'll get over it, John, or should I say Johnnie?" Annie remarked, glancing with a smirk towards at Bobby.

"Well, you can't stay in there all day, it's John's turn now," said Bobby, tactfully disregarding her taunt.

"Yeah, I know that. I was just sitting here for a second. It was pretty scary, you know," confessed Annie as she was crawling out of the cart. "Well, now I know what a whirling dervish is. And thanks for all the help," she appreciatively said to Bobby. "And you too, John, I know you got up early for me," she added respectfully.

"Enh, you're okay Annie," John passively acknowledged. "I really thought you did great, though, —for it being your first time," he conditionally complemented. "But, just watch a pro in action," he then boasted as he got himself into the cart. "Any time you're ready, Bob. I'm ready to lay down some rubber," he announced, taking hold of the steering wheel.

"Okay, here goes," announced Bobby, wrapping the pull cord around the starting wheel and ripping the little engine alive again. And as if someone had just fired a starter pistol into the air, John took off like a shot while Bobby and Annie took a step back onto the grass to observe without being in the way.

"Boy, he's pretty good," Annie said when John had managed to slide the machine sideways in the first turn without slowing down.

"Yup! He's pretty good, all right," Bobby conceded. "But I'm better," he stated like the cock of the walk. "After all, I built the thing, you know," he pointed out.

"I know that, silly," said Annie, playfully poking him on the shoulder to get his attention away from John. "And I want you to know, too, I only wore this blouse for *you* today, not for him," she coyly mentioned. "So, do you like it?" she questioned, provocatively arching her back with unfettered enticement.

"Oh, yeah, you, ah, look great today, Annie," Bobby sheepishly muttered, now shifting his eyes down towards his shoes in embarrassment.

"I look great today? Is that all? I look great today?" Annie repeated, amused at Bobby's reaction, while willfully continuing to captivate his full attention. "Look at me," she coaxed him, putting both her hands on her hips in a demanding stance. "Now, I am going to ask you one more time," she said to him expressly as her emerald green eyes were scrupulously searching to ensnare his very soul, "Is that all you have to say to me?"

"No," Bobby honestly responded. "You look more than just great today," he said. "Actually, I think you are the most beautiful thing that I've ever seen, today or any other day," he admitted. "And just so *you* know, —you might of thought of me when you put that blouse on today, but *I* thought of you the instant I got up," he attested in total abandonment of any lingering inhibitions that might have previously held him at bay.

Then, without saying another word, he put his left hand around the side of her waist and pulled her torso dead against him, and after taking his right arm to secure her even tighter, and pausing a moment to look straight into her eyes, he kissed her with every ounce of his passion. It was the first time that Annie had ever felt helpless but, to her utter amazement, she discovered she did not mind at all.

"Yoohoo! It's me, Barbara!" a voice then called out from over by the tree. "You're supposed to be spotting Johnnie, Bobby, not makin' out!" she clamored loudly, approaching from over by the tree.

Just how is it that I can hear her over the noise of the engine? thought Annie, as Bobby instantly released her from his grasp.

"Hi, Barb," Bobby casually reacted as he went back to paying attention to John, who by now had negotiated the cart over to the school's ball field and was presently rounding third base.

"Did you get to ride in the cart, Annie?" Barbara then asked excitedly, as if someone had just flipped her demeanor switch over from AC to DC.

"Yeah, I rode in it," Annie responded aloofly, turning her total attention over to where John was racing the cart.

"What's sa matter? Didn't you have a good time?" asked Barbara.

"Yeah, I had a great time," Annie responded tersely, still annoyed that her romantic interlude had been interrupted.

Meanwhile, as the two girls talked, Bobby simply moseyed away, consciously likening himself to be Steve McQueen in The Great Escape.

"Well, you won't get *me* into that thing. It's too dirty for me," Barbara maintained. "I might get some of that dirt all over my clothes. And besides, I don't have the shoes for it anyway," she dismissed. "And by the way," she inanely continued, "which was more exciting for ya, smoochin' Bobby, or ridin' in the cart? My God, you guys looked like one of those movie scenes where the guy picks you up and carries you away, cept'n he ain't got no mansion to take you to, —all you guys got is a tree, and it don't hide you very good, either! Ha, ha, ha," she witlessly chattered.

Doesn't she ever shut up? Annie reflected, trying her best to ignore the nonsensical prattle.

For the next two hours, Bobby and John had challenged each other for the coveted title of "King of the Road," and after each of them had performed a various number of turns and maneuvers to each other's satisfaction, John had finally taken claim to the honor. The truth was, however, that each of them traded off the title every other week, and this week was nothing more than John's turn to receive it, regardless of their performances.

"I'm going to ask Annie to help me push the cart home, so I can be alone with her. You got something you can do with Barbara?" Bobby stealthily asked John while beginning to wrap up their operation.

"Sure, I can take her over to the mall, and then I can go over to her house," John said. "Her old man's got a pool table in the cellar," he added while putting the screwdriver back into the supply crate. "Yeah, I can find plenty of stuff to do," he confirmed.

"Great. That's cool. That really helps me out, man. I appreciate it, pal," Bobby thanked in a low tone of voice, proceeding to go over to where the girls were patiently standing on the grass about twenty feet from the edge of the tarmac.

"You want to help me take the cart home, Annie?" Bobby asked her specifically. "And John says he wants to take you to the mall, Barb," he continued, before Annie had a chance to respond.

"Oh, he did?" said Barbara in complete delight.

"Sure did," remarked Bobby. "Go and ask him yourself," he advised with a grin on his face.

Immediately upon hearing this news, and as fast as her heeled shoes could carry her, Barbara promptly negotiated herself away to where her "Johnnie" was still diligently putting away the last of the supplies back into the crate.

"So, do you want to help me push the cart back to my house?" Bobby asked Annie once again. "It's only a couple of blocks," he noted.

"Of course, I'd be happy to," Annie responded. "You know, I guess John must like listening to her yap all the time," she commented facetiously, glancing over toward the cart where the two of them could still hear Barbara's never-ending twitter.

"I don't think John listens to anyone, that's what I think, Bobby replied. "And, I also think that we had better go over there before he changes his mind," he heedfully concluded.

"I got all the stuff in the box, so you're ready to go, buddy," reported John as soon as Bobby and Annie had reached the tarmac. "Me and Barb are off to the mall. I'll catch you later Bob, and you too. Annie," he stated, expeditiously taking Barbara by the arm and steering her away.

"See ya in gym class, Annie!" Barbara yelled back over her shoulder.

And as the two lovers stood silent for a second to watch their compatriots leave beyond their sphere of intimacy, it had become quite apparent that Bobby could no longer be bound by the probationary rules of his youth, for today it was as if the angel of adolescence had granted him clemency.

Chapter Twelve

"Well, we're all alone now," stated Annie. "Just you, me, and the cart," she said as John and Barbara began to fade away in the distance.

"Yeah, you're right. So, let's get rid of the cart," Bobby suggested. "If you sit in the cart with the box on your lap, you can steer it while I push," he proposed.

"Can't you just drive it home?" Annie asked.

"No, you can't ride it in the street. It doesn't have a license plate," Bobby informed her factually.

Finally, after Annie had situated herself in the cart with the box directly on her lap, Bobby began to push the cart home.

"I'm going to speed up just before we get to the hump in the sidewalk and then my driveway will be the next one you come to," Bobby called out loudly from the back of the cart, steadily pushing it on. "Just so you know," he emphasized further.

"I hear you," replied Annie, while only a few moments later Bobby did exactly as declared.

And over the hump she went, leaving him heavily breathing behind. Annie, now believing in herself to be a "seasoned driver," negotiated the left turn into Bobby's driveway like an expert and was quite proud of herself when she finally engineered the cart to come to a full stop, precisely before the opened door of the garage.

"Good work, Annie, good work," remarked Bobby coming up trotting behind. "Like my dad says, you do good work, —not much of it, but it's good," he funned.

"Hey, I already get that from my dad. I ain't gonna take it from you," Annie explicitly replied.

"Just kidding, Annie, just kidding," Bobby responded apologetically while Annie was removing herself from the cart.

"That's going to cost you a kiss, and it better be a good one," Annie declared. "Go on, go on. Keep on going," she repeated, playfully pushing Bobby into the garage until his back was against the refrigerator door in the corner.

Then, as soon as Bobby had recognized that his retreat had ended in a complete and utter failure, he compliantly, and not altogether begrudgingly, acquiesced by opening his arms to her in a welcoming gesture of appeasement. In the end, with nowhere to escape, Annie ravenously grappled him into submission and proceeded to collect her due with all the fervor and determination of an enraptured Aphrodite.

Annie could not gage the time that had elapsed, nor did she even try, but as their lips parted, she had learned one thing, —that the true nature of eternity was a fragile thing to be treasured, and that the timeless and magical moment of this fleeting kiss had now become a sacred image, emblazoned within her breast to be immortalized forever. In this, she felt that the infinity of time was indubitably on her side, and hence this cherished moment would never die. *But was it also true for him?* she wondered.

"Well, did I pay my bill in full?" questioned Bobby evenly, after the two of them had stopped to catch their breath.

"Almost," Annie sighed, before flatly pinning him back against the refrigerator again. This time, however, she removed her hands from his neck and began to run her fingers through his wavy chestnut hair, intently looking directly into his eyes in the hope of seeing her own reflection. In reciprocation, Bobby's ardor had fed his courage to such a degree that he had slowly inched her torso aside, just slightly enough, to take his right hand from the small of her back and slide it up under the front of her unsecured blouse. Slowly, Bobby rose his hand up higher and higher on her bare skin, and in very moment he approached her breast, Annie suddenly pushed herself back and broke off the embrace.

Not truly understanding the ramifications of his actions, and his courage now in total abandonment, Bobby pretended to be stupefied as he immediately stretched out both his hands in astonishment and feigned innocence, exclaiming, "You told me you wore the blouse just for me. I couldn't help myself!"

"Well, you were about to!" Annie admonished. "Do you think I play helpie-selfie with just anybody?" she scolded him.

"No, I never thought that," Bobby avowed.

"Well, exactly what did you think?" Annie vehemently questioned.

"Well, honestly, I thought you wanted me to," Bobby revealed, somewhat embarrassed, but honestly forthright.

"Well, I might want you to, that is, it would probably be okay, if we were going steady," Annie caveated, toning down her furor in recalling one of Barbara's confessions.

"You mean you want to go steady?" Bobby asked, caught completely off guard.

"I might go steady with you, that is, if you asked me to," Annie flirtatiously suggested, enlisting the help of her large and most beguiling eyes.

Then, as the bell of lost wills tolled, and the lamb came forth unto its slaughter, those fatal words were came forth, "Annie, would you go steady with me?" Bobby sheepishly asked.

"Of course, I will!" Annie elatedly accepted, hugging on to him tightly, only to then abruptly stop and push him back once again. "But you still have to get me a ring first, you know," she postured conditionally, completely stopping her advances to hear his reply.

"Sure, I'll get you a ring," Bobby confirmed, sealing the commitment with another kiss.

Alone to the world they were, until the notice, "to be continued" flashed across the silver screen of their minds, precisely when a voice from the home's back porch called out, "Bobby, are you going to leave that thing in the middle of the driveway, or are you going to put it away?"

"I'm puttin' it away now, Mom!" Bobby called back, unseen from the garage while the two lovers had immediately released each other from their bonds.

"Well, when you're done with that, you can ask your girlfriend in there if she wants something to drink. I just made some iced tea," his mother announced, before retreating back inside the kitchen to let the wooden screen door slap loudly closed behind her.

"I guess I will never have any privacy," Bobby decreed out loud in dismay, while Annie was thrilled with the prospect of meeting his mother.

"So just give me a little peck, and I'll help you put the cart away," Annie whispered supportively, putting her hands upon both sides of Bobby's face and smacking him with a short kiss. "Come on, let's go, she's waiting for us," she prodded with an eager smile.

Aside from this current annoyance, it could not be said that Bobby was totally unhappy. He only wondered how long it would take to comply with Annie's wishes before he would be allowed to receive his end of the commitment. In any case, he respectfully put the cart away and brought Annie into the house for some iced tea.

"Annie, this is my Mom. Mom, this is Annie," Bobby announced, entering the house through the same screen door that his mother had used.

"Hello, Annie. Would you like some iced tea?" Bobby's mother asked her pleasantly.

"Yes, I would, Mrs. Taylor," Annie politely replied in turn.

Karen Taylor was a petite woman, no taller than Annie at about five feet two. She wore her light brown hair short with a moderate amount of curls that had been produced by using a Toni Home Permanent Kit. With sky blue eyes and a profuse amount freckles, she had a child-like appearance that seemed to fade into adulthood when she spoke.

"Come on and sit down at the table," Bobby invited, pulling out one of the chairs from under the kitchen table for Annie, and taking a seat as well.

Karen went over to the Frigidaire, took out an aluminum ice cube tray, and placed it on the counter next to the sink. She then took down two glass tumblers from the cabinet above, pulled up the handle on the ice cube tray, dislodging the cubes, and one by one placed them in the glasses. Going back to the Frigidaire, she removed a pitcher of tea and poured it over the awaiting ice.

"Here you are," Karen pronounced, placing the drinks upon the table. "I made it this morning, so it's fresh. I hope you like it," she amiably stated, placing pitcher on the table. Then, after putting ice cube tray in the sink, and with no further ado, she promptly left the room.

"Is that all?" Annie whispered to Bobby in surprise. "Isn't your mother going to ask me any questions?"

"No, I don't think so," Bobby told her, unconcerned with his mother's deportment.

"Are you sure? Doesn't she want to know anything about me?" Annie continued.

"Nah, she's just trying to be nice, —after all, she already knows that I don't go around trying to play helpie-selfie with just *anyone*," he sedately chuckled.

~

Bobby was now on a mission. Not having saved much money from his chores, he nonetheless took what he did have and purchased a small silver ring with a black onyx stone, paying additionally to have the sterling letter 'B' monogramed upon its face. He hoped she would like it, and although Annie had sincerely told him that she truly loved it, he still could not help from feeling that it was greatly insufficient as to the fairness their covenant.

I can do better that that, he knew of himself, and consequently by the end the week, he went down to the corner gas station and asked Mr. Barilla for some regular hours. He also had started power mechanics shop in high school and was now determined to become sufficient unto her needs. He was also seriously falling headlong in love with her.

In January of his senior year, Bobby had obtained his driver's license, and as if a magic dragon had seemed to fly in out of nowhere, *whoosh*, his Whirling Dervish had gotten instantaneously transformed into a 1958 Chevy convertible. It was white, it was cherry, and it was all his. He had obtained it from a customer who had expressly wanted Bobby to have it, specifically in citing his congenial disposition towards everyone who had come to the service station in need of some personal attention.

The special price offered was one that he could afford, and everyone was happy to see him as its proud new owner. The interior was spotless and candy apple red, while outside it sported a pair of twin side mirrors and a set of matching rear antennas to boot. The car was even equipped with a rear speaker in the center of the back seat, which gave it the illusion of having a stereophonic sound system. To top it all off, the show car also came with a set of rear skirts and a continental kit that made it appear to be half the length of a football field. *Now I can drive Annie past that stupid bike rack in style,* was the first thought in his head the very instant he had gotten the title to the car in his hand.

He drove Annie everywhere she wanted to go. She was the vindication of his lust for life, and he was both proud and humbled by it. The car was his showpiece, and when the time came to attend the senior prom, he figured he had it all under control, except for one small detail. Jolanda had relayed to Annie that Bobby first had to seek her father's permission before being allowed her to go.

This of course, would involve him coming over to her house one evening when the "Old Man" had time to see him. Bobby had already taken Annie to the movies, bowling, and even to her church cake sale, but this was different. Annie's Mother had already asked him a million questions, and never missed a chance to feed him every time he came by, either, but even after all that time, her father had never so much as said 'boo' to him.

How many other guys have to go through this? Bobby cogitated. *I thought all parents would be happy to see their daughter have a date for the prom. What problem could there be? He never said anything to me before, so what'd I do? He rarely talks to me at the station. He always talks right to Mr. Barilla. Is he really going to say no?* Unendingly, Bobby fretted over being summarily turned down, until precisely at seven o'clock on one solemn and deathly quiet evening, he rang the front doorbell of the Russo residence to formally ask for Enrico's consent.

Immediately, Bobby's ordeal had begun as Capricia, who had been peeking out from the white flowered curtains in the living room, called out loudly to her mother in the kitchen as if she were Paul Revere warning that the Red Coats were coming, "Ma, it's Annie's boyfriend Bobby. He's here to talk to Daddy now!"

Even Bobby could hear Capricia from outside on the doorstep and cringed at the sound of the announcement.

Oh God, please spare me from complete humiliation, Bobby prayed as Annie unlocked and opened the front door.

"Hi, Bobby, come on in. My Dad's in the kitchen," Annie smiled enthusiastically.

"Do I have to?" Bobby whispered as he came in while she shut the door behind him.

"Yeah, you have to," Annie replied, shooing him with her hands in the direction of the kitchen with a devilish grin.

"Hello, Mr. Russo," Bobby greeted politely upon entering the kitchen, noticing Enrico sitting at the table and Jolanda standing by the sink.

"Do you want a cup of coffee, Bobby?" asked Jolanda before Enrico could reply to Bobby's greeting.

"Sure, Mrs. Russo," Bobby nervously responded.

"Just sit down at the table, then. He's not going to bite you," Jolanda said informatively, turning to take out a cup from the cupboard.

"So how long you been at the gas station? About a year or so? Is that right?" Enrico straightforwardly questioned, taking a drink from his coffee and easing back in his chair to leisurely observe his guest.

"Yes, sir, about a year," Bobby answered politely, sitting directly opposite the husky Italian.

"Here's your coffee, Bobby. The sugar and milk are on the table," Jolanda interjected. "Well, I've got some laundry to do, so I'll leave you two in peace for now," she imparted, putting the percolator on the table and exiting without saying another word.

Bobby, now feeling totally abandoned, was completely mortified in having to face the dreaded inquisitor all alone, and was thus afraid to say anything. Enrico took another drink from his coffee, but also sat silent in his chair for a moment, continuing to study the boy before him.

"Barilla says you do good work," Enrico then finally commented.

"I try to do my best, sir," Bobby responded seriously.

"Well, they all say you do a good job down there, especially Peterson, the guy who sold you that car of yours," he said revealingly.

"You know him?" Bobby asked, taken aback.

"Sopresa? That's Italian for surprised," gesticulated Enrico with his right hand, theatrically enlightening the boy. "He owns the hardware store downtown," he further noted.

"Yes, I know," Bobby responded, trying not to look like a complete ignoramus, while unconsciously adding three sugars to his coffee.

"But, what you probably *don't know* is that I paved the back of his store for him about five years ago and, so I asked him for a favor." Enrico continued to apprise him. "You don't think I want you driving my daughter all over town in some hunk of tin, just to end up at Finelli's soda shop, do you?" he rhetorically stated. "That car of yours has got to weigh two tons. I only want my daughter to be safe, that's all," he said as a matter of fact. "And, of course you can take my daughter to the prom. That's why you're here isn't it?" he asked the young man expectantly.

"Yes, sir," Bobby respectfully acknowledged.

"Well, what kinda guy wants his daughter to be dateless on her prom night?" Enrico stated rhetorically. "Just make sure that your intentions are all good, okay, son?" he candidly requested.

"Yes, sir," answered Bobby, thoroughly stunned by the magnitude of Enrico's empathy.

"Now, there is one more thing that I do want to ask you," resumed Enrico in a more inquisitive tone. "You goin' to college when you graduate?"

"No, I'm taking power mechanics. I like to work on engines," Bobby concisely answered.

"Just engines, or any machines?" Enrico inquired in a curious tone.

"Well, I guess any machines," Bobby thoughtfully clarified, finally taking his first drink of coffee.

"And what about paving machines?" Enrico specifically asked.

Oh, I know where he is going now, Bobby concluded to himself, beginning to feel a little more comfortable.

"You need me to fix one of your paving machines, Mr. Russo?" Bobby affably responded.

"No, not right now," Enrico replied, "but I could use a good mechanic, so I'm askin' you, do you want the job?" he solicited plainly.

"Well, I have a job right now," Bobby ruefully pointed out.

"I know that," Enrico stated with the emergence of a thin smile across his face. "Remember who you're talkin' to?" he casually remarked. "I meant full time, when you graduate. You want me to teach you the business? I'll teach you the business," he offered, holding out his two hands, palms up.

And then it just popped out. "Are you sure you're not just giving me the business right now, Mr. Russo?" replied Bobby with a grin.

"That's a good question, son," Enrico chuckled lightly. "I could be, and that's a good point too, but no son, I'd be happy to teach you the business. And I mean that," he sincerely confirmed, not expecting an immediate response. "Well, let me know after you take my daughter to this prom thing, okay?" he stated, rising up from the table. "Right now, I got some stuff I gotta do out on the back porch," he casually mentioned, while turning to leave. "Oh, and by the way, Annie said she'd be wait'n for ya in the livin' room," he mentioned in finality, before disappearing through the back door completely.

And thus, the great inquisition of Bobby Taylor was one for the history books.

Was that it? It's all over? Bobby aporetically pondered as he stood up, completely alone in the kitchen. *My poor head! What exactly just went on here?* he reflected, beginning to wander back to the living room in a daze.

"Well, did he say you can take me?" questioned Annie, as soon as Bobby had come into sight.

"Oh yeah, I can take you alright," Bobby responded, still in a fog. "He also asked me if I wanted to work for him," he added in bewilderment.

"He did? Oh, well, that means he really likes you," Annie verified enthusiastically, removing herself from the couch.

"Well, I gotta go," Bobby numbly stated, ambling on over to the front door.

"Here, I'll walk with you out to the car," Annie offered, opening the door.

Slowly, in pensive reflection, Bobby began to walk down the front walkway with such solitude that the only thing to be heard was the explicit sound of his footsteps as they landed flatly upon the flagstones beneath his feet. It was not until the two of them had finally reached the end of the walkway that the silence was broken by Annie when, after latching onto his arm, she provocatively asked, "Aren't you going to kiss me tonight?"

"Right in front of your house?" Bobby all but exclaimed.

"Yes, right in front of my house," Annie definitively answered. "Where else do you think we are, on the moon?"

she questioned facetiously. "Don't you think that my father knows you kiss me?" she taunted.

"I think your father knows everything about everything, that's what I think," Bobby maintained, despite having been overwhelmingly confused.

"Well, I think you're just chicken, that's what I think," Annie challenged as she pushed against him playfully.

"Oh yeah, so I'm chicken, am I?" Bobby responded, suddenly clasping his arms around her and whisking her completely off the ground to pin her directly against the side of his car. "So, I'm chicken, huh?" he repeated. And with total unconcern over anyone who may be watching, he kissed her with all the passion of an untamed tiger. Responding in kind, Annie kissed him in return with equal, if not greater, voracity, reveling over the concept that it was *her* passion which needed to be tamed, not his.

Chapter Thirteen

Unabated, their zeal for each other not only endured past their graduation, but persisted to grow while Bobby had accepted the employment offer from her father. They became a known "item" in the community. Sanctioned by both of their families, their union was accepted by everyone as the perfect marriage in having blended the unadulterated quality of respectful intentions, a natural concupiscence for each other, and a boundless enthusiasm for life.

Everything was copacetic until that bright summer day when Bobby came home from his job at the Russo Paving Company and his mother presented him with a letter that began, "You are hereby directed to present yourself for an armed forces physical examination to the local board." He was given a date two weeks later in which to report. He had been drafted.

Overwhelmed with a myriad of possible future scenarios, induced by this dilemma, Bobby went straight to his room to solemnly contemplate his fate. He was the oldest of the Taylors' three children. He had a younger two-year-old sister named Margaret, and a brother William who was six years his junior. Because he was the senior male, Bobby felt that it was his mantle to be the most responsible and as such, it was his duty to serve his country for his namesake. He was an honorable young man and respected his father for serving in the in the Pacific Theatre, who was schooled as a navy welder.

Perhaps he could be assigned to a mechanized unit as a mechanic, he speculated after a great deal of thought. This alone had given him some solace to be upspirited about, and so all was fine again as his trepidations began to wane. He had taken a bad situation and had made the best of it, *and that is something to be proud of,* he told himself. But nevertheless, this feeling of pride disappeared as quickly as it came upon him, for inevitably his ruminations turned to, *Oh my God, what about Annie?*

After a quiet dinner at which his father, who never spoke much, advised him that he should simply "do his best and keep his nose clean," and that, "the whole family would be proud of him," Bobby drove off in his Chevy convertible to inform everyone concerned of his unfortunate change in destiny.

The weather is so beautiful, Bobby thought, putting the top of the car down. *I am going to enjoy this ride,* he added in a peaceful appreciation of all for which he was grateful. Precipitously and inexplicably, he verily found a new clarity in what was, and what was not, truly important. It was as if, mystically appearing, the very phenomenon of life had been revealed to him personally. Epiphanized, he truly felt the exhilaration of the shear magnificence of a sultry summer's night.

For the first time, Bobby pellucidly took notice of the heavens around him. And, as if drawn into another realm, he now surveyed the sunset's creamy crimson sky, that had briefly caught the day before it closed its eyes. And just when its eastern half did turn the swirling clouds at last, into a faded hue of royal blue, it left them there to dissipate and die, —and Bobby did not wonder why.

"Annie, your boyfriend is comin' up the driveway," Capricia called out from the dormer in her room.

"Mind your own business!" Annie yelled out, bounding down the stairway. "Well, what'cha wanna do tonight?" Annie blissfully asked, letting Bobby in the house by the kitchen door.

"Well, I guess I just gotta give you a raise now, so that when you come back you'll still want to work for me," Enrico gratuitously imparted.

"Well, thank you sir, but I don't think you will have to worry about that," responded Bobby.

"Anyway, it's yours," Enrico discharged. "And by the way," he added in comradery, "as a word of caution from one grunt to another, keep both your socks and your dick dry, and you'll do just fine, —just passin' it on," he smiled thinly.

"Yes sir," Bobby courteously replied, as a small shade of embarrassment had encompassed his face.

"Listen, we want you to come home in the same condition that you left in, son, that's all," Enrico stated in all sincerity. "Anything else you need?" he questioned.

"No, sir, I just wanted you to know first, because of my job," Bobby answered dutifully. "Oh, and by the way, I'm going to try to get into a mechanized unit. That way, I can still be a mechanic. I just thought you'd like to know," he mentioned on an upscale note.

"Well, son, I have to tell you, your time's gonna go by a lot faster than you think," Enrico projected optimistically. "And I don't want you worrin' about what you're gonna do when you come back here, either. Your job'l be right here waitin' for ya," he definitively reinforced.

"I know, sir," Bobby acknowledged, "but first thing first, —I haven't told Annie yet," he confessed. "So, I guess I'd better go and do that," he said dismally, glancing over in the direction of the kitchen.

"Yeah, son, I think you might as well get it over now, rather than later," he supported. "And I don't envy you for that, but you still gotta do it," he offered sympathetically.

"I know," Bobby fatefully replied, turning to protractedly leave the room.

God damn it! Enrico said silently to himself as soon Bobby had gotten fully out of sight. *No wonder they put all the bad news in the newspaper. If the town crier came to my house with that piece of news, I'da shot the bastard myself. Well, I got through it in one piece, I suppose he will, too. I just hope he'll be okay,* he prayed within the solitude of his mind.

"You done talkin' to my Dad?" asked Annie, as soon as Bobby had entered the kitchen.

"All done," Bobby reported. "And good evening to you, Mrs. Russo, how are you tonight?" he specifically asked, seeing her sitting at the table with Annie.

"I'm fine, Bobby," Jolanda replied. "Do you want something to drink? I still have some coffee on," she offered, getting up from her chair.

"No, thank you, Mrs. Russo, I'm okay," declined Bobby graciously, to then ask of Annie specifically "Do you want to go out to the breezeway for a little while?"

"Sure, let's go, it's already gotten dark out, but it's still nice," Annie responded spritely, immediately rising from her seat at the table.

Then, seizing Bobby by the arm, Annie usher him over towards the back door of the kitchen.

"Good night, Mrs. Russo!" Bobby courteously called back over his shoulder on his way out.

Once entering their own private terrace, the two of them instinctively took their anointed positions upon the brightly cushioned glider, which unobstructedly overlooked the expansive back yard.

"You know, on a bright night like tonight, you can see all the way down the hill, just from sitting right here," Bobby observed pensively. "Look at all the lights on in those houses down there. You can even see the traffic on the highway from here. I never noticed that before," he openly mused.

"When I was a kid, I used to camp out here in an old tent that my dad would put up for me. Sometimes, after all the people had put their lights out to go to bed, you could actually see the stars more clearly than ever. I mean, the sky is really filled with them. It is so awesome," reflected Annie.

"Here, I have something for you to read," Bobby said in a more somber tone, leaning back in the divan while taking out the draft notice from his pocket. "Here, go ahead and read it," he pressed her, holding it out in his hand.

Looking at Bobby apprehensively, Annie accepted the paper from his hand, disengaged his right arm, and sat forward to read it.

"Oh, Mother of Jesus, I don't believe it!" Annie cried out while bolting up, so loud that it could be heard from the house, scrunching the detestable notice in her hand.

"I guess she found out," Enrico commented sadly to Jolanda, who had joined him in the living room.

"You know our Annie is in love with him," Jolanda said softly.

"Who doesn't know?" Enrico remarked in communion with everyone else's feelings. "And don't forget about his own family, either. His father's just a hard workin' stiff like the rest of us. It's his cross to bear the most, —it's *his* son, you know," Enrico commiserated.

"I think that we should give a special beneficence to Saint Jude this Sunday and ask Father Bernardino to say a blessing for Bobby. Do you think we should?" Jolanda petitioned.

"Sure, why not? It can't hurt," Enrico said agreeably. "You know, of course, that Bobby is an Episcopal, not a Catholic," he mentioned as he got up from his chair to lean over and kiss his wife on the cheek.

"I know," Jolanda confirmed sadly.

"Well, I'm going to bed now. I've had enough for today," Enrico stated in total exasperation, to then plod off for their bedroom.

"I'll be up in a minute, as soon as I'm done cleaning up," Jolanda faithfully replied.

"I don't believe it, I just don't believe it," Annie repeated, now in a lower tone, defiantly shaking her hand that still clutched on to the crumpled notice. "What's going to happen now?" she questioned as she sat back down on the glider, with her contemptuous attitude beginning to wane.

"I have to report for a physical in about two weeks, and then I will know more. Until then, I go to work like everyone else," Bobby explained as a matter of fact.

"But I love you! What's going to happen to *us*?" Annie cried out again while the tears of desperation began to fill her eyes.

"After I serve my time, I'll be back," Bobby reassured her, adjusting his position to cradle her as she compulsively clenched on to him for dear life.

"You do love me, don't you?" Annie asked in complete and utter anguish, softly sobbing.

"Of course, I do," Bobby answered attentively.

"I mean, do you *really* love me?" Annie prompted, directly looking at him and fearing the worst, the vain recognition of an unrequited love.

Releasing his right arm from his gentle embrace around her, Bobby brought his left hand up to the side of Annie's cheek, wiped off a tear from the side of her face with his thumb, gazed intently into her eyes, and momentarily paused until she had stopped weeping. Then, with the sincerity of a man condemned, he said, "I love you with all my heart, Annie. Don't you *know* that? I think about you all the time. I can't *not* think about you. I think about you when I get up in the morning. I think about you when I go to bed at night. I think about you all day long. I think about you so much at work that I worry about forgetting to put a bolt in somewhere, and then I have this vision that the transmission falls right on my head and kills me. And after that, I even have a dream where you bury me along with that stupid transmission that did me in!" he additionally confessed.

"Come here," Bobby then softly submitted, moving his right hand from Annie's cheek to the back of her neck. And gently drawing her even closer, he subsequently proceeded to kiss her with the tenderness of a celestial cherub. "Now, do you understand that I love you with all my heart?" he petitioned beseechingly.

"Yes, I think you do," admitted Annie, recovering some of her composure.

"So you just *think* I do? Is that it? You don't *know* I do?" Bobby questioned in feigned disbelief.

"Well, I'm not gonna ask you to drop a transmission on your head just to prove it, if that's what you want," Annie replied as she finally managed a smile, still wiping off the last of the tears from her face.

"Well, just don't bury me with it, okay?" Bobby requested lightheartedly.

"I promise you I won't," Annie pledged, her catharsis coming to a close.

Emotionally exhausted, each in their own manner, they had been so overwrought with emotion that an eternity of at least three minutes had silently passed by as they simply snuggled together before the next inevitable question was eventually brought up.

"So, how long do you have?" Annie finally asked.

"Two weeks before my initial exam," was Bobby's simple reply.

"And how long after that will it be before you have to actually go in?" advanced Annie, in trying to gage what little time they had left together.

"I don't know. I'll guess I'll find out when I get there," Bobby answered in full resignation unto a destiny to which he had no control over in the slightest.

~

"I have an idea!" announced Annie excitedly, sitting once again on the breezeway glider on the day after Bobby had completed his examination. "Since we have almost two months before you go in, that still leaves us plenty of time to do all kinds of stuff," she declared. "For example, you can take me up to my Uncle Tony's cabin on the lake this weekend. I have a key, and we could spend the whole day together. You'd like it. My uncle has a dock and a boat there. You could take me out onto the lake, and..."

"Okay, okay, I'll take you, Annie," Bobby interrupted, unclasping his free arm around her and leaning forward in a futile attempt to induce some emotional restraint to her giddiness.

"We need to go early, so you better pick me up by six o'clock," Annie instructed, reaching over and tapping him on the shoulder to ensure his undivided attention.

"I'm gonna need directions," Bobby sensibly reminded her.

"Oh, that's no problem. I've been there a lotta times," Annie offered.

"Oh, ho... no, no, no," Bobby told her forebodingly. "I have to get the directions from your father," he said with a definitive smile.

"Well, that's fine by me," Annie shrugged.

There was no power on earth that could now subdue the rapture in Annie's heart. Even her father, who had reservations about their aquatic adventure, upon the intensity of Annie's demand, relented, and forthwith surrendered the directions to Bobby and wished them both a good trip.

~

The sun was just beginning to rise as Annie was awaiting Bobby at the kitchen door, and at exactly six o'clock on that next Saturday morning, the long white convertible drove explicitly into her driveway. Once Bobby had secured the car in place and had gotten out, he quietly approached outside the steps leading up into the kitchen, whereupon Annie opened the door and pointed down to a wicker picnic basket on the floor by the entrance and whispered, "You take this out to the car, and I'll be out in a second."

"Okay," Bobby responded quietly, picking up the basket and noiselessly retreating. Annie went over to the kitchen table, retrieved her purse and personal bag, which had been strapped over the corner of one of the kitchen chairs, and then snatched up her keys. Turning about, she surveyed the room for one final time to see if she had forgotten anything, and then closed and locked the door behind her.

There was no traffic on the road until they had gotten on the highway, and even then, the cars were few and far between. The peripheral daily sounds that were normally induced by the plethora of people going about in the performance of their daily activities were notably silent. This, in turn, suggested that this gracious sense of serenity was the reward due the entire city for having survived another struggling week of insecurity to thankfully live another day. The only exception to be heard was the light orchestrated commotion which was generated by the local delivery trucks, who were always regarded as a naturally peaceful inclusion that was to be expected in the normality of a Saturday's sanguine routine.

And so, equally serene to their own surroundings, the two lovers traveled on together in an individual meditative attempt to adjust to the early morning's proprieties. It was a whole new experience for them. While becoming totally absorbed in trying to take in all of the various sights, sounds, and smells of the lackadaisically awakening city, each of them in their own way began to discover a new awakening within themselves. Never, ever before had they experienced the full and uncompromised sensual aroma of the bread factory in full production without having it tainted from the daily noxious pollutants that were produced by the prodigious number of cars, trucks, and buses that were always congested about the plant on the weekdays.

The occasional tractor trailer was yet another thing to be reckoned with. Without the usual cacophony of sounds that seemed to otherwise disguise their existence, these behemoth freightliners were now raucously passing them by without the slightest regard, for there were no other vehicles in front of them to slow them down. Belligerently, one after another, they would bluster on past the two pilgrims in an apparent attempt to sway them from their destination, but the two-ton Chevy had valiantly stood its ground.

"It'll take us about an hour or so to get up to the lake," Annie projected pleasantly, as their pensive silence had now come to an end. "Also, there's a small town about ten minutes from the cabin that has a diner. We can stop for breakfast there, if you want," she suggested.

"That's cool," Bobby said, turning onto another state road, which was predetermined to be the most scenic route to experience.

"You know, it's really nice sometimes if you get up early on a Saturday morning. You see all kind of things that you never see during the week," Bobby noted as the two-lane road had become less defensive to negotiate.

"Oh yeah, I know," concurred Annie heartedly. "Did you smell the fresh bread when we passed by the factory?"

"Yeah, it was outrageous," declared Bobby. "And did you see the brightness of the sun coming up over the river when we were going over the bridge?" he commented more than he asked. "My dad was in the navy, and he said that a red sky in the morning was a sailor's warning, but a red sky at night was a sailor's delight. And so, according to him, it looks like today should be a pretty good one," he optimistically prophesized.

"Oh, I fully intend it to be. In fact, I intend this day to be the most fabulous day of all," Annie resolutely declared.

"Annie," Bobby addressed in a curious tone, "since there is no more traffic on the road, and I don't think there is going to be anymore, why are you still sitting way over there?" he asked in bewilderment.

"I don't know. Where *should* I be sitting?" Annie teased, pulling her legs up and wrapping her arms around them, cornering herself coyly against her door.

"Well, I actually don't know, either, but I wouldn't be leaning against that door where I had to kill this big ugly spider this morning, just before we left," Bobby revealed in a serious tone.

"What?" Annie cried out, jettisoning herself away from the door. "I can't stand spiders!" she clamored, brushing herself off to confirm that none of those "wretched insects" might still be upon her.

Eventually, after calming down, Annie settled herself precisely against Bobby in the middle of the bench seat, reactively causing him to stretch out his right arm to snugly secure her even further.

"Why didn't you tell me that had to squash that spider when I got in the car?" Annie eventually questioned in all seriousness.

But Bobby did not respond. He just kept his eyes attentively on the road before him, not uttering a single word.

Hey, wait just a minute. He's up to something. I've seen that little smirk before, Annie thought, while trying to read his countenance. Then, as his smirk turned into a full-fledged grin, the entirety of it all hit her like a Mac truck.

"There wasn't any spider, you jerk! —was there?" Annie challenged. "It was just a story you made up to get me over here, —wasn't it?" she conclusively asserted, for his subtle mischievous chicanery had now become all too obvious.

"Well, there could have been," Bobby burst out laughing. "You never know," he added in sheer amusement, glancing over a second and clenching her even closer.

"Well, I guess I teased you first," Annie openly admitted in good sport.

Chapter Fourteen

The temperature was already approaching the eighty-degree mark at only nine o'clock in the morning when the Chevy convertible precipitously descended upon the small town named Crossville at the bottom of Hope Mountain. There was a white Texaco two-pump gas station on the right-hand corner that shared a large asphalt parking lot with a ramshackle summertime vegetable stand which had not yet opened for the day. The corner to the left of the intersection opposite the gas station supported the classic chrome plated diner along with its neat grey stoned parking area that was encompassed by a natural rail fence. The third corner, opposite the gas station and kitty corner to the diner, displayed a huge sign that was mounted over a long and expansive porch to the entrance of a monumentally sized two-story building that clearly boasted it to be the home of "Jimbo's Jumbos!" *The World's Largest and Most Tasty Worms and Peanuts, Your Choice!*

The old clapboard building, which had last been painted over twenty years earlier with a coat of dark red ship primer, had a genuine "rustic" appearance that had been accentuated with a row of black enameled shutters and matching trim that transversed the entire upper story of the building.

At one time, the structure was obviously built as a home, but now the front porch, which ran the entire length of the structure, only served as a junk repository. To the right side of the porch, proudly hung by a couple of rusty chains, was a shoddy wooden plank, which advertised its eclectic pile of dilapidated articles that had been strewn about in a higgledy-piggledy fashion upon its deck to be antiques.

Besides the worms and the peanuts, once inside, there was also a small grocery section and a local mailing station where the tourists could send off their postcards.

The forth corner, opposite the diner and Jimbo's Jumbos, could not be built upon, for the bare rock from the base of the mountain rose up contiguous to the curve in the road.

"Pull in to the diner," Annie directed as Bobby slowed down on approaching the crossing. "I'm hungry," she declared.

"This place looks okay," Bobby said pleasantly as he pulled into its parking lot. "You know, there's got to be over a dozen cars parked out here. Where in the heck did they all come from?" he wondered out loud.

"There's a lot of people that live on the lake in the summertime," Annie explained. "And the other reason they're here, is because their food is pretty good. It's owned by the Greeks, like most of all the other diners are," Annie annotated as Bobby put the car into its park position.

Once inside, the couple was immediately addressed with a passing "Good morning," from a red aproned waitress, scurrying by with a glass carafe of coffee in her hand.

"Sit anywhere you want," the waitress said, not slowing down her gait. "All the seats by the window are taken, but there's an empty booth down there on the end," she pointed out with her free hand, "Or, youse can sit at the counter if you want. Anyways, somebody will be with you in a sec," she asserted, continuing on her way.

"You want to sit at the counter?" Bobby asked, leaving the choice to Annie. "The service might be faster," he reasoned.

"We're not in a hurry. Let's go sit in that booth down there over on the end," Annie decided, tilting her head and shifting her eyes in its direction.

"Sure, that's cool," agreed Bobby, while Annie took the lead.

And so, down past the long row of counter seats they went until coming to the single empty booth, whereupon Bobby reached out and latched onto Annie's arm, keeping her from taking a seat.

"Wait a minute," Bobby cautioned, now leaning over and whispering quietly in her ear, "Are you going to be sitting next to me, or across the table on the other side where I heard there were spiders?"

"I'm not falling for that again," Annie smartly asserted, "but I am going sit next to you anyway, even if it's just to keep you in line. It's for your own good, you know," she explicitly added, sliding over into the booth.

Finally, once they had comfortably situated themselves down, not a minute had gone by before the same waitress stopped by to place two menus on the edge of their table and announced she would be back shortly. Handing one of the menus over to Annie, Bobby picked his up and began to determine his selection.

"I can't imagine how a small place like this can have a four-page menu. And you know, *all* these diners are like this. How can they possibly know how to cook all of this stuff anyway?" Bobby wondered out loud.

"Like I told you, they're all owned by Greeks. That's what they do. They all own diners like this. There are some that are owned by Italians, but my father said that the only difference between the two, is the feta cheese, —if it's owned by an Italian, they have an antipasto salad on the menu, and if a Greek owns it, they add feta cheese to it and call it a Greek salad. That's how you know," explained Annie. "See here on the second page, just like I said, a Greek salad with feta cheese," she pointed out.

"Yup, you're right, all right," Bobby agreed, continuing to peruse the menu.

"Have you ever even tried feta cheese?" Annie enticingly probed.

"No, I never heard of it before," Bobby responded dismissively. "I'm just going to have the two eggs with some home fries and bacon," he decided plainly. "Oh, and by the way, how far are we from your uncle's cabin?" he asked inquisitively, deliberately changing the subject in detecting that something was afoot from the very tone of her question.

"Oh, it's just around the corner and up the next hill," Annie answered casually, putting down her menu and shifting her eyes to the waitress, who had now come back to take their order.

"So, ya know what you guys are gonna have?" the waitress addressed them, pad and pencil in hand.

"Yeah, I'm gonna have two eggs over easy, bacon, and home fries, please. And a cup of coffee," Bobby ordered.

"What kinda toast ya want with that, sweetie?" the waitress asked.

"Just some white toast," Bobby mechanically responded.

"And I'll have the French toast and a coke. Also, could I have a side order of feta cheese with that, too?" requested Annie politely.

"Sure honey, you got it," the waitress confirmed, flipping the page of her pad over and leaving the table.

"You drink a Coke at breakfast time?" asked Bobby in amazement.

"Sure, you drink coffee for the caffeine, and so I have my Coke for the same reason. Besides, I can't stand coffee, it's yucky," Annie stated cogently.

"So, you also eat feta cheese in the morning too?" Bobby questioned suspiciously.

"No, that's for you," Annie outright specified. "I got some so you could try it. It's pretty good. It's something like cottage cheese," she explained lightheartedly. "And it isn't going to kill you, I promise," she sustained.

"Here you go," interrupted the waitress, "One Coke, and one cup of coffee," she verified, putting down Annie's soda and Bobby's coffee before him. "The milk is over there by the sugar shaker, and I'll be right back with your breakfast," she succinctly stated, abruptly leaving again without another word.

"So, did you bring your swim suit with you, like I told you to?" Annie questioned.

"Of course I did. You know I always do what you tell me to," Bobby answered satirically. "And anyway, I figured I had to bring it, just in case your uncle's boat sinks on us," he goaded her with a small grin.

"Do you even *know* how to row a boat?" Annie threw at him, "Cause if you don't, I can teach you," she countered.

"I don't think that will be necessary. I've gone fishing with John and his dad every opening day since I was about ten, and a lot of other times too," Bobby testified.

"Oh, really?" Annie commented in doubt.

"Well, wait till you hear this one," Bobby said eagerly, intending to prove the veracity of his proclamation. "There was this time this guy forgot to put his emergency brake on when he had gotten out of his car after he had parked it backwards on the boat ramp to put his boat into the water. He had only gotten about ten feet away to ask this other guy who had come with him something when, all of a sudden, the other guy yelled out, 'Holy crap, your car is rolling backwards!' And then the guy turned around and just freaked out.

"The funny thing was that, instead of running over and trying to get back into his car to put the break on, all he did was run around and wave his hands in the air, screaming 'Oh Lordy, Oh Lordy!' as his boat trailer continued to roll down the ramp, boat and all, and pulling his car with it too, until they both ended up sinking right into the lake. It was the most hilarious thing that I ever saw.

"It was just like out of one of those old Laurel and Hardy movies, except for one thing," he qualified now in a serious tone, "he had his little boy with him, and so we felt really bad for the guy," he added sadly. "Anyway, Pete's dad took a rope and attached it to *his* trailer hitch, and then we all helped him pull his car out of the lake. Unbelievably," he stressed, "after we got it out, the car actually started. So, we let it run for a while to let it dry out, while we put *our* boat in the water. After that, we all got their boat in the water, too, and everybody went fishing. But I gotta say, it still was the most hilarious thing I ever saw," he repeated, chuckling in recalling the incident.

"Well, that was nice of John's dad," Annie applauded.

"Well, we helped, too, I mean me and John," Bobby reminded her.

"I know, that's why I love you," Annie validated, commending his actions by leaning over and planting a kiss on his cheek.

"Two eggs over easy for you," the waitress broke in, "and the French toast for you, honey," she presented, putting the plates down before them as they sat back in their booth to be served. "Anything else?" she plainly asked.

"Could you heat up my coffee for me?" Bobby requested affably, moving his cup over closer to the edge of the table.

"Sure thing, sweetie, I'll be back in a jiff," she replied, hesitating for a second to remark directly to Annie, "and he sure *is* a sweetie, ain't he?"

"He sure is," Annie certified while Bobby only raised his eyes to the ceiling in inescapable torment.

"Well, I'll be right back in a minute," the waitress then said abruptly, promptly leaving again.

Going back behind the service counter again, the waitress reached up to the pass-through window of the kitchen, picked up a small salad dish with her right hand, and with her left secured a coffee carafe from the hotplate below and returned to their booth.

"Here, I almost forgot. Here's your feta cheese," the waitress apologized, placing the salad plate on the table in front of Annie. "No one ever ordered it for breakfast before," she admitted candidly while refilling Bobby's empty coffee mug. "Now, you guys let me know if you need anything more. By the way, —my name is Maggie," she imparted before going to attend to her other customers.

"Whoa, they sure give you plenty of food here, look at the size of this pile of home fries," Bobby remarked, pointing to them with his fork.

"Yeah, and look at the size of my French toast too. I've never seen it this thick," Annie extolled, leaning back and displaying her plate.

It wasn't long after the shared praises over the virtues of a Greek diner and the accolades of efficiency concerning their waitress that the two sojourners had effectuated the cleaning of their plates. Coincidentally, as both of their forks had resoundingly clanked finished onto their plates in unison, they each had ominously fallen silent while simultaneously shifting their eyes in the direction of the untouched feta cheese.

"Like I said, did you see that pile of home fries they put on my plate? Man, I just can't eat another thing," Bobby declared again, leaning back and rubbing his belly in complete satisfaction.

This time, quite ready for a myriad of Bobby's inevitable excuses to come, Annie was completely determined not to be out maneuvered.

"Why, you still haven't tried the feta cheese yet," Annie mentioned thoughtfully, reaching over for the salad plate.

"Oh, thank you, but I just can't eat anymore," Bobby said politely, breaking off eye contact and looking away as he gently rubbed his belly once again for extra credit.

Annie, putting her hand firmly upon Bobby's shoulder, thus forcing his attention from elsewhere in the universe and back into the reality of her presence, now proceeded to notch up her advance.

"Oh, can't you just try a little bit? I'm sure you'll like it. You like cottage cheese, don't you?" Annie demurely asked in a cajoling manner.

"Yeah, well, I mean it's okay," Bobby accepted, "but still, I just can't eat another thing," he steadfastly asserted, respectfully continuing to rebuff her entreating request.

Undaunted, Annie moved his finished plate away with her left hand, replaced it with the salad plate, and then shamelessly scooch directly against him to put her right hand softly upon on inside of his thigh. Then, after steading herself with her left elbow upon the table, she leaned over, looked directly into his eyes, and dropped the bomb.

"You mean you won't try some, just for me?" Annie lovingly pleaded, only to immediately and mercilessly follow up her request with the coup de gras of all irrefutable phrases, "You want to make me happy, don't you?

Petrified, Bobby just sat there.

"Aw, come on, don't you want to make me happy?" Annie repeated seductively. "Just a little bit, for me? Okay?" she reinforced affectionately, while now taking her fingernails to the inside of his thigh.

"Okay, okay, I'll try some," Bobby surrendered, but not before attempting to salvage his dignity by qualifying, "But I can't eat much. I told you I was stuffed."

"You don't have to eat all of it, just try a little bit. You'll see, you might like it," Annie sparkled, halting her attack in knowing that she had won.

Apprehensively, Bobby brought a forkful of the cheese to his mouth. Benignly, after tasting it briefly, he thereupon swallowed the curds with practically no reaction at all.

"Okay, so I ate some. Are you happy now?" Bobby said in appeasement, putting down his fork with no further comment.

"Sure, now I'm happy," Annie asserted victoriously. "That makes me *very* happy," she smiled, gently petting his leg as one would reward a good dog.

"I don't know what the big deal was, anyway. It didn't have much taste, other than it was somewhat salty," Bobby now testified in being totally unimpressed.

"Well, now you know what it's like," Annie said brightly. "Now, you can add it to all the other stuff that you know, except that it was *me* who taught you this time," she flaunted. "And you can't learn that in one of those fancy car magazines you read all the time, either," she stipulated, sitting back to finish her soda.

"No, I guess you can't," Bobby credited.

"Of course," Annie added as she rolled up her eyes and impishly looked away, "who else in the world could have gotten you to eat some old goat cheese but *me*, anyway?"

"What?" Bobby exclaimed, trying to subdue his surprise. "You gotta be kiddin' me! That cheese was made from a goat?" he said, flabbergasted beyond belief.

"Well, it could have been a sheep. Sometimes they make it from sheep's milk, too," Annie said informatively, trying not to smirk. "But, I don't know exactly, maybe they mix 'em?" she simplemindedly proposed. "But, in any case, I can tell you one thing, the milk they make it with, sure don't come from a cow!" she unashamedly laughed.

"Oh my God! That's disgusting! Bobby said with a sour look on his face, sticking out his tongue and shaking his head downward while uttering, "Euch!"

"Aw, it's not so bad now," Annie consoled him. "At least it wasn't spider milk. I hear that it's *really* salty," she laughed again.

"So, that's it," Bobby concluded, crossing his arms and looking away.

"Oh, don't be that way, Bobby," Annie beseeched him. "Listen, how about I make you a deal," she offered practically, "No more teasing me about the spiders and I won't ask you to eat anymore any more feta cheese, okay?" she offered in a truce.

"Well, I guess I deserved that one," Bobby admitted, looking straight back at her again. "Okay, you got a deal," he accepted with a smile of relief.

"And I agree, too," Annie said, once again moving her hand over to pet his leg.

"You guys want the check now?" Maggie then asked, seeming to appear out of nowhere.

"Yeah, you can give it to me," Bobby instructed, snapping back to reality as he promptly got up from the booth and held out his hand to receive the bill. "Here, this should cover it," he told the waitress, handing her back the check with some folding money that he had taken out from his pocket. "You can keep the rest," he added graciously, "We gotta go now. We're going up to the lake," he chatted while waiting for Annie to join him.

"It's gonna be a hot one today. It should be great out on the lake though. I hope you guys have a good time today," wished Maggi while Annie was exiting the booth.

"Thank you," responded Bobby, as immediately Maggi began to clear the table.

"Now, when you pull out of the parking lot, you need to turn left and go around that big rock that sticks out against the road. Then go straight up the hill for about a half a mile until you come to a split in the road. And then, once you turn to the left, my uncle's place is only a short way away down, right on the same road," Annie explained on their way to the car. "Don't worry, it only should take about ten minutes now," she added.

"Good, it already took longer to get here than I figured," Bobby asserted.

"Yeah, I know. It always seems that way," Annie replied as they both got back into the car.

"You know it's going on ten o'clock already?" Bobby noted, pulling out of the diner's driveway.

"Yeah, I figured as much," Annie stated when passing the protruding rock formation at the corner of the intersection. "Well, once we get over this hill you will be able to see the lake," she offered encouragingly, as onward the two romantics began to marvel at the surrounding forest.

The mountains were covered in a carpet of variegated shades of green, while the mottled patchwork of the birch, oak, and maple trees had become one with the landscape. And as the multi-shaded leaves were rippling brightly in the morning breeze and the road had narrowed, and the canopy of greenery had completely engulfed them in their quest to share together a moment in eternity, they reverently drove on. From the sunny strands of light that had intermittently peaked through canopy above them, to the crunch of the tar and gravel road beneath them, their senses had truly become alive.

But they were not alone, as they soon found out, for the lingering aroma of bacon and maple syrup could not be denied as it wafted through the air. Then, came the sound of iron griddles clanking to the attack of the steel spatulas while the immutable chatter of the omnivorous children was demanding to have more. The campers were now seen to be everywhere, bustling about in the business of trying to commune with mother nature as they, too, were seeking to enjoy their lives to the fullest.

"Wow, look at all those people," observed Bobby.

"Oh yeah, I told you there were a lot of people up here," reasserted Annie while Bobby was extensively taking note their omnipresence. "And look over there behind those bushes," she pointed. "There are more of them. I guess they're just popping out of everywhere, like little moles from their hidey-holes," she said in an animated fashion with a grin.

Propitiously at last they arrived at the top of the next hill, and just before the road spilt, as Annie had said it would, there came an opening in the trees to where Bobby could get his first glimpse of the lake. Slowly he pulled the long white convertible over to a quiet stop on the mountainside road, turned the engine off, and rested there silently to embrace the moment.

Then, as the breath of Zephyrus did blow upon them a complementary tribute in the winds of a summer's passion, and the bounty of Persephone in the recognition of their harmony had blessed their unconditional union unto the influences of Aphrodite, the entire world stood still beneath their feet.

"You know, I love you so much," attested Bobby so sedately and with such an unquestionable surety of presence that Annie had been rendered speechless. Then, reaching over with both of his hands he gently twisted her around until she had faced him directly and proceeded to kiss her so firmly and with such resolute solemnity that it virtually petrified her unto the core of her very existence.

"So, is this what the country air does to you," Annie remarked as soon as Bobby released her, fanning herself in the style of Scarlett O'Hara. "I hope you don't take any other girls up here, they won't have a chance," she frivolously commented without thinking.

"Oh, now that's not fair," Bobby despondently replied, taking her comment to heart.

Hurtfully retreating to the driving position, Bobby turned away in silence, casting his eyes down the mountain side towards the lake in the wounded reflection that his most sacred expression of love had been taken as a trivial thing, a simple matter to be toyed with.

"I was just teasing, silly," Annie submitted in a small tone of remorse, moving over securely clasp onto his arm.

"Well, just tell me where I'm supposed go now, okay?" Bobby dolefully asked, while continuing to look away as to hide the hurt that her proposed insinuations had caused him.

"I'm sorry," Annie apologized.

"Well, you know I love you, and you go and say a thing like that and hurt my feelings," Bobby vented sadly, as his eyes misted over.

"I'm sorry," Annie emphasized sincerely again. "You know I didn't mean it," she stressed pleadingly. "Oh, come on, I know you love me. I'll never talk like that again," she repentantly implored. "Oh, come on Bobby," she pleaded once more, "I didn't mean it. I'm sorry. Let's not spoil the day, please?" she begged in final desperation in truly feeling shameful over the consequences of her behavior.

Slowly, after taking a deep breath and exhaling slowly to regain his integrity once more, Bobby turned around slowly and said to her forgivingly, "Oh, I guess it's okay. I know you didn't mean it."

"So, we're still going to the lake, then?' Annie asked in hopeful anticipation.

"Well, if you can just tell me where the hell it is, I guess we can still go, pilgrim," Bobby replied in his best John Wayne imitation he could muster, still trying to manage a smile.

"Well, if you put it that way, I guess I'll just have to tell you," Annie smiled back in relief, kissing him on the cheek for his forgiveness. "It's exactly six houses down," she then disclosed to his surprise, promptly moving away so he could drive.

"Is that all?" Bobby questioned, turning on the ignition to get the car centered back on the road again.

"Well, first of all, there *are* no houses on the right, because the mountain goes straight up," Annie apprised him. "Now, on the left, if you look just under the tree tops, you will be able to see the cabins down on the lake side... you see, there's the first one," she pointed out as it came into view. "Also, if you notice, the driveways veer off the road at an angle before you get to the actual cabin. That's because they kinda circle around as they go down the hill, because it's so steep that if you went straight down, you wouldn't be able to stop, and then you'd end up ploop! —right in the lake," she grinned humorously.

"Just tell me when we approach the right driveway, okay?" Bobby requested seriously, carefully winding the car around the narrow road.

"There it is," Annie suddenly flashed out as if she was a newscaster calling out to her cameraman.

And so, with a great respect for the goodly decline before him, Bobby reduced his speed to a crawl as he began to negotiate the entrance to the property. Slowly, the car descended as it half circumscribed the cabin until eventually reaching a grey stoned parking area towards the right bottom of the lot, which extended all the way to the edge of the lake.

"Whew, well, we made it," Bobby announced with a proud sense of accomplishment, while edging his car onto the stone and putting it into park.

"Oh, yes we did," Annie officially ratified with a kiss on the cheek.

His vitality restored, Bobby now sat back straight up in his seat, took a deep breath, put his right arm around her shoulder and pensively perused the land around him like a conquistador over his province. Thoroughly content with his artful achievement, Bobby then turned his attention to his duties at hand.

"What do we do now?" Bobby addressed Annie.

"Well, the first thing you can do is back the car up a little, turn it towards the cabin, and then back it up right here again so it will face it up the hill. That way it is easier to get out when we have to leave later," Annie suggested. "Then we get the stuff out of the trunk and bring it into the cabin. And, that's all there is to it," she instructed with such a smile that Bobby felt he could not be more grateful to the very God that gave him life.

~

The lakeside cabin was a two-story building with the back of the lower story completely buried against the hillside, presenting the illusion that from the top of the hill, the bottom level did not even exist. Painted spring green and trimmed in white, at times when the sun had shone directly into the eyes of the observer and the dogwoods were in bloom, the secluded cottage would virtually disappear against the backdrop of the landscape.

A vine covered sundeck extended out and over a concrete patio off the upper level at the back of the cabin which provided an unobstructed view of the lake from the colorful patio chairs that were often appointed on top. There were potted plants everywhere, both artificial and real, that were not only hanging in clusters from the underside of the covered patio but situated in every nook and cranny inside the happy little cottage as well.

The upper level was entirely composed of the master bedroom. The eastern side of the room showcased a large panoramic set of windows that overlooked the deep blue lake all the way to the impending mountain on the other side which rose abruptly from its shoreline. An access door to the deck was directly to the right of the windows, and adjacent to it was cornered a white iron circular staircase that led to the lower floor.

Next to the staircase on the room's south side wall sat a long, mirrored vanity, and to its right was a door to the outside that led up the hill, which was kept locked and never used. Along the back wall on the west side first came the door to the bathroom, and then followed a recessed area that sheltered a lowboy dresser with a large mirror and matching armoire adjacent to it in the corner.

The king-sized bed had its antique white headboard and matching twin bed stands situated flat against the north wall, while opposite the foot of the bed was the iron staircase and vanity. The panoramic windows were to the left of the bed. Finally, as to leave no doubt as to who the owners of the cabin were, a large Romanesque countryside painting had been preeminently mounted above the bed's headboard.

Under the vaulted porch, and on top of the concrete patio beneath it, was centered an eight-foot picnic table. On the patio's left side, looking out from the lower level windows toward the lake, was a brick and mortar charcoal grill, while on the opposite side of the table, with its back to the parking area, hung chained a weathered porch swing, which freely swung to and fro from the rafters whenever the breezes from the lake would command, causing it to creak like the bones of an old man.

There were four large windows and a half-windowed door on the lakeside of the bottom level, which were dedicated to let in as much light as possible. It also was comprised of a single room, with the exception of another bathroom in its northwest corner, that had been built directly under the one in the upper level. The working area of the kitchen had the refrigerator stationed in its far-right corner, in tandem with a matching white porcelain stove that sat adjacent to its immediate left.

Along the rest of the back wall, between the bathroom door and the stove, stretched a long row of cabinets with a white tiled counter and sink. Directly mounted above the counter was a line of matching cupboards that took the brunt of the responsibility to store the tableware and extra food supplies for the copious amounts of voracious visitants who would expectantly arrive with the most ravenous of intentions. A large rectangular oaken table with six matching chairs had been conveniently positioned lengthwise in front of the cooking area, just a few feet away.

Opposite the kitchen area and under the lakeside windows was a multi-flowered couch, and to its left was a corner coffee table. Directly next to the coffee table, with its back to the north wall, was a well weathered cream-colored recliner that, when extended, appeared to separate the busy kitchen area from the more tranquil and relaxing section of the room.

Next, following on from the flowered couch and past the half-windowed entrance door, came the iron spiral staircase, thereafter being followed by an old pea-green sleeper sofa.

And although the sofa was quite frumpy in appearance, from its obviously heavy usage, it nonetheless was clean. Then came the door to the lower bathroom.

Bright, sunny, and comfortable, it was a happy little cottage that seemed to canonize to one and all, that in the joy of a summer's day, eternal love shall find its way.

Chapter Fifteen

"Is this good enough?" asked Bobby, after re-parking the car in the graveled area, now with its tail directly facing the lake.

"Yeah, this is perfect!" excitingly declared Annie.

Then, hurriedly moving aside, Annie latched onto her large personal bag, having been indiscriminately thrown on the floor, and ejected herself out the passenger side of the car. And upon leaving the car door wide open, she jaunted over to the shore of the lake next to where the boat dock began, dropped her bag, outstretched her arms, and cried out to the heavens above, "Oh God, it's going to be a beautiful day!"

Turning and continuing to spin around, Annie was the quintessential essence of a dancing fairy, displaying herself in all her glory before the chromatic backdrop of the opalescent lake and the summertime's malachite mountains. Having gotten out of the car to position himself against the passenger's front fender, Bobby had no other thought but to give God his thanks for this truly magnificent situation to which he was a part of.

Moseying over to the passenger door, and closing it after Annie had left it ajar, Bobby attentively repositioned himself by the back-quarter panel of the car while waiting a moment or two before loudly calling out, "I don't want to interrupt your show over there, but do I have to carry all this stuff in by myself?"

"Sure, I'll help," Annie replied cheerfully, putting an end to her little dance of joy to once again reclaim her bag she had cast upon ground by its handle.

Buoyantly jogging now, Annie beelined over to where Bobby was patiently standing. Then, once she had gotten in range, again she cast aside her bag, jumped up high into the air, and precipitously secured a hold around his neck. She now simply hung there with her feet bent back and off the ground, while Bobby had quickly latched on to her in his best effort to stabilize himself from the veritable attack.

"Well, are you ready to go out into the lake?" Annie asked excitedly.

"Aren't I allowed to put my bathing suit on first?" Bobby responded while grinning like a thief who had just secured the Mona Lisa for his very own private viewing.

And, as "well," was the only word that Annie could utter before Bobby had whimsically tried to silence her with a kiss, she nonetheless refused to be stifled. Determined not to have her agenda slowed down any further, and tenaciously as ever, she only responded by pushing back upon his chest and wriggling herself free from his grasp.

"Come on, *I'll* carry the basket *and* my beach bag, and all you have to do is get *your* stuff," Annie dictated as she flitted over to the back of the car and waited for him.

Following Annie over to the trunk, Bobby unlocked and opened it, obediently standing back while she reached in to get the basket. Then, bending over the extended continental kit, Annie clutched on to the handles of the weighty basket and in one swift motion whisked it out and placed it upright onto the ground. After opening the basket up for a moment to inspect everything and verify that its contents were still intact, she looked up and realized that Bobby had not moved so much as an inch. He was still standing in the same spot, but with his arms crossed, seeming quite content to do nothing but observe her in all her glory.

"So, aren't you going to get your bag out of the trunk? I can't handle everything else all by myself, you know," Annie said. "I don't mind bringing in the basket, —I have to unpack it, anyway, because it's got some of my other things in it too, not just the food that my mother made for us, —but can't you get yours?"

"Oh, I can get my bag out of the trunk by myself, all right," Bobby answered nonchalantly. "I'm just standing here watching *you*, that's all," Bobby shamelessly admitted. "Why, you are something, just to watch I mean," he clarified. "You know, you are so pretty, just like in that Roy Orbison song, 'Pretty Woman,'" he mused out loud to her.

Oh, God help me. I want to attack him right now, Annie thought, suddenly dropping the lid to the basket. And as her passion for him had completely erased any idea of what she was presently doing, she simply stood up and vacantly looked askance in trying to recover what little mental cognizance she had left.

"Okay, I'll get my things," Bobby abruptly acceded, unwittingly breaking her trance while going over to retrieve his bag from the trunk.

Finally remembering what she was going to do next, Annie went over, picked up her tote bag, and placed it on top of the wicker basket. Then, sighing in relief to have regained her emotional constitution, she reached down to pick it up with both hands. Bobby, mistaking the graphic nature of her sigh as being attributed to her expected physical struggle with the basket, could no longer just stand by and amuse himself, for he knew that the decent thing to do was to offer his help.

"Annie, this is ridiculous. I'll carry the basket and *your* stuff, and then all you have to carry is *my* gym bag, okay?" asserted Bobby, firmly closing the trunk of the car.

"Okay, so you want to be the man? That's fine by me," Annie laughed. "I hope you know what you are in for," she tagged, backing away from the basket while reaching out for his bag.

"I think I can handle it," appended Bobby while the two of them subsequently began to head to the cabin, each with their own load to bear.

"You can put the basket down now while I look for the keys," Annie instructed, once they had gotten to the lakeside door of the cabin.

After putting down Bobby's gym bag, Annie rummaged through her own bag until she had located her keys, and after unlocking and opening the door, she then announced, "Well, this is it," and stepped aside. "You can put my stuff on the table, and I'll bring in yours," she officiated, following thereafter to put Bobby's bag upon the floor by the iron staircase.

"Boy, this place is all painted like the Garden of Eden. All you need now are those parakeets you got at home and you'd have a regular jungle scene," Bobby noted smartly, putting the basket and Annie's tote bag on the kitchen table.

"Doesn't it make you feel like we're Adam and Eve?" said Annie, suddenly embracing her arms around him.

"Are you sure we're not just hiding out, like Bonnie and Clyde?" Bobby laughed.

Thoroughly surprised with Bobby's analogy, Annie promptly pushed back at him for his declarative faux, and punitively took a swipe at his arm. Smartly, she then turned away and started up the circular stairs while exclaiming back, "You could have at least said Robin Hood and Maid Marion!"

Bobby, now pausing for a second to watch the very object of his desire navigate right up the stairs above him, along with those "tiny little shorts," he instantly realized that he was heading in the wrong direction. Hastily, he moved to correct his position by calling out frantically, "I meant Romeo and Juliet," scrambling up the staircase in desperate pursuit. Ultimately, by the time he had reached to top of the stairs, Annie had already taken a stance before the picture window which looked out over the lake.

"Come over here," Annie dictated, knowing that she once again had the upper hand.

"I was just kidding," Bobby remarked repentantly, still seeking forgiveness as he approached.

"Just take a look at that," Annie said in a disciplinary tone, half turning while she pointed out the window. "Are you really going to tell me that this place isn't beautiful, and that we weren't meant to be here together?" she wistfully proposed in searching for a romantic moment from her beloved suitor.

"Of course we were meant to be here together," Bobby affirmed gently, wrapping his arms snuggly around her from behind. And, yes, it really is beautiful," he reinforced. "This is the most beautiful place I have ever been," he emphasized, "But, you know, no matter wherever I go and no matter whatever I'll see, I know that I will never see anything more beautiful than you," he resolutely testified, softly kissing the side her neck with all the tenderness of a celestial seraphim. Then, pulling back from her a tad and turning her around to face him directly, he put his hands securely on her shoulders, looked straight into her eyes and in complete tenderheartedness, asked her face to face, "Is this all you wanted?"

Instantly becoming almost completely and uncontrollably captured by the spirit of his love, Annie cautioned, "Okay, that's enough for now," and in trying to retain her emotional integrity, delicately removed his hands from her shoulders and turned to go back down stairs.

"You can change into your bathing suit up here, and I will get into mine in the bathroom downstairs," Annie pronounced, toddling over to the stair's iron railing with her hand upon her chest.

Bobby, following Annie her to the bottom of the stairway, grabbed onto his gym bag still lying on the floor beside it, and bounded back to the upper room to outfit himself, while Annie went over to the table where Bobby had placed the wicker basket. Pushing down its handles and opening the lid, Annie removed a shoebox full of eatables that Jolanda had packed for their welfare and put them in the refrigerator, briefly verifying that the old Kelvinator was indeed yet working and sufficiently cold. She then withdrew a small travel case, closed the basket back up, and placed it empty upon the floor next to the table. And with tote bag and travel case now in hand, she went into the lower bathroom.

Perhaps, after only three or four minutes had gone by, and with feet faster than Gene Kelly could have wished for, Bobby tapped down the iron spiral staircase, considering himself to be, "ready to go."

"Boy, these stairs are really cool," Bobby called out to Annie while she was still changing in the bathroom. "I'll wait for you outside on the swing," he called out, leaving through the back door leading to the covered patio.

"Okay, let's see if I have everything," Annie murmured, setting her tote bag upon the top of the commode and her travel case upon the counter next to the sink. Item by item, in the hope that her fairy godmother did not fail to remind her just exactly what would be needed, she began to paw through the tote bag's contents. "Humm, it seems everything is here," she said out loud. "So now, I guess all I need is my smock and swim suit," she added, taking these articles out from the travel case. Next, she completely disrobed, hung her current attire on the clothes hook that was mounted on the back of the door, put on her swim suit, her sneakers once again, sans socks, and donned her smock.

"Well, I guess I'm all ready now," Annie concluded out loud, making one last perusal of her bag. Fully satisfied with the entirety of her appearance, she now opened the bathroom door, put out the light, and left the bathroom with her tote bag slung over her shoulder, again to return to the kitchen area. Opening the refrigerator, she took out two cans of soda and added them to her bag. Closing its door, she reached over to the nearest drawer under the counter to her left, took out a washcloth and a church key, and added them to her collection as well. Finally, after closing the drawer, she hustled over to the patio door.

"I see you found a home," Annie proclaimed, coming out onto the patio and turning to lock the door behind her.

Bobby, reclining quite comfortable on the porch swing, with one leg up and one leg down, seemed ever the picture of contentment, and after chucking her keys back into her tote bag, Annie proceeded to negotiate herself over to the side of the swing, where she deliberately began to toy with the curls in his hair.

"You know, I am going boating on the lake today. I wonder if you know of some handsome young man around here that would like to go with me," she solicited enticingly.

"You know, I do know of such a man, and he is not very far away," he apprised her. "So, what does it pay?" Bobby inquired, as if being interviewed for a job.

"How about I give you a down payment right now?" Annie offered as she bent down and gave him a short kiss.

"Okay, I'll take the job right now!" Bobby exclaimed, spryly removing himself from the swing to accept the offer.

Thereupon taking Bobby by the hand, Annie led him down to the landing where the johnboat was docked. The boat was a decent twelve feet long and had been covered over with a canvas top, except for the outboard motor that was clamped onto the back of the transom. Bobby walked down to the prow of the craft, which was facing out toward the lake, and began to remove the canvas. Once he had untied the rope from the bow cleat, he pulled back a portion of the cover and climbed into the front of the boat.

Beginning to roll up the cover, Bobby climbed over the center seat until he had reached the stern, tossing the rolled-up cloak atop the pier. Next, after fetching a couple of rope ties from a wooden storage bin sitting next to the outboard engine, he nimbly hopped back onto the dock. Finally, after tying up the roll of canvas and securing it to a couple of mooring cleats on the landing, he stood back up. Completely proud of his efficiency, Bobby then stretched out his left arm back in the direction of the boat and officiously announced, "All aboard that's going aboard."

"I wanna go, I wanna go," Annie appealed, acting like an impudent child while stomping her foot.

"Okay, the children may board at this time, but you must sit in the center seat, and remember, do not stand up in the boat, or Captain Bob will be very angry," Bobby announced in character.

Holding on to his hand, Annie stepped out onto the boat's decking with her left foot, thus causing it to slightly rock sideways. Waiting a second for the rocking to subside, and after letting go of Bobby's hand, she quickly brought over her right foot and steadied herself by holding onto the gunwale, punctiliously sitting herself down upon the center seat, facing the stern. Once Annie had secured her position, Bobby descended onto the vessel's back quarter to neatly take the seat directly next to the engine's port side, facing Annie.

"So, do you know how to work the engine?" asked Annie provocatively.

"Are you kidding me? It's an engine, isn't it?" Bobby commented back. "The first thing is, I hope your uncle left some gas in the tank," he said hopefully, while opening the gas cap at the top of the engine. "Yeah, it's full. That's good," he reported, putting the cap back on the tank.

It was a clean wooden craft that was painted forest green and kept in good condition. A simple boat, it had been constructed with a seat for one in the prow, room for two in the middle, and a single seat in the stern on the larboard side for the pilot to sit and command it. On the starboard side of the engine was a red spare gas can, a wooden bin containing an extra can of oil, miscellaneous tools, and a small first aid kit.

Directly in front of the supply box lay the anchor. It was about a ten pounder and attached to a coil of rope, which was in turn attached to an eyehook bolted through the back top corner of the transom. Under the center seat, a set of four orange cushions were stored to either sit upon or use as a flotation device, if ever the boat sank. Opposite the sides of the center seat were a set of turned down oarlocks with twin oars secured beneath them by a set of chromed hooks that were screwed into the side of the boat's frame.

Bobby released the catch that kept the engine propped up and lowered its shaft and propeller into the lake. Choking the engine to prime it, after turning up the idle, he pulled on the wooden handle of the starter cord in a fashion no different than he had done, many a time before, to the Whirling Dervish.

Abruptly, the mighty three horse Johnson sputtered valiantly for a few seconds in trying its best to start, but nonetheless, just as abruptly, it quit. Indomitably, Bobby gave a second pull on the cord, and it was all that was necessary to bring 'the little engine that could' roaring back to life. This time, in a most concerted effort not to die again, it kept on sputtering and chugging along sporadically, refusing with great determination to succumb unto the silence of its own demise.

"We'll have to let it run a little for it to warm up, but it seems to run just fine," Bobby assessed.

"I know," Annie concurred. "You forget, it's *my* Uncle's boat. I've been on it plenty of times before, you know," she reminded him.

"Yeah, but did he ever trust you to handle the engine?" Bobby questioned in doubt.

"No, he never did," Annie honestly confessed.

"Well, *this* guy will," Bobby trumped with his thumb pointing to his chest. "So, who's the guy that's most important to you now?" he exhorted pretentiously.

"My dad, of course," Annie quipped back quickly with a wide grin.

"Okay, you got me," Bobby admitted with an accepting smile. "Well, it looks like the engine is all warmed up now, so if you turn around and reach over and untie the bow line, I'll get the one back here, and we'll be off," Bobby instructed pleasantly.

Once the lines were unwound from the cleats on the pier and thrown into the boat, Bobby reached over to the throttle, turned it up, and at almost high noon, the two young mariners sailed away from the dockside in search of the panoptic rapture which had given the secluded mountain lake its fame.

"So where do we go, Matey? asked Bobby, awaiting his orders.

"Well, we're on the north side of the lake. You see the beach over there?" Annie pointed out. "We passed it by where the road split," she referenced.

"Yup, I see it," Bobby answered.

"We can start by going over there, where the mountain comes right down to the water," Annie further instructed, now pointing over to the right of the beach. "That's where the stream comes down from the mountain that feeds the lake. The dam is at the other end of the lake about two miles down," she further noted, stopping to think for a second if there was anything else of importance that Bobby should be aware of. Accordingly, after looking askance for a moment she concluded, "Um, anyway, that's about the size of it."

"Okay, here we go, then," Bobby announced as he turned up the engine to full throttle.

Remarkably, the little three horsepower Johnson engine pushed the boat along quite formatively. This unexpected speed in turn had produced a most appreciated cooling in addition to the lake's summer breezes, for the temperature by now had well passed the ninety-degree mark.

Bobby, who had reached the opposite end of the lake in no time, now began his lackadaisical tour of the lake's eastern shore beneath the mountain's omnipresent vaunt of greenery that appeared to miraculously spring up right from the lake itself. It was from this vantage point that he could see the entire lake and had become completely immersed in a kind of natural peace and self-reflection which, both suddenly and surreptitiously, enveloped him in a mystical blanket of benevolent wishes come true. He felt blessed that he was there.

And while Bobby was busy puttering along aimlessly, Annie had taken off her smock, applied her Coppertone, finished brushing her hair, and had put her Yankees baseball cap on over her designer Wayfarer Ray-Bans, all being produced from her tote bag.

"Do you want to steer the boat now?" Bobby offered pleasantly. "The captain is now ready for a boating class," he announced cheerfully.

"No, that's okay," Annie declined politely. "I'm happy right here, and besides, I trust you," she mocked with a smile. "No, I'm going to look for my transistor radio and see if I can get something in," she annotated in a more serious tone.

Picking up her bag once more, Annie again began to rummage through its contents as Bobby watched her in amusement.

"How much crap do you actually carry around in that thing, anyway?" Bobby commented rhetorically in simulated amazement.

"None of your beeswax, mister," Annie responded shortly, still searching through her bag of unlimited contents. "You know, if you ever even just look into a woman's handbag, you will lose your soul forever. You know that, don't you?" she emphasized expressly. "It will simply disappear into the bag, and it will never be found again. So, you never, never, ever, look inside," she continued on, flush with the personification of a mischievous pixie while she glanced up at him with her hand still inside the bag. "Why, it's even one of the few things that even the Holy Father can't forgive you for," she defiantly added.

Suddenly, stopping dead in the middle of her diatribe, and looking directly upward, Annie announced, "Ta da," miraculously pulling her right hand out of the bag with the radio held out in full display. "See, here it is," she announced triumphantly, waving it high in the air. "Now, we can have some music!"

Oh, thank God, the crisis is over, Bobby thought to himself, but this time, he knew enough not to make his remark out loud.

Eagerly, Annie turned on her radio and began to fuss with the tuning dial until discovering, to her complete amazement, that it could in fact pick up her favorite station.

"Oh, I can't believe it. I got my station in. And listen to what's playing!" she squealed as she held out the radio for Bobby to hear it above the modulation of the motor.

"Well, I'll be darned, you really got the station in," Bobby said in astonishment. "And listen to that," he said in hearing the little leather-cased radio broadcasting faintly, *Come on down to my boat baby, come on down and sail away.* "You know, that was played just for us. You realize that?" he asserted in being totally blown away by the odds of it all.

"Oh, I believe it too," Annie radiantly agreed. "You know, why don't we just go out to the middle of the lake, turn the motor off, and just drift for a while? We could just relax and work on our tans," she recommended.

"Sure, that sounds good to me," agreed Bobby. "I could even get a little snooze. After all, we got up early this morning and it did take over an hour and a half to get here. I think that's a good idea," he certifiably agreed.

Once they had reached the middle of the lake, which was about a half a mile between either shore, Bobby turned off the engine as proposed, and handily reached down to pick up the anchor atop a coil of rope on the deck next to the wooden supply box.

"Anchors away!" Bobby announced dramatically, tossing the anchor overboard and pausing for a second thereafter before admitting, more buoyantly than the anchor itself, "I always wanted to say that."

"Well, now you can," supported Annie.

"Boy, this lake must be pretty deep. The anchor didn't even hit the bottom," Bobby observed out loud. "Oh well, it'll still keep us from drifting too fast," he remarked for Annie's benefit. "Okay, now pick up your legs," he instructed, leaning forward to remove the flotation cushions out from under the middle seat on which Annie was perched.

Taking out two of the cushions, Bobby put them flat on the deck between the center seat and back of the boat. Next, taking out the second pair, he propped them up against the engine, rear seat, and supply box.

"You can put your legs down now and come over here," Bobby invited as he took off his shirt, sat down on the cushioned deck, and comfortably reclined back to survey his good fortune.

Carefully Annie got off the center seat, and while holding on to the gunwale to her left, she crawled over atop the decked cushion, laid her smock down first, and then situated herself directly next to Bobby.

"Hey, this is pretty nice," Annie proclaimed once she had finished fidgeting about. "It's almost like being in a cradle, —Whaaa, I want my Maypo!" she parodied the commercial.

"So, are you comfortable?" Bobby asked attentively as he disregarded her levity.

"I sure am," Annie expressed, while rolling over closer to give him a peck on the cheek. "You know something?" she then said, "I think I'd just rather have it quiet, what do you think?

"Oh, that's fine by me," Bobby replied complacently.

Turning, Annie clicked off the transistor radio, still nestled atop her handbag, and again returned to her former position as the two of them now lay in a quiet repose, snuggled together against the endless lapping waves of time.

Drifting about, the two love hearts were at total peace while the midday sun intensely shone directly down upon them. Occasionally, a lazy cloud would float on by to briefly relieve them from the veracity of the heat as it passed overhead, but soon enough, the blazing brilliance of the sun would once again return. With eyes closed, the two of them simply drifted about, introspectively describing the intense images which randomly appeared against the backdrop of their eyelids in a myriad of panoramic psychedelic colors which constantly changed form as the radiation from the direct sunlight overhead would cascade down upon their inner thoughts, stored within their minds.

Faintly, off in the distance, the chipper revelers about the beach area could still be heard cavorting about the water's edge. With the exception of being intermittently interrupted by the occasional sound of another motorboat skimming about the vicinity, it was completely peaceful, as peaceful could be. Even the subtle scent from Annie's freshly applied coconut tanning oil was in tune with the wafting aromas which occasionally would meander across the lake from the plentitudinous barbeque grills that had been festively fired up for the unbridled feasting of the day.

It was a fabulous day for them upon the lake, and as they drifted, so too did their conversation. From their abstract sensuous perceptions to the realities of their impending separation being only four weeks away, nothing was left unattended.

"So, how much do you love me?" Annie asked, as all young girls in love do, in trying to quantify the value of their surrender.

"Enough to want to marry you, you know that," Bobby answered placidly.

"I know, but can't we get married before you go?" Annie gently pleaded, propping herself up on her left arm and curling his chest hair with her index finger.

"I would love to do that with all my heart, honey, but we can't," Bobby factually responded. "Your father has been too good to me and I just can't ignore that. And besides, it would kill your mother not to have a proper wedding. I even told her that I'd join the Catholic Church.

"And my mother wouldn't be very happy, either. And nor would my dad," he asserted plainly, "For a lot of reasons," he added. "No, the only one that would be happy would be your sister, because you'd be in the dog house," he realistically pointed out. "And besides, there just isn't enough time and I don't want to hurt anybody's feelings, especially when all they want for us is to be happy," he definitively explained.

"Anyway, I've requested to be in the motor pool, which I will probably be assigned to, and then I'll be sent to Vietnam for about year to repair the vehicles over there," he further noted. "After that, I'll get transferred someplace else to train the next guy to take my place. That's how it works. And I might even get sent back here for that," he said, now with a degree of optimism. "Look at it this way," he offered, "it's not that long, and by that time I will have saved up a bunch of money and we can get married right. Then *everyone* will be happy," he proposed.

"You know, that might be fine for you, but what exactly am *I* supposed to do while you're gone?" questioned Annie despondently.

"Why don't you go work for your father?" Bobby proposed. "He told me he needed somebody else in the office. You could answer the phone and maybe help him with the accounts. You know, send out the bills, answer the mail, go to the bank. All that stuff. Somebody's gotta do it, and right now he's paying that bookkeeper lady extra to do it, because it's gotta get done.

"Or, you can always take some courses at the community college if you want to," he submitted. "You were always pretty good at that stuff in high school. Take up something you like. I don't think you want to be a waitress or work in a factory, do you?" he asked straightforwardly.

"No, I'm not going to do that," Annie said flatly.
"Well, I don't blame you," Bobby concurred. "You shouldn't have to. Besides, think about it, who does your

dad have anyway?" he questioned. "Sure, he's got your Uncle Tony and your Uncle Marco, who are a couple of great guys, and I know they are all your family, but let's face it, he doesn't have a son to take over the business.

"*You're* his favorite, and you know it. Everybody knows it I guess he likes me fine because I always try to earn my pay, but I also know it's because I try to make you happy, and that's why he gave me my job in the first place. I'm not that stupid," he interjected. "He also didn't want his daughter going out with some hippy bum. He told me so. You know your dad, —he tells you flat out what he thinks. So, I kinda got an unspoken agreement with him. I do my job, he pays me good, I don't become a bum, and I make you happy. And so, as you full well know, when your dad is happy, *eeeverybody's* happy," he stressed.

"Now, since I am not going to be working for him for the next two years, it should be your job to fill in for me," he suggested practically. "That way, he will be happy while I'm gone, and I get to keep my job. So, in the end, I figure I have to come back to you, not just for my job, but because I love you, and it's you, and only you, that makes *me* happy." Then, turning sideways and looking at her directly, he candidly admitted, "After all, I want to be happy too, you know!"

"I love you so much!" Annie avowed softly, reaching over to caress the side of his cheek in not breaking the fixation between them. "And you know I have no choice," she conceded, "I realize that I can't make that many people be unhappy just because of me," she said in all decency. "But still, it is you I want to make happy the most, because it is you who makes *me* the happiest. I guess I'll just have to work for my dad for a couple of years, that's all," she fatefully accepted in a sad tone.

"But you know, there is still one thing I guess I should tell you," Annie now mentioned, changing her countenance to that of a naughty girl. "My father already asked me if I would work for him when you went for your physical. And I told him then that I would," she admitted with a sly grin.

Annie never ceased to fascinate him. To him, she was an incredible enigma, and it was far beyond his comprehension to think of her possessive terms. That she was to be his and his alone was a responsibility that Bobby had sometimes shuddered to think about.

"Well, that's nice to know," Bobby acknowledged, fully accepting her conniving ways. "Well, I don't know about you, but we have been out here for a couple of hours already and I've had about enough. What do *you* think?" he then asked in changing the subject.

"Yeah, I've had enough too, let's go back," Annie agreed, promptly sitting back up. And after picking up her smock and latching onto her handbag, she carefully crawled back over to the center seat once again and put up her feet.

Bobby took no time in putting the cushions back in their place, thereafter proceeding to reel in the anchor by pulling up on the old hemp rope, hand over hand, to which it was tethered. Finally, when the anchor appeared from the depths of the lake and was tossed forthwith upon the deck of the boat, they were now free to return from whence they came. Adeptly, Bobby again took control over the little engine's prowess and speedily put the craft on its destination home as the lake had all but relinquished its momentary hold upon its altogether satisfied excursionary visitants.

The afternoon midday sun had already peaked, and while the intensity of its heat began to wane, the added breeze which now began to blow across the little boat's prow was notably welcomed. Then, in no time at all, the Arcadian campestral cabin had come into view over the glittering ripple of the silver topped waves.

Upon approaching their destination, Bobby guided the boat in a semi-circular fashion toward the northern side of the dock so that he could come in at an angle from the shoreline. Slowing the craft down to an idle, he then turned it hard to its starboard side and killed the engine completely. Noiselessly, they now progressively drifted sideways until the vessel lightly docked itself succinctly against the side of the pier.

"A perfect landing," Bobby asserted, boastfully standing up to wind the rear mooring line around its dock cleat.

"I got to hand it to you. It most definitely was," Annie testified brightly, reaching over as well to secure the bowline to the pier. "And speaking of handing it to you, I'm going to hand you the responsibility of covering the boat back up by yourself while I go to the cabin and get your lunch ready. You are hungry, aren't you?" she stated more than asked. Then, tote bag and smock in hand, she climbed out onto the dock and expeditiously left on her way.

"Sure, I'm hungry," Bobby called out. "And besides, I don't want to disappoint your mom. After all, I already know she was the one who really made it!" he taunted, while Annie had already stepped off the dock.

By the time it took Bobby to refill the tank on the top of the engine from the spare gas can, recoil the rope attached to the anchor and place it neatly into the supply box, recanvas the boat, and tightly secure its mooring lines, Annie had his lunch on the table. Coming in through the door with his tee shirt put back on, Bobby could plainly see that Annie was already sitting patiently at the table. Again with her brightly colored smock back on, she was the picture of readiness, while the table was completely set before him.

"It sure looks good," said Bobby as he approached her, "but you look better," he added, leaning down to kiss her on the cheek.

"Okay, that's enough for now. Go over and wash your hands first, and then come sit down," Annie dictated.

Compliantly, he did as he was told, and upon finally sitting down, he briefly took a moment to examine the fare. Sitting on the plate directly in front of him was a large sandwich on sliced Italian bread, along with a veritable mound of macaroni salad, which was garnished on the side with three of the largest black olives Bobby had ever seen. Upon further inspection after picking up the top of his sandwich, and under the lettuce and tomato, to his delight was staked all of his delicatessen favorites, —boiled ham, Swiss cheese, and mortadella. Then, as if at a panic, he suddenly halted his examination and cast his eyes about the table in pursuit of his most cherished condiment.

"Aha, there it is, the mustard!" he exclaimed, pointing over to the center of the table. "I knew you wouldn't fail me," he told Annie as he beamed like the boy who had just been given the Red Ryder, Carbine Action BB Gun for Christmas.

"You didn't really think I would forget a thing like your favorite mustard, did you? Listen, my mother might have made all this stuff, but don't you forget it was *me* who made sure that you had your mustard," Annie correctly pointed out.

"Don't worry, I won't," Bobby acknowledged shortly, reaching over for the Gulden's jar of mustard in the middle of the table. "Oh, good, I see she made some ice tea," he commented, having to negotiate around the tall glass in front of him to obtain the galvanizing object of his bounty. "Oh, great, I see your mom also made those almond cookies with the powdered sugar on them, too. I love those things," he happily proclaimed again.

"Well, if you really want to know, *I* made those cookies, too" Annie additionally disclosed, while intensely studying his every reaction.

Bobby, however, was now oblivious to everything, for his afternoon feast had consumed his entire concentration to the abandonment of all else. Transfixed in observing the immense pleasure that he was experiencing by simply having a good meal set before him, Annie could not help but think it that would be her to give him an even greater joy to experience, one he would never forget.

She also realized that she truly loved seeing him happy, especially if it was because of her efforts. These feelings had now propagated within her a great sense of spiritual accomplishment, which in turn had only fueled within her an unquenchable passion to altogether consider dismissing the foreboding social boundaries that she had been warned not to disregard so lightly.

"You haven't eaten very much," noticed Bobby, after washing down the last of his sandwich with a large drink of his iced tea.

"No, I'm not very hungry. I'm not much of a lunch person," Annie decreed. "I'm going up stairs to change. When you're done, come on up and we'll go out on the deck and watch the people out on the lake," she pleasantly proposed as she got up, took her bag off the corner of the back of her chair, and jaunted up the spiral staircase to leave him alone with his thoughts.

What a good life, Bobby mused, reclining back in his chair to savor one of the almond cookies. *I have a beautiful girl, it's a fabulous day, and I don't have a care in the world! I guess I gotta go in the army, but then, all I need to do is my job for a couple of years, and after that, I get to come back to this. That's not so bad. I don't really want to go, but, I guess I don't have any choice. Oh well, I'm damn sure I have it a lot better than most other guys. She is so beautiful. Oh... and I do believe in serendipity,"* he grinned to himself in remembering that he had learned the word from Annie. Patiently, he waited for a few moments longer until his apprehension had finally gotten the best of him, and thus curiously went over to the bottom of the iron stairway.

"Are you ready for me to come up?" Bobby then called out.

"You can come up and go out on the deck if you want, and I'll be out in a minute," Annie answered back from inside the upstairs bathroom

Taking the stairs two steps at a time, Bobby virtually bounded up to the second floor, and going directly over to the outside glass door he smoothly slid it open and advanced to the outside deck, as specifically instructed. And then, standing casually against the outside rail for perhaps only a minute or two, still relishing the thoughts of his good fortune, he heard Annie calling out softly, "Bobby, would you come in here for a second?"

"Sure," Bobby responded, and upon entering the room, he beheld the most amazing sight he had ever seen. Beside the corner of the bed stood Annie, the celestial fairy queen of his desires, bearing the most impish, naughty, and frolicsome smile upon her face, which by no means detracted in any way from the baby doll negligee that she had put on.

"Don't just stand there, come here," Annie summoned.

Beguiled, like a fly to a noiseless patient spider, the victim crept ever closer to his inevitable surrender, and once within her grasp, she reached out, clasped her arms tightly around him, and with her head pressed firmly against his chest implored, "I want you to have me. Right here, and right now," she posed with all her heart.

Until this moment, after three years of companionship, and with the sole physical exploration of playing patty fingers, Bobby was mortified to think of the consequences now confronting him. *What if I fail to please her?* was his first thought, and secondly, "What if you become pregnant?" came next, as it uncontrollably just popped out of his mouth.

"Don't you worry about that," Annie spoke assuredly, "it's not my time. But, it *is* the time for you to make me happy. And this is what I want. You said you loved me, and only me. So, love me and make me happy," she implored him once again. And so, as it was ordained to be, he took her as commanded.

Chapter Sixteen

Dusk was slowly approaching as the long white convertible with its canopy open to the heavens above meandered back gracefully past the fork in the mountainside road as the two lovers, who were now one, manifestly relinquished the connubial cabin of their dreams behind them. The sounds from the lake's festivities had become noticeably subdued from earlier in the day, for the ruckus that had been produced from the multitudes of exuberant merry makers in attempting to conjoin themselves directly with nature itself had since become quietly absorbed into the vastness of the forest about them. Intertwined, the spirit of the mountain and the mountaineers alike had become completely melded together as every participant to the day's events was ardently trying to commit to memory their most affectionate and cherished moments, while fresh within their minds.

"So, what are you thinking?" Bobby curiously asked as the midsummer night's gardenias had taken full charge of their senses.

Annie, who was lying back leisurely in her seat with her right arm stretched out over the side of the car, lackadaisically trying to catch the wind in her hand as the waning sunset had all but surrendered the last of its dominance behind the crest of the mountain, upon hearing Bobby's request, whimsically responded in tune, *"Will you still need me, will you still feed me, when I'm sixty-four?"*

"So when did you learn how to sing?" smiled Bobby softly.

"Just now, how'd you like it?" complacently replied Annie, adjusting herself in a more upright position.

"Not bad, not bad at all," Bobby complimented. "So, you're happy then?" he asked in turn.

"I am now what you call captivated," Annie replied. "Yup, —that's it, captivated," she confirmed. "And you are the one who did it to me," she accusatorially stated, before pausing a second to observe his reaction. Next, in seeing none, she noted, "Why, of course I am happy, silly. Just look at all the money we saved. My dad will be ecstatic," she declared.

"What do you mean?" asked Bobby.

"Oh, when I tell my dad what we did, he won't have to pay for a big wedding anymore," Annie fortuitously replied.

"What! Are you nuts?" Bobby cried out, trying to keep his attention on the road.

"I'm only kidding, silly" Annie confessed. "I still want a big wedding, and I'm going to have one. I wouldn't ruin that. I'm not *that* stupid," she said reassuringly.

"Well, that's a relief," Bobby sighed.

"I'm only going to tell Barbara, that's all," she then muttered with a grin.

"Oh my God! That's even worse! What have I done?" Bobby lamented vociferously unto the heavens above.

"Oh, come on, I'm still teasing you," Annie asserted in consolation, while moving over to snuggle directly against him. "Now, put your arm around me and don't let me go until we are home, and I promise I won't give you anymore conniptions, okay?"

"Okay," Bobby replied, securing Annie with his right arm. "You know, you could cause a guy a heart attack with talk like that," he asserted while she loved against him.

So together, each with their own reflections of the day, they continued on with their trek home while a blanket of silence had fallen softly upon them in the sultry summer air.

It was then that Annie chose to ask about the one question that Bobby had managed to avoid answering, to anyone.

"What do you *really* think about the Vietnam War?" Annie lightly asked as philosophically as possible, in trying not to unnecessarily upset him.

"I try not to," Bobby answered matter-of-factly. "Do I believe in all that domino crap of losing the world to the commies like Eisenhower said? Hell no, —that's just a load of crap. Do I think we even need to be over there at all? Hell no, —that's just a lot of crap, too. Do I have to go over there because I was drafted? Hell yeah. It's either that, or go and get called a coward, and I ain't no coward, so off I go," he said flatly.

"And by the way, it's also too late for me to go to the new community college to get a deferment. Besides, if it wasn't, I'd probably flunk out, anyway. And then I'd still end up going. Either way I go, so I might as well go now and get it over with," he said conclusively.

"Listen, everyone knows the whole thing is a lot of crap," he continued. "There's nothing *I* can do about it. So, I try to mind my own business and do the best that I can. Look at it this way," he appealed, "this has been the best day of my life and I love you with all my heart, but you know, I guess some of the others are also right," he flatly reasoned out loud.

"Okay, so who *is* right?" questioned Annie.

"All those who say we should fight for our country, that's who," Bobby answered. "See, you have to admit that I wouldn't have you here today if my dad and yours hadn't fought in the Second World War, and so now it's my turn to do *my* part," he explained. "Hell, if it wasn't for them we'd probably still be in The Depression. Who knows?

"Well, that's the attitude, for a lot of them, anyway," he qualified, "You know that. And that's why I try not to think about it, because there aren't any good answers to any of it. Now, you can go on thinking about it, all by yourself, until your head hurts. That would be your problem, but as for me, *I'd* rather spend my time thinking about you, and that's *my* problem," he stated with a slight grin.

"Besides, it makes me feel a whole lot better," he stated in an optimistic tone. "After all, why would I want to be thinking about that stupid old war, when I can be thinking about you? In fact, I'm thinking about you right now," he smirked, "and you're completely naked too!" he laughed loudly in amusement.

"Is that all you think of me?" Annie frowned at him sadly.

"Of course not, but don't worry," Bobby comforted, "I won't tell Barbara," he laughed again.

"I really don't think either of us wants that," Annie agreed, while the two of them now settled down to face the inevitable.

~

The summer of sixty-seven was a magical and mystical time. The country was basking in the radiance of the greatest economic period in its history. Union wages crept ever higher as huge sums of money transferred hands from the treasure trove of taxes generated by the greatest industrial might the world has ever known, all to support all the new social programs that were created for the lower classes of people who believed themselves to have been denied their fair share of the abundant prosperity.

The Great Depression was all but a memory as caskets of money were virtually exploding everywhere from the successful warring economy. A man could get a job, and in a few weeks, buy a car, —it may have had maypop wheels, the muffler tied on with coat hanger wire, and went through a quart of oil a week, but it ran, and he could get a much better job once he had it.

Perhaps the starving masses of the thirties were no more, but there were still plenty of poor folks still looking for a better life. And as the access to mobility had become significantly more affordable, masses of these people who had been heretofore tethered to their rural lifestyle began flocking into the cities in to improve their lives where the union paychecks were the highest and the public welfare the greatest.

Everyone had a public opinion and had fought to be heard. Freedom was the word of the day, and not just for those *"who had nothin' to lose."* The women fought for the freedom not to wear a bra in public, the hippies fought for the freedom to make love in the streets, and Dr. Martin Luther King Jr. fought for the freedom of everyone to peacefully try and solve their problems in the *"sweltering summer of the negro's legitimate discontent."*

As everyone seemed to have a beef about something, every faction imaginable, nonetheless, did absolutely agree on one thing, —they all had the unalienable right to protest that they had no freedoms. Also, regardless of the depth of the disparities between the discontented and disillusioned, everybody, with perhaps the sole exception of the politically connected military elite, had come to hate the very concept of why the war in Vietnam was being waged. Undaunted, nonetheless, the draft continued to press on while its system of arbitrary deferments vociferously fell under attack.

It was *"hot town, summer in the city,"* all over America, and as The Supremes, the Turtles, the Association, Dion Warwick, Bobby Vinton, Frankie Valli, and even Frank and Nancy Sinatra had encapsulated the passions of love, the Beatles, the Doors, the Rolling Stones, and Peter Paul and

Mary were expressing their observation of man's social behavior. And while Bobby Gentry, Aretha Franklin, Procol Harum, and Ray Charles had all embraced their inner struggles, the Fifth Dimension, the Mamas and the Papas, the Electric Prunes, the Grass Roots, and the Strawberry Alarm Clock gave everyone all the time that was needed to escape them.

The people were alive with life and the consequences of death alike. They loved with wide eyes open and fought to better themselves in a world from which they could not escape. Everyone had also come to the conclusion, that if given the choice, no decent man would go to war simply to improve another man's country while his own family was suffering at home.

It thus became no secret, that when a government can show no plausible danger to its people in the support of a foreign war, over which its combatants would gain nothing but their own demise, it has a problem. And with the politician's nefarious intentions aside, when the struggle over a man's decency becomes greater than the struggle for him to escape the pernicious will of his own government, that government will then inevitably and justifiably fail, for the very underpinning of a forced draft has been, and will always be, forever repugnant to all decent men who full well know that honor consists of much more than a politician's declaration.

Bobby Taylor had now but four weeks left until he had to report for his formal induction at Fort Dix. Until then, he and Annie were at one with the enchantment of life itself. Annie had given herself to him fully and Bobby could think of nothing else but to pleasure her. Together they had become inseparable as the war was trying to do its best to put asunder that which no man could.

It was on an early September morning when Bobby's father had pulled his Buick Le Sabre over to the curbside in front of the Russo home. It felt curiously strange for Bobby to get out of the passenger side of a car and have to walk up the same driveway that he had been so accustomed to driving upon. *I guess I won't be coming over here for a while,* he thought, approaching the side door to the kitchen. It was no sooner than he had gotten within ten feet of the door then Annie came running out and into his arms. Nothing was said at first as both had just embraced each other in silence.

"I'll be back in about eight weeks. That won't be so long," consoled Bobby, while Annie continued to cling onto him in total desperation.

As hard as Annie tried, she could not remove from her mind a particular childhood tune which seemed to play over and over again in her head, *"With tears in eyes, she said and sighed, and you could hear her say, —I'm sorry playmate, but I can't play with you,"* while in sad departure, the song had further gone on to pledge that regardless, they would still be, *"jolly friends forevermore."*

"But I don't want you to go," Annie franticly appealed as if some sort of miracle would happen while the tears of the impending reality were uncontrollably streaming down her cheeks to aimlessly fall upon the ground.

"Listen, I'll be back," Bobby told her compassionately, "and when I do, I'll be in better shape than ever," he reassured her.

"I like the shape you're in now," Annie continued to cry.

"You know I have to go," Bobby said sedately, gently turning up her head and affectionately wiping the tears from her face.

"I know," Annie fatefully acknowledged in resignation.

"Well, I expect my goodbye kiss now," Bobby said delicately. "You see, my dad's waiting and I have to go," he reminded her.

Compliantly, Annie then threw her arms around him one more time to mournfully kiss her most sacred possession goodbye. Then, after again professing his love, he left to surrender himself unto his awaiting destiny.

"See you in a couple of months," Bobby called out from the end of the driveway, stopping momentarily to record her image against the backdrop of all his treasured memories.

And as the car door had profoundly closed behind him with a thud, his boyhood had come to an end. *May God have mercy on my soul,* Bobby said to himself, accepting that from this moment forward he was to march to a different tune.

Neither Bobby nor his father had anything to say for the entire trip on their way to the downtown bus station. Each man knew of his place and had respectfully acknowledged it in the reverent solitude of ride. It wasn't until the car had finally gotten parked and the two of them were standing next to where the bus was stationed that the silence was broken.

"Well, Dad, I guess I'm off to join the circus," Bobby said as he put his gym bag down on the pavement for a moment.

"I only have one thing tell you," his father began advisedly, "and that is, when *I* was in, I had this guy in my outfit we called 'The professor,' mainly because he *was* one, and secondly, because he always had some kinda philosophy about everything," he said. "Anyway, he used to say that every man in his life, sometime or another, would be faced with a dilemma, and that a dilemma was a situation you find yourself in where *all* your choices are distasteful.

"Now, the way I look at it, it's even simpler than that. Sometimes, you'll be damned if you do, and just as damned if you don't, so what's the difference? In any case, son, before you leave, I want you to know that I have always been proud of the decisions that you have made, that's all," he told him straightforwardly.

And so, with a shake of a hand and a pat farewell upon his back, Bobby got on the bus and disappeared down the road to fulfill his obligations.

Annie's plight was a different story. She didn't have the minutia of the boot camp's regimentation to occupy her mind while working at her job, and thus the ensuing phone calls and weekly letters of unbridled love which she received only exacerbated her unhappy situation. She had taken up working in her father's office, as she had mentioned she would, in order to learn the paper work involved in running his business, but spent most of her time pining over her condition and re-drafting her letters of adoration to her beloved soldier, —and no one seemed concerned about it, either.

It was actually just over nine weeks when, without any warning at all, that a strange young man appeared in an olive-green uniform outside the Russo residence at eleven o'clock in the evening, incessantly ringing the door bell, which thereupon had disturbed the entire household.

"Oh my God," Capricia's voice shrieked out, peering from the front dormer of her bedroom. "There's a white Chevy convertible parked in our driveway!"

"Stay out of my way and mind your own business!" Annie reprimanded, flinging open her bedroom door and bolting past her sister at the top of the staircase. And virtually cascading down the stairway onto the lower floor like a tidal wave from a broken dam, with her Chantilly robe aflutter behind her in the breeze, she appeared to have never even touched the ground.

Expeditiously, after flipping open the dead bolt atop the door knob with her left hand and opening the door with her right, she flung herself unreservedly against him with the force of a class five hurricane. Remarkably, however, the smartly dressed soldier stood his ground against all odds from being ravaged beyond recognition by the most fierce and furious onslaught of unrestrained passion in the annals of military history.

And I haven't even made Corporal yet, Bobby thought.

For the next two weeks, Bobby tried over and over again to martial his forces in defense of his military composure, only to be outflanked time and time again. Consequently, in the battlefield of love, it became mutually resolved that it was Annie who had the unequivocal and indefensible attack advantage, and that Bobby, in order to salvage what little integrity he had left, had little choice but to sue for peace by promising to take her to church. It was also stipulated that he do this in full-dress uniform as well.

"Before God and everyone?" Bobby cried out.

"Yes, that's it exactly, before God and everyone," Annie annunciated most clearly.

It was eleven o'clock on the following Sunday morning when Bobby kept his promise as the last of the gilded autumn leaves clung desperately to the hope of seeing another day. Annie couldn't have been more pleased with herself as together they passed through the impending ornate doors of the Saint James Catholic Church on that bleak November day. And although it may have been a dreary day outside, once inside, the couple was surely a radiant sight to be reckoned with.

Outfitted in his immaculately pressed army uniform, he presented Annie to its congregation in an emerald green ruched skirt with a ruffled hem which gently waved as she walked on by. A shimmering white-on-white, long sleeved pearl buttoned silk blouse revealed a small golden crucifix that ostentatiously glittered around her neck. Her stunning beauty had all but appeared to reverently beg for humility from underneath the white laced mantilla that she had pinned upon her crown, right down to her single buttoned matching pumps upon her feet.

If any sins were to be forgiven that day, then the entire church should have been given absolution for being guilty of empathetic hubris in every manner imaginable. Father Bernardino himself, in the church's announcements, made sure that he condescendingly thanked both Annie and Bobby for attending, in not wanting the message of the true nature of the church to be upstaged by his parishioners dwelling over the sins of the flesh.

And as the Bobby had kept his promise to take Annie to her church, so too was he going to keep his promise to his military commitment, for after he had finished rendering to God what was expected, his leave was ending and his obligation to the Caesars had become due. He still had the rest of the day, however, and afterward, without half as much angst as their last separation had produced, he began to say his goodbyes.

"It actually isn't so bad," Bobby told Annie late that afternoon, "I only have to go to Knoxville this time. After about six weeks of A.I.T. training, I'll be back again," he said good-naturedly, now accepting his training as a good thing. "After that, I'll be able to fix anything that moves, I suppose," he positively contended.

"I guess that's not so bad," Annie said evenly, knowing there wasn't a single thing she could do to change this still objectionable situation. *At least if I act somewhat pleasant this time, Bobby won't have to worry so much*, she thought, and so she did.

All seemed to be at peace with the universe now, as Bobby had been granted the peace to apply his efforts toward the one endeavor that he truly loved, second only to Annie. This time, his return to active duty had absolutely no melancholy affect whatsoever on their zeal for each other, for they had learned to cherish without passion, to love without lust, and accept upon faith that the true concept of love exists far beyond their corporeal desires.

Bobby's absence had now become accepted as a natural course of events, instead of an unavoidable catastrophe. Thus, the next six weeks drifted by fairly pleasantly, absent of the woe-be-gone despair which had been excruciatingly experienced the last time he was required to leave. Finally, when the end of January had eventually come around, and on one of its coldest and otherwise colorless Friday mornings, Bobby Taylor was again temporarily discharged from his duties.

Having completed his training, Bobby had been promoted to the rank of Specialist First Class for his outstanding performance in the field of mechanics, and although he was personally thrilled with his progress, he saw no purpose, other than one of self-aggrandizement, to vaunt his promotion before Annie, or anyone else, by mail *or* by phone. He did, however, notify everyone this time exactly when his arrival at the bus terminal would be.

Decisively, having commandeered her father's Cadillac, and with no one else's objection, Annie appointed herself with the responsibility of having to pick him up. Thus, armed with the instruction to be at the station at exactly one o'clock in the afternoon, she left early, intending to find a parking space that was precisely across from where Bobby's bus was assigned to stop.

It read exactly twelve fifty-five on the dashboard clock of the Cadillac when Annie had accomplished her goal, and in less than five minutes later, the bus rolled smoothly into the station. Then, as the coach's airbrakes squealed it to a stop in its lined-off space and the pneumatic doors discordantly screeched open to disgorge the beleaguered travelers out onto the awaiting pavement, a thankful silence fell about the terminal as the bus's mighty diesel engine had finally ceased to cantankerously belch out its noxious fumes.

Not possibly being able to ignore the imperious emerald green El Dorado that was parked opposite the bus stall, Bobby, duffel bag in hand, immediately bee-lined it over to where Annie had been patiently waiting. Also cognizant of the car's conspicuous presence, Annie did not feel that it was necessary to sound its horn at whatsoever, for she knew that soon enough, Bobby's wandering would be over, and her one and only soldier boy would report to her front and center to once again to resume his commission as her most cherished, and now altogether experienced, lover.

Chapter Seventeen

"Well, hello, my love," Bobby addressed Annie as he opened the passenger side of the car. Then, leaning the front seat over and tossing his duffel bag in the back, he wasted no time in getting in to immediately slide over on the car's plush leather seat and then halt, just short of contact, and ask with the grandest of smiles, "Ja miss me?"

"What do you think?" Annie rhetorically said, requiting him with a prolonged kiss in the conformation of her love. *Oh my, I still have to drive,* she suddenly reminded herself, breaking loose from the embrace. "Now, you sit there and behave," she smiled, admonishing him lightly for her own thoughts while turning on the ignition. "Do you want go somewhere to get something to eat first?" she considerately offered before taking the car out of park.

"Yeah, that sounds good," Bobby said amiably. "Why don't we go over and give old Dr. Fizz a visit? It's been a long time since we've stopped by his place. What do you say?" he proposed.

"Sure! Wait till he sees us in my dad's Cadillac," Annie responded, amused by the thought.

"A-ten-tion!" subsequently blared out from behind the soda fountain from where Dr. Fizz was standing upon the very instant Bobby followed Annie through the soda shop's door. "All hail to Major Cool!" the doctor continued, giving Bobby a gratuitous and unofficial salute.

"That's Corporal Cool, for all those too blind see my stripes," Bobby replied with a light censure. "You haven't changed your name from Dr. Fizz to Colonel Corn, did you?" Bobby then retorted with a grin as big as Texas while taking a seat with Annie at the counter.

"How's it goin' for you, kid? You sure look great. What's it gonna be? The usual? And are you goin' to introduce me to your woman, or what?" Dr. Fizz asked in a quizzical fashion, rather than responding to Bobby's obvious gibe.

And with the coolness of a gambler holding a pat hand, Bobby slowly replied as he figured the Duke of Drama would, "Yeah, you can say I'm doin' okay. And sure, I'll have the usual, —and this? This is my woman Annie," he stated casually. "And although she's kinda little, I still want you to know, she's still a dead shot," he clarified. "And right now, she's with me, pilgrim, just so you know," he proclaimed, his right thumb pointing against his chest.

"Whoa ho, you're good kid, very good. I almost think you're ready for an Oscar," announced Dr. Fizz, thereupon turning away to get their glassware. "That was coffee, right? And for you, it's a hot fudge sundae with all the stuff on it, isn't it Little Miss Oakley, ah, I mean Little Miss Annie?" he corrected, glancing back over his shoulder.

"Aw, I guess I will let you live, —this time, pardner. But don't let it slip again," remarked Annie, getting into the act with a smirk.

Then, as Annie more intently watched her confection being prepared, she noticed that her long-time friend seemed to be a little slower than his usual self. At first, she thought perhaps he just might be under the weather, but then, when he placed her sundae in front of her and she got a better chance to observe him closer, she realized that there wasn't anything wrong with him at all. He had just become an old man.

And after the doctor put down Bobby's soda in front of him, without the magical straw appearing, Annie almost began to feel sad. She also noticed that his face had now become sort of droll, less animated, and that his hands were beginning to reveal the truth of their age. Then, there were the age spots, which before she never noticed, either.

In silence for a moment, the vigilant patron stood as the obvious disparity of their ages brought to light the inevitable end of all things, as no longer were Annie and Bobby the children whom he had once entertained as such. They had become adults, right before his very eyes, and he an old man before theirs. It was in this quiet enjoyment now that they had all become truly respectful of each other as equal participants in the story of their lives together, without the levity.

"I want you to know I am very proud of you, Bobby," Mr. Finelli told him sincerely.

"Thank you, sir," Bobby answered without fanfare. "I want you to know the US Army doesn't have a clue on how to run a decent soda shop, sir, and probably never will," he offered kindly. "I think of you and this place every time I see their dessert selection, if you want to call it that," Bobby testified as he took a drink from his soda.

"And what about you, Miss Annie? How do you like workin' for your dad? I see he lets you drive the Caddy now," Mr. Finelli remarked.

"It's okay," Annie said plainly. "You know my dad. He's easy to get along with. You show up, do what you got to do, and then you go home. I never see the guys, except for on Fridays when they get paid, so it's just me and Mildred the Bookkeeper. I just can't wait until this whole Vietnam thing is over," she ended disdainfully, while Bobby just looked off away in the distance.

"I don't think anyone likes it, Annie," Mr. Finelli agreed.

It was then that the threesome began to hold their first conversation as true commensurates in the eyes of each other. They laughed and joked for over an hour as they reminisced over their past experiences, each from a different point of view, until the subject of their concerns again began to approach Bobby's current situation. And as the scent of melancholia had now began to tinge the air, an equal sense of impending stress had also become germane to Annie when, after taking notice of the Coca Cola wall clock behind the counter, she suddenly exclaimed, "Oh no, It's almost two o'clock. I've got to get my dad's car back."

"Well, I guess we have to go now," Bobby noted in a regretful tone, rising up with Annie to say their goodbyes.

"Well, Corporal, keep your head down and come back to us in one piece. You got that?" Mr. Finelli emphasized, while Bobby's took the offered hand from across the counter and shook it firmly.

"I intend to," Bobby expressly replied, laying a five-dollar bill on the counter and leaving to open the door for Annie, who had already passed by the juke box.

"See you later, Mr. Finelli," Annie cheerfully called back with a small wave of her hand.

It was the first time that Annie had called him by his surname in a very long time. And it was the first time that the professional fountaineer did not try to argue with Bobby over leaving a tip, either, —for all three of them had now accepted each other for their own independent statures.

"Why don't you drop me off at my house first?" Bobby suggested. "I need to check in with my mom, and then I need to check out the battery in my car. Is that okay with you?" he submitted politely.

"It's okay by me. I should to get back to work, anyway," Annie replied. "There is only one thing, though, —where are you going to take me tonight?" she asked, seductively biting the corner of her bottom lip and glancing in his direction.

"Well, since I don't get paid very much, I thought McDonald's would be good, or perhaps, if you want it your way, Burger King is okay, too, I guess," Bobby teased.

"I am going to pretend I didn't hear that," Annie countered as she tilted her head up and away from him.

"All right, I'll tell you, then. I made reservations at D'Agostino's," Bobby conceded. "So, listen," he expressly continued, "I am going to be wearing the uniform I have on now, so you might want to put on something nice, like that dress you had on at church the last time I was here," he proposed. "This is supposed to be a pretty fancy place, you know," he added.

"So, you like that dress?" Annie smiled coyly.

"Gimme a break, even Father Bernardino liked you in that dress, ha, ha, ha!" Bobby chuckled out loud. "That dress would be perfect for tonight," he certified as Annie pulled the Cadillac into the driveway at Bobby's house. "I'll see you tonight, then," he confirmed, leaning over to give her a gratuitous kiss. "I love you," he told her, "and I am so happy to be home," he sustained.

"I love you, too," Annie echoed. "And I don't want you to leave again, but I know you have to," she said sadly, pausing to stabilize her emotions while she chose her next words carefully. "So, what time do you want me tonight?" she asked leadingly with her eyebrows raised.

"Nineteen hundred hours will be fine. No later and no earlier. That means about seven o'clock to you civilians. You got it?" Bobby responded as he totally ignored the innuendo in her question.

"Yes sir, Mr. Army Man, your package will be ready for your inspection at exactly seven o'clock on the dot," Annie saluted mockingly from behind the steering wheel.

"Oh, I give up," Corporal Taylor commented, simply shaking his head and shutting the car door behind him.

~

"Whoa, it sure is cold out here," Bobby commented to himself, once arriving at side door of the Russo home at exactly seven o'clock that evening. Being expected, the door opened almost immediately, and as soon as it did, Annie grabbed him by the lapels of his coat, pulled him inside, and kissed him before he could utter another sound.

"Come on in. You have to say hello to my parents before we go," Annie insisted, taking him by the hand and hauling him off into the living room.

"Good evening, Mr. and Mrs. Russo," greeted Bobby formally.

"I heard you were back, Corporal. Congratulations on your promotion," Enrico applauded, rising from his easy chair to shake his hand.

"Thank you, Mr. Russo," Bobby respectfully replied. "They taught me how to fix a tank," he smiled congenially. "So, in case you want to buy one, sir, I'm all prepared," he joked.

"If it's got a track on it, I could probably use one," Enrico smiled as he sat back down in his chair again. "Enh, anyway, we can talk about that later," he dismissed, further adding "I don't want to hold you two up. Go out and have a good time at D'Agostinos. We'll see you again before you go," he sustained, fondly shooing them away with his right hand.

"It's nice to see you in your uniform again Bobby. It makes you look so handsome," Jolanda complimented.

"I think you're handsome, too!" Capricia yelled out from the top of the stairs.

"Thank you, Mrs. Russo," Bobby responded gracefully, now being tugged away by Annie while not responding to Capricia.

"You've got to find your own boyfriend, Cappy, —this one's taken!" Annie smartly called back in substantiating her claim.

Fortunately, the engine had remained warm enough to turn the heater on the moment the car had been restarted, for outside they could see their breath practically freeze in the air before them. Having next turned on the radio, Bobby reclined back and reached over with his left arm to embrace Annie, who had snuggled tight against him while waiting for the chill within the car to wear off. Finally, by the time the Beatles had figured out whether they were actually saying goodbye or saying hello, the white chariot had become well within their comfort zone and they were ready to go. Thus, after unwrapping his arm from around Annie, Bobby shifted the car into gear, slowly backed it out of the driveway, and off they went.

Bobby thoroughly expected the night to be a showcase of new experiences, but once arriving at their destination and walking with Annie from the side parking lot, he suddenly saw something that he never could have imagined. Directly outside the front entrance to the posh restaurant was a long red-fringed canopy and underneath it was vigilantly standing the most ornate uniformed doorman ever thought possible.

Apparently impervious to the bitter cold, the man was dressed in a full-length, immaculately white overcoat, which had been baroquely embroidered in a bright crimson red about its upper bodice and set off with a pair of forest green epaulets, trimmed in gold. Complete with a matching visored hat and wide red belt, there was no question that his charge was to specifically and most decorously greet the guests.

"Welcome to Poppa D'Agostinos. I trust your evening will be a pleasurable one," the doorman greeted in the smoothest of baritone voices, holding open the door for the two of them as they entered.

"May I take your coats, please?" a black and white uniformed woman then asked from behind a counter to their right of the waiting area.

Turning and facing the attendant, the couple took off their coats and placed them upon the counter. Reaching across the counter, the woman handed Bobby two numbered wooden chips and cordially said, "Thank you."

"You're welcome," replied Bobby, pocketing the chips and escorting Annie over to a lustrous mahogany podium that was guarding the formal entrance to the dining area.

"Welcome to D'Agostinos Ristorante Italiano. Do you have a reservation?" a tall, thin Maître'd petitioned as they approached.

Exhibiting a pencil thin moustache and dressed in a black-tie tuxedo, the shiny black-haired man reflecting the very essence of formality then paused, patiently awaiting Bobby's response.

"Yes, sir, Specialist Taylor, for two," Bobby replied in a mannerly fashion.

"Yes, Corporal, I see we have you right here," the Maître'd confirmed from the register lying open on the highly polished escritoire before him. "Right this way," he gestured with his right hand, leading the way over to the table which had been exclusively reserved.

"My name is Enzo," he announced, once Bobby and Annie had been seated. "If you should need anything at all, perhaps some special attention that I might be able to provide for you, please do not hesitate to ask your waiter to request me," he instructed. "His name is Romero, and he will be with you shortly. And here are your menus," he ceremoniously presented. "Signorina, e'esatto?" he politely asked in Italian, presenting Annie hers first and attentively pausing for her response.

"Yes," Annie confirmed, taking the menu from his hand.

"And Signore," he addressed Bobby in the same manner, thereafter bowing slightly and promptly taking his leave.

Bobby Taylor had no idea they had been seated in the "Sweetheart Booth." From their vantage point they could view the entire dining room, but did not realize that everyone else had an unfettered view of them as well.

The walls of the rococo styled dining room were decorated in a dark red, velveteen flocked wallpaper. Gold accents were everywhere, from the sparkling crystal chandeliers imperiously hanging from the ceiling, to the handles of the flatware that were uniformly displayed upon the tables.

The tables themselves were all topped in white linen. Crimson red, fanned cloth napkins were set atop the gold trimmed service plates, while a matching single red rose, center vased upon each and every table, had solicitously dominated all else. Every single chair, as well as all the booths, were upholstered in a wine-colored leather, rolled, pleated, and buttoned.

The cornered booth, to which they were assigned, sat the both of them next to each other with their backs to the wall and their table positioned before them. This way, the table's purpose was more than just something to eat off. It also served as a buffer between their personal solemnity and the rest of the patrons, as well.

Truly ornate, the little alcove was flanked by two six-foot privacy panels and secured at their front edges by a matching pair of eight-foot high, elaborately carved posts. These posts not only formidably sentried its entrance, but also doubled to support the overhead arched cornice, which circumscribed the entire booth. Also hanging from the center of the cornice was a set of white and gold trimmed wedding bells, awaiting to proclaim their purpose.

Completing its color scheme, the entirety of it all was painted in a lacquered, candy apple red, while the fascia of the cornice was affixed with a small troupe of golden cupids on either side of the celebratory bells. Finally, for to wholly encapsulate its guests, an intricate network of grape vines was intertwined over the top of the small gazebo. This provided a convenient resting place for a small flock of errant white doves, whose sole purpose was to deliver unto all who were situated beneath their domain the peaceful blessings of true love.

No longer than a minute or two passed by since the Maître'd left then a slight young man in a white jacket and red bow tie came over and filled the water glasses on the table. Another young man who had been dressed exactly as the other followed right behind him and placed an iced relish tray in its center, right in front of the vase with its single red rose, leaving without a word along with the first one.

"Boy, this is pretty fancy," said Bobby, picking up an olive from the glass tray.

"Yeah, my dad took everybody here once before, a long time ago," Annie said. "And, I know he still takes my mom here every now and then, too," she casually added.

"Would anyone here care for a cocktail before dinner?" requested another man, this time in a black tuxedo like the Maître d was wearing.

"You must be Romero, is that right?" questioned Bobby politely.

"Yes, exactly. My name is Romero and I will be your waiter for this evening," he confirmed in a pronounced Italian accent. "Now, would the Signorina or Signore care for a cocktail this evening before dinner?" he repeated.

"We're not old enough to drink, sir," Bobby replied in all honesty.

"I did not request your ages, Corporal, sir," he replied in the collective. "I only asked if the Signorina or Signore would care for a cocktail before dinner, that is all," was his simple reply, pausing a moment for Bobby to absorb his statement before once again asking, "So, would the Signore or the Signorina care to order a cocktail, or not?" the stocky waiter again pleasantly asked, with his eyebrows up and his pencil at the ready in the anticipation of an order.

"Well, what do you think, Annie?" Bobby asked with a devilish grin, attempting to put the weight of the decision upon her.

"Oh, whatever you think is best, sweetheart," replied Annie, submissively and quite deliberately dogging Bobby's attempt to ensnare her into accepting the responsibility for the latent consequences.

"Excuse me, Romero, that is right, isn't it?" asked Bobby respectfully, in not wanting to mispronounce the waiter's name.

"Yes, Signore, that is quite right," Romero answered factually.

"What would you recommend, if you were me?" Bobby asked, searching for some small degree of support in his effort to become sophisticated.

"A Singapore Sling is quite popular now, sir. It is made with a variety of fruit juices and a couple of different kinds of rum and is considered to be one of our more exotic libations. It even comes with a small umbrella and a straw," Romero enticingly disclosed. "Signore, I am *most sure* that the Signorina would enjoy one," he then smoothly proposed.

"Okay, Romero, we'll both have one of those," Bobby officiously decreed, this time without any consultation.

"Yes, Signore," Romero smartly replied, expeditiously leaving with his order.

"Yeah, this place is great all right," Bobby noted, now picking up his menu.

"I hope you brought enough money," Annie whispered surreptitiously, after noticing the prices on the menu.

"Sure, I brought enough. Get whatever you want. I expected this," Bobby whispered back assuredly.

"And here are your cocktails," Romero announced, placing the first one in front of Annie and the second in front of Bobby. "I shall be back momentarily while you enjoy your cocktails," apprised Romero, promptly leaving them to their own devices again.

"Oh yeah, this *is* a great place," Annie corroborated after tasting her drink.

"Yeah, and this thing is really good, too, isn't it?" Bobby remarked in absolute contentment.

"It sure is," Annie reemphasized, taking another sip from her straw. "Can I have your umbrella for Cappy?" she then asked.

"Heck no," Bobby replied abruptly. "Let her get her own boyfriend to get her one. This is mine, and I'm going to keep it. It's *my* souvenir," he said protectively.

"I just thought you might want to be nice," Annie cajoled.

"I am nice, but this is the only one I got. Besides, I want to keep it to remember *you* with," Bobby adamantly stated. "Unless you want me to take Cappy here the next time instead," he submitted flatly, briefly pausing with no remark from Annie. "Well, do you?" he specifically questioned.

"Naaahh, forget that idea," Annie dismissed with a casual wave of her hand. "Well, that was a pretty stupid idea, anyway, wasn't it?" she provocatively offered.

"I'm not going to answer that question," Bobby laughed, "I know your game," he self-assuredly proclaimed.

"Has the Corporal made his decision yet?" Romero now politely interjected from across the table.

"Not really," Bobby replied, "But since you gave us some good advice on the drinks, what do *you* think is good?" he asked.

"Well, Signore, I would start by having Enzo make you a Caesar Salad, which is a house specialty. Then I would follow it up with a Chateau Briand, complete for two, and then we can discuss the dessert later, Signore," Romero recommended efficiently.

"What the heck is all that? Because, I don't have any idea of what you just told me," Bobby truthfully admitted.

"Signore, a Caesar Salad is prepared for you at your tableside by Enzo. It is made from chilled romaine lettuce and tossed before you in a Caesar dressing, along with some fresh baked croutons and then topped with some grated Romano cheese," the waiter explained.

"Now, the Chateau Briand consists of a choice, center cut beef tenderloin for two, and is broiled to perfection according to your own personal taste," Romero continued. "Then it is carved tableside on an oaken platter by the Maître'd himself. It comes garnished with duchess potatoes and the Vegetable del Giorno, which today is asparagus with hollandaise or, if you prefer, a mixed medley of grilled roasted tomatoes and zucchini in a lemon basil butter sauce. I personally would recommend the second choice, Signore," he suggested in closing.

"I'm hungry already, Romero, I think we'll have that," Bobby established without hesitation. "That is, if that's what you want Annie?" he then asked considerately.

"That sounds good to me, only I want my meat done medium rare," Annie qualified.

"Good. That's okay by me too," Bobby confirmed. "Then it's settled, Romero, that's what we'll have," he finalized. "Oh, and there is one more thing," he brought up, "What are duchess potatoes?"

"They are twice baked potatoes, sir," Romero responded respectfully. "They take a baked potato and remove the insides, adding together some cream, eggs, butter and salt, whip up all the ingredients, and taking a pastry cloth they decorate the edges platter, browning them off in the oven. They are quite tasty and absolutely delicious, Signore," he certified.

"Now, one last thing, Signore," Romero gestured with his index finger in the air, "Do you or the Signorina desire an appetizer first?" he politely asked.

"I don't know," answered Bobby. "What do you think, Annie?" he asked politely.

"I want a shrimp cocktail," Annie answered without any hesitation.

"Okay, she would like a shrimp cocktail please, Mr. Romero," Bobby ordered compliantly, "And what else do you have?" Bobby further inquired with interest, while the waiter was writing down Annie's request on their guest check.

"We have fried calamari, which is fried squid served with our own tomato basil sauce. We have escargot baked in garlic butter. We have gazpacho, which is a tomato and vegetable soup served cold. We also…"

"Excuse me a minute, Romero," interrupted Bobby, as graciously as possible, "I think I'll just have the shrimp cocktail, too, okay?"

"That is fine, Signore, two 'Jumbo Shrimp Cocktails,' then," Romero acknowledged. "I will submit your order now, and return with your appetizers in un memento," he pronounced. "Oh, and one last thing, Signore," he said, "Did you want the asparagus or the roasted tomatoes and zucchini?" he asked.

"I want the tomatoes," Annie interjected.

"Sure, that's fine," Bobby confirmed.

"And, by the way, Signore, I forgot to ask, are your cocktails satisfactory?" Romero questioned hospitably, after making a final notation on their check.

"Are you kidding? They're great!" Annie burst out smiling, as her drink was obviously having an effect.

"I'm happy to see you are enjoying yourself, Signorina," Romero remarked, exiting their table.

Chapter Eighteen

"So, you're having a good time?" Bobby asked as he sipped on his drink in one hand and twizzled with his toy umbrella with his other.

"Just look at this place. It's like we're in our own little garden. It's so cool," Annie reflected.

"Well, I'm happy that you are happy, Annie, because you know I love you," Bobby doted.

"Oh, don't start that, you'll make me cry again. Let's just have some fun, okay?" Annie lightly pleaded.

"Sure, I can do that," Bobby said agreeably, noticing Romero on his way back with the shrimp cocktails balanced upon a small round tray.

"One for the Signorina and one for Ill Gentiluomo," Romero announced as he adeptly placed the appetizers before them. "Enjoy," he added succinctly, leaving without any further comment.

"Holy cow, look at the size of these shrimp!" Bobby remarked, picking one of them up by its tail from the glass supreme dish.

"You're supposed to use that little fork that's stuck into the lemon wedge, not your hands," counseled Annie quietly, "but that's okay, no one ever does," she then admitted candidly. "First, you take the lemon wedge off the fork and squirt the juice on them, and then you're supposed to dunk them into that red cocktail sauce in the middle, like this," she explained, adroitly demonstrating her dunking technique before munching one down.

"So that's it?" questioned Bobby.

"That's all there is to it," Annie repeated, picking up another. "Are you going to eat yours or just sit there and watch me eat mine?" she asked with a grin.

"No, I'm going to eat one, see," Bobby replied, and then he did. "Oh, these are good," he outright determined, "especially with that sauce."

"You mean you never had one before?" Annie inquired in wide eyed amazement.

"Nope," Bobby said shortly, "I saw what they looked like in the fish store, and that was enough for me. I guess they don't look so bad once they are all cleaned and cooked. And with that sauce, I have to admit, they really are good," he conceded.

As soon as they had finished their appetizers, one of the white jacketed young men came over and whisked away their empty supreme dishes, while the second bus boy wheeled over a small table sized wooden cart, and after placing it directly in front of the table, attentively remained.

On top of its left side sat a large wooden bowl, and directly to its right was placed a multitude of mysterious artifacts that were all but hidden under a brightly colored red and white gingham towel. Enzo, coming over, inspected the cart and said, "Grazie," dismissing the lad, while Romero once more returned, replacing the young assistant.

"Good evening again, Signore Taylor and Signorina. I see you have chosen one of our all-time favorites. I trust you are having an enjoyable time," spoke Enzo smoothly.

"We are having a great time, Mr. Enzo," Bobby assured him.

"Since I have prior knowledge that you have never had a Caesar salad before, courtesy of your waiter Romero," Enzo acknowledged with a slight nod in the waiter's direction, "I will explain its preparation as it is made."

Once the maître d' had removed the white and red checkered towel, not only were all the various preparatory accoutrements revealed, but to the cart's far right he had also uncovered a large crystal bowl cradling a white cheesecloth bundle, packed in crushed ice. Neatly centered towards the front of the cart, and directly to the right of the wooden bowl, were positioned a set of four matching curettes of various colored liquids, while behind them a half-dozen crucibles of all sorts of exotic ingredients were stationed at the ready. Finally, on a large white pressed linen napkin, and directly behind these various compounds, lay a whole set of cutlery and other various silver implements, methodically displayed in awaiting their intended purpose.

Gee, this guy must have gone to dental school, Bobby thought to himself in amusement when taking notice of the extensive array of utensils but decided to not make the comment.

Next, the Maître'd reached under the cart and placed upon its right-hand corner the largest peppermill ever known to be in existence and stopping for a minute to survey his assembly of accoutrements necessary to his trade, he then formally began his show.

"The first thing, now, is you take a pinch of chopped fresh garlic and put it into the bottom of the bowl, and then you take one of these large table spoons and mash the pieces with its back side, right into the wood itself, like so," Enzo demonstrated. "It is critical that you have an unfinished turned wooden bowl, and not a finished ply one, because the surface of the ply one is too slick, and the garlic pieces will only slide about each other, and not be 'pressed into service' as they need to be, with no disrespect to you, Corporal," Enzo commented, drawing a thin smile across his face, while briefly shifting his eyes to Bobby.

"None taken," Bobby smiled, quite entertained by Enzo's levity.

"Well, next," smiled Enzo in return, "you add a little virgin olive oil, mix it around like so, —and now the bowl is ready," he declared, momentarily tilting the bowl for their inspection. "Then, I take a couple of croutons, place them in the bowl, and to that I add three nicea fata anchovies, —just as they do in Italia, he animatedly continued.

"Now, you see, the unprofessional man tries to dice them up with a set of forks pressed against them but, in doing that, the little pieces can still be seen in the dressing. Then, what would happen sometimes is that the customer would say that he or she does not care for anchovies at all, and wants the entire dressing completely made over," he problematically explained.

"Well, if you don't have them in it, it is not a Caesar salad," Enzo stated definitively. "They not only provide the natural salt needed, but their oil contributes to the flavor and texture of the dressing," he maintained. "So, like I said, since a Caesar is not a Caesar without them, what are we going to do, I ask you?" he posed rhetorically. "To this, the answer is simple," he mildly stated. "You hide them, of course!" he smiled with a gesture from his right hand.

"Now, the first thing you do is to toss into the bowl a few of these little crispy croutons," he continued. "Then, I crush them against the anchovies with the back of my fork against the wooden bowl, like this," he skillfully exhibited. "The croutons will act like sandpaper and the mixture will now form a paste, so 'Aha,' —there are no small pieces of anchovy to be seen in the dressing!" he proudly displayed, again turning the bowl towards them to see the blended mixture.

"Next, you add a small amount vinegar, a pinch of English mustard, a dash or two of Worchester sauce, some nicea olive oil, from It-aly of course, and now comes a fresha squeeze of lemon," he ceremoniously announced with a casual glance to Romero.

And as Romero mysteriously took his leave, Enzo then picked up a whole lemon from one of the crucibles and began to roll it hard across a small cutting board next to the tray of accessories.

"Now, I am going to cut the lemon in half," declared Enzo, "save half over here, and then wrap the second half here in this piece of cheese cloth. You then twist the back of the cloth closed, and now when I squeeze it, look at all the juice," he commented, "and with no seeds in the dressing, either," he established with a broad smile.

Romero, now swiftly returning with a single egg in a white ceramic cup of steaming water on his tray, stealthily placed it on the wooden cutting board precisely next to where Enzo was mixing his concoction. Then, picking up the spent lemon rind, along with its discarded other half, he deposited them both underneath the back of the cart, and once again retreated in silence.

"Most places introduce a completely raw egg into the dressing, while *we,* however, prefer to ever so slightly coddle the egg first," Enzo resumed. "This procedure allows the dressing to congeal and will allow it to adhere better to the romaine lettuce for a superior result," he additionally explained, putting down the two forks.

"Now I will take out the egg, dry it off with the towel so it doesn't slip from my hand, crack it lightly on the cutting board, and then add it to the rest of the ingredients," he seamlessly continued. "So, now we need to add a little more virgin olive oil, a dash of red wine, and a dash of white, — for vigah, as President Kennedy liked to say, —and now we are finally ready to mix it all together," he proudly declared.

Picking up another silver fork with his right hand and holding the wooden bowl askance off the table with his left, Enzo then proceeded to briskly stir the mixture together. Lastly, upon reaching satisfaction with the viscosity of the dressing, he placed the bowl upright and reached over to the glass bowl to his right. Flipping the ice packed cloth upside-down, so that the ice fell to the bottom of the bowl, he thereupon unwrapped it from the top, and with a pair of silver tongs, removed the romaine lettuce, gingerly placing it in the wooden bowl.

Romero, who had now returned, methodically picked up the emptied glass bowl and spent towel, deposited them under the cart and replaced them with place a pair of chilled salad plates brought back from the kitchen, once again to withdraw to his standing position.

"Now, we can complete the tossing of the salad," stated Enzo. "First, we must turn it over gently in the dressing a few times, being careful not to break its delicate structure that keeps it crisp, while allowing the mixture to cling to the lettuce evenly throughout the salad," he demonstrated with a pair of matching wooden utensils. "Then, we add the croutons, sprinkle everything with a mixture of freshly grated and Romano and Parmigiano cheeses, give the salad another toss or two, and finally, voila! —we now have our famous Caesar salad," he eminently displayed, tilting the bowl for his customer's inspection.

"Very nice," complemented Bobby.

And upon being approved, the Maître'd proceeded to apportion the salad atop the two chilled plates, sprinkled them once again with some additional grated cheese, and gracefully moved away from the cart.

"Romero, Sir," addressed Enzo, yielding to the attentive waiter.

Without a response, the waiter slightly bowed, picked up the plates and placed them in front of the guests. Finally, with no further ado, Enzo himself, slightly bowed in respect to his guests, politely wished them "buon appetito," and tout de suite, left to reattend his station by the podium.

Romero, after fetching the monster pepper mill from the corner of the cart, had come back to the side of the table to vigilantly stand there in silence, like a nut cracker with scepter in hand, awaiting his guests' attention while they intimately reviewed their creations.

"Would Signorina or Signore care for some fresh pepper on their Caesars?" Romero eventually solicited in a stately manner.

"I'd love some," Annie replied.

And, as requested, the dutiful waiter reached over the table with the business end of the pepper mill, and from where he was standing, twisted its top of it a few times.

"Is that sufficient, Signorina?" Romero asked.

"Yes, that's fine," replied Annie.

"And you Signore?" Romero further questioned.

"Sure Romero, I'll try some," Bobby told him eagerly.

"Is that sufficient?" Romero asked again, following a few more twists.

"Yeah, that's good," Bobby accepted.

"Then, buon appetito," Romero concluded, turning to attend to the cart.

Finally, after putting the gargantuan peppermill back under the cart and checking to see that all was accounted for and in good order, Romero again raised his index finger into the air and, in two shakes of a lamb's tail, the fellow who had first brought the cart to their tableside came over from the across room and expediently took it away. Thereafter, the waiter turned back to face the table, courteously bowed in silence, and summarily left the two lovers alone.

"You know, this food is really good," Bobby expressed after having tasted his salad. "I used to think that coming to a place like this was just a lot of boloney, but it's not. This food is really great, and I don't know of anyone that could make this stuff at home," he openly admitted, continuing to ravenously attack his salad.

"It's actually more than that," Annie began to expound. "A lot of people waste their money by eating a bunch of crap out all the time. And like you said, most of the stuff that everyone buys out you could make at home, and it would be better for them, too, —but they're just lazy, that's all. If they simply saved all that money they threw out on the street by eating that ridiculous fast food junk, they could afford to eat here a couple of times a year and have a great experience that they would always remember, like we're having now," she justified.

"I have to say Annie, that you are one hundred percent right," Bobby agreed after putting down his fork, having finished his salad to the last. "And you know, if only you weren't such chatterbox tonight, you might have time to eat your salad, too," he poked at her in amusement.

"And, if you only read more, you would know more about manners as well," retorted Annie.

"What do you mean by that?" asked Bobby indignantly.

"Well, for instance, when you are done eating, you don't put your used fork back on the clean table cloth. You place it upside down in the middle of your plate. That way the waiter will know that you are finished, even if there is something left. Watch," Annie instructed, putting her fork upside down on her plate and reposing in her seat.

Then, faster than a disappearing cannoli, one of the white jacketed men popped up out of nowhere, and with hardly a sound, *whoosh,* the plates were gone. His partner then also abruptly appeared, refilled their water glasses, and with the sole exception of the ice cubes clinking, unobtrusively disappeared like the other.

"Well, do I have to say you're right again!" exclaimed Bobby with a soft smile, "but you can't tell me that you learned all that in a book," he appended.

"No, I didn't," admitted Annie. "I learned it from Manners the Butler, you know, that little Kleenex guy who always picks up your napkin off the floor," she commented smartly.

"Yeah, sure," Bobby acknowledged in amusement.

"I understand you ordered the Chateau Briand, Signore?" Enzo cordially cut in with a congenial smile, reestablishing himself before their table.

"Yes sir," answered Bobby, endorsing his choice without hesitation.

Again, with that single finger in the air, the cart from the kitchen reappeared, along with Romero in close persuit.

"Sir," Romero simply addressed the Maître'd, turning to face Bobby and Annie to formally acknowledge, "Signore Taylor and Signorina."

This time on the cart was the largest silver domed cover Bobby had ever seen, and beside it sat an organized set of cutlery, serving utensils, and two white and gold trimmed plates. Then, as both Enzo and Romero took their usual positions next to each other behind the cart, Romero briskly lifted the dome straight up and readily whisked it away, revealing the 'Piece de Resistance' of the entire restaurant. Enzo, now centering himself at the back of the cart, picked up the heavy oaken board on which the culinary display was set, and tilted it carefully toward his guests to inspect.

"Does the Chateau Briand meet with your approval?" requested Enzo professionally.

"The Corporal Specialist and the Signorina believe it to be a work of art, Enzo," Bobby replied, grinning at Annie and thinking, *I believe I'm really beginning to get the hang of this, and I'll be darned, it's pretty cool!*

Placing the platter back down, Enzo picked up a set of serving implements and removed the duchess potatoes from the sides of the board and deftly placed them on the side of their plates. Then, after picking up a large black handled knife and giving it a few short strokes on a sharpening steel to hone its edge, he was ready to carve.

"The original Chateau Briand was made from a piece of center cut choice sirloin," Enzo began explaining, while proceeding to slice the beef into thin medallions and alternately place them upon the center of their plates. "It was later substituted with a single strip of center cut tenderloin, sacrificing the succulence of the sirloin, for the tenderness of the tenderloin. We here at D'Agostino's Ristorante Italiano have skewered the two meats together before broiling to ensure that you will receive both the maximum succulence of the beef alongside its exceptional tenderness as well," he explained with pride, laying aside the carving knife and fork.

Next, after portioning the medley of colorful vegetables onto their plates and opposite the duchess potatoes, Enzo picked up a small silver gravy boat and zig-zagged the top of succulent beef with a translucent demi-glaze.

"This is the house's special dressing, prepared especially for the Chateau Briand," Enzo further expounded, coming to the end of his presentation while making a final perusal of the plates before him. "And now, I will leave you two to enjoy your meals, —and so, buon appetito," he courteously tendered, relinquishing his position once again to Romero, who had returned as inconspicuously as he had left.

Removing the two platters from the cart, Romero placed them directly in front of his guests and stepped back with a small respectful bow, allowing the two young assistants, who had also appeared when Romero had returned, to remove the relish tray and replace it with a cloth covered wire basket of hot rolls and a crystal butter dish that had been sprinkled with ice chips. Then, as efficiently as they had appeared, the two assistants whisked the cart away and dissolved into the now bustling commotion of the room.

Left to attend the diners alone, Romero picked up the silver-wired bread basket placed on the table, pulled back its cloth covering, revealing its variegated assortment of rolls, and after subsequently showcasing them for his guests' approval, formally asked, "Would Signorina care for a hot garlic bread stick, or perhaps a Parker House roll?"

"Yes, I would," answered Annie, taking out a long fresh garlic stick from the basket and placing it gingerly upon her bread and butter plate.

"And you, sir?" Romero questioned, offering the same to Bobby.

"Yeah, I'll have one of those, too," Bobby responded pleasantly, taking out a Parker House roll for himself.

Putting the basket back down upon the table, Romero then studiously surveyed the entirety of the fare for anything that he might have missed, and being completely satisfied that all was in order, saluted, "Signorina, Signore," and with his usual bow, courteously left them to the privacy of their own proclivities.

"I have to tell you, these people really know what they're doing," Bobby remarked, picking up his dinner fork.

"I told you it was worth it," Annie reinforced. "Can you actually imagine never having an experience like this, just because you spent all your money every day at Burger King? You know, —where you wanted to take me in the first place?" she taunted.

"I can still take you there if you want," Bobby proposed in an accommodating tone.

"No, I think I'll pass this time," Annie affably declined.

"Well, I can tell you, *I'm* having the best time of my life, —and that's for sure" Bobby testified in changing the whole tone of the conversation. "And it's all because of you," he affectionately confessed, to then smoothly lean over and give Annie a small peck upon her cheek. "You know I love you," he whispered, instantly draining her frivolity.

"Enough of that now, or I won't be able to eat," Annie fetchingly appealed. "Let's enjoy our meals first. There will be plenty of time for that later," she proposed, customarily patting his leg.

Finally, after Bobby had consumed the last morsel known to ever have existed upon his plate, and after having retired his fork upside down along with his knife, as previously instructed, he comfortably reclined back to victoriously declare, "Well, *I'm* finished."

"Well, I'm not," Annie responded, even though she had little left.

And so, while Bobby was considerately waiting until Annie was completely finished her meal, suddenly he came to the bright conclusion that "now" was the best time to make his next move.

"You know, I think I'll get out that little gift I have for you, —that is, if I remembered to bring it with me," Bobby teased, while unbuttoning the top left pocket on his shirt.

"You have a gift for me?" exclaimed Annie in a muted tone.

"Well, I don't know if it is a gift or not, but it's something that I thought you might like," Bobby presumed.

"Well, what is it?" asked Annie anxiously.

"Now, just hold on a minute, are you sure done eating? Bobby questioned explicitly.

"Oh yes, I'm all done," Annie replied, squirming about in her seat.

"I don't think so," said Bobby in doubt, smiling smugly.

"What do you mean? I'm all finished," Annie expressly declared.

"Well, I don't see your fork turned over on your plate," he replied like a teacher in a third grade-class.

"Oh, you jerk!" Annie burst out, playfully slapping him on the shoulder.

"I don't know, what's a gentleman to do now?" Bobby questioned, looking up and away to an imaginary spirit with his arms crossed.

"Well, you better give me my present now, or I'll, —I'll, cry on you right now, —right here in front of everyone," Annie pouted.

"Well, we just can't have that now, can we, little lady?" Bobby responded in his John Wayne fallback position.

"No, we can't!" Annie feistily responded.

"Okay then, if you just sit back for a moment, I'll give it to you," Bobby agreeably capitulated with a smile. "I got this from one of the guys in my platoon. He wrote it himself," Bobby testified, reaching into his unbuttoned pocket and taking out a small folded piece of paper. "He took all those extra English classes in school, like you did, and he wrote this poem. He said it's about the draft, but I don't get the connection. To me it's more like something Bob Dylan wrote than anything else," he admitted while holding it out.

"Just give it to me, soldier," rambunctiously ordered Annie, snatching it from his hand. "So, you brought me some poetry, huh?" she now said affectionately. "Why, how sweet of you," she chirped, starting to unfold her present.

"I don't think you understand," Bobby cautioned, "It's not all that lovey-dovey stuff, —just so you know," he reinforced.

"I don't care. Poetry is poetry. I love poetry," she responded gratefully. "So, let's see," she began,

Rewards

The summer's heat was in full force
As Caesar's August took its course
Upon the weak and old

But for the strong and young at heart
The summertime is best to start
The conquest of their souls

Like pocket watches made of gold
Allegiances are cheaply sold
With aspirations to behold

How can a mind be so controlled
To make a man to be so bold
To give his life to fit the mold
Of a greedy politician's goal

When shiny medals are so cold?

Chapter Nineteen

"Boy, this guy is heavy," Annie said, after putting down the poem.

"I told you, it isn't all that lovey-dovey stuff," Bobby reemphasized in observing her reaction.

"Still, I think it's beautiful," Annie commented. "No one ever gave me a poem before," she added. "Anyway, I like it," she validated gratefully. "Can I keep it, is it mine?" she humbly asked, looking at him directly.

"Sure, it's for you. The guy gave it to me, and now I'm giving it you," Bobby verified.

"Why thank you," Annie said graciously kissing him upon the cheek and putting the poem into her purse. "I have to go to the little girl's room now," she then noticed, while clutching onto her purse and sliding out from her side of the table. "You should escort me and then wait for me to come out," she whispered back across the table, apprising him of his expected duty.

"Okay, okay, no problem," he delicately consented, getting up from the table, thinking it would be the perfect opportunity for him to get a complete tour of the rest of the place.

After exiting under a large archway towards the back of the room, Bobby noticed that the restaurant was a lot larger than he had imagined. Once past the arch, they subsequently found themselves in a small room which served as an antechamber to another three archways.

"The room over there," Annie nodded to her left "is where they have their weddings. The doorway over there," she gestured to her right, "goes back to the kitchen, but we're going straight ahead," she said, leading him straight through the arch under a baroque sign that read "Restrooms and Lounge."

"I *can* read, Annie," Bobby replied with a small smile, demonstratively raising his eyebrows.

While Bobby's intention was to simply take Annie down an access corridor and wait for her outside the bathroom door, once passing through archway at the back of the room, he was astonished to see, however, not just a hallway with a couple of doors, but what appeared to him to be a spacious living room, entirely filled with a multitude of leather upholstered chairs and couches, all with their corresponding end and coffee tables bedecked with a variety of ashtrays for the convenience of the smokers. Lastly, one could not ignore the opulent crystal chandelier centered in the room, whose warm reflections gave off a pensive touch to the legion of Renaissance paintings which were tastefully displayed upon the walls for the perusal of the guests.

Copies, naturally, but oils just the same, there was the Primavera by Botticelli, Raphael's Madonna and Child, Leonardo da Vinci's Last Supper and Mona Lisa, and even a large reproduction of The Creation of Adam on the ceiling of the Sistine Chapel by Michelangelo. There was even an exact replica of Donatello's sculpture of David, displayed in a corner alcove of the room.

"This doesn't look like a bathroom to me," Bobby leaned over and said to Annie, "it's more like a museum."

"This is a sitting room. It's where you're supposed to wait for me," she clarified. "The woman's room is over there to the left," she noted with a slight nod, "and the men's room is over there to the right," she additionally gestured.

"Well, I'll be right here when you get back," Bobby assured, releasing her from his arm to go on by himself to the men's room.

It was to no surprise that Bobby, when returning to the waiting room, did not see Annie anywhere, and so, quite amiably, he decided to find the most comfortable chair in the room and simply sit down relax. It was then, once ensconced in the respectful repose of the moment, that he took the time to appreciate the obvious purpose of the room.

"Yes sir, this is surely a swanky place, all right," Bobby said to himself, while looking about after further reclining in the over-stuffed chair. *"You know, I wonder how long it will be before I ever get back here?"* he questioned to himself. *"Well, I guess it's gonna be some time, anyway, so, —oh what the hell, why bother thinking about it,"* he summarily dismissed. *"Humm, I wonder how much longer she'll be?"* he then further mused, languishing into oblivion before the Renaissance masters of antiquity.

"Well, are you going to walk me back to the table, or are you just going to sleep right there?" Annie both questioned and challenged at the same time.

"Oh, there you are," replied Bobby, collecting himself a moment before getting up. "You know, they got some guy in a tux, —right there in the bathroom, who offers you a fresh towel, —and he has all sorts of cologne too, if you want," he disclosed to Annie, retaking her arm.

"That's the bathroom attendant. You're supposed to tip him," Annie mumbled under her breath.

"Yeah, I figured that, because he had a big glass on the counter that was half stuffed with money, so I tossed in a buck, but I didn't want any of his cologne," he added. "And that was only because I am so sweet smelling now, that I didn't want you to pass out on me," he chuckled.

"Oh, don't worry about that, I can take it all right," Annie assured him with a smirk.

Happy and well fed, the two lovers now began to feel a little more at ease, and thus began to pay attention to the many other goings on about them.

"You see? The fork thing worked again. The plates are all gone," Annie lightly noted in vindication, after they both had repositioned themselves at their place settings.

"They sure are," recognized Bobby. "And look over there, that looks like some guy with a violin," he spoke out in fascination, pointing across the room.

"Yes, Signore, he will begin to play for us in a moment," Romero informed them as he cordially interrupted their rapport. "Would the Signore or the Signora care for some coffee?" he then asked, running across the table a small hand-held device, which magically removed any of the occasional bread crumbs that may have gone errant.

"Yes, I would," answered Bobby, "definitely."

"And Signorina?" Romero acknowledged.

"Oh, yes. I would like a demitasse, please," Annie ordered.

"Right away," Romero responded cordially as he put the devise back into his jacket pocket and left.

"What is a demitasse?" candidly inquired Bobby.

"A small cup of coffee," responded Annie smartly, with a little smile of "advantage hers" upon her face. "It's served in a pretty dainty cup, for pretty dainty girls, just like me," she colorfully correlated for his amusement.

"Yeah, I can see that," smiled Bobby agreeably. "And Corporal Cool prefers this 'dainty pretty girl' to all the other "dainty little girls," —just so you know," he responded in kind for "advantage his."

"The demitasse for the Signorina," Romero expeditiously then announced, proceeding to put down the now famous "small and dainty" flowered cup, along with an equally "small and dainty" tea spoon directly in front of Annie.

"And a regular coffee for the Signore," he continued, placing a gold trimmed saucer and cup down before Bobby. "Does the Signorina and Signore care to hear the dessert choices?" he cordially solicited after adding to the table a small creamer and matching sugar bowl, beginning to pour their coffee.

"Yes, we do," replied Bobby.

"We have Cherries Jubilee, Bananas Foster, Crepe Suzettes, Peach Melba, and Baked Alaska," Romero recited systematically, finally appending, "and of course, I can return with the pastry gueridon, if you like."

"What is a pastry gueridon?" questioned Bobby.

"A Geneva Gueridon is the proper name for the wheeled carts we have been using to present and prepare our more exotic foods for you," explained Romero. "The particular gueridon I am talking about now, displays our pastry selection. We have Cannoli, Neapolitans, and Boconnotti, — that sort of selection Signore," he informatively answered, assuming Bobby understood itemized examples.

"Oh, I see," Bobby vaguely acknowledged. "What do you think, Annie?" he asked.

"What is a Peach Melba?" Annie inquired.

"It is a peach, poached in a sugary syrup, cut in half, with a scoop of natural vanilla ice cream on top, and covered with a melba raspberry sauce," Romero factually replied. "Then, it topped off with some fresh whipped cream, almond slices, and finally finessed with a touch of Amaretto. It is quite a favorite with the ladies, Signorina," he enticingly proffered.

"Do you want one?" Bobby asked.

"Sure! It sounds fantabulous," declared Annie.

"Okay, Mr. Romero, we'll both have that," said Bobby.

"Well, sir, since we have become rather busy in the last half hour, I'm afraid that it will be a few extra moments before Enzo will be free," Romero graciously disclosed.

"That's okay," Bobby responded agreeably.

"Then, Signore, I will make sure the bus boys will keep your coffees filled," Romero courtly confirmed, slightly bowing before leaving them once more in seclusion.

"I always wondered how people could take hours just to eat a meal when they went out," Bobby admitted frankly, in picking up the conversation.

"That's why it costs the money. It's not just a meal, like I've been saying all along, it's the whole experience," Annie reiterated expressly. "So, are we having fun yet?" she then taunted, playfully poking him in the side.

"Lean over here for a minute," Bobby mysteriously replied. "I want to tell you a secret."

And the very moment she complied, Bobby quickly pulled Annie closer, kissing her full on the lips until he felt her respond. Once she had, he quite abruptly broke off the wistful embrace, just as quickly as it was initiated.

"Now, are we having fun yet? You tell me," challenged Bobby with a grin.

Before Annie could utter a word, a short and colorful man, dressed like a wandering gypsy with a bright red bandana on his head, and a large gold earring dangling from his right ear, abruptly popped his head into their alcove. He pleasantly asked, while gesturing out with his violin, "Have you any requests, Signore?"

Snapping back to an upright position from his preoccupation with Annie's attentions, Bobby paused for a second, looked off into the air for a moment, stroked his chin in thought and then proposed, "You wouldn't know, 'Bird on a Hill' by the Beatles, would you?" he asked, not believing in his wildest dreams that the little gypsy with the goatee would have even heard of it.

"So, Signore, you say this song of yours was made by, eh, bugs?" the entertainer asked politely.

"Oh, no, no, no," replied Bobby in all sincerity. "The Beatles sang it. They're a rock and roll group. They're not bugs," he amusedly informed the slight man.

"Oh, not bugs, huh?" the gypsy responded, scratching his head for a moment. "Hum, let me see what I can do," the violinist pressed on, standing back from the table, while putting the fiddle to his shoulder and softly beginning the ballad:

"There were bells on a hill
But I never heard them ringing
No I never heard them at all
Till there was you

There were birds in the sky
But I never saw them winging
No I never saw them at all
Till there was you

Then there was music and wonderful roses
They tell me in sweet fragrant meadows of dawn and dew

There was love all around
But I never heard it singing
No I never heard it at all
Till there was you

Then there was music and wonderful roses
They tell me in sweet fragrant meadows of dawn and dew

There was love all around
But I never heard it singing
No, I never heard it at all
Till there was you

Till there was you"

Instantly, the couple was mesmerized, for their senses had come to a complete and unconditional halt unto one of the most perfect instruments in the world, the violin. The resonance elicited by the violinist's dulcet tones transcended their souls unto the spirit of the muses themselves. In perfect tenor, the tender ballad was pitched into the fray as the last vestiges of a doubtful love were swept away in a tidal wave of passion. Anointed before God and everyone, by the time the virtuoso had finished, the very concept of true rapture had been sanctified before all who were in attendance that evening.

Thereupon, following the precise second to which the performance had ended, a complete and utter silence befell the room, while every eye and every spirit in the house had become committed to their cause. Love was truly all around, and in the very moment that the strolling minstrel had concluded the ballad, there wasn't a single person in the house who did not applaud. It was a moment for all to remember as the colorful gypsy respectfully stood aside, formally presenting the loving couple to the houseful of guests, while courteously taking no bow.

Finally, by the time the thunderous applause dissolved away into the evening, and the slight statured musician had wandered off to vindicate his purpose once more, there was no doubt left within the souls of both Annie and Bobby that a single violinist could have the power to move world. And as the audience's interest in the two lovers also began to dissolve in favor of their own pleasures, the intimacy that had been put aside during the public performance before them had now returned with a vengeance.

"Boy, that was amazing," Bobby proclaimed, reclining back into the seclusion of the booth. "It really blew me away. You could really feel the vibrations from the violin going right through you," he testified.

"It made the hair on my arm stand up," Annie said in wonderment, while also reclining back to once again lean lovingly against her beau.

"I presume you enjoyed Aldo, our gypsy violinist, Signore Taylor?" Enzo asked smoothly, presenting himself in tandem with Romero again.

"Mr. Enzo, he was really great, sir," Bobby pronounced categorically.

"Are you and the Signorina ready for dessert, then?" Enzo inquired.

"Yes, sir, all ready," Bobby answered directly. "Are you ready, Annie?" he attentively asked.

"I'm ready if you're ready," declared Annie, while both their attentions turned to being served a new performance.

Once again, like clockwork, as Enzo merely raised his finger, the gueridon was heralded into place. This time, however, on one side of the gueridon was a highly polished brass and copper chafing stand, while directly on top of it sat a large flat-bottomed frying pan, also clad in copper.

On a tray next to the chaffing dish, and situated towards the front of the cart, again was placed a full set of colored curettes and crucibles containing all the ingredients that were considered necessary to accomplish the task. Directly next to the chaffing stand, lay the utensils. Differently on the cart this time, however, there were three distinctive bottles of liquor, and next to them a pair of cut glass supreme bowls, all patiently waiting to be put in service.

Romero, after removing the frying pan from atop the chafing stand, stood back a moment while Enzo took out a long wooden match and lit the Sterno can beneath, replacing the pan for the Maître'd to begin his new show.

"The first thing is to put a generous amount of butter into the pan," established Enzo. "Then, after the butter is melted, you add the fresh peach halves and let them slowly simmer, while adding in the sugar. Next, as the mixture slowly becomes caramelized right before you, we add a dash of pure vanilla, a pinch of nutmeg, and a hint of ginger," he articulated, thereafter tilting the pan slightly with one hand and ladling the mixture over the peaches with his other.

"Now that the peaches have been poached sufficiently, so that they are tender, yet firm, we will make it all come together like so," he continued, discharging the ladle in favor of one of the exotic liquor bottles that had been positioned to his right.

Steading the pan with his left hand, Enzo then rained down an even stream one-fifty-one rum across the peaches, causing it to sizzle across the surface of the mixture. Next, after withdrawing the bottle, while simultaneously tilting the pan slightly to its side, —*whoosh*, the cloud of steam which was emanating from the pan suddenly burst into flames.

"This process is called a reduction," explained Enzo, retaking the ladle in hand. "The alcohol itself actually burns off, but it causes the sauce to come together in a nice sugary gravy that will cling to the peaches better," he explained, stirring the mixture until all the flames had died out.

"Now, I will place the peaches into the supreme dishes with the halved side up, and after pouring the caramelized mixture over the top of them, I will begin to address the Melba sauce," he declared, thereafter standing back for Romero to pick up the used pan and associated utensils, promptly to return them to the kitchen. Next, after replacing the pan with yet another from under the cart, the Maître'd again resumed his performance.

"And now, moving on," Enzo thinly smiled, "I shall make the Melba sauce. First, we introduce some butter to the pan, so the fruit doesn't stick, and while it begins to melt, I will crush the fresh raspberries in this mortar with a pestle like this," he began to demonstrate. "Then, after making sure they have been thoroughly mashed, I pour them into the pan and add an ample amount of sugar, like so, —while all the time stirring the mixture until it begins to boil," he stressed. "Now, as the rolling boil begins to crackle, I am going to sprinkle in some powdered arrowroot to help thicken the mixture, and next we will amplify its attitude with a little Cherry Herring, thereby complementing the fruity goodness of the berries," he touted, pouring in the full-bodied liqueur with all the finesse of a maestro conducting the Overture of 1812.

Once more returning from the kitchen with his tray, Romero brought with him a small crystal bowl of freshly whipped cream, along with a second bowl containing two snowball-sized portions of vanilla ice cream. Subsequently, and as unobtrusively as possible, after having placed the bowls upon the cart, he picked up a set of silver tongs, removed the two ice cream balls, one by one, and put each atop the hollow of the awaiting peach halves. Finished with this task, the waiter deposited the empty bowl under the cart and once again stood back as Enzo unabatedly continued.

"And as we shall see, if poured slowly, the sauce will harden and encase the ice cream in a most delightful shell," Enzo successfully established, hastefully replacing the pan atop the chafing stand and extinguishing the Sterno. "Now, we add a most generous amount of whipped cream, top that with a few sliced almonds, add a little accent of Amaretto, —and magnifico!" he theatrically declared, holding out his hands in finality.

Romero, reaching over to the cart while Enzo had stepped aside, picked up the two desserts, one at a time, and after placing them carefully upon a pair white snowflake doilies atop their gold trimmed plates, delivered them forthwith to his patrons. Bobby was so impressed with the art work in front of him that it took a goodly three minutes before he realized that Romero was now by himself, with the Maître'd nowhere to be seen.

"Huh, I guess Enzo had another dessert to make," Bobby noted in looking around. "You know, that guy is harder to thank than the Lone Ranger," he grinned in a boyish manner towards Annie.

"Is everything satisfactory, Signore?" Romero asked.

"Everything is okay by me," Bobby replied.

"Me, too," Annie concurred.

"Then, enjoy your desserts, and I shall be back momentarily," Romero imparted politely in retreat.

"You know, every time you think you've eaten the best thing that you can possibly eat, that Enzo guy comes along and tells you about something else that's even better. I wonder how long it would take for somebody to actually eat everything they could make in this place?" Bobby wondered out loud.

"Your ice cream is melting," Annie reminded him. "And, it isn't going to eat itself," she goaded him playfully.

"Okay, okay," Bobby answered compliantly, picking up his dessert spoon.

It did not take even five minutes for Bobby to completely ravish his dessert when, to no surprise, Romero reappeared with his bar tray in hand once more.

"This is Liquore Galliano, a most interesting after dinner cordial from Italia," he announced, proudly presenting his guests with a petite pair of footed glasses which had been filled with the shimmering golden libation. "Please accept these as a token of our appreciation for dining here this evening at D'Agostino's Ristorante Italiano," he proffered. Then, without further repartee, he placed the two ponies of the salubrious digestives before them.

"Thank you, Romero," Bobby politely acknowledged.

"And I want you to know that everything was just perfect," complemented Annie, as Romero cordially nodded again in silent acceptance and left.

"What an evening," Bobby proclaimed, after finishing his after-dinner drink. "What about you? You've gotten awfully quiet, suddenly," Bobby remarked.

"Oh, I'm as happy as I can possibly be, my little soldier boy," Annie serenely mused while reclining back in total complacency.

"Well, I'm finished too," Bobby also sustained. "So, I guess we better get up now and give someone else a chance," he courteously suggested.

"Yeah, I guess it's time to go," Annie agreed with a small sigh, struggling a bit to slide over and out of the booth.

"Excuse me, Romero?" Bobby hailed from the corner of the booth, as soon as he had gotten up.

"How can I be of assistance, Signore Taylor?" Romero said as he approached from two tables over.

"Can I have the check, please? We are ready to go," Bobby announced.

"Oh, no Signore, you are on account with us. It will be billed like always," Romero respectfully affirmed.

"But, I don't have an account," Bobby straightforwardly declared.

"Signore, your evening has already been charged to the Russo Paving Company, —by the wishes of Signore Russo himself. I cannot change that," Romero explained as a matter of propriety.

"Did your father pave everybody's parking lot in the entire city?" Bobby questioned Annie.

"Maybe, —you know my dad," Annie grinned in amusement. "It was you who told him where we were going, not me," she testified, as if to exonerate herself.

"Well, here, this is for you Romero, okay?" Bobby said, reached into his pocket and offering out a ten-dollar bill.

"Oh, thank you, Signore, but you don't have to do that," Romero declined politely. "Like I said, all has been taken care of, sir."

"No," said Bobby evenly. "I understand that. I want you to have it, sir," Bobby reinforced, physically putting the bill into Romero's hand.

"Why, thank you very much, Signore," Romero recanted, graciously accepting the tip. "I wish you all the best, and of course, —the Signorina as well," he specifically addressed. "And so, for the last time, thank you again," he repeated, retreating in finality to attend to his other duties.

"Well, I guess, all we have to do now is just leave," Bobby concluded, holding out his arm for Annie to take.

"I think that we should say good bye to Enzo first," Annie mentioned.

"I intend to, sweetie pie, I intend to," stated Bobby, affectionately patting her hand upon his arm.

"Well, we hope to see you again, Signore Taylor. We certainly enjoyed having you as a guest tonight," attested the Maître d' as the couple reentered the lobby.

"Thank you very much, Enzo," Bobby replied, "We had a wonderful time," he said appreciatively, shaking Enzo's hand, while also palming another ten-dollar bill.

Unlike Romero, however, Enzo did not protest in the slightest as the additional gratuity all but vanished before the appreciative "thank you" could be uttered.

"It was our pleasure to have you, Signore Taylor, and we hope to see you again," expressed Enzo. Just give your coat chips to the attendant by the door, and she will retrieve your garments. Once again, Corporal, thank you sharing the evening with us," he postscripted respectfully, officiously returning to the podium.

Chapter Twenty

As the satiated couple sauntered over to the coat check room and placed their coat chips on the counter, the attendant came over, picked up the chips, went through the line of hanging coats, and returned with their garments without saying a word. Then, after first helping Annie with her coat, Bobby took his from the counter, put it on, and tossed two dollars into the tip chalice on the counter. Finally, after putting put his arm tightly around Annie, together they exited D'Agostino's Ristorante to the belated declamation, "Thank you, come back again," from the coat check girl.

The door man, still with his hands in his pockets from the cold, once noticing the couple was leaving, took out his right hand and advanced toward them from the outer corner of the awning where he was still on the job, and before the sentry had been given the opportunity to speak, Bobby spoke first.

"I thank you very much," Bobby announced. "We had a wonderful time."

"We thank you very much for coming, Signore," the man politely responded.

"No, here, thank *you*," Bobby said, shaking the doorman's hand with another gratuity in a final goodbye.

Then, after the pair had rounded the corner of the building, and just when they thought their dining adventure had come to a complete end, the doorman was still heard to call out resoundingly, "Don't forget, you are always welcome back here at D'Agostino's Ristorante Italiano."

Nonetheless, oblivious to all else and with only the sound of the crushing ice beneath their feet, the two lovers, now consolidated as one against the frigid air, resolutely trudged on. Then, once again sheltered within the Chevy fortress,

Bobby assertively pumped on the gas pedal a few times, turned on the ignition, and the mighty "348 stone crusher" came back to life. Waiting patiently for the car's heater to become functional, the two lovers now huddled together, beginning to romantically fantasize over getting home to the warmth of their igloo after having to endure a hard and brutal day of ice fishing.

Naturally, they first thanked God for having another successful day in which neither of them had been eaten by a polar bear or had fallen accidentally into an ice hole, there to be eaten by an itinerant killer whale, all the same. Secondly, after anointing themselves Na-Nook and No-Nook of the North, they both categorically agreed that the worst way to die was to be eaten alive by a wild animal, completely alone in the wilderness, —with only one exception, and that was to be only half-eaten, and still be left alone to experience an even greater agonizing death.

"Yup, and that's an even worse fate than to die at the hands of Dangerous Dan Mc Grew, the notorious outlaw," Na-Nook pointed out. "Reputedly, he would just steal the clothes off your back and leave you standing there all naked and frozen like a Greek statue before God and everyone," she elucidated.

"Yeah," No-nook agreed, "And that's because I think it would be much better to freeze to death first, and then be eaten, rather than the other way around," he soundly pointed out.

Finally, after the two spiritually conjoined Eskimos had finished debating their funeral arrangements and had kissed their adventure into the wilds of the Yukon goodbye, they had come to realize the coldest reality of all, —that time is but a luxury that no one gets to keep for very long, regardless of how you die. They also realized it was quite another thing for a car to have a good heater.

Two weeks and only two weeks was all the time they had left together, this they knew. And so, on the very next day after mass, sitting on the settee in the rec-room of Annie's basement, together they sought to tackle their situation head on.

What do you do when you know you only have two weeks left before being unavoidably cast into that chasm of emotional severance? That was the very question to which they still had no answer, but try they did to alleviate their pain. The very definition of the word "future" was on trial, for how it equated to every aspect of their being was now as nebulous as the very "present" itself, for its own ambiguities could not be accounted for either.

Thus, the two beloveds fought together to find an acceptable solution that would at least attempt to satisfy their hopes and dreams, and therefore afford them some degree of relief from their anxieties, but for every plan there seemed to be a flaw, and for every dream a harsh reality, until only one solution appeared to be acceptable.

"Why don't we just have a good time while I'm still here and leave it at that?" Bobby finally concluded. "What if this, and what if that, is just depressing. Nobody can take away your wants and dreams," he established. "And if that's all you got, what's so wrong about that? That's all anybody's got, anyway," he argued. "Right now, for example, I'm a happy guy. Aren't you happy? Didn't we have a great time last night?" he asked, in trying to cheer Annie up.

"Well, I'm still not happy with the war," Annie confessed truthfully.

"I didn't ask you if you were happy with the war," Bobby now scolded. "Forget about the war, okay? You're not the one who's got to go, I do."

"Okay, I won't mention it again," Annie proclaimed, putting up her hands in surrender.

"Good! Now that you've forgotten all about 'The War,' tell me, exactly, what do you think about it now?" Bobby asked in no uncertain terms.

"Eh, what war?" Annie cluelessly replied.

"That's it exactly! Bobby emphasized, "So, I don't want to hear of *any* war, *anymore*," he explicitly stressed. "Pretend it doesn't exist, okay? The only thing that I know exists right now is you. *You* are the only thing that is real to me, and right now, that makes me happy, not sometime in the future, but right now. Don't you know how much I love you, and only you? That is all that matters. That's it. No more. Can't you be happy with just that? Like I said, *I'm* the one who has to go," he reminded her solemnly.

"Oh God, I love you so much!" Annie cried as she clutched on to him while the tears of anguish again began to trickle down her face.

"So, this is being happy? Because it sure doesn't look like it to me," Bobby contended skeptically.

"That's why I am crying, stupid!" Annie whimpered, "It's because I am so happy, that I don't know what else to do. Don't you know anything?" she dolefully chided, clinching on to him even tighter.

Oh boy, what kind of nutty logic is that? Bobby thought, nevertheless feeling remorseful in perhaps he had been too overbearing with her. *Maybe I should just go about this another way,* he then considered.

"Well, since you are so happy, and I'm such a happy guy, too, why don't we just go out then and have some fun," Bobby whimsically proposed, trying his best to console her.

"Because it's freezing outside right now, that's why, silly," Annie said, pushing herself back from him for a second to repeat, "Like I said, don't you know anything?"

"Well, not much as you. At least I know that," Bobby admitted, cuddling her gently. "So, I guess, all that means is, is that we're going ice skating, then," he lightly reasoned with a smile.

~

For the next two weeks their woes had been put into remission as the two of them went to revisit all the familiar places that had left them with a cherished memory, and nothing was ever mentioned about the war again.

"Yeah, there it is," said Annie, as the old elementary school came into view from the warmth of the car. "Remember the day that I got my first ride in the cart?"

"Oh, you mean the old 'Whirling Dervish?'" Bobby mused.

"Was there any other one?" Annie commented.

"Nope, it was one of a kind," Bobby declared.

"Where is it now?" Annie asked.

"Oh, it's got a tarp over it in the back of the garage," Bobby said.

It was when driving past the old brick high school, to which they had attended, now eerily vacant for the day and in the very the dead of winter, that both had come to the realization that the institution was no longer the same without them. Sure, every brick was there, —but they were not, and together they concluded that it was them who had made the school come alive, and not the other way around.

Before, the school was their security in the projected promises of a good future, but since their future had become most tangibly the present, it was now but a fond memory of their past, redundant as baby's carriage is to a toddler. Thus, it had become all too apparent that the entire business of security was a myth, for bricks by themselves, no matter how they are stacked, do not have a memory, only people do.

They then met with John that evening and reminisced at the soda shop after he had finished his shift at the cold rolled steel plant where he had gone to work along with his father. A few days later they met Barbara at the bowling alley with her new boyfriend, who she had acquired after John had "dumped" her. She informed them that she was now working the shoe store in the mall, and she had enrolled in a cosmetology school, "In order to better my life," as she phrased it. Her demeanor had not changed in any perceptible way, and she had not lost her knack for transforming the story of her life into one gigantic soap opera, either.

Both Annie and Bobby were learning that to be in love with life itself was the only force which could conquer the insignificance their own mortality, and as such, were now at total peace in the purity of life eternal. Bobby was even looking forward to having his last meal before leaving to return to duty, for Jolanda had offered to make him his favorite, and he knew it would be quite some time before he would get another that was even remotely the same.

Bobby loved a good meal, and although it was announced over the six o'clock news that due to the icy driving conditions outside, that everyone was requested to remain at home, it deterred him not in the slightest. There was no possible way that he was going to be cheated out of his just desserts before leaving, and in this he was resolute.

While the daytime sun did its best to melt away the snow from the center of the plowed streets, it also produced a myriad of frozen rivulets along the curbs and intersections once the evening freeze had come into play. Even in the center of the streets, where the natural dips and hollows lay, there lay slick sheets of dangerous ice that were also formed. It was not to be denied, it was indeed a perilous thing to be on the road that evening.

Undaunted, however, Bobby left the warmth and comfort of his own home for the warmth and comfort of the Russo home in the anticipation of his sumptuous goodbye dinner that had been extended to him. Annie had already reported to Bobby that her mother was in fact making the lasagna, and stuffed with plenty of sausage, too, so not to show up was the only thing that wasn't on the table.

Accordingly, Bobby drove along at a snail's pace with as much caution as could possibly be expected, and as this exercise still afforded him plenty of time for amusement, he began to ponder, *Am I really going to the Russo's just to see Annie again, or am I going just because I better not insult Mrs. Russo by not showing up, or, is the real reason simply, it's the lasagna? Man, that stuff is so good, especially when Jolanda makes it.*

And just who am I going to blame if I get into an accident?" he then began to consider, *"Well, I certainly can't blame Jolanda, that's out. And there is no way I would try to pin the blame on Annie, either, that would be suicide. Well, I guess the easiest thing to do is, if anything goes wrong, I'll just blame the lasagna. After all, how can you offend a lasagna?* he thought to himself rhetorically. *And besides, I'm only going to end up eating it, anyway. I'll just be eating my own excuse, so how's that going to work for any evidence?* he laughed, pulling into Annie's driveway.

~

"Hello, Bobby," Jolanda said affectionately, opening the side door to the kitchen.

"Good evening, Mrs. Russo," Bobby replied, mannerly as always, while closing the door behind him.

"You can go sit in the living room with my husband, Annie will be down in a minute," Jolanda said. "Dinner will be ready in about fifteen minutes, and you can hang your coat in the hall closet," she pleasantly instructed.

"Hello, Bobby," Capricia greeted from over by the stove, grinning like she had just received a front row ticket to see Gone with the Wind.

"Hello, Caprice," Bobby replied pleasantly, knowing he was being visually scrutinized while leaving the kitchen for the living room.

"Good evening, Mr. Russo. Specialist Taylor reporting as ordered, Sir," Bobby announced heartily the moment he entered the room.

"Hope you are a specialist in finishing everything on your plate, Corporal, or you will have a major problem on your hands," Enrico noted amusingly.

"The Corporal is aware of the kitchen protocol, Sir," Bobby joked back, taking a seat on the couch askance from Enrico's Stratolounger.

"Well, I guess you're off tomorrow," Enrico said with finality, putting down his newspaper.

"Yes, sir, Mr. Russo, tonight's my last night," Bobby affirmed. "Then I'm off to join the circus to be a broken-hearted clown," he paraphrased. "Well, I'm going to miss everyone, Mr. Russo, I want you to know that," he then said more sincerely.

"Enh, we're all clowns in the circus of life, Bobby," Enrico answered philosophically. "It's like we're all on one big merry-go-round, and the people get on, and people get off. You can count yourself lucky if you get on a horse next to somebody that you actually like. It makes the ride a whole lot better," he expounded.

"You're right about that," Bobby agreed. "I pity the poor guy who has to spend the whole ride next to the obnoxious clown, always honking his horn," he added light heartedly.

"And sometimes you think that you might be able to better your position by changing your horse, but then again, you realize that you still can't predict who gets on and off beside you, for there are no guarantees, no matter where you are in the race. So, like I've said before, sometimes you just luck out," Enrico fatefully declared.

"Dinner's ready!" Jolanda called out from the kitchen, promptly putting an end to these not-so-Sophoclean observations.

"Well, before we go into the kitchen, Mr. Russo, I have a question I want to ask you, if you have a second." Bobby asked reticently, after Enrico had risen from his chair.

"Well, go on," Enrico replied invitingly, leaning forward to offer Bobby a degree of confidentiality, "ask away."

Putting his hand into his right pants pocket, Bobby withdrew a small blue hinged box and held it out for Enrico to take.

"My question is," Bobby began sheepishly, handing the box out, "do I have your permission to offer this to Annie?" he asked apprehensively.

"Oh, I've seen one of these before," Enrico stated cautiously, taking the box from Bobby's hand to open it. "What is this, a half a carat?" he asked, guessing its weight like a stumper at a carnival.

"Yes, sir, it's a half a carat, at least that's what they told me," Bobby answered.

"So, what's your question?" elicited Enrico.

"Well, the fella at the jewelry store told me it was an engagement ring, and I was going to ask Annie if she wanted it, but, since you are her father, I thought I should ask you first," Bobby timorously asserted.

"Robert, are you asking my permission to marry my daughter?" Enrico petitioned directly, in trying not to cause the young man any further discomfort.

"Yes, sir," Bobby humbly replied.

"Then, I only have one question for you," Enrico stated explicitly, pausing with an expectant look.

"Yes sir?" asked Bobby in a dead pan manner.

"What took you so long? I was beginning to think you was a mouse, not a man, heh, heh, heh," Enrico quietly kidded, grasping on to Bobby's hand to practically crush it. "Of course, you have my blessing, son," he decreed. "And now, the rest is your problem," he jokingly added, soundly patting Bobby on the shoulder and offering back the ring.

"Well, what's taking you two so long in there?" Jolanda called out again from the kitchen.

"We're on our way," proclaimed Enrico, arching his eyebrows at Bobby in denoting that their pact of silence was in effect.

"Bobby, you sit at the end of the table opposite my husband," Jolanda directed, the moment he and Enrico had come into the kitchen. "And Caprice, honey, will you see what's taking the princess so long?" she asked, closing the door to the refrigerator and picking up a large wooden spoon from a plate on the counter.

"Okay, mom," Capricia responded cheerfully, leaving to be heard trotting up the stairs after her sister.

"Everything is ready. We're just waiting on Annie now," Jolanda announced to all. "You can pour the wine if you like," she said pleasantly to Enrico, glancing over in his direction from her station by the stove.

"I got it," Enrico replied supportively, getting up from his chair and picking up the opened bottle of Chianti off the table. "Some vino, Corporal?" he asked Bobby politely.

"Sure, I'll have some," replied Bobby, moving his wine glass closer to Enrico.

Then, while Enrico was reaching directly across the table and beginning to pour the wine into Bobby's glass, Annie, at long last, appeared from the hallway door with Capricia close behind.

"Would you put some in my glass too, Daddy?" Annie requested spritely.

"Are you sure you can handle it?" Enrico teased her with a smile.

"Daddy?" Annie addressed back in an admonishing tone.

"Okay, okay," responded Enrico in atonement, to then pour some wine in her glass at the setting to Bobby's right. Next, after attending to all the other wine glasses, his own included, and with no further ado, he comfortably reclined back in his chair at the head of the table. And so, the table was set.

Chapter Twenty-One

"Girls, would you help me put the dinner on the table?" Jolanda asked, taking the lasagna out of the oven with a red potholder in each hand and placing it on top of a white and red checkered towel on the counter next to the oven. "The salads are in the refrigerator, Annie. And Capricia, here is the bread," she added, holding out a cloth covered wicker basket.

After putting the basket on the table, Capricia next took the salad plates one by one from Annie as they were handed to her and placed them down in front of each of the place settings.

"What is this, feta cheese on my salad?" Bobby amiably asked Capricia when his was placed before him.

"What? I heard that. Do you think we are Greeks now, Soldier? That's not feta cheese. We're not Greeks here. No decent Italian puts feta cheese on their salad," Enrico decreed. "That's Provolone and Parmesano, so that you know, son," Enrico apprised Bobby authoritatively.

"Oh, yes sir, I was just kidding," Bobby responded respectfully, "Annie has already given me that lesson," he explained with a respectful grin.

"Pretty fancy uniform you have on, Bobby," Capricia noted in a provocative manner.

"It's what they give me, Caprice," Bobby replied indifferently.

"I think he is so handsome in his uniform," Annie chimed in, brushing her hand across his back on her way to take the chair on his right.

"Is everyone seated now?" officiously inquired Jolanda in taking charge, to which all three in unison replied, "Yes."

"Well, here it is, I hope everyone likes it," submitted Jolanda, placing the large white ceramic baking dish upon a wooden cutting board centered directly in front of Enrico.

Considerately, they all now sat in silence while Jolanda put down her oven pads, washed her hands, took off her apron, primped her hair for a second, and seated herself beside Enrico.

"It is as beautiful as our two daughters, Mi Amore," Enrico proclaimed for the benefit of Jolanda, praising her efforts. "And so, we will all do what we must," he solemnly said before bowing his head in silence. Then, after longer than a pause and shorter than eulogy, he offered openly, "We all thank the Lord for this great meal and ask for the safe return of Corporal Taylor, amen."

"Amen," declared Jolanda, followed by all else, which ended what was considered to have been the meal's grace, a rarity performed by the patriarch of the family himself.

"Corporal Taylor, if you would hand me your plate?" Enrico moved on politely.

"I guess this is going to be your last home-cooked meal for a while," commented Annie, passing on Bobby's plate over to her father.

"I'd say for about a year or so, give or take a month," Bobby estimated. "But there is one thing that I *can* definitely say, and that is, I'm sure not going to having any lasagna like this when I'm gone. It looks delicious as always, Mrs. Russo," Bobby complimented, taking back his plate back from Annie, heaped with a mountain of food.

"Why, thank you Bobby," answered Jolanda.

"So, what are you now, some sort of super mechanic?" twittered Capricia to Bobby, sportively grinning while she handed her plate to her mother. "Is that why you got that patch on your sleeve?"

"Caprice, it's called a chevron, and I have the rank of a specialist because I am trained in something else besides just shooting at annoying people. You do understand that, don't you?" Bobby rhetorically grinned back. "But in answer to your question," he continued in a more serious tone, "yes, I am a certified super mechanic, and from now on, you have to address me as 'Super Specialist Taylor,' and that's an order," he goaded playfully.

"That was a super what again, Bobby?" Capricia bantered in return.

"I want to tell you, my bride, I don't know how you manage to always make this better than the last time, but you did it again," interceded Enrico, deliberately changing the direction of the conversation.

"You sure did, Mom," supported Annie.

From the day they had met at the school yard, the history of Annie and Bobby was now on review for all at the table to reminisce over and enjoy until the final dinner fork had fallen fallow. Jolanda and Capricia finished removing the dinner dishes from the table and placed a stack of dessert dishes and forks in its center, while Bobby and Enrico enjoyed their coffees. Then, after Capricia had retaken her seat at the table, she proceeded to scoot over her chair a little, so her mother could present Bobby with the largest chocolate cake that she had ever made.

"Bobby, since it is your day, you get to cut the cake," Jolanda officiated, placing it down decisively in front of him. "Now hold on one second while I get you the cake knife," she stipulated, turning back to the counter behind her. "Now Bobby, you get to make one wish before you cut it," she ruled, putting down the cake knife directly beside the cake. "And you can't tell anyone your wish, or it won't come true," she cautioned. "Not even Annie," she noted specifically.

"Well now, let me think. Humm, now let me think some more," Bobby dramatically paused with the knife at the ready. "Now what could I possibly want?" he openly mused, now looking up to perhaps receive some divine inspiration.

"You had better know what you want by now," Annie warned.

"Okay, I got it!" declared Bobby, climatically plunging the knife directly into the cake. "So, now that I have my wish, and before I cut the cake again, there is still one little thing more that I need to ask of you, Annie," he said with a pause and a smile.

"Oh, yeah? and what is that? Annie asked suspiciously.

"Here," was Bobby's one-word response, reaching into his right-hand pocket to take out the little blue box, which he then gingerly placed upon the table before her.

"And, what is that?" Annie asked cautiously.

"Open it up and you tell me," Bobby replied, leaning back in his chair while Annie slowly opened it up.

"What is it Annie?" petitioned Capricia impatiently as Annie sat frozen with her mouth open while gazing fixedly upon its contents. "Well, what is it?" Capricia clamored again.

"Here, you look," Annie said to Capricia, displaying it out across the table.

"Oh my God! Oh my God! It's an engagement ring!" squealed Capricia, bouncing up and down in her chair with excitement.

"Well, is that what this is, Bobby?" questioned Annie in mild disbelief, now presenting the ring back to Bobby.

"That's what the man at the jewelry store said it was," reassured Bobby in a hapless way.

Did you talk to my father about this?" slowly questioned Annie in a presumptuous tone.

"I sure did," Bobby testified proudly, thinking that he had done the right thing. "And when I did, your father said, 'what took you so long?' and then he even shook my hand. I think he likes me," he grinned elatedly.

Then, as a sudden silence fell, Annie now appeared to be infuriated as she looked back and forth the table in trying to determine exactly who she should censure first.

"So, the two of you were conspiring against me, huh?" Annie fumed. "Now don't get me wrong, this is certainly a beautiful ring," she certified, "In fact, to me it appears to be the most beautiful ring in the world, but just who are you trying to get engaged to, Bobby, my father?" she peevishly chastised.

"Well, I thought that ah, we could get engaged now," Bobby warily replied.

"I don't know, could we?" Annie mockingly replied. "I don't see how I could ever get engaged to anyone who didn't ask me properly, because I can guarantee you one thing, if I am not, it ain't going to happen," she stated as firmly as if she was Martin Luther hammering his thesis to the church's front door.

"Don't you want to get engaged?" Bobby asked meekly, pandering for an escape.

"Wrong question!" Annie responded vehemently, casting her eyes away from him as she crossed her arms in rejection.

"Okay, okay," Bobby addressed her repentantly. "Annie, will you marry me? I do love you," he affirmed with all the humility he could muster.

Slowly, and without any discernible expression, Annie then scrupulously faced him directly, shifted her chair to the side, placed the blue box carefully on the table, and up she jumped to quite unexpectedly pounce squarely upon his lap. And now, clutching on to him as tightly as the law would allow, she categorically replied, "Of course I'll marry you, my little soldier boy!" and then kissed him full on the lips. Next, as quickly as Annie had seized the moment, she just as abruptly pushed back from him to say, "Hey, wait a minute, there's still one more thing I need to know."

"What is it now?" asked Bobby, beleaguered obviously to the point of mental exhaustion.

"Why *did* take you so long?" Annie grinned while glancing over to her father, who was now pretending to be as unobtrusively innocent as the proverbial fly on the wall.

Finally, after the ring had been ceremoniously put on Annie's finger and the clamorous behavior had subsided, the cake demolished, and the coffee dispatched around the table, Bobby decided that it was now *his* turn to assert himself, and so he then relaxed back in his chair for a moment to gather his thoughts.

"Well, I guess I have to say, I do have a confession to make," Bobby then imparted as Annie's ears perked up in interest. "I guess you should know that I knew all the time that you had no choice but to accept my proposal," he stated casually. "Yup, no choice at all," he reinforced, looking up and away in a pronounced sigh of self-satisfaction.

"What do you mean? I could have said no," Annie objected flatly, "If I wanted to," she magnanimously replied.

"Oh no, you had no choice," Bobby said dismissively. "You forget, *I* had the wish," he stressed.

"Aww, why are you telling me that? Now the wish won't come true somehow," Annie sadly complained.

"Well, that's not actually true, either," Bobby corrected. "You see, I actually wished you to say no, because I knew you would try to worm it out of me somehow, someway, some day. So, now it's a done deal," he proclaimed with great satisfaction. "I guess Bobby wins again," he declared most contentedly, to then lean back to ceremoniously pat his belly like an exalted Buddha.

"Wait a minute now," Annie objected, "It was my mother that gave you that wish, and therefore, —" she began before being interrupted.

"Well, you two, I'm going into the living room to relax with your mother now," said Enrico, getting up from his chair. "Honey, are you coming with me?" he asked his wife.

"As soon as I take off my apron," Jolanda responded from over by the sink, whereupon she immediately pulled upon one of its strings, releasing it from around her waist.

"Caprice," Enrico then called back in his magisterial tone, once he and Jolanda had gotten out of sight.

"Okay, I'm on my way," Capricia begrudgingly replied, not wanting to be deprived of her own personal soap opera. "Well, I guess I won't be seeing you for a while," she said to bobby fatalistically.

"Nope, I'll be gone in the morning," Bobby confirmed.

"Anyway, I hope you have a good trip and I'll see you when you get back," Capricia offered in a considerate tone, finally removing herself from the table.

"Thank you, Cappy," Bobby considerately replied, while Capricia wandered away to her upstairs room.

Alone, the sobriety of time had finally come to take it due. Even after enumerating all the anticipated times of joy they intended to have together once Bobby returned, it did little to help the prevailing sadness. The cold reality was that the futility of fighting time had been poignantly foisted upon them, and there was nothing in the universe that could be done about it.

There were no exaltations, no cheerful revelations, no effervescent expressions in the declarations of their love to each other, as only a profound sense of compassion for the welfare of each other had overwhelmingly filled their hearts. The time had come for him to take his leave, and after one long, passionate kiss, they left the kitchen and went into the living room so that young soldier could give his final farewell to her parents.

"Thanks for everything, but I've got to be going now," Bobby regretfully said to both Jolanda and Enrico, sitting in their respective easy chairs.

"You take care of yourself, Bobby, and make sure you write and let us know how you are doing," Jolanda requested warmly.

Standing up from his chair, Enrico clasped onto Bobby's hand once more, shook it heartedly, and pronounced officially, "I have nothing more to say, soldier. Just be proud in what you do and have a good tour. We'll be here when you return."

And there they were again, back at the kitchen door where they had parted many a time before. The unavoidable pain and anguish over their separation had now permeated the air to such a degree that once the door was opened and Bobby had turned to say goodbye, Annie simply grabbed his hand tightly and said, "Don't say any more. There is nothing more to say until you return." Then, in a last gesture of Annie's undying love for him, she placed the softest of tender kisses upon his cheek, and amidst a torrent of silent tears, released his hand.

Finally, as door closed behind him, she watched him leave through its window while the unimaginable will of a dispassionate God, despite her pleas for mercy, had given her no quarter. It was only in the hope of his return that she found herself able to fend off a complete and utter crushing of her soul.

~

At seven o'clock in the morning, it had already become a strikingly bright day. The sun's brilliance sparkled its rays in a kaleidoscopic panoramic array of colors that danced its way across the sheen of the hardened snow which had blanketed the landscape. The air was crisp, clean, and cold. There wasn't a cloud in the sky. The morning day was as pure as if being seen through a polished looking glass. The trees reflected a silvery glitter off the frozen icicles which hung copiously about their heavily laden branches. There was no breeze at all and not a sound to be heard on this winter's day, for this was the day that Bobby Taylor went off to Vietnam.

Almost three weeks went by from that day before Annie had received his first letter. Not professing to be a writer at all, Bobby's correspondence was short and for the most part merely an itinerary of his trip. It then professed his love for her, a greeting to the rest of her family and, all in all, that was it. It wasn't much, Annie thought, but still she treasured it.

Then, after another week had gone by, Jolanda called Annie at work to tell her that Bobby's mother said she was going to stop by at about seven o'clock that evening after dinner. Completely surprised by the phone call, Annie left work early. She had become so preoccupied with the news that she could no longer function at her job. *Maybe she has another letter for me, or he got a promotion? Or even still, maybe he sent me some kind of gift?"* she thought. She was dying of anticipation, and after eating nary a thing for dinner, swiftly retreated to her room to vigilantly station herself by her dormer window, anxiously awaiting the arrival of Karen. Patiently, she sat there for over an hour while reading her one and only letter, —over and over again.

It was five minutes past seven when Mr. Taylor pulled the Buick into the Russo family's driveway and parked it in precisely the same spot that Bobby had, many a time before. Exiting out of the passenger side of the car, Mrs. Taylor walked over to the side door, while Jolanda, after having noticed the car's arrival from its headlights shining through the kitchen's windows, had gotten up to let her in.

"Hello, Mrs. Taylor, I'm Jolanda, Annie's mother. Would you come in?" she greeted graciously.

"I'm not going to be long, my husband is waiting for me in the car," Karen said as she sniffled a bit in a crumpled handkerchief. "I just came by to see Annie for a minute," she spoke somberly and using the handkerchief again. "Oh, I'm sorry," she then apologized, "my name is Karen, I'm Bobby's mother," she said while Jolanda closed the door.

"Here, why don't you sit in this chair?" Jolanda offered respectfully in sensing that she was in distress.

"No, thank you. I won't be but a minute," Karen answered plainly.

"Annie, Mrs. Taylor is here!" Jolanda called out loudly as Annie, already on her way, instantly bounded into the room.

"Did Bobby call you? Did he send you a letter? He sent me one last week!" Annie exclaimed excitedly, letting loose a barrage of questions all at once.

"No, Annie. Would you sit down for a minute, please?" Karen asked her solemnly.

"Well, what did he have to say?" Annie continued on excitedly, respectfully taking her place in the chair.

"Just try to be quiet for a second, would you, please?" Karen asked sedately, obviously still trying to hold onto her composure.

"Don't you feel good, Mrs. Taylor?" Annie now asked in concern.

Not responding directly to Annie's question, Mrs. Taylor then took in a deep breath, paused for a second, and simply delivered the news.

"This morning, about ten o'clock, a nice lieutenant from the Army came by my house and politely informed me that about three days ago my son, Bobby, was killed while he was on duty."

Chapter Twenty-Two

"What?" Annie said in shocked disbelief.

"They told me that my son was killed when a rocket hit his barracks about three days ago," Karen confirmed as she bit her bottom lip to keep herself from crying again.

"Oh God no!" cried out Annie. "No! Oh God no! Oh God no! Oh God no!" she hysterically kept repeating, clenching her fists and beating them against her breast while Jolanda turned quickly to her daughter and held onto her tightly in consolation. "I can't believe it! I can't believe it! Oh no! Oh God! Oh no!" Annie convulsively kept repeating as she clutched tightly onto her mother's waist, still seated in her chair.

"Well, I'm going to go now," announced Karen despondently. "My husband is waiting for me in the car outside. The officer said it would be a few weeks before they would bring him back to us. We will let you know when he's here," she apprised them bleakly. "I can find my own way out, Mrs. Russo, thank you for everything," she acknowledged. Then, in failing to constrain her weeping anymore, she left the Russo home.

Horrified to the point of complete collapse, Annie still clung on to her mother, gasping for her breath amidst a flood of tears. Virtually becoming consumed by grief itself, she then swooned and slumped listlessly in surrender against her mother while her very spirit seemed to dissipate from her constitution. Scared to death herself, Jolanda shook her daughter by her shoulders and cried out her name, "Annie, Annie!" and prayed to God for the forgiveness of her sins, in now clutching onto her daughter for dear life.

Next, as if a demonic spell had been instantly exorcised from trying to destroy her will to live, Annie sprung to life again with a vengeance, and spontaneously pushing her mother away, she abruptly stood up in complete defiance of the very concept of death and violently swept the flowered centerpiece cleanly off the table, causing it to crash in pieces across the floor.

"It isn't fair! It isn't fair!" Annie screamed out as she stomped her foot, still crying in pain and misery. "God damn it! It just isn't fair! It just isn't fair!" she kept repeating as she stormed up to her room and slammed her door behind her.

Enrico, who had heard everything from his chair in the living room, only sat in silence as he put his head in his hands.

Capricia, in trying to mind her own business when the commotion had started, did not come out of her room until she had heard the ensuing silence of the dead that had followed. Gingerly, she then went down the stairway and into the kitchen to see her mother quietly cleaning up the glass shards of the annihilated centerpiece that had become strewn throughout the entire floor.

"Mother, what's wrong?" Capricia asked as sedately as possible, while Jolanda stood upright to address her directly.

"Bobby was killed in Vietnam, honey," Jolanda collectedly replied.

Reactively latching onto the nearest kitchen chair to steady herself, Capricia was in complete and utter shock, and struggling to keep her equilibrium. Transfixed, she had become overwhelmed in having both a fond remembrance of him and at the same time cope with the tragedy of it all.

Within the bounds of decency, Capricia had always fancied Bobby and had dreamed that she, too could find another boy just like him for herself. She had always been happy for Annie, but now she felt only a profound sadness left in her heart. Overcome with grief, she tried and tried to

331

comprehend the reality of Bobby's death, however, she could not. Emotionally exhausted, she could think of nothing more than to accepted her lack of understanding and muttering sadly to her mother, said, "Well, I'm going to go to my room, too," and slowly ambled away.

After the kitchen was eventually put back in order, Jolanda finally gave out a sigh of despair and went quietly into the living room to sit down next to her husband. Enrico was now sitting with his head back and his eyes closed in repose, his evening newspaper still in his lap and his hands now folded together on top.

"Ricky, are you okay?" Jolanda asked compassionately, after resting herself for a few moments.

Then, in not perceptively stirring an inch, and with his eyes still closed, Enrico began his argument about fate itself.

"You know, the minute that you start to think that life is great, some crap like this happens. You believe that all you have to do is work hard and keep your nose clean, and eventually you will be rewarded," Enrico postulated. "But sometimes a man can't even work hard enough to make his own family happy. It's always somethin'," he said in exasperation.

"Just when you think you're getting somewhere, some outside force comes along and changes your whole life around. What's the point in even trying to play by the rules? They only stack the odds against the honest man. I might just as well be a crook, like those sleazy politicians who give me those contracts," he said in disgust.

"They don't give a damn about the roads I build, or the people who pay for them. Unless it's a road that they need personally drive on, they couldn't give a damn less, —oh, but when it's finished, that's a different story. They get their picture taken, standing right on top of it, and outright lie and say, 'I built this road for you,' when he didn't build a damn thing. The only thing that he really did was take old Joe's money and lie to them on how it was spent. Those bastards steal more money from the people with their white shirts and ties in one year than Al Capone could steal in a million, and they don't need a machine gun to do it, either. It's like I said, I might as well be a crook and take my chances. The odds are better," he detestably noted.

"Oh, honey, don't talk like that. God can hear you. We all loved Bobby. These things just happen. I will go to Father Bernardino and ask him for his blessing. I can even see if we can get a novena said for him. It wouldn't hurt to ask," Jolanda proposed. "I'll have Annie take me to buy some candles, and then maybe I can get her to talk to the father by herself. I think that would be good for her," she said hopefully, while Enrico made no reply to her intentions.

"Come on, Ricky, I think we should go to bed now," Jolanda recommended sympathetically, standing up from her chair. "Come on, honey, let's go," she urged further, now placing her hand on his shoulder and gently stroking it.

"Yeah, I guess you're right," Enrico responded with a heavy sigh of exhaustion, his enmity beginning to wane.

Annie did not come out of her bedroom the entire next day except to go to the bathroom and summarily return. The only response Jolanda could successfully solicit through her locked door was, "Go away!" while one could still hear her sobbing miserably through her door. Not Capricia, nor even Enrico would even attempt to knock on her door. On the second day of her seclusion, after Enrico had left to work and Capricia had gone to school, Jolanda again made a plea at Annie's door for her to come out.

"Honey, you need to eat something. It's just the two of us. There is no one here but us. You can talk to me. I will understand," Jolanda tenderly implored.

"I don't want to talk to anyone!" Annie snapped back defiantly.

"Okay," Jolanda agreed, "You don't have to say anything. Just come downstairs and I'll make you some scrambled eggs and toast, that's all. You still have to eat. Then you can go back to your room, and I won't bother you," she promised once again, quietly leaving to retreat back down the stairs.

Jolanda, not knowing what else she could possibly do, aimlessly sat herself back down at the kitchen table, and in total desolation, remained there for the better part of an hour with an untouched cup of coffee before her on the table. From the time of her childhood, to her marriage with Enrico, to the birth of Capricia, she sat there and revisited it all.

To be alive another day, to still be of use to others in their time of need, was a good thing, Jolanda believed. There was nothing bad in death, there was only the life that God had given her and everyone else, to live happily while they could, according to His plan.

And so it was, that, in the middle of all these thoughts, Jolanda suddenly felt that the whole universe had shifted. Instinctively, she cast aside her own personal grief, stiffened up in her chair, and then spontaneously looked over to see that Annie was standing directly behind her under the archway that led to the hall.

Disheveled as never seen before and still in her pajamas, Jolanda was shocked to see the horrific toll that Bobby's death had taken upon her daughter. Devastated beyond recognition, Annie was standing there under the archway, motionless, and leaning against the door jamb like a ravaged and neglected husk doll that had been thrown away upon a trash heap. The manifestation of her anguish had etched within her countenance the cadaverous vacant stare of a lifeless and worthless shell of a former human being whose soul had been ruthlessly trampled upon without mercy.

Jolanda had no idea of what to do. Slowly, she stood up, but said nothing. Together, they stood there in silence for a moment, each in their own worlds, not knowing how to begin to describe their own struggles, even to themselves. It didn't take but two steps forward by Jolanda to approach her strife-ridden daughter when, in total anguish, Annie had all but collapsed against her mother in a desperate attempt to find some degree of deliverance to soothe her tortured soul.

"Oh, Mommy, what am I going to do?" Annie wailed out uncontrollably, grasping onto her mother more pathetically.

"It'll be okay, it'll be okay," Jolanda repeated while she held on her daughter in trying to console her. "Come on, why you don't sit here," she coaxed, gently releasing herself from Annie's grasp and pulling out a chair from under the table. "Come on, take a seat," she repeated, as she delicately corralled her daughter over to the chair.

"You need something to eat. I'm going to make some eggs and toast for you now," Jolanda said delicately. "Do you want some orange juice, honey?" she then asked softly while turning toward the refrigerator.

"No, I want some coffee," Annie responded, stoically situated with her head down and her crossed arms in front of her.

"Sure, I still have some left from this morning," Jolanda replied attentively, going over to the cupboard and taking out a cup and saucer.

"Could you just give me a mug? Don't bother with that stupid china right now, okay?" Annie directed tersely.

"Okay, sure, honey. Do you want the milk, too?" Jolanda asked in a stewardly fashion.

"Yeah, I want the milk, too," Annie responded flatly, as her mother silently complied with the request.

Jolanda went about the chore of preparing the breakfast as simply as possible. She said nothing regarding the fact that Annie had never wanted coffee before and was content with simply having her out of her room. Jolanda had full well experienced the feeling of being mortified with disappointment, and knew that over time, its intensity on the inside would subside, but for how long Annie's demeanor on the outside would be affected was a different question.

For now, at least, Jolanda had assessed that Annie would physically survive her tragic loss when she observed her daughter finally taking a drink of her coffee, and that, for the time being, was all that she had prayed for.

It did not take but a few minutes for Jolanda to fix the light breakfast, and after having turned off the burner on the stovetop, placed the plate of scrambled eggs and toast in front of her daughter, along with a knife and fork. Silently, going over to the refrigerator to supplement the breakfast with a jar of strawberry preserves, she then sat down at the opposite end of the table to pray in silence, while neither of them uttered a word until Annie declared, "Well, that's all I want. I'm going back to my room," and did exactly that, while Jolanda did not respond in the slightest. And it was there that Annie stayed for the rest of the day, without any further disturbances from her mother, until Capricia and Enrico had both come home from their daily exercises.

"Dinner's ready, Annie," Jolanda eventually called out and up the stairway to Annie's room after everyone else was seated for the evening meal, but there was no response. Consequently, not wanting to cause any further problems for the evening, and accepting the non-reply, she then simply decided to go back to the kitchen and began to serve the meal without her.

Subsequently, however, after the dinner had been put upon the table and Jolanda had taken her seat, Annie, at long last, appeared through the doorway of the kitchen and went over to take her usual place at the table, still dressed in her pajamas. Regardless, proceeding altogether once again, the Russo family finally began the evening meal, and with the exception of the dishes clanking and the usual requests to pass the condiments around, the meal was still exceptionally quiet until everyone had eaten what they wished, while no one even mentioned the topic of dessert.

"Well, I'm going into the living room," was the only thing that Enrico ever said, before standing up to promptly lumber off to the solemnity of his living room chair.

This left the three women alone to commiserate with each other as they continued to dawdle over the unfinished food on their plates.

"Annie, when your father comes home for lunch tomorrow, would you take me to the church so I can buy some candles?" Jolanda eventually asked in the softest tones possible.

"I guess I could," Annie answered dismally. "That is, if Daddy will let me drive the car," she amended.

"I'm sure it will be okay, honey," Jolanda lightly assured her.

"Well, I'm going back to my room now," Annie announced dourly, getting up and leaving without another word.

"I'll help you with the dishes, Mom," Capricia offered supportively, although she was not in much of a good mood, either.

~

Upon the very next day, Jolanda, after having prepared lunch, stood quietly at the side kitchen window to see exactly when her husband would arrive, and upon first seeing Enrico pulling in the driveway, ritually wiped her hands off on her apron and hastened directly over to the bottom of the stairway.

"Honey, your father's here," Jolanda called out, returning to the kitchen to greet her husband.

Closing the door behind him, Enrico trudged over to his chair with nothing to say as he took off his coat, placed it on the back of his chair, and then sat down quietly while Jolanda poured him his usual cup of coffee.

"Can I have one, too?" Annie plainly asked, coming into the room and taking a seat at the table, having finally gotten out of her pajamas.

"Sure, just give me a second," Jolanda responded, going back to the mug tree on the counter, percolator in hand.

Next, after pouring Annie her coffee, Jolanda went back over to the stove top, dished out another bowl of minestrone, matching hers and her husband's, and placed it in front of her daughter, thereafter taking a seat at the table herself. Quietly, they all sat at the table and ate their meal until Enrico had finished his soup, along with one of the sandwiches that had been stacked on a plate in the center of the table, and then the silence was broken.

"Are you okay to drive the car?" Enrico inoffensively asked his daughter as a matter of concern.

"Yeah, I'm okay, Daddy," Annie answered glumly.

Enrico reflectively studied the swirls in his coffee for a moment and feeling that the best thing he could do for her was to get her out of the house, he thus both ominously and optimistically decided to let her go.

"Well, are you two ready, then?" Enrico asked, getting up from his chair to put his jacket back on.

"I'm finished," declared Annie as she rose up from her half-eaten soup.

338

"I'll get the dishes later," Jolanda asserted, standing up as well. And without delay, she took off her apron, put it on the back of her chair, and left the room to go to the coat closet by the front door. "Okay, I'm ready," she notified the two of them when she came back into the room, noticing that Annie had already gotten her all-weather jacket on and was standing forbearingly by the back door.

It was cold, bleak, and chillingly dank outside that day as the wrath of winter, in its last attempt to not give in to the vicissitudes of spring, was irascibly nasty. Splattering the icy slush about the sides of the street, the stately green Cadillac eventually arrived at its appointed parking space outside the offices of the Russo Paving Company.

Not a word had been spoken since leaving the house, for the atmosphere within the car had matched the outside atmosphere in spades. "Miserable," was the unspoken word of the day, for all three had fully accepted that God had clearly granted Mother Nature as much free will as he had given man and full well knew that to pointlessly complain over their present conditions would only prove to exacerbate everyone's anxieties.

"Just take it easy and be back here with your mother by five," Enrico directed to Annie the moment he got out of the car.

"I will," Annie responded obediently, sliding over on the bench seat to take control of the car while Enrico closed the car door tight and trudged back to his office.

"So, where exactly do you want to go, Mom?" Annie asked in a bland tone, while putting the car in reverse.

"It would be nice if you could take me to "The Shrine of Saint Patrick." They have a much better selection of candles and things than we do at our church," Jolanda replied.

"If that's what you want," Annie responded indifferently, while backing the car up to get out of the driveway.

Slowly, as they slogged along in solitude, the mournful pair dedicated the dismal day unto the distasteful task of preparing themselves for both the public and private mourning of their grief. Nothing was said, because there was nothing to say. The beatitudes of life seemed to be had nowhere on the highway of life that day as they traveled along. Everyone appeared to be aimlessly sloshing about, concerned only with their own survival in the not-so-hopeful expectation that their lives would have better times to come.

Then, while Annie noticed the massive tractor trailers unconcernedly propelling an ungodly wave of nasty sludge upon the defenseless smaller vehicles, it only reinforced her newly acquired supposition that the plight of the weak, small, and humble was not a pretty one to behold at all.

At least I have the comfort of my Dad's Cadillac, Annie thought while she watched a truck pass her by, callously careening a caliginous mass of road muck upon some poor slob who was standing by the side of the thoroughfare. *I guess that's just the way it is,* she resolved to herself in being devoid of any pity that she previously might have had for the undeserving and unfortunate fellow.

It took about forty minutes for Annie to reach their destination, anticipating some form of relief from her woes, but once entering the meticulously mannered grounds of the shrine, it had become all too obvious that the ravages of Old Man Winter had an effect on everyone, regardless of their circumstance. Normally bustling about with all sorts of people seeking to enjoy its natural bucolic setting, it was now virtually devoid of any activity, festive or solemn.

Yet as the emerald green El Dorado passed through the arched brick towers which were imposingly guarding the entrance, a sense of serenity was still felt within the constitutions of both Annie and her mother, regardless of the inclement weather. Perhaps it was the stoic black iron fence that had surrounded the entire grounds of the shrine that seemed to distinctly imply that all within its grounds was holy, or perhaps it was the intimidating stone entrance into the complex that projected that their souls were safe once past its gates, but it mattered not, for once they had gotten inside, it was as if each of them had been granted a blanket of solace which now seemed to cloak them from their agonies.

For them it was a major comfort to be there as they looked about the entirety of the shrine. To their right stood the white Corinthian columned rectory that had been vaingloriously appointed against the backdrop of a terraced hillside garden, which had gone somnolent for the season. The statue of Saint Patrick himself, with nary a snake to be seen, was centered in a wishing fountain directly in the middle of the shrine, it too being dormant for the season.

Traveling around the lucky Saint, the solace seeking parishioners now proceeded past the majesty of the shrine's gargantuan brick-and-mortar stained glass cathedral and its equally gargantuan, but less majestic, parking lot. Lastly, when they had reached the end of an almost endless carpet of macadam, they finally came to the particular object of their quest, —Saint Patrick's Fellowship Hall and Sister Linda's Shop of Religious Supplies.

"Good afternoon," a cheerful voice spoke out, unseen from behind a barricade of free standing shelves of small statuettes and brightly colored figurines of piety, the minute Jolanda had opened the door.

"Hello?" Jolanda responded, seeking to physically match the voice with the person behind it.

The small store, being perhaps only twelve feet wide and about twice as long, was crammed with all sorts of religious artifacts. Annie had come in behind her mother and, as the silver doorbell vatically tinkled above her, she tightly closed the door behind her as to shut out the cold and promptly stationed herself by the front counter next to the cash register.

"Can I help you?" the cheerful voice spoke up again, revealing its source to be an elderly nun, now rounding the corner of one of the six-foot high, fully stocked partitions.

"Yes, —I am looking for some candles for a Shrine of Novena," Jolanda requested humbly.

"How large is the shrine to be?" asked the Sister in trying to be mindful of Jolanda's needs.

"It will only be a small shrine. Just one for my home," answered Jolanda.

"Will the candles be burning through the night?" the nun politely inquired.

"Yes, they will," Jolanda informed her.

"Well then, you need the candles that are poured into glass. They, of course, are much safer than the free-standing candles. They will also last much longer. Come this way," advised the Sister, leading Jolanda over to a shelf which displayed a plethora of glass candles with all sorts of saints and religious scenes pictured upon them, while Annie stayed behind.

"As you can see, there are many to choose from," the nun continued, "The taller ones should last two to three days. Sometimes they can last up to four days if there is no breeze about. I will leave you to your selection now. If you should need anything else, I will be over at the counter," the pleasant shopkeeper stated, leaving Jolanda with the privacy to make her own decisions.

After Jolanda had made her selections, one by one, a total of ten candles were chosen, along with a one-half ounce of frankincense oil, and an ornate silver "Mass Card."

"Will that be all? the helpful nun asked pleasantly as Jolanda began to carefully place her purchases on top of the checkout counter.

"Yes, I believe that will be all," Jolanda answered in kind, opening her purse to pay for what she had picked out.

"I'll carry them, Mom," offered Annie after the clerk had run up and bagged the sale.

"Thank you," Jolanda said to the clerk, turning with her daughter to exit the shop as unpretentiously as they had come in.

Jolanda decided that there was no sense in requesting for a mass be held for the salvation of Bobby's soul by Father Bernardino, since it was something that he could not grant, being Bobby had never been ordained a Catholic. But this did not, nonetheless, exclude her from praying to her own shrine for Bobby's sake, and for the salvation of her daughter's soul, as well.

It was a simple shrine. The ornate silver gilded "Mass Card" with a picture of Jesus amongst a flock of lambs had been centered between two of the tall glass candles atop the living room credenza and under the hanging cut glass mirror above it. In front of the card Jolanda had also placed her best set of rosary beads for anyone to use, if the spirit within them had suddenly moved them unto prayer. The small bottle of frankincense had been placed on the right of the shrine to perhaps provide some solace and healing within the sorrowful hearts of all the beseechers who further sought to attain some additional comfort. It was a most reverent and considerate shrine.

Chapter Twenty-Three

The funeral attendees were both voluminous and dismal inside the St. Andrew's Episcopal Church on that Saturday afternoon when Bobby's funeral was held. Despite the emergence of a clear and placid day outside, the sadness of the event still cast an overriding shadow of insecurity upon all who were there in reverent attendance.

Built in 1789, the white and single steepled tabernacle was constructed in the classical design of the day. Its large front doors led directly to the lobby which, in turn, led to its main chapel. There were a set of twin stairways constructed on both sides of the entrance area, leading straight up to the balconies, which stretched the entire length of the inside walls of the worship area.

Open coat closets were constructed under the stairwells on either side of the lobby, and centered between the two opposite doors, which lead directly into the chapel, was positioned a vine-covered grey stone planter with a small running waterfall, whose basin was adorned with a half-dozen white doves who were all peacefully congregating about its edge. Painted above this was a pastel fresco of Jesus delivering his Sermon on the Mount in beatifying all who sought to be uplifted. It was a serene area that had truly made everyone feel welcome.

Inside the main sanctuary was a row of center pews with an aisle on either side, separating them from the side pews, which stretched over to and under the balconies above. This gave a sheltered feeling to all who sat beneath the vaunted veranda, as the stained-glass windows along the side walls projected aesthetic warmth throughout the entirety of the room, especially on a sunny Sunday morning.

The pulpit area was elevated, and positioned behind it was a twelve-foot gold cross which hung from the ceiling. A hundred-year-old gilded pipe organ, which covered almost the entire back wall, was simply a wonder to see. The dedicated choir's section, also elevated and positioned to the left side of the pulpit, was further denoted by a two-and-a-half-foot privacy railing of white enameled wainscoting. To the right side of the pulpit was a matching elevated area where the organist sat.

The lectern itself, having endured many a coat of white gloss enamel itself over the years, was original and had been built with the church itself. Neither overly impending nor underwhelming, the entirety of the pulpit area had sufficed, quite properly, to take the room's center attention from whence the minister was ordained to address all who came before it in humble worship.

The front pew had been reserved for Bobby's immediate family, while the rest of Taylors sat to the right of the first pew and the Russo family was invited to sit on its left. The amount of Taylor family members that were in attendance paled in comparison to the multitudes of the Russo clan, who were there in full force. It was standing room only in the medium sized church that day, for the entire high school body had come to pay their respects to the first one to fall in military service from the class of sixty-seven.

Up until the service itself, the ushers were frantically scurrying about to find some additional room in which to place the never-ending stream of flowers that had been arriving by the minute. The flood of flowers had enshrined the altar to such a degree that even the vacant choir section had been overcome with a cascading carpet of vibrant colors.

The covered casket was centered in front of the pulpit and had been draped with an American flag. Standing sprays of red and yellow roses, offset with Stargazer lilies, were placed behind the casket as its backdrop, while off to the right end of the coffin was a large military portrait of Bobby, displayed upon an easel.

After the Twenty Third Psalm was recited, and the Gloria Patri doxology had been sung by all, the pastor began the eulogy. Bobby, having attended the small-town church on a fairly regular basis when growing up, was familiar to the Reverend, who had become quite taken by the gregarious boy. And so, the service was begun with a personal reflection of the young soldier. From childhood, the pastor related to all how Bobby had always given of himself cheerfully in attending the many church functions, from the summer carwashes to the cake walks at the annual carnival, while especially helping out during the holiday season.

Then, as the Reverend concluded his litany of the many other memorable moments to which Bobby had been associated with, along with citing the more commendable highlights of his character, he tactfully changed the eulogy's deliverance from the exaltations of the deceased to the salvation of the souls at hand.

"As all our passion burns within us, telling us that it is wrong of God and the natural laws of nature to take away a soul so young in life, we must also now be ever grateful for the gift of life that he still grants within us all," the Minister began. "The tragedy that a parent must witness the early retirement of their child's mortal life before them is a cross to bear unlike any other. For God giveth and God taketh away, and as I stand here, a servant unto God, I can truly testify that the Lamb of God that taketh away the sins of the world will have mercy upon him," he attested boldly.

"And as his body is entered into the earth, his soul will still flower within us all, for as long as we all shall live, his fond memory will always be alive within us," he declared.

"Is this not a gift from God?" he then challenged rhetorically. "Are not all these flowers about us here today, a gift from God as well?" he emphasized. "So, is it not the same loving God that needed Robert William Taylor's soul the same loving God that left us with his fond memory to grow and bloom within us, just like these flowers bloom here before us?

"When we become lost in times of trouble, and beginning to doubt our own life's destiny, will not Bobby Taylor be there to comfort us? I say that he is the one who is trying to comfort *us* right now. And if you can feel this, is it not proof of an everlasting life within all who seek God's clemency?" he again proposed rhetorically. "So, I am going to now ask for a minute of silence, so that we all might reflect unto the glory of God's divine will and the salvation of Bobby Taylor's soul," and with this he folded his hands before him and bowed his head.

Then, in silence, the entire congregation prayed until an "Amen" was heard from the pulpit and a resounding "Amen" was responded in turn.

"Now, being a man of the cloth," the pastor continued on again in a more familiar tone, "I usually try to conduct my services in the sole light of the Holy Scriptures, as I have been entrusted to do, however, there are certain times that I feel that as an individual, and before God myself, that I should make a small contribution of my own.

I now confess to all of you that I could not prevent myself from feeling a great sadness in my own heart over the passing of Bobby Taylor," he admitted somberly. "And so, I wish to share with you the end of a secular poem that I once had to read as part of my studies to become a minister of God. It is considered a romantic poem written over a hundred years ago by Percy Shelly. I hope that in this poem's final verse you can gain an understanding about the nature of God, which I perchance could not adequately convey. It has always been a great comfort to me in times like this, and I wish to share it with you.

Its title is '*Ode to the West Wind,*' and its last lines read:

Scatter, as from an extinguished hearth
Ashes and sparks, my words among mankind!
Be through my lips to unwakened earth

The trumpet of a prophecy! O wind,
If winter comes, can spring be far behind?"

Then, in finality, the ceremony was closed with, "May the Lamb of God that taketh away the sins of the world have mercy upon you. May the Lamb of God that taketh away the sins of the world have mercy upon you. May the Lamb of God that taketh away the sins of the world have mercy upon you. Amen." Thus, the sermon of the flowering soul was concluded.

Now although the church was not considered large, it did have its own cemetery on its grounds, and so the entire multitude of mourners went outside to witness the military burial. Then, following the 21-gun salute, everyone was invited to walk over to the church's fellowship center for some refreshments and respectful condolences to the family.

While many a good-natured friend and relative brought covered dishes and copious platters of food to eat and helped in serving them, still others milled about, renewing old acquaintances while waiting in turn to visit in sympathy with the immediate family.

Annie had been graciously seated at the Taylor's table, along with her mother Jolanda, as a natural part of the family. Enrico, Capricia and the other members of the Russo family considerately chose to sit apart from the main table so as not to interfere with the Taylor family's personal grief.

The senior visitors had gravitated generally toward the elder folks, while Bobby's and Annie's high school aged companions stopped by mostly console Annie. It was agreed by all that the food was most complementary to the occasion, but as the time trudged on into the late afternoon and the refreshments dwindled, so too did the bereaved guests. Thus, at conclusion of the day's most somber event, at four o'clock on April the thirteenth, nineteen hundred and sixty-eight, Bobby Taylor's Rite of Passage had been consecrated, honored, and dedicated unto the ages.

Annie talked little to anyone after the funeral and thereafter only responded in turn with one-word answers. She expounded upon nothing. Her countenance became void of any expression whatsoever, and she had ceased to question anything. Except for her meals, she stayed in her room in a state of mournful grief that manifested itself into a hopeless despondency that drove her into a continuous dreamt reality of her past.

Sleeping only in an emotional state of exhaustion, Annie spent her entire time awake hoping in vain that she could just magically instill herself into the fantasies that she had so envisioned. She even stopped attending church with her mother, choosing to stay at home alone with only her misery as her sole companion.

Neither Jolanda nor Capricia risked trying to engage Annie in any convivial conversation in fear of stirring up an uncontrolled emotional response. Even the evening meals, although now relatively enjoyable, were entirely absent from any frivolity whatsoever.

It took almost two weeks for Enrico to summon up enough fortitude to even think about having to confront the anticipated stress that he knew he would have to endure in directly having to address Annie's depression. Eventually, however, after noticing that Annie filed her fingernails down to where she had none, and she had lost ten pounds or better, he decided that he could wait no longer, and on the next Friday evening after dinner, he decided that would confront her.

After Enrico had apprised both Jolanda and Capricia of his intentions ahead of time and was poured his after-dinner coffee as was planned, instead of offering up some type of dessert, both Jolanda and Capricia simply got up, excused themselves from the table, and left the room. All alone now, except for Annie, Enrico began his appeal.

"Honey, are you coming back to work in the office next week?" he asked tenderly, trying to avoid the possibility of her misconstruing his concern for her welfare with an authoritative directive.

"No. I am not going back to the office," Annie answered respectfully, but still in a tone of resolution. "I don't know what I'm going to do now, but I am not going back to the office, that I do know," she fixedly reinforced.

"Well, you don't have to, but you just can't stay in your room forever," Enrico told her with a little more force. "Your mother is worried about you," he stated flatly. "Now, I'm not going into work tomorrow. I can take you anywhere you want to go, even if you just want to get out of the house. It's up to you. Wherever you want to go, I will take you," he offered, looking directly at her with the obvious expectation of a dutiful reply.

"You could take me over to visit Bobby in the morning," Annie responded antiseptically.

"Okay then, we'll leave about ten o'clock after breakfast, okay with you?" Enrico affably suggested, trying to accommodate to her wishes with a minimal amount of tension.

"Yeah, that's fine. Can I go now?" Annie asked.

"Sure, no one's got a rope around you. I'll see you in the morning," Enrico responded, rising from his chair.

~

"I'll stop at the flower shop first, if you want," Enrico thoughtfully proposed to Annie, exiting the driveway the next morning after breakfast, as agreed.

"Thank you, Daddy," Annie sincerely replied, for the first time in a while.

Spring was now definitely in motion on that day they traveled to the Garden of Eden Flower Shop, as the weather outside was now pleasant enough to only require the donning of a sweater. The air was still cool and breezy, but once underneath the direct influence of the sun, a sort of coziness could be felt beneath its radiant warmth as the chilling coattails of a winter's past elusively wisped around them in a crisp and intermittent burst of a forget-me-not solicitation.

The shop was small and well stocked with all types of both popular and exotic flora which had been gratuitously displayed for all to leisurely peruse. Dish gardens, potted peace lilies, wedding arches, portable kneeling benches, and a complete selection of silken sprays and wreaths were all arranged decorously for the selective viewing of the prospective customers.

Upon entering the florist shop, an entire wall of greeting and sympathy cards were displayed against the store's right-hand wall and extended uninterruptedly to the end of the room. To the left of the door was the sales counter to pay for the buyer's selection when leaving the store.

Behind the sales counter was a large work space allowing an unfettered access to the twelve-foot work counter against the far-left wall, which was shelved with all kinds of supplies necessary to the trade. Bolted on the far-right end of the work counter was the pick machine, —a cast iron monstrosity for fusing barbed tin spikes onto the stems of silk flowers for the purpose of harpooning them into an unsuspecting green block of foam, intended to become the base of the "natural-looking" arrangement.

The very front of the store was virtually one large display window, and against the back wall, butting against the end of the long card rack, stood a lighted four door glass cooler with a live promenade of arrangements in vases and various pastoral baskets of spring colored flowers.

Enrico quietly informed the florist as to the nature of their presence, and being fully aware of Bobby's funeral, it was agreed that Annie should make her own selection, without any outside influence. Once past the front counter, her journey began. She had never been in a flower shop before, and was astonished to see the scope of events to which flowers could be dedicated. Not only were their flowers to be given at births, deaths, and weddings, but for every holiday and occasion imaginable.

Both Enrico and the proprietor remained by the counter, while Annie went on by herself to make her own selection and again be alone with her thoughts. This time, however, Annie was under the influence of the Garden of Eden, where her empathy for the perishable flowers all but made her own personal grief, by comparison, seem to be a trivial thing.

What a brief life they have, Annie reflected. *But what a life of brilliant color and happiness they provide to so many others, as year after year the same flowers come back to be in full bloom for everyone to enjoy, just like a cherished memory. I guess it really is exactly like the Reverend said in his eulogy,* she concluded, now beginning to feel some small degree of comfort.

It was at this point that Annie was struck with the idea that she was actually blessed to have the sanctity of Bobby's soul yet flowering within her. This thought was at least one good thing that she could salvage from his passing, she now justified.

And it was in this revelation, Annie postulated, that to select some lilies for Bobby's gravesite would be the wrong choice, and accordingly picked out a simple spring bouquet from the glass cooler. Then, removing the batch of posies from its container, Annie brought them over to the check-out counter and laid them down.

"Is this your selection? the florist politely asked.

"Yes," Annie replied to the aproned woman.

Picking up the flowers, the florist took them over to the work table, and after deftly mixing in some additional baby's breath, some fresh green ferns, and tightly taping the bundle together at bottom of their stems for it to fit precisely into the bronze vase ensepulchered at the head of the gravesite under the shadow of Bobby's tombstone, the arrangement was complete, for she was thoroughly familiar with the uniform requirements of the church's gravesite. Finally, after wrapping the arrangement in a green floral tissue paper and tying it tightly with a curled yellow ribbon, the floral artist handed it to Annie.

"Just unwrap the flowers from the paper and put them, exactly as I have them taped, into the metal vase by the headstone. You should be fine," the florist concluded.

"Thank you," Annie replied, while Enrico put down a twenty-dollar bill to pay for them.

"That will be five ninety-five and three percent sales tax," the florist said, ringing up the sale.

"That's fine," commented Enrico, holding out his hand to receive the change. "Thank you," he then courteously added.

"Thank you," the florist replied in return.

Following a short and silent ride over to the Episcopal church, Enrico smoothly pulled the Cadillac into the parking lot betwixt the main sanctuary and the modest community graveyard. Guarded by a pair of six-foot-high brick-and-mortar columns parting a four-foot evergreen hedgerow, its opening gave way unto a blue gravel walkway that wound its way about the insides of the grounds. To each side of the columns sat a matching pair of wrought iron benches which, when sat upon, brought absolutely no comfort to anyone, alive or dead. A flagstone walkway had been laid in the front of the iron benches and ambled along the hedgerow to the back of the property to where the maintenance shed was located.

After getting out of the car and nearing the cemetery's entrance, Enrico placidly said to Annie, "I'm going to stay out here, if that's alright with you. I'll be out here on this bench," he sustained.

"That's fine, I can go by myself," replied Annie as she walked on alone.

After about half an hour and two cigarettes later, and precisely as twelve o'clock church bell tolled the noontime hour, Annie emerged back through the vine covered Pillars of Hercules, ostensibly into new world.

"Okay, I'm ready to go," stated Annie to her father, still sitting on the bench with his head down after just having lit his third cigarette.

"Do you want me to take you home now?" questioned Enrico, looking up and directly at her.

"No, but I would like you to take me to Saint Margaret's College, if we have the time," Annie requested.

"It will take over an hour for us to get there, you know," Enrico briefed her factually, not questioning the request.

"I know," was Annie's two-word answer.

"I can take you if you want, but I hope you realize that we have to be back for your mother's dinner by six, so we can't spend a whole lot of time there," cited Enrico out of respect for Jolanda's efforts.

"No, I don't want to be late for dinner, either. I just want to take a look at the campus there, that's all," replied Annie, being openly cognizant of the parameters.

"Okay. Let's go, then," agreed Enrico standing up and crushing out his cigarette on the flagstone walkway beneath his feet.

"So, you have a reason for wanting to see the College of Saint Margaret?" Enrico asked, once he had gotten the car onto the highway.

"Yes, I do. I thought I might go there, that is, if you would let me," Annie submitted. "I really don't want to go back to the office, and I don't want to go to that ridiculous community college, either. I just want to go someplace that I don't have to think about the whole stupid town," she rattled off tempestuously.

"It just makes me sick to be reminded every day about Bobby," she continued. "I can't go anywhere that doesn't remind me of him. Everywhere I go, I have been there with him. And everyone I know, asks me the same stupid questions, —'How are you feeling Annie?' 'What are you going to do now, Annie?' —and it just makes me sick," she outright declared.

"So, yes, in answer to your question, I do have a reason to go to St. Margaret's, —even if it's just to get away," stated Annie definitively, only to add in a much softer tone, "and besides, I'm sure Mother wouldn't mind it at all."

"Okay, sure, that's fine by me. If you want to go there, then you can go there," Enrico told her, "I only asked what your reason was, that's all," he stated plainly, tactfully disengaging from his daughter's barrage of emotional victimization. "Well, now that we have that settled, why don't we just enjoy the ride, okay?" he proposed after a short silence, reaching over and turning on the car's stereo to an easy listening station.

~

The college was located in the foothills of the mountains and was the main employer of the small hamlet which surrounded it. For over a hundred years, the ivy-covered administration building had dwarfed the other buildings in the town and carried on a good reputation for providing a fine parochial education to the women of the Catholic faith.

With fourteen-foot ceilings on every floor, technically being only a three-story building, it appeared almost five stories high. Its massive stone façade commanded a righteous admonition upon the entirety of all those who dared speak critically of its dominate position in the community.

A large round stained-glass window was centered on the third-floor elevation between its two impending square stone towers, cornered on either side of the front of the structure. This architectural presentation of the Chancellery gave everyone the distinct impression that its sole and specific purpose was to keep a vigilant eye upon all those who were under its auspices, and in reverence to the substantial contribution that the institution had made in the growth and prosperity of the town over the years, the city council had respectfully passed an ordinance that no other three story commercial buildings were to be henceforth built within the city's limits.

A small Abbey to the rear of the grounds was connected to it by means of a meandering covered brick walkway, and from there the walkway went on to connect the abbey to the main chapel on its other side. These three preeminently matching grey stone buildings thus formed a frontal courtyard, replete with a set of corresponding stone benches, manicured greenery, and a life-sized statue of the Madonna at its center. The chapel's steeple, adorned with an eight-foot gold cross mounted atop a twelve-foot copper spire with a green patina, actually achieved a height much greater than the Chancellery, but the massive size alone of the college's administration building easily appeared to contradict this fact.

The grounds themselves had become completely intertwined within the city itself as a considerable amount of non-contiguous property over the years had been gifted to the burgeoning institution as it grew. The town was the college and the college, the town.

It was about one thirty in the afternoon when Enrico Russo had pulled his Cadillac off the state highway and quietly rolled it into the downtown area of the diminutive municipality. Following the arrowed signs that read "The College of Saint Margaret," Enrico was able to park on the street directly across from the entrance to the main campus. There were a sparse number of students that were seen to be leisurely milling about the grounds and a few more clustered upon the benches in the central garden area when Annie and her father got out of the car to survey the main campus from the gum-spotted sidewalk contiguous to the school.

"Could you tell me where the administration building is?" questioned Annie of the first uniformed student they had come into contact with.

"Are you kidding me?" the short haired girl laughed. "You must be new around here," she smiled in amusement. "Well, you see that giant building behind me? That's it, in all its glory. It's only the largest monstrosity in the whole town, that's all," she quipped. "It's pretty much closed this afternoon, —after all, it is a Saturday, you know," she noted smartly. "Now, you may be able to find one of the Sisters over at the Abbey, though," she then suggested helpfully. "That's that smaller building at the end of the courtyard," she physically pointed out. "Well, I've got to go now, lots of luck," the young girl ended dismissively, promptly turning to continue on her way.

"Well, what do you want to do now?" asked Enrico, waiting for instruction.

"I just want to walk around for a while and see if I like it," Annie replied. "Come on, let's go on over to the covered walkway over there," she proposed, moving in its direction.

"So, you think that you might want to go here? It seems nice enough," Enrico offered affably.

"Well, it's far enough away, and like I said, I think it would make Mother happy if I went here," Annie responded in a more considerate tone than one in resolve. "And I do agree with you, it is pretty nice here. This garden sure is well kept, and I guess it's quiet enough, alright," she observed out loud while they continued to leisurely amble away.

After strolling about the meticulously kept grounds for about twenty minutes, Annie and her father eventually reached the Abbey at the back of the complex. Then, after entering through a covered alcove and passing through an arched wooden doorway marked "Office," they came upon a small reception area with one of the Sisters punctiliously seated at a highly polished and particularly ornate, antique escritoire.

"May I be of some help?" asked the Sister dutifully.

"Yes, I was looking for someone who could give me some information about going to college here?" inquired Annie politely.

"Are you Catholic?" the Sister asked imperiously.

"Yes, sister, I have been baptized and confirmed in the St. James Cathedral," Annie courteously replied.

"Well, I guess that certainly must qualify you as a Catholic, my child, doesn't it?" the Sister decreed in an officious attitude, while Enrico stood silently by.

"Yes, that is what I've been told, Sister," Annie responded in a like kind manner. "Well, anyway, I was wondering if there was someone here this afternoon who could help me get a pamphlet or a catalogue, or at least something that would help me apply for admission here in the fall. I was told there was no one at the administration building this afternoon, so here I am. Am I in the right place?" she asked respectfully.

"Yes, you are in the right place, young lady. The administration building does close at twelve o'clock on Saturdays," the officious nun affirmed. "But I do believe that I can help you," she stated assertively. "I always keep a few admission packages in my station here in the event of a situation occurring exactly like this," the Sister related, rising from her chair to go over to a tall wooden filing cabinet in the corner of the room behind her. "I would recommend that you make a proper appointment the next time," she proposed without looking up, still searching the cabinet for an admission packet, "You will find that we can be of a much greater help if we are prepared ahead of time to attend your special requirements, as I believe you are in need of," the Sister spoke up prophetically, now glancing sideways at Annie momentarily before finishing her search.

"Thank you very much, Sister," Annie replied appreciatively, imagining the sister could actually feel the anguish within her.

"By the way, child, I am Sister Sara, the Mother Superior's first administrative assistant. Now, should you need any further help with your application, please do not hesitate to ask. That is one of my functions here," she offered with a small pleasant smile, handing over a large manila envelope to Annie's awaiting hand.

"Well, I thank you for everything, Sister Sara, and I will certainly let you know if I do," Annie responded most appreciatively.

"Thank you for your help, Sister," added Enrico, as the two of them took their leave.

"May God bless you both," the sister then imparted, making the sign of the cross in the conclusion of their visit.

"I want to go here, if you don't mind, Daddy," Annie almost pleaded the instant they had gotten back into the car. "Do you think I can?" she asked without the overtone of her grief showing for the first time since the death of Bobby.

"Like I said, if you want to go here, then you will go here," Enrico pronounced clinically. "Will that make you happy?" he asked in concern.

"It will help," she said frankly.

"Then, if you really want to go, you still have one more thing to do," Enrico stipulated.

"What is that?" Annie asked in puzzlement.

"You have to ask you mother, that's what," he told her as he glanced over to her with a smile.

"Is that it?" Annie questioned in disbelief.

"That's all there is to it," Enrico confirmed.

"Oh, thank you Daddy! I will try to be happy, I promise," Annie replied in making her best attempt to allay his concerns.

"Now, this I just want you to remember, Annie," Enrico said in a sincere tone. "No matter how far you travel, no matter where you end up being, you will still never be able to run away from yourself. You understand that?" he questioned assertively.

"Yes, Daddy, I know, I won't forget," she acknowledged.

Chapter Twenty-Four

Mahoney Hall, the dormitory to which Annie had been assigned, was where all the first-year students who did not commute were placed. Upon a second visit, after being accepted to attend, Annie was encouraged to visit one of the vacant rooms in preparation of her intended stay. The "suite" consisted of two rooms, each attached together between a common bathroom with a separate access door from each side. Each room was designed to house two students.

The spartanly decorated rooms had two large sliding door closets which could be locked, matching twin wooden beds with side stands, and two oaken study desks with a set of bookshelves which were mounted on the wall directly above. A matching chair had also been provided for each of the desks and a fluorescent light fixture was affixed under the overhanging shelf for the individual's evening study. A small brass lamp was placed on the top of each of the side stands. These were the complete furnishings that had constituted the entirety of the room's decor.

After witnessing the frugal atmosphere that inherently pervaded all the rooms in the building and in conversation with one of the older residents of the hall, Annie got her first taste of what her new "dorm life" would be like. It was also then she first learned that the hall was rumored to be haunted by "Saint Margaret the Virgin herself," and that all of the girls there must be pure, or suffer in penance for as long as they lived under her auspices. Annie did not think that the story was the least bit amusing.

Orientation for the fall admissions was traditionally held every year in the Saint Augustine cafetorium on the first Saturday in September. On one end of the large room was the school's cafeteria, and showcased at its opposite end was a curtained stage of dark violet, suspended on high from its proscenium and extending its entire length. Ending at either side of the raised stage was also a low set of stairs for frontal access.

The facility was designed to hold five hundred students at a time, a scooch less than the entire student body. The eight-foot dining room tables were customarily folded up and removed when the room had to be arranged "theatre style" for any significant event, and such was the case for all the school's orientations.

It was precisely at nine o'clock sharp on that next Saturday morning in September of sixty-eight when Sister Elizabeth tapped upon the microphone protruding up from the cherry lectern in front of her and announced, "Attention, class, attention," while the room's chatter slowly fell into silence.

"The orientation for girls who will be domiciled here at Saint Margaret's will now begin," it was decreed.

Sister Elizabeth was a serious nun who stood about five-foot ten. Thinly featured and standing erect as a board, she was always perceived to be much taller at a distance. Her perfectly starched wimple added an immeasurable amount of stature to her character, lording over her entire presence.

When closely encountered, however, it was her seasoned facial caricature and dead pan deportment which would completely trump any errant concerns one may have had in considering there may be even the slightest weakness of resolve within her. With her intense and piercing dark brown eyes, she was known to stop an altercation simply by casting a discerning look upon its participants. Indomitable, she stood before her flock and commanded their presence with the surgical grace and ease of a superlative administrator.

A woman of conviction in her early sixties, she bore a countenance which reflected an acquired wisdom that had become naturally etched into her total character by the serious burden of her invocation. She was considered by all to be earnest in every respect. Her face projected neither sternness nor compassion, as officiousness was her charge, and she performed her function flawlessly.

"I am Sister Elizabeth. Since we do not have an Abbot overseeing our most humble abbey anymore, anyone who is interested in the blessings of Father Mc Gregor's Order may find him over at the church on site. The Father also delivers the Sunday Mass, at which I expect every student of the Catholic faith here to attend.

"I have been given the duty of head administrator for this college, and I also hold the title of Mother Superior, responsible for the school's parochial matters, as well. For all others who are not of the faith, I am the Dean of this institution. For unceremonious matters, I do not mind being addressed as Sister Elizabeth, or Dean, as we are all loved equally in the eyes of God.

"Now, the first thing that I feel we must address is the newly reported sighting of the apparition of 'Saint Margaret the Virgin' in the dormitory. I cannot witness that I have personally seen this phenomenon, however, it has been rumored that the spirit of Saint Margaret speaks to every young woman that first walks into her dorm room," she stated, pausing for a moment while she seemed to scan the room for anyone who was not paying attention.

"For all those who doubt this, when you first finished your initial surveillance of your living quarters, did not someone mysteriously whisper into your ear, 'You mean to tell me that the only place in here that has a mirror is the bathroom?'" she quoted to a snickering audience and pausing briefly. "That, my children, was the spirit Saint

Margaret the Virgin herself, or so I am told," she officially reported. "Did anyone not hear her?" was then asked pointedly, as the interrogative had efficaciously produced nary a single denial.

"There is a curfew that is in effect for all who reside in the women's dormitory and is enforced by the locking of the facility at ten o'clock in the evening, Sundays through Thursdays, and eleven on Fridays and Saturdays by the Resident Sister who is also quartered in the dormitory on the first floor. Permission for any girl to stay out later can easily be obtained from the Resident Sister simply by request with an acceptable reason," the Mother Superior annotated assertively. "Sister Ruth, what would you say would be and acceptable reason?" she questioned directly over to the stout and stern looking nun standing by the side exit of the room.

Without moving her brick-like stature, which was in fact blocking the door, and without changing her hard-shelled appearance, Sister Ruth looked up in reflection at the ceiling and then replied to the student body in a notable German accent, "Vel, I zink dat if de girls ver out looking up at Gott's stars, unt Professor Schmidt vas vif dem az a chaperone for her astrology class, unt she vas explaining die accepted rules uf der heavenly bodies, I vud zink den, dat vud be okay," she advanced out loud. "Ya, dat vud be acceptable," she additionally reinforced.

"You see, girls, *that* is an acceptable reason," Sister Elizabeth confirmed with great look of approval upon her countenance, nodding her head over to Sister Ruth in concurrence. "Continuing now," the Mother Superior began again, "each dorm room will be shared by two students companioned together for the academic year. You will be roommates. In turn you will share your bathroom facilities with a second set of roommates which will become your suite mates. Based upon your applications, we have tried to suit everyone together by their shared commonalities. Reverence to God and to each other in all matters shall be observed.

"Now, there is only one regulation to which there is no dispensation under any condition, and to violate it *will* result in immediate dismissal," she stated resolutely, "and that is, under no circumstances are men allowed to enter the women's dormitory. If it is burning down, it is the duty of your Resident Advisor to be the last one to leave. Then, and only then, will the firemen be allowed to enter the women's dormitory," she decreed, as Sister Ruth, still standing vigilantly at her post, suddenly exclaimed out loud, "Oh, Gott in Himmel!" while she frantically held up a large wooden cross that was prominently secured to her cincture. This, as a matter of course, again drew a number of random chuckles from the audience, as well as a harsh look of censure from the lectern. Then, as soon as the respectful decorum had been restored, Sister Elizabeth continued.

"When you leave here, there will be a package on the table next to the door with your name on it. You will see that the first thing in the packet is a map revealing all of the campus buildings which are part of the college.

"The administration building will be open until five o'clock today, where you can obtain the keys to your rooms for you to begin your move in. You are then all expected to return here at eight o'clock on Monday morning to begin your class selections. Sister Ruth has a staff that will be more than happy to attend to your needs and will be available to help you after eleven o'clock today in the lobby of Mahoney Hall after picking up your keys. She will be your Resident Advisor. And now, that concludes your instructions for today, so ladies, together," The Mother Superior bowed her head, "'Hail Mary, full of grace, the Lord is with thee. Blessed art thou among women, and blessed is the fruit of thy womb, Jesus. Holy Mary, mother of God, pray for us sinners, now and at the hour of our death. Amen."'

~

After leaving the cafetorium, packet in hand, Annie went directly over to the courtyard area where her mother, father, and Capricia were patiently seated.

"I have to go to the main office in the administration building to pick up the keys to my room, and then I can move my stuff in," Annie announced upon arriving.

"Don't you think we can get something to eat first? You have all day to move in, and after today, your mother and I won't be seeing you for a while," Enrico pointed out without getting up. "Besides, do you want to fight that line over there for an hour just to get your keys?" he noted, glancing over in the direction of the administration building.

"No, I guess I don't," Annie sighed in accepting the situation.

"So, come on," Enrico said pleasantly, standing up and offering his hand to Jolanda. "I think I want some pancakes. I saw an International House of Pancakes down the street by that new mall, just as I got off the interstate," he suggested.

"I want the apple pancakes," Capricia spoke up eagerly.

"You can have all the apple pancakes you can eat, sunshine," responded Enrico, trying his best to make light of the times.

It took about an hour and a half for everyone to be fed to capacity and give Annie their best wishes, as well as the usual unwanted advice, before promptly returning to the campus for everyone to say their goodbyes.

"Oh, I just know you are going to have a good time here!" Capricia predicted enthusiastically, once everyone had arrived at the front door of the Mahoney Hall.

Although the comment was particularly irritating to Annie, she ignored it, for she did not feel that she was going to the college for a "good time" at all. She only felt that the unfair world had forced her to be there, and dictating it should be so did not make her happy in the least.

Eventually, after there was nothing left to say, Annie pledged to write, or at least call, and then hugged her mother and sister. Then, driven more out of grateful appreciation than anything else, she kissed her father on the cheek, and with her luggage trolley in tow, promptly became consumed by the institution itself. She did not look back.

Mildly surprised when Annie finally got to her dorm room, she noticed that the door was standing ajar and stopped for a moment to wonder why. Slowly, after she had pushed the door open a little further, she saw a very tall and thin girl bent over the bed against the farthest wall, tucking in its sheets. Startled, the girl spontaneously stood upright and revealed that she was nigh on six feet tall.

Her jet black, tousled hair surrounded her light freckled completion as if she had just been caught frolicking with a windstorm on a summer's day. With a tiny turned up nose and the wisp, of a smile she reflected the picture of innocence, while her pale blue eyes and naturally arched eyebrows also gave her the inquisitive look of a child.

Her willowy figure, which flowed from the long, graceful line of her neck in traversing the entirety of her form in delicately accentuating the thirty-six-inch curvature of her hips, was unavoidably noteworthy and could not help but felicitously accent the tightness of her jeans. The one single anomaly which presented itself to be incongruent to the aesthetically rhythmic continuity of her most slender and supple pliancy was the size of her feet. They were only a half an inch from becoming a true "foot" in every sense of the word. And that was with her shoes off, which they were.

Diametrically opposed, physically, the two girls now stood there in a brief silence while both of them could not believe their eyes. *What commonality could I possibly have with her?* each of them had instantaneously thought to themselves.

"Hello. My name is Jill," the tall girl said, first to politely introduce herself.

"Well, everyone calls me Annie," she slowly responded, becoming transfixed on the size of the girl's bare feet. Then, suddenly snapping out of her daze, she quickly turned away to briefly glance over her shoulder, and looking back said, "Well, I'll go bring in my stuff now," while promptly retreating to the hallway to wheel in her luggage.

Banging and clunking the cumbersome trolley through the doorway, Annie eventually negotiated it directly next to the vacant bedside opposite Jill's, and then began to unload her belongings, one piece of luggage at a time.

"You can have this side if you want," offered Jill amiably. "I don't really care. I just got here first, but it really doesn't make any difference to me."

"No, that's okay, I'm good over here," Annie said shortly.

Jill Jillian seemed to have been born tall. For as long as she could remember, she was the tallest girl in her class, both in grammar and high school. Consequently because of this fact, she had to sadly endure a relentless torrent of ridicule. Her feet did not escape their fair share of attention, either. Cruelly, she was called a "Flat Foot Floozy" and laughed at, when ironically, she'd never even been on a date. She was indeed the girl that sat at home on the night of the prom and read a book.

Jill Jill, or Jill Sillyan, as she was also nicknamed, could never catch a break and no one came to her rescue. She was made to feel like a clown for the sport of others, and its effect had a most decisive influence on her psyche. The constant barrage of abusive taunts from the other students did not, however, cause any adversarial thoughts of retaliation. Instead, it only manifested itself in the installation of a complete aloofness within her demeanor towards everyone.

An only child, Jill was born unto parents who embraced the "intellectual approach" to raising her, and consequently dismissed their daughter's feelings of inferiority as simply not germane to her educational melioration. In fact, they dismissed their daughter's feelings altogether. "For your personal feelings just get in the way of a good education," they would remind her whenever she had sought some degree of solace from them. "All you need to do is mind your studies," they would reiterate, while totally rejecting her emotional pleas without any apparent concern.

It was difficult to discern which one of the girls spoke the least. The entire first semester was mostly spent in silent acclimation to their surroundings. They went to vespers together occasionally out of boredom and attended the church services with the same benign indifference towards each other as they did when they went to the cafetorium to eat their meals. It was something to do besides study.

Scholastically, having no outside distractions, the two of them had no problem in receiving an invitation to join the honor society, and together made the Dean's List in their first semester. They both went home for Thanksgiving. They both went home for Christmas. And they both went home again after their final exams, each marking the end of their first experience away from home.

Well, I survived that, at least, the two of them now thought independently, as they each vowed to themselves with certitude that they would return.

It was after they did return to start their second semester that the hundred-dollar question was finally asked: and that was, "How come you decided to go to Saint Margaret's?" And its answer actually lay in the "commonality" to which Sister Elizabeth had alluded, for each of them, perhaps for different reasons, were quite equally, absolutely, and most unequivocally, miserable.

It was finally after they had settled down to attack their second semester that they began to speak to each other in personal terms, and after spending an entire weekend of describing in detail to each other the essence of their suffering, they came to a quandary to which they could not resolve.

Was it worse to live your life with the suffering of little harpies poking at you constantly to remind you of life's impending doom, or is it better to live your life waiting to be mashed on the head severely, only from time to time, by a giant ogre until the same fate was achieved? Subsequently, because they could not come to any definitive answer over that particular conundrum, they decided they would take a philosophy class together with the intention of finding out the answer to another age-old question, and that was, "Is it better to have loved and lost than never to have loved at all?"

Unsatisfied, yet still dauntless in their endeavor, after becoming thoroughly disappointed in failing to extract a finite answer from their professor, they immediately moved on to explore their own set of values in an effort to solve this controversy by comparing their own particularisms.

"So, you mean to tell me that I have it better than you because I had Bobby to love me and now that I don't, somehow I should still be happy in just knowing that I once was? Is that it?" Annie proposed about an hour past midnight on one Friday night, looking up at the ceiling from her bed.

"Oh, no, by no means should you be happy at all, either way," responded Jill clinically. "You see, my misery has always been there, like I said before, like little harpies always poking at me," she contended, "and I put to you, the only difference between the two of us is that you just happen to be whacked on the head with one gigantic disappointment all at once, that's all. But not to worry," she said with assurance, "another one will come along soon enough. It may be bigger or smaller than the last one, but you will see, it will come along all the same, I guarantee it," she prognosticated.

"You have to understand, the little happiness that you think you have is only the relief you feel when you believe that the pain in life has briefly stopped. Now, sometimes these feelings last longer than others, but eventually the misery always comes back.

"Therefore, because I have always been in constant pain, and don't expect it to change any time soon, and you have had only intermittent pain, you naturally have it a little better than me, that's all," Jill further rationalized. "But, nonetheless, we are all suffering here on this earth, and that is precisely why I am a Catholic, because it is my lot to suffer, and I accept that," she stated in complete conviction.

"Well, I don't know if I agree with that, entirely," Annie ruminated out loud. "Granted, I'm not happy now and haven't been since I lost Bobby, but I should accept my suffering as a vindication of my life in all its misery because to suffer is the true reason why I am a Catholic? Is that what you are saying?" she questioned.

"That's about right," Jill responded in the affirmative.

"So, as I understand it then," Annie continued, "when somebody thinks that they're happy, they are really not, for they should realize that their situation is only temporary and, sooner or later, another disappointment will only come along and ruin any kind of happiness that they thought they had in the first place? And that's as good as it can get?"

"Pretty much, I would say," Jill confirmed.

"I guess, then, to sum it all up, that all happiness is, according to you, nothing more than like trying to survive an earthquake, —you are happy that you survived it, but you also dread the aftershock. Then, you are happy for a while you survived the aftershock, but you still dread the next earthquake and so, on and on it goes. Therefore, all you are doing in life, then, is waiting for the next earthquake of doom to hit you and in accepting this fate, this becomes the very essence what being a Catholic is all about? Is that correct?"

"Correct," affirmed Jill.

"Okay, I only have one more thing to ask," Annie persisted.

"Okay, go on," said Jill.

"Well, if only various degrees of pain exist to prove to you that you are indeed alive, and being a Catholic is supposed to be a joy, then how can you even define happiness at all?"

"Well, like I've already explained, happiness is only the absence of pain, and since the absence of anything is, by definition, a void, and 'from the void we come and unto the void we shall return,' then it must follow that the only way we can know true happiness is to reunite with the void. And you know what that means," Jill ominously put forth.

"So, in other words," Annie submitted, "no one can truly define happiness at all while they are still alive, and therefore by it being totally undefinable, it is unobtainable."

"Exactly!" Jill declared, ecstatic in that someone could finally understand her self-justifications.

"But on the other hand," continued Annie, "if happiness is truly undefinable, how could you ever know when you have it in the first place, even when you do become one with the void, as you put it? Also, how can you even possibly prove this whole theory of yours, anyway, unless you yourself come back from the dead to tell us about it? And somehow, I doubt that's not going to happen," she challenged.

"I don't have to," replied Jill flatly. "All I have to do is have faith. My faith is my salvation, and that my ticket to happiness," she proclaimed. "Everybody suffers the pain of life, some more, some less, so what? I'll have my happiness in the end, and right now I am content with that. I have accepted and become numb to my pain. I have confessed the sins of my desires and have been given absolution by the Church. I have accepted the fact that I cannot have, nor can I give, true happiness to anyone.

"So, may God have mercy on my soul, but I have no feelings for the sufferings of others. I have my own to deal with, and outside of charity, they can deal with theirs. Now, I don't fault *you* for trying to be happy Annie, but as for me, I have already passed through the gates of hell that read 'Abandon all hope, ye who enter here,' and I accept that," she puissantly certified.

"Well, thanks for your support," acrimoniously replied Annie, "but, as Scarlett said, 'Tomorrow is another day,' and right now, I'm tired, Jill, so I guess I'll just see you in the morning," she said in conclusion, turning over to get comfortable with her pillow.

"See you in the morning," replied Jill.

Chapter Twenty-Five

When the entire country had finally managed to say its goodbyes to 1968, in no uncertain terms, did anyone consider themselves to be happy, Catholic or not. The Tet offensive had begun the year in earnest, while the might of a half a million troops tried to enforce a philosophy of days gone by. Like dominoes falling in a different respect, one after another, as Martin Luther King Jr., Robert Kennedy, and even Jackie Kennedy had gotten up from the table at Alice's Restaurant, they left behind a meal that would never be fully digested to everyone's satisfaction.

Then, as if to add to the distaste of the repast, the Catholic Church itself threw in the towel, officially sanctioning the dissolution of its obligation to profess a moral or religious high ground within its own educational institutions as it all but abandoned the sanctity of its decreed independence. The Church's outright desire to garner its share of shekels from the public trough by compromising the religious integrity of its parochial schools now began the incantations of its own decline.

It was in this environment that the two champions of misery now found themselves united in the pursuit of understanding the justification of their lives. Was their fate predetermined by God, as defined by the Catholic Church, to persevere in their suffering while, at the same time, the church itself was changing its own definition? Or was it the dawning of the age of Aquarius that would determine their future in accordance with a heavenly star chart? What about their own individualism? Was it even considered? Did anyone even ask them? And so, the cards were on table.

The student lounge was premeditatedly located akin to the campus library and had naturally become one of the college's focal points, whose main purpose became the primary place to champion the student body's collective ruminations and political persuasions. This function was alive and well in the spring of 1969 when the Vietnam War was the paramount concern on everyone's mind.

Publicly espousing its adversity to the war, the Catholic Church's generally liberal institutions, for the most part, had successfully been able to avoid the many physical confrontations that began to spring up at the larger state sponsored schools, especially those with an ROTC program. Nevertheless, without having any significant altercations at Saint Margaret's, the vehemence of the outraged students toward the war unabatedly continued whenever and wherever the students were assembled in any significant numbers.

In approaching the end of their second semester, whether it was a conclusive result of the complete sharing of their intimate suffering, or simply the feeling of comfort gained by the fellowship created in the melding of their intellectual proclivities, the overriding feeling of misery that pervaded the lives of both Jill and Annie had now become upgraded from the gross feelings of self-pity, to an unmitigated expression of acute cynicism. Metaphysically, both Jill's aloofness and Annie's social antipathy were resultantly, and most assiduously, transformed into a strikingly capricious, and sometimes even outspoken, opinionated force to be reckoned with.

It was just after Daylight Savings Time had begun one evening that the two cohorts decided to avail themselves of the student union to see exactly what was "happening" there. Previously, neither of them had left their room much at all, except to go to class and Mass, but now figured that it would probably be a good thing to see firsthand how all the other students were occupying their free time.

One of the newer buildings on campus was the Student Union, which had been attached to the library by a short breezeway, and in good weather collected a variety of egocentric student philosophers who would casually sit outside about its planters and benches in the adjacent patio area to pontificate their thoughts.

The lounge itself was a flat topped single-story square building that defied all attempts of artistic persuasion to provide or promote a single ounce of leisurely comfort or relaxation, the rest of college's general aesthetics ignored. The systematically placed mismatched couches and chairs, which were donated to the institution by the local Society of St. Vincent de Paul, had been stationed in such a manner that everyone seated was afforded an unobstructed view of the brand-new color TV that was positioned atop a large four-foot-high oaken dresser in the far-right corner of the room.

A side door to the left of the patio entrance opened to the breezeway area, and upon entering through it was a slate grey Formica service counter, which stretched all the way to the left rear corner of the room. This area sectioned off a door to a supply room and a back-counter area with a wash sink for the dispensing of refreshments whenever an official social event would provide them.

To the counter's right, and against the back wall behind the mismatched collection of couches, coffee tables, and easy chairs, stood a long row of glass locked cabinets that displayed a multitude of trophies aggrandizing the institution's self-image of having an aggressive sporting behavior.

The highly polished linoleum floors provided the finishing touches of the utilitarian necessity to keep the facility clean and tidy. It was a place to let the students congregate where they could "keep an eye on them" for the welfare of all.

Once approaching their intended destination, both Annie and Jill, who normally did not have a habit of aimlessly strolling about the campus, noticed for the first time that they were in the minority to still be wearing their uniforms. Amazed by their discovery, they began to feel that they had entered another dimension. *How long has this been going on?* they thought in unison, looking about in surprise.

"You know, I thought we were attending a Catholic girl's college, but this is ridiculous," Jill outwardly observed.

They were aware that the University had not been strictly enforcing the dress code for over a year in light of the new social acceptances embodied within the decrees set forth by the Vatican II Convocation, however, having cloistered themselves in their room since attending, they were unaware of its direct effects. It was always universally accepted that the secular students would never wear the uniforms, but what really surprised them was that hardly any of the other girls were wearing them either. Hip hugger jeans, flowered Mumus, tie-dyed t-shirts, and even a healthy amount of bright and braless caftans were observed to be everywhere.

"They all look so comfortable," Jill additionally noted to Annie in a low whisper. "Wow, do I feel out of place," she whispered again as they continued to ramble on through the coterie of females loitering about the breezeway.

"How do you think I feel?" responded Annie. "I hate this pleated woolen skirt. I can't stand it. It scratches you when it's dry, and it stinks when it's wet. Come on, let's see what's going on inside the union," Annie directed in leading the way.

No sooner had the door closed automatically behind them, cutting off the outside peripheral noise, than the two girls heard the television in the corner announce, "And that's the way it was…" as the CBS evening news had poignantly come to an end.

"Well, I've heard enough. This so-called war only makes me sick," remarked one of the girls, getting up from the easy chair she had been lounging in, while most of the others surrounding the TV also followed suit.

"There is no reason for us to even be over there," charged another girl in response.

"Yeah, there is," rebutted another girl argumentatively. "It's just another way to make money for the military industrial complex which is running this country."

When overhearing these opinionated outcries, Annie thereupon began to advance her position in sympathy for their cause, until a short chubby girl in a bright multicolored tunic with straggly long blond hair yelled out, "And all those soldiers over there are only just a bunch of baby killers, anyway."

Horrified, Annie went directly over to the girl and demandingly asked, "What did you say?"

"You heard me! I said that all of those soldiers over there are nothing but baby killers, because they are!" she decried voraciously.

Then, unexpectedly, as if a lightning bolt had been instantaneously hurled from the right hand of Zeus himself, Annie's fist hit its mark squarely upon the left side of the mouthy impertinent girl's jaw. Fully knocking her clean off her feet, she landed with a hard thump upon the even harder floor and lay there senseless, moaning as she held the side of her face. Aghast, the other girls stood back as Annie lorded over her adversary. Then, with the ferociousness of a lioness whose cubs were in danger, she figuratively pounced upon her helpless prey.

"Who the hell do you think you are?" Annie screamed down at the girl. "I ought to kick you right in your damned head right now!" she continued as the girl on the floor covered her face with her hands and curled into a ball.

"Don't hurt me anymore," the girl on the floor cried out weakly.

"You miserable piece of shit! My boyfriend was killed over there, and he didn't want to go, but at least he wasn't a cowardly piece of shit like you! How dare you judge my boyfriend in his grave off a damn stupid TV report! You're too much of a skank to even have a boyfriend! You have no damn concept of my misery and my suffering, but I'm gonna give you some of it right now and see how *you* like it!" Annie asserted as she drew her right foot back.

"Please don't hurt me anymore, I'm sorry!" begged the besieged girl again.

"Hold on a minute, Annie," Jill interjected as she placed her hand upon Annie's shoulder. "I think she already got the point," Jill emphasized, while perusing the shocked spectators, one by one, with the finality of a sports referee.

"But I want to hurt her so bad! I want to hurt her just as bad as she hurt me!" Annie cried out with her tears streaming down in torrents from her face, then grabbing onto Jill in emotional exhaustion.

"That's okay, that's okay," supported Jill as she stroked and patted her back. "Let's go back to the dorm now," Jill consoled, to then lead Annie away.

Then, it was over.

"No doubt you had cause, Annie," Jill supported, now walking back to their room while Annie's tears began to subside, "but didn't you ever hear that 'the meek shall inherit the earth?'" she alluded.

"Yeah, I heard of it," Annie answered contentiously, "but if the meek shall inherit the earth, and the righteous the kingdom of heaven, then I would rather spend my time being righteous," she bantered back with conviction. "And besides, right now, I don't give a rat's ass about the weak."

There was no doubt left in the room that day over who garnered the most sympathy, and it wasn't the downed girl. The anguish which had cried out in pain from the soul of Annie Russo in an unrestrained rage was far more to be pitied than the insignificant punishment bestowed upon the irreverent dissident who provocatively caused the altercation in the first place.

Ironically, it was precisely in the public recognition of her silent forbearance of pain, which heretofore had only been shared with Jill, that Annie, thereafter this incident, unintentionally achieved a goodly degree of admiration throughout the campus. Seen as a frontline surviving victim from the terrifying collateral damage caused by the universally agreed upon unjust war, in one fell swoop, Annie had achieved her Associate Degree in Martyrdom. She also acquired the title of "The Little Slugger," which alone carried its own share of respect.

As eventually the days of Annie's self-pity began to recede, her quest for an emotional peace had caused her to realize that perhaps she was not alone in her frustrations. She hence determined that peace was an inherently elusive concept that was often misconstrued for simply being comfortable. For some, she reasoned, that to be physically comfortable perhaps was good enough, but for others, it was not.

Annie also concluded that there was a big difference between comfort and contentment, especially when gauged against her own experiences. Contentment denotes a degree of finality, she figured, while to be comfortable is only perceived as being temporary. True peace itself, on the other hand, she concluded, was neither. To her, it was a concept unique to one and all, and given time, it would come to her regardless. All she had to do now was wait for its arrival.

So I guess I'm not in Hell after all, Annie said to herself, *Nope, I guess it's more like purgatory,* she then deduced, raising up her emotional state from being despondently morose to only now being in a state of melancholia.

~

Thrilled the country had landed on the moon, as well as monumentally astounded at the success of Woodstock, the entire nation witnessed a new brand of national unification: Space. Whether it was the space above, the space within their hearts, or the space within their minds, everyone was passionately alive in seeking to expand themselves in one form or another.

Two things, however, had to happen first before a true expansion of the society was to happen. Peace was at the top of the list, and although everyone by now was espousing it was desired, the methodology of how to obtain it was still unresolved. The second on the list was that the past had to be left to die, for trying to build a new future when obsessed with the miscarriages of the past only tends to hamper the creative spirit from progressing in a healthy form.

In this spirit, Annie realized that her initial reasoning for applying to Saint Margaret's was now moot. At long last, she was accepting that "the past was the past" and there was nothing she could do to change it. *'Perspective in thinking' is the primary lesson to be learned here,* Annie embraced now, willfully beginning to reshape her thinking.

Annie had also felt guilty for the perceived abandonment of all her "friends" which she had left behind in her quest for solace. Nonetheless, she cheerfully looked forward to returning home on her first summer break. She couldn't wait to inquire as to their welfare, but to her complete surprise, once she did return, her welcome back was nothing like what she had expected.

After witnessing that everyone she had gone to school with was more caught up in their own struggles, pleasures, and personal endeavors, than being even vaguely concerned with *her* welfare, she gained an entirely new point of view about life. Friends she felt they would always be, but after witnessing the prosaic nature of their small-town existence, a profound and almost profane sense of self-worth came over her.

Thomas Wolfe was right, —you can't go home again, Annie thoughtfully considered in a new appreciation of his postulates. She did not, however, share his observations as to pertaining to everyone. *What about all those who never leave home at all?* she literarily mused in trying to apply the author's supposition to all of her "friends" that she, herself, had left behind.

To them, where is the relevance? Annie began to think. *Also, where is the relevance to those who have left home and had already accepted their fate as being a lonely one? And what about all those who do not wish to ever return at all? Plus, you add to that all those who just crave adventure simply for adventure's sake, and solely view going home as merely another undertaking to support their own particular concept of individuality, —that might be something to be happy about, not necessarily sullen. I guess not every great book applies to everyone,* she critically determined.

Ultimately that summer, Annie accepted that she was no longer one of "them" when their comments seemed to denote her to be more of a news item than that of a friend. Subsequently, she reached the determination that she was indeed a better person for leaving. *After all, I at least have the thrill of adventure,* she concluded.

386

It was then that Annie began to count the days until the fall semester was to begin, as now her only thinking was, *For God's sake, I hope that Jill hasn't gotten any taller.*

Happier than ever to be back, the very minute that Annie had entered the dorm room, she could not help herself from sharing, detail by detail, everything she had experienced, both real and philosophically, leaving not a single thing to the imagination. Then, after Jill had shared the same, quite joyously the pair of kindred spirits laughed until the cows came home, —their home.

~

It took every ounce of Annie's pertinacity to convince Jill to go with her to the peace march that was planned to be held at Mall of Washington in D.C. that year.

"If I am to accept your theories of misery, then you should accept mine of unrepentant suffering," Annie argued. "And that means you have to witness the application of these theories. You just can't mouth off about them and not know what you're talking about. That only makes you look like an idiot," she manifestly declared. "Besides it is your duty as a good Catholic to witness God's attempt to save mankind. After all, you took the same English class I did. And you had to memorize Pope's lines, same as me. You remember how it goes,

'Hope springs eternal in the human breast;
Man never is, but always to be blessed;
The soul, uneasy and confin'd from home;
Rests and expatiates in life to come.'

"So, you have to go, or recant your teachings!" Annie challenged.

Annie won the argument, and thus had gotten her way, for on Saturday, November the 15th, 1969, she took her soul mate in hand and after putting on a backpack, went to attend the greatest assembly of people to publicly, peacefully, and respectfully protest their disgust over the unbridled abuse of power by the very politicians elected to guard the integrity of the world's greatest democratic republic ever known.

"Well, how long will it take?" asked Jill as soon as they arrived by the Capital's tidal basin and had gotten off the train.

"How long does it take for what?" replied Annie, while they now proceeded to thread themselves through the already substantial crowd of dissidents.

"How long will it take for you realize that your efforts to be happy are futile, and that coming here is just another stupid attempt to prove me wrong?" flatly postured Jill, glancing over to Annie with the wryest of smiles.

"I don't know, maybe all day, maybe never. You never know," Annie answered elusively, their forward movement, now being halted by the multitudes of squatting malcontents who were literally lying down on the grass before them.

"We're still going over to visit the Catholic University of America tomorrow, aren't we?" Jill presumptuously asked.

"Sure, we can do whatever we want. I said we'd go there and we will," Annie confirmed, starting to get frustrated with the disorganization of the entire matter, coupled with the fact that she and Jill couldn't move any further without having to push past or trip over somebody.

"Okay, I'll just chill out then," Jill conceded. "But, what good is this doing, anyway?" she added. "I mean they're just up there giving speeches, no different than the politicians they hate do, and so what is the point, other than just being here? It seems to me that we are just another sardine in the can. Can't we go somewhere else, where at least where it smells a little better?" she suggested, trying not to grin.

"I don't have a problem with that. At least I will be able to see something else besides the backside of this guy in front of me," Annie grumbled discreetly.

"Well, come on, then, let's go over to where the Supreme Court is. Maybe there are less people over there, and we can at least see something historical while we're here," Jill suggested.

The fact was, however, there was no place that it wasn't crowded. Even the Capitol Building and all the streets leading up to it were crowded, as well. People with signs were everywhere, and not just the college students. It was as if every sector of society was there, including some parents who even brought their children.

The intake was incredible. Who, what, where, when, and why, were all asked; while not even how escaped the questioning either. But what really drove the crowd that day was not an interrogative, whose answers were only producing more snakes than the head of Medusa, —it was an adverb, and that adverb was, now.

"Now" was what the multitudes demanded, ramifications be damned, but who was there to grant them anything anyway, regardless of their protests, now *or* later? It was rumored that President Nixon had clandestinely come out late in the evening to talk to some of the protesters, to the conniptions of the Secret Service Agency, however, his impromptu foray never made it into the six o'clock news.

And where were all the other politicians, on both sides of the issues? On the golf course, presumably. Finally, after witnessing this pitiful abdication of responsibility, it became Annie's conclusion that cowardice could come in many forms, and that political cowardice was perhaps its worst. *All politicians should be required to read All Quiet on the*

Western Front, she thought to herself as she and Jill continued to push their way back through the unending crowd.

"You know, Jill, I read *The Ugly American*, and I just realized that it's not the Americans who are ugly, it's really the sleazy politicians who represent them that are," stated Annie, once they had finally gotten to the street on their way to the Capitol building. "It's as if they spend all their time reading Machiavelli instead of Thomas Paine, or even St. Thomas Aquinas."

"I believe that you are one hundred percent right about that," Jill categorically supported. "Theoretically, we should all pray for those politicians who did not show up to accept their responsibilities, but since the only politician with a soul and a true passion for the people was shot to death, who do you even pray for? I, myself, have enough to pray for, just in having to pray for other Catholics like you," she said smartly. "I say they will all end up in Dante's inferno. You know, way down there to be eaten alive, over and over again, for all of eternity. Don't you agree?" she trenchantly proposed.

"That's too good for them. That's what I think," responded Annie, as her ire was beginning to rise.

Then, in realizing the gravity of her leading statement by the bellicose tone in Annie's response, Jill immediately decided to change the subject with the confession that she was getting hungry and that they should find a place to eat.

"Well, why don't we just check in to our room first?" said Annie, now turning to Jill with a devious smirk upon her face.

"Check in where?" questioned Jill suspiciously, to no reply. "Come on, you can tell me, I won't get pee'd off. I know you, remember? I'm okay with your wackiness. Just lay it on me. Don't try to make me happy by causing me to suffer even more than I already do. I told you. I know you, you little imp. Where are we going?" Jill clamored on incessantly, still to no response, while Annie continued to steadily walk along in silence.

"Right over there," Annie suddenly responded, pointing across the lawn past the White House. "Come on, let's go. It's after four o'clock, anyway," she added while both of them kept trodding in the hotel's direction.

Finally, once getting in clear sight of the building and seeing its opulence and grandeur, Jill could not believe her eyes.

"How can we afford to stay there?" Jill asked in great concern. "I agreed to stay over, but I can't afford to stay there. I thought we were going to stay at a youth hostel or something like that. Besides, they probably don't have any room for us to stay there anyway," she flatly conjectured.

"Oh yeah they do," Annie certified. "For *us* they do," she emphasized. "I already made the reservations under the name of my father's company. My family isn't exactly poor, you know," she reminded her. "They took them last week, and I've got the money on me right now. I guess you are just going to have to suffer the guilt of living like a queen for a change," Annie teased her with a grin. "And like you said before, don't worry about it, —sooner or later, you'll be miserable again," she laughed whole-heartily.

Once situated in their room on the fourth floor, the view of the city seemed to be worth every cent that was spent. As crowded and noisy as the city was, once inside, one could even hear a pin drop as it hit the floor. *What a picture,* they thought to themselves as they first peered out the front window of the suite.

"And so, in the midst of all the turmoil, the two young wayward souls found luxury in the bastion of an old nearby castle, where all of the servants were oh so nice," chronicled

Jill, flopping down upon the first neatly fitted bed she came to.

"What book is that from?" asked Annie, sashaying over to the other bed and flopping down on hers as well.

"The Book of Jill. That's what," she amusingly took credit for.

"That's really not so bad," Annie complemented. "So, you are going to be a writer now?" she asked serenely, while grinning up at the ceiling

"Well, *I am* an English major, silly," Jill reminded her redundantly.

"Oh yeah, that's right. I almost forgot about that," Annie responded facetiously. "It's not as if I'm an English major too you know," she pointed out. "You know, it's nice you want to be a writer, and maybe will be a good one too, but I know *I'm* sure not going to be one," Annie professed in total contentment. "Maybe you can write a story about me. I can give you plenty of material," she then submitted in jest.

"You've already given me plenty of material, and I appreciate your offer, I really do," Jill acknowledged in kind. "You know, no one has ever been concerned with my welfare before," she stated, changing the subject. "At least you make an effort to contribute to my misery instead of just ignoring me, and you know how grateful I am of that," she chuckled.

Experiences, if survived, become their own reward, Annie and Jill were beginning to comprehend. They are the building blocks of life which, when skillfully arranged, become the foundation upon which wisdom rests. And in this concept, the formidable pair of persecuted souls set off together to find some bedrock.

From the empathetic depths of agony and pain, to the compassionate heights of exaltation, the two pilgrims marched on to find a new look at an old world which was rapidly changing around them. What was then, is not now, they were beginning to accept, and to continually live in the past would be to surrender all that is creative, casting aside the very marvel of being alive. They *had* to move on, they now realized, especially while the winds of youth were still behind their backs.

And so, after a sumptuous breakfast in the regal dining room the next morning, they quietly toured as much of the Capitol as time would allow, concluding their journey with a visit to The Catholic University of America, as planned. "Oh, what a trip to be remembered," they both agreed.

Chapter Twenty-Six

As all things have an effect to be dealt with, once having returned from their trip, neither Annie nor Jill could see any compelling reason they should continue to wear their school uniforms, specifically because most of the other girls were not wearing theirs. To wear the school's uniform now would only draw them more attention than if they didn't, they concluded, and they liked their anonymity.

Another thing they noticed was that the number of nuns who were staffed to teach at Saint Margret's appeared to be waning in comparison to the non-Catholic employees, as the aftermath of the 1967 Land O'Lakes Statement now began to become apparent.

Instead of "biblical fact" and the "gospel of truth" being cited as part of an educational process in which to better understand the world, the stature of the bible itself was reduced to be an allegorical simile of interpretation by many of secular professors who did not even have the capacity to understand or accept the lessons contained within it, let alone ever having read it in its entirety.

Also, regardless of the statement declaring, "the Catholic university must have a true autonomy and academic freedom in the face of authority of whatever kind, lay or clerical," the statement's duplicity did not reveal that the government's authority was to be superimposed over all things financial concerning the school's administration. "What a great thing," it was declared, —for as long as the Catholic universities had now allowed the government to dictate their hiring procedures, including a plethora of other dictatorial regulations, they would be approved to "cash in" from the public grant system.

The unbridled stupidity that hiring a secular professor, who never had anything published independently, solely because the government had authorized that person to have the intellectual judgement to reinterpret and critique the greatest book ever written did not escape even the most moronic of all. Nonetheless, the teachers took the money, the school's administration took the money, the Diocese took the money, and the dignity of the Catholic Church took a hike.

All the religious artifacts chthonic to the Catholic Church were removed from its classrooms, and the requirement for employing a specific number of secular teachers was also enforced. To the average student oblivious to the intricacies of the school's administrative policies, these changes were of little concern. Sadly, the only contentious point of interest which garnered any of the public's attention was the debate over what the proper length of a nun's habit ought to be.

"Sister Ruth, don't you find that to be humiliating?" asked Jill one evening while she and Annie visited her in the Resident Advisor's quarters.

"Ach no, I don't conzern myzelf mit dos matters," Sister Ruth responded. "Bezides, you can't humiliate me at my age. I am content mit my life. Gott has been gut to me, unt now I do vut I like to do, unt dat is to teach you girls vut ist really important in life. You zee, everyvon ist different unto Gott, but each von of you should still vork to der fullest, because if you don't, you only cheat yourzelf out uf die joy dot only Gott can give you. Unt die greatest joy of all, uf course, ist to be happy mit your own efforts unt accomplishments, fer no von can take dot from you, no matter how short your skirt is," she smiled whimsically.

"Well, what about the war? How do you feel about that?" Asked Annie with genuine concern.

"Vell, you liddle von, I vill tell you," Sister Ruth began. "Der are millions uf people around der vorld. Der country I vas born in hass lost two vars in my lifetime. I had to pray for der souls on boat sides. Ve all die, unt den ve all vill push up die zame daises. I can only pray for dose who do not appreciate dem. At least I do not haff to pray zo hard for der vons who do appreciate dem, for dey are already de schildren of Gott. I believe you haff a zong dot asks, ver haff all die flowers gone? Am I correct, liddle lieb kuchen?" Sister Ruth asked of Annie.

"Yes, that's right," answered Annie respectfully.

"Vel, das ist all in Der Bible. I alzo believe you haff taken a course in schournalism, nicht war?" the nun further questioned.

"Yes, Sister Ruth. Sister Anker teaches the class," Annie responded factually.

"Vel den, I suggest you put your education to vork," the Sister advised. "In der vords from your own newspapers, you should read all about it den. It ist all in Der Bible, unt it vil answer more of your quevestions den I can," she submitted.

"Sister Ruth, what do you think of Vatican Two ? Do you think it will ruin the church?" asked Jill.

"Vell, my fater vas in der horse buziness," Sister Ruth began, as Annie could feel one of her stories coming on again. "He owned a schtable unt bought unt zold horses. He alzo had der delivery vagons, vich ran between der liddle villages around Der Kournigheit. Vel, along kompt das automobile. Unt den he hat gefunden dat he vas not in der horse buziness at all. He vas in der freight buziness. Zo, now my fater, unt my three bruders, vorked mit der trucks instead of mit der horses."

"Den, after der first verld vor, my fater unt my two surviving bruders continued on in der buziness uf freight.

Den, vouden't you know dat von day, von of my bruders zed dat, 'I sink dat ve should buy an areoplane unt go into zie transportation buziness of people, too. Ve need to be more modern in our zinking.

"Vel my fater unt my udder bruder zaid, 'Oh no, Ve should yust schtick to vat ve know, —after all, it makes us a gut living now. Ve should yust be happy viff vut ve already haff.' Vell, unhappily, my von bruder left by himself unt vent into der airoplane unt people buziness, all by himself. Dis, uf course, did not make my mutter happy at all.

"Vell, Gott vas very good to him unt his business, unt he made a lot of money, but yet he vas lonely for his fater unt his bruder. Zo finally, dey all got togezer unt vent into a new business, —der freight, die people, unt der mail delivery buziness. Den, dey ver all happy vunce again, especially my mutter. Vell, voudent you know dat after all dat, day yust go unt buy anudder horse farm again? Unt now, you zee, after all dey had been trugh, dey had gone novare, for in das ende, der greatest joy vas to yust ride their horses von more time."

"You see, Miss Jill, Der Catholic Schurch ist der Schurch of Jesus Christ, and all of die udder Christian schurches are like die vayverd schildren from die mutter who bore dem all. Now, all of deese schurches are just like being in der transportation buziness. Ve are all going in the zame direction, unt eventuality ve vill all arrive to be judged in die zame place, unt how you get there, by die grace of Gott, ist die only quvestion dot ist unanswered venn you are born.

"Now den, der Schurch alzo hast to make decisions," she continued. "Let's yust say dat der Schurch ist like a railroad for die people to ride on. If ve are to maintain the railroad, it must have zome regulations, or it von't run at all, nicht wahr? Unt den, der regulations haff to schange mit the times. It ist zeese schanges dot test the visdom of der engineers. Den finally, die judgment of deez decisions can only be measured by die satizfaction of die passengers. If dey are happy, dey stay on the train, unt if dey are not, dey get off unt travel by oder means.

"Zo, it appears to me, dat by der new regulations adopted by der Zecond Bishops Azzembly, dot it haz become more important to the Schurch to increase the size of der railroad over die quvality of der ride. It ist not my place to judge dat decision, arber I can guarantee you von zing, der railroad itself vill outliff its regulators. Does dat answer your quevstion?" Sister Ruth directly addressed Jill.

"Well, it certainly gave me something to think about, Sister Ruth," Jill answered reflectively.

"It sure does," agreed Annie.

"There is only one other thing, though, —is your family still in business?" asked Jill out of curiosity.

"Ach no, I am zie only von left uf my family. None of dem survived the zecond vor. Unt, zoon enough, I vill be pushing up die daisies along by dem too," the Sister sighed in a pleasantly fateful tone.

Then, after pensively pausing for a moment, Sister Ruth slowly got up from her chair and politely announced, "Vell, I haff now to begin my prayers, so ladies, if you please," she said in adjournment.

And so, after thanking Sister Ruth for her most intriguing revelations, the two students left the small apartment with a point of view that would carry with them for the rest of their lives.

~

In the fourth semester, by the time the rigors of their lives had become habitually familiar, the college culture in all its trappings had completely rebranded the two girl's identities. It was also at this time that the Kent State atrocity became a national day of shame. And while the ripples of discontent became a shockwave of horror that was felt across the entire nation, the emotional outrage over the war had finally and unequivocally reached its critical mass. From the largest of the state schools and private universities to the smallest artisan collage, the ultimatum to end the war had now become exacerbated tenfold, and the attitude to make it so at Saint Margaret's was no different.

"You know, the argument of cause and effect is irrelevant to the dead," Jill noted realistically, while she and Annie were sitting in the courtyard on the day after the Kent State Massacre. "So, it just goes to show you, you can argue all you want about the miserable conditions that surround you, like they did, but does it really do you any good? It didn't them. If you ask me, as I see it, they simply felt that their lives were miserable, in one way or another, and then decided to spout off about it in public, that's all. Unfortunately, however, the worst mistake that they made was to outright personally condemn the whole school's administration. Obviously, the administration got tired of listening to their badgering, because it made them just as miserable, and took action to stop it, —and there you have it. Nothing at was solved at all, and everyone is even more miserable than before. Anyway, at least that's how I see it," she annotated clinically.

"Don't you ever have any compassion at all?" admonished Annie. "What about their parents? What about their friends and their families? What about all of the other students at Kent State? Don't you have any feelings for them?" Annie empathetically questioned.

"For them, or their cause? There is a difference, you know," Jill pointed out philosophically.

"For both," qualified Annie.

"Of course I feel compassion for their friends and families, but in as much as I don't even know them, what do you expect me to do?" Jill responded ascetically. "Listen, if it were you and me that were killed, I believe that they too would feel the same way in spirit, but they would hardly be at our funerals, either. If you really want to know, I have already said a prayer for their souls. Have you? Or have you been so busy being pissed off you forgot?" Jill proposed, while waiting silently for a reply.

"Well..." Anne dragged out.

"That's what I thought," said Jill in vindication. "Oh no, I forgot!" Jill sardonically pantomimed, putting her hands to her cheeks with her mouth open in disorientation. "Well, Jill forgives you. For Jill said a prayer for *you* too, so you're covered," she declared in the first person.

Then, momentarily waiting for a response which did not come, Jill continued.

"Now, as far as their cause is concerned, is it not the same as ours? Did I not go to Washington with you? Just because I don't try to take the bleeding-heart mantle from the Virgin Mary doesn't mean that I have no feelings about the war. It's an abomination in all its forms. So, if you want to become the face of this cause, then honey, I'm right behind you. But how can I facilitate your emotional needs when at the same time I'm supposed to be going, 'oh whaa, whaa, whaa, my feelings are all hurt. I just can't seem to be able to get anything done!'" she parodied again. "You don't really think that kind of childish behavior would actually help to advance your position, do you?" she interrogated in a tone of indignation.

"No, I guess it wouldn't," conceded Annie.

"Well, now I'm waiting," stated Jill, fractiously facing away with her eyebrows raised.

"Okay, I'm sorry I accused you of having no feelings at all," offered Annie apologetically.

"That's better," accepted Jill formally.

"Anyway, I still think she still needs to work on her feelings," Annie muttered under her breath over to the bush planted next to where she was seated.

"I heard that!" exclaimed Jill. "And are you so deluded that you think that the stupid plant next to you is your friend, too?" she resentfully questioned. "Well, that's it! I don't mind praying for your misguided soul, but I am not going to pray for the soul of a dumb bush, too!" she categorically declared. "You're on your own now," she apprised Annie in feigned abandonment. "And by the way," she then sedately added, as if now telling Annie a secret, "the bush doesn't agree with you, anyway."

"You know, Jill, —seriously, what can anyone do, or better, what is anyone *going* to do about it?" Annie questioned in earnest.

"I really don't know, Annie. What do you expect? You can complain all you like, and you can have all the protests you like but, in the end, there are only two things that seem to be able to make any difference at all, one is power, and the other is money," submitted Jill.

"Power, you see, is only the ability to cause an effect on something or someone," she additionally delineated. "Now, the only way to gauge the amount of power that a person or any group of people has is to equate its effects into monetary terms so that its degrees can be measured in the secular world by quantifiable means," she further proposed.

"Then, the intangibility of having more power now becomes a concrete benefit to those who believe that they can buy all the comfort that they need. In essence, power is money, and money is power, and to gain it for its own sake is one of the greatest sins of all. And since when did you ever see anyone who declared they 'had it all' be all that comfortable, anyway?" she stated more than questioned.

"Now, what is comforting to one may not be to another, and perhaps never will be," she continued. "Then, the only question to ask yourself is, 'Am I satisfied with the comforts that are bestowed upon me by God or others, or, do I want the self-satisfaction of being able to accumulate enough power unto myself to create my own sense of comfort?" she posed.

"You see, I believe that you are the kind of person who will never be comfortable until you feel that you have some sort of power over your own destiny, and that is why I admire you. God did give us free will you know. I, on the other hand, would be most comfortable to just to help you in your quest to find whatever comfort you feel you need. I think that would be neat," she offered with a congenial smile.

"So, in other words, just to be my Sancho Panza, then, is all that you need to be happy? Is that what you're telling me?" questioned Annie.

"Sure, I'll join your crusade," Jill agreed with a grin, "just as long as it's not *me* who has to personally suffer from your wacky adventures."

~

It was the final assignment given in Annie's poetry class that caused the decision to be made. Professor Willis was short and thin of stature. Roughly five and a half feet tall, he was one of the first male secular teachers to be hired under the new standards of integration as adopted by the administration's adoption of "The Land O'Lakes Statement" declaring the school's academic independence to be free from any of the church's religious doctrines.

A self-important man, Professor Willis continually had made references to his great achievements in life. His favorite story about himself was that, because of his superior intellect, he was one of the few selected elite chosen to serve on a submarine during "The Big One."

"Only men of great mental acuity and courage are allowed to serve on a submarine, and I had the privilege of being one of those men. It takes great mental discipline, and that is what it will take to pass this course," was the standard proclamation he gave at all of his orientation speeches.

Professor Willis had dyed his straight, short hair a dark chestnut brown in a feeble attempt to hide his age, but only succeeded in appearing as if a bowl of chocolate pudding had been dumped upon his head. Under the pallid countenance of a garden gnome, he wore a various number of different bow ties. They were always of a plaid variety, and for some unknown psychological reason only he, in all his brilliance, had the capacity to understand their significance. His suit was never ironed, nor his shoes ever shined. "Does he really think that everyone believes him to be the Einstein of literature?" the students would laugh behind his back.

Sadly enough, the students did not laugh when they found out that Professor Willis had the propensity to enjoy threatening to fail his students simply for the sport of it. Annie did not like him, and therefore sat in the back of the class. He ridiculed the students individually as well as en masse through innuendo, adversarial hyperbole, and outright humiliation whenever a student had the tenacity to voice a different point of view that ran counter to his own. The altogether patronizing manner in which he conducted his class had coarsely grated against Annie's sense of fair play on a daily basis.

Although she detested the professor, she still felt that if the other students were willing to put up with his behavior, it was their decision to make, and thus it was none of her concern. This acceptance of non-intervention seemed to work out just fine for Annie until the day that Professor Willis noted out loud at the beginning of the class, "Why, Miss Russo, I see that you are no longer wearing the school uniform any more. Is there some significance to this new behavior?"

"The only significance here, Professor Willis, is that you are the only one to remark about it," Annie responded indignantly.

"Well, I'm sure that everyone else has noticed this 'change' as well, and I was just wondering if you wanted to share your thoughts about it with the rest of the class," Professor Willis pushed back imperiously.

"No, Professor Willis, I do not," replied Annie in an even greater indignant tone.

"Well, then, I guess since you have nothing worthwhile to contribute to the class today, Miss Russo, we might as well continue on where we left off last Tuesday, without your less-than-stimulating myopic outlook on life," the professor insultingly retorted.

Then, after picking up the textbook that lay in the center of his desk before him, he dispassionately instructed, "Class, we will all now pay attention to the words of John Keats on page one-forty-nine," as he proceeded to read the poem *Ode on a Grecian Urn*

Thou still unravish'd bride of quietness,
Thou foster-child of silence and slow time,
Sylvan historian, who canst thus express
A flowery tale more sweetly than our rhyme:
What leaf-fring'd legend haunt about thy shape

Of deities or mortals, or of both,
In Tempe or the dales of Arcady?
What men or gods are these? What maidens loth?
What mad pursuit? What struggle to escape?
What pipes and timbrels? What wild ecstasy?

Annie was furious. She was livid. She would have dropped his class in a heartbeat if it was not past the time where it would penalize her record. Undaunted to retain her self-worth, she decided that if he wanted to play the personal attack game that she would most sincerely respond in kind. *I'll just wait until after the next exam when he gives everyone back their graded papers. Then I want to see how he will answer MY questions,* she said to herself with conviction. *Did he not think that his reputation had preceded him?*

Annie was all but waiting for him the next time he had to pass back everyone's graded exams. Then, as usual, while he wrote down the general results upon the chalk board, he proceeded to demean the entire class.

"There is one A, there are no B's there are two C's, three D's, and the rest of you have failed. Now, those are the grades that you deserve," the Professor categorically announced. "However, since the school is determined to show that it can provide at least an average education to everyone, I am going to be gracious to you people and employ the bell curve in adjusting your grades. I therefore have averaged the grades of all twenty-eight of you, so that the majority of you will receive a C for the course. The rest of you will receive a proportionate undeserved raise in your grades, so don't worry, only the truly pathetic will fail."

"Excuse me?" signaled Annie as she raised her hand from the back of the class.

"Yes, Miss Russo? I believe you were one of the two to at least received a C. You have a comment?" Professor Willis asked of her officiously.

"Oh yeah, I have a comment," Annie began fearlessly. "Well, first of all, I also happen to think that the bell curve is a joke, but I don't know if it's for the same reason that you do," she stated leadingly.

"Then, why don't you elaborate more for us, Miss Russo, so we *all* have the benefit of your unique insight this time?" the Professor superciliously requested.

"Well, the way I see it, the bell curve was made up for the benefit of those teachers who are just average, not the students. If the teacher had the ability in the first place to do what they are paid to do, then no student should be in fear of failing in the first place. It therefore follows that 'the employment of the bell curve,' as you so succinctly put it, is nothing more than a cheap device invented to keep the teachers from being seen as failures, —not the students. So, my question is, Professor Willis, do you agree with that assessment or not? I am sure that the whole class will be very interested to hear your thoughts, sir," Annie mockingly declared.

"My thought is that there is always an opposing view, Miss Russo. Now, the only relative thing for *you* to understand, is that before you make such suppositions, you had better first determine from which end of the tunnel you are looking through, especially when you have no choice but to pass through it," the professor pompously cautioned.

"Now, I think we should be getting back to our discussion of Shelly, Byron, and Keats, which is where we left off last," he moved on dismissively, addressing the rest of the room as a whole.

I guess he doesn't like eating his own words, Annie said to herself contentedly, while the professor continued on with his critique of Lord Byron's "Ozymandias."

"Now for your final," Professor Willis next declared as the end of the class was nearing, "Everyone is to submit a poem. There are no special requirements as to the poem itself. Whether it is free form or has a rhyme scheme is up to you. The different tools of the trade such as alliteration, onomatopoeia, and cacophony are encouraged, but they are also not required. Your work will be graded totally and subjectively by me, and me alone. Naturally, I will first have to decide if it even qualifies as a poem, which I sincerely doubt anyone in this class is capable of producing, but nonetheless, I will read it." he disdainfully noted. "Then, I will assign it *some kind of grade*, as I am required to do."

"Excuse me again, Professor," interrupted Annie, "could you please tell us exactly why you feel that no one in this class is capable of writing a good poem?" she questioned.

"Oh, that's easy to explain, Miss Russo," the professor phlegmatically began, "You see, you have to have some genuine inspiration to create a work of art, and I don't see that in any of you. Now, a work of art, such as a painting, is more than just the sum of its parts. It is more than its canvas, and pigments, and the frame around it. It has the inspiration of the painter within it. This makes it greater than the sum of its parts, just as a poem is more than simply some insipid words which have been written upon a piece of paper in some type of descriptive or emotional fashion. So, to sum it up for you, young lady, I do not believe that there is *anyone* in this class that has any inspiration at all, let alone enough to write a decent poem, if you must know, Miss Russo," he declared flatly.

"Now, are there any other questions concerning the final?" Professor Willis then openly asked the entire class, while peering about the room in search of anyone else who might have had the perspicacity to risk the consequences of his reprisal. Finally, after a dead silence had sufficiently passed, he declared conclusively, "Then you are all dismissed," causing everyone to promptly scramble from the room.

With only three weeks left in the semester, Annie finished her assignment early and decided to hand it in almost a week before it was due. This time, however, she decided to wait until everyone had completely left the classroom, for then she could not be so easily be dismissed.

"So, you have some sort of problem with your assignment that requires my special attention, Miss Russo?" Professor Willis coldly addressed her, looking up from his desk over the top of his half-framed glasses.

"No, I don't have any problem, Mr. Willis. I came to hand in my final, which I am sure you will find deserves an A," Annie stated matter-of-factly, placing a manila folder directly upon his desk before him.

Putting down the red grading pen in his hand, Professor Willis languidly reclined back in his chair, took off his glasses, and slowly proceeded to visually scrutinize the obstinate student before him from top to bottom in a contemptuously vain attempt to instill within her a feeling of futility in the face of his dictatorial intimidation.

"So, you think so, do you?" the Professor pejoratively questioned. "Well, I'll tell you what. Without even looking at it, I will give you a B for the course, and that will be the best I will give you. I am still convinced that you simply do not have inspiration to write a good poem, and therefore, I would advise you to take the B before I actually decide to read it and rule that you don't even deserve that," he decreed, proffering it back to her with the sardonic smile of impunity upon his face.

Taking back the folder, Annie emphatically re-tossed it back upon his desk and stated in an evenly controlled, but intensely upset tone, "No, Professor, this is an A poem, and I will not accept less for the class. I do not like the manner in which you degrade my religion, and I especially do not like the manner in which you sexually degrade all of the girls in this class. You make me sick in trying to compromise the integrity of their virtue too!"

"You see, I know why you always give that one girl in the class an A, and I find you to be disgusting, both as a human being *and* in the manner in you teach your course. You are the worst kind of extortionist, and believe me, I do know how it works."

"Now, *this* is an A paper," Annie told him in no uncertain terms, tapping her index finger on the top of his desk. "And I am not coming back to your final class, either," she told him flatly. "Now, I hope to never see you again," she added brazenly. "But, if I do not see a final grade of A posted on the wall next week, *I will*, and mark my word you won't like it, expose you for exactly what you are," she avowed with the seriousness of a coroner's report. "And now, I hope you have a nice day, Professor Willis," she finalized flippantly, to then stalk out of the room with both her books *and* her integrity.

412

Chapter Twenty-Seven

At eight o'clock sharp on the very next Friday morning, having given himself a few days in which to compose his final assault against the impudent and unworthy child, Professor Willis appeared at the door of the Dean's office.

"How can I help you, professor Willis?" Sister Elizabeth asked of him pleasantly.

"I have a situation with a certain problem pupil that I think you should be aware of, and I believe that she was also the same one that caused the altercation in the student lounge last year," was Professor Willis's opening line.

"Oh, my dear, this sounds quite serious," Sister Elizabeth acknowledged, rising from her chair.

"I can get the door for you, Dean," the professor offered politely.

"Oh, don't worry Professor Willis, I can get it, but thank you just the same," Sister Elizabeth responded in kind as she seemed to glide over toward the office door.

Once the Mother Superior had reached the doorway, however, she did not merely close the door. Instead, she addressed one of the officious nuns who had been diligently attending to her duties in the next room.

"Sister Sara, you are schooled in the art of short hand, are you not?"

"Yes, Mother Superior, I am," replied inconspicuous nun whose desk was stationed by the entrance to the office.

"Would you please come in here with your notepad for a moment?" Sister Elizabeth asked plainly.

"Of course, Mother Superior," answered Sister Sara, picking up the spiral bound book that was sitting upon the back corner of her desk.

Once behind the now closed door to her office, Sister Elizabeth took her usual position behind her desk, while Sister Sara placed herself at a small student desk that was quartered unobtrusively in the far corner of the room.

"I apologize for this, professor, but with all of the new regulations, these types of concerns are required to be recorded now. You probably know better than I the reason it is required, having practiced in the secular world, whereas I have not," Sister Elizabeth commented politely.

"I understand all too well and that is precisely why I am here, Dean," offered Professor Willis in his best academic posture.

"Well, then, so that is good. Please, have a seat," Sister Elizabeth gestured to one of the two mahogany chairs in front of her desk. "So again, how can I help you Professor Willis?" she officially proceeded.

"It is about Annette Russo. Are you familiar with this student at all?" Professor Willis specifically questioned in trying to denote Annie's insignificance.

"I am aware that she is a student here," answered Sister Elizabeth benignly. "Now, what is this about an altercation that you mentioned?" she politely asked in clarification.

"I believe that it is common knowledge among the students that she actually knocked another girl to the ground and physically hurt her one day last year in the student union over a political debate. It is because of the mental problems which can be caused amongst the other girls by Miss Russo's behavior pattern that is my main concern. I don't think that this school needs that type of reputation to go on uncontrolled. Do you not agree with me?" the professor solicited.

"I follow exactly what you mean, Professor. Go on," replied the Sister attentively.

"In any case, I feel sorry for the poor girl," Professor Willis proceeded. "Not that I am concerned about myself, being trained to handle such matters in the submarine command, however, she actually had the audacity to threaten me," he efficaciously contended.

"That's almost unbelievable, Professor," the seasoned administrator incredulously noted.

"I know, Dean, I was just as shocked," Professor Willis emotionally endorsed. "That is why when she came to me and demanded that I give her an A for the course or she would make up that I had sexually confronted her, I was beside myself. I was flabbergasted. What about the school's reputation, I thought? And what about the other girls? And that is why I am here today, Dean. What do you recommend I do?" he ended beseechingly in his closing performance.

"I understand that this girl does not deserve this grade? Is that correct?" the Mother Superior asked in verification.

"That's the whole point, Dean. It's my passion to be able to give my students the best grades possible, but as you know, it would be unfair to do that at the expense of those students who really deserve it," Professor Willis testified. "I even employ the bell curve, which is as you know, is the recommended manner of helping the disadvantaged, so that students like this Russo girl can at least go away with something for her efforts.

"When she made her demand, after turning in her final assignment, I even offered to raise her grade to a B, which is the best that I felt I could morally do, simply to avoid this distasteful situation for the good of everyone. But she summarily tramped out of my office in a fervor after having threatened me," he asserted.

"Do you think that her final exam could have any bearing upon her receiving an A for the semester? Elizabeth then questioned.

"Not at all, Dean," Professor Willis responded with conviction. The final exam was simply a poem, and she already handed it to me when she came in with her outrageous demand. Dean, her poem was so pathetic that I felt bad for her. That is when I offered her the B regardless, — at least for her effort in not missing a class. And you see, I still plan on giving her the B which she doesn't deserve, and that is the real reason why I came here, —to rest my good conscious," he feigned to confess. "Do you think that even though she doesn't deserve it, that for the good of the school and the welfare of the other girls, that I should simply keep the peace and unfairly award her the B?" he questioned in a most sincere tone.

"Well, I do have a few questions to ask you first," Sister Elizabeth answered, pausing a second to assemble her thoughts. "That is of course, if you don't mind, Professor," she qualified.

"Oh, of course, Dean. What is it that I can help you with?" Professor Willis dociously responded in being quite content with his performance.

"Well, first of all, I would like your professional opinion on something," Sister Elizabeth requested, leaning back to open the center desk drawer before her.

"I would be happy to give you any assistance that I can," the professor congenially replied.

"Well, very good," the Mother Superior stated, "since this has to do with a most germane aspect to this situation," she disclosed, handing over a copy of Annie's poem from the manila folder retrieved from her desk to thereafter intently wait for the poetry professor's expected commentary.

The Artists Charge

When poetry defines the poet
And art defines the artist
Does inspiration really show it
Or is their truth the farthest
Thought within their minds?

For rhythm, rhyme and meter are but rules,
As paint and clay and canvas are but tools
To help the spirit of the work prevail
The verity of its message must entail
The soul within its times

The song of life belongs to one and all
Composer or conductor matters not
To give a pound of flesh is small
When sacrifice indeed becomes your lot
To share with all in kind

For one's creations are but born alone
Unique from God, in every artist's soul

In instantly recognizing the poem, although he tried his best to act unaffected, the professor's eyes could not hide his obvious surprise. And while pretending to peruse the paper, the Mother Superior sat silently before him, simply counting the ticks in the clockwork of his mind until such time as the professor was ready to respond. Finally, after Professor Willis had coalesced his thoughts as best he could on the spur of the moment, he quietly laid Annie's work back upon the Mother Superior's desk and said candidly, "I see that you have already spoken with Miss Russo."

"Yes, Professor Willis, indeed I have," confirmed the Mother Superior. "Now, what is your opinion of her poem?" she questioned dispassionately, referring to the subject at hand.

"Well you see, Dean, that's exactly it. I didn't want to bring it up, but how pathetic can it be to plagiarize another person's work, and then pass it off as your own? Besides committing a crime, it's outright immoral," he indignantly advanced. "Surly you must agree with that, Dean," he righteously postulated.

"Why, naturally plagiarism is a dismissible offense, Professor," the Mother Superior factually recognized, "and so, I wondered about that as well," she acknowledged. "Now because the poem *did* seem to be an exemplary composition for a first-year student to hand in, as you also seemed to surmise, I felt it was my duty to investigate this matter. So, all things considered, I had the Society of Jesus, —in lay terms, the Jesuits, —research the poem," she revealed to him clinically.

"And since factually the Jesuits are unquestionably one of the world's foremost experts in the field of art and literature for the last five hundred years, I have no reason to question their conclusion that this poem has not been plagiarized from any source whatsoever which could be found. I have also had the privilege of having a witness testify before me that Miss Russo did in fact absolutely write this poem, as she witnessed it being written. Therefore, in conclusion, I have no doubt in my mind that this poem was indeed composed by Annette Russo," she decreed, while the professor made no reply.

"Now, this matter of the poem is one thing," the Mother Superior proceeded, while the tone in her voice had now become decidedly more austere, "but I also have another problem that concerns your situation which was also brought to my attention, and that is this," she then openly displayed in her hand for his viewing an additional piece of paper that she had removed from the manila folder upon her desk.

"This, Professor," The Mother Superior began again, after putting back the paper into the folder, without actually having handed it to him, "is a list of signatures of all the 'girls,' as you refer to them, who are in Annette's class who attest that you have sexually harassed them in one form or another, including the one girl who dubiously always received an A for her work, who, in my opinion, certainly could have never written a poem such as this," she decreed.

"Now, Mr. Willis, this office will be reviewing *all* of the final grades intended to be given out to your class *before* being finalized. And you will also submit to me all of the academic records and literary material written by these same students that you have in your possession immediately after they have handed in their final exam papers," she officially demanded.

"Also, Mr. Willis, I am going to request from you a response paper as to whether or not I should implore, to use one of your terms, 'The Laws of God' or 'The Laws of Man' in the prosecution to be wrought upon you in seeking out the validity of these allegations against you, or instead, you can feel free to request a kind recommendation from our establishment in the quest to find employment elsewhere, with the submission of your resignation. In that particular case, I will not require the paper," the Mother Superior discretionally decreed.

"So, you have recorded Mr. Willis's testimony and my instructions to him explicitly, have you not, Sister Sara?" the Mother Superior then asked the all-but-forgotten scribe in the side corner of the room.

"Yes, I have, Mother Superior," Sister Sara dutifully acknowledged.

"Well," the Mother Superior concluded most officiously, "that will be all, Mr. Willis. You are dismissed."

Then, without uttering another word, the professor quietly stood up, turned, and began his trek toward the door, a beaten man. And not hearing nor really even expecting any further remarks from the professor, Sister Elizabeth finalized this additional opportunity to advise him before he had completely exited, "Whatever your response is going to be, Mr. Willis, please remember to keep it short, —I have a lot of praying to do, sir"

Thereafter, it only took Professor Willis the weekend to clean out his office, never be seen on the campus again, summarily abandoning his post. The final week of the class had now been assigned to Sister Ruth to finish. And what a last week it was.

~

"Vell, class, ve only haff von more day after dis, unt den you should haff all your assignments in order for your final grades. I haff no problem mit dos schtudents who haff already completed der vork viff maybe helping die udder vons vich are haffing zome trouble," Sister Ruth announced compassionately while winking at Annie, who did return to take a seat in the very front row. "Unt now, I must earn my vages as a poetry professor unt teach you ad least von poem. Unt ya, unt it yust zo happens to be a Churman von, unt it goes like dis," she grinned, "Am morgan, morgan, nur nicht haute, sagen alle faulen laute!"

"Sehr gut, ya!" Sister Ruth proudly smiled to a totally bumfuzzled audience. Then, after sensing that something was indeed awry, she exclaimed out loud, "Ach du libber, Ich ferguesse! I forget dot I am not in Chermany!" she exclaimed with her right hand to her face and her mouth wide open in surprise. Finally, after the class had finished being amused by her antics, she again resumed her lesson. "Zo classe, en English it says, 'Tomorrow, tomorrow, unt not today, is vut die lazy people say!' Now, dot is a gut lesson, ya?" the jovial nun grinned once more, still to no discernible response.

"Oh yes, Sister Ruth. There sure is a lot of truth in that. I'm sure that we all understand that lesson," Annie offered appreciatively on behalf of the other students.

"Gut! Fir now, I haff a final azzignment to help all uf you perhaps receive a better grade," Sister Ruth announced, proceeding over to the chalkboard behind her to write down the poem in both German and English. "Now, any von dot turns in a paper viff my poem written down on it ten times vill receive an extra five points credit to der final grade for der verk, unt any von who writes it down anudder ten times in Churman vill receive an indulgence of a full final grade higher. Zo, der ist no reason for any von to fail dis class, untless of course you are yust a bunch of lazy bones like da liddle poem says," she said in feigned admonishment. "Now, does any von in dis class not understand die azzignment?" she sternly concluded.

"No, Sister Ruth, we all understand," the entire class now responded, jubilantly appreciating being commuted from the dreadful sentencing that was about to befall them.

~

"Jill, you should have been there," attested Annie in vindication, after retelling the story in front of the Sisters Sara and Ruth, while the Mother Superior was hosting them in her office on the last day of classes.

"Vell, liddle Annie, unt Jill, you too, I yust vont you to be avare of der sin of pride. It vos not out of pride dot I had my liddle poem recited, unt it vas not out of ill vill unto der odder teacher, eader, but it vas truly for die zake uf die message uf die liddle poem.

"You zee, I learned it as a liddle girl, unt my mutter before me, unt now, all uf the girls in die poetry class haff it to tell der schildren. Unt so finally, if it is de only ting dot ist remembered from die class ist dot little poem, I haff done my job, az directed by Sister Sara here und our Mutter Superior," she explained humbly.

"I think that Sister Ruth is now somewhat 'bending the boloney,' as she says from time to time, girls," Sister Elizabeth softly smiled. "In many cases, it is Sister Ruth that is more superior than me, or my title. But now, so that you fully understand, when you were in orientation and it appeared that I was annoyed with Sister Ruth for interrupting me with her 'Oh, Gott in Himmel!' routine, well, that was all Sister Ruth's idea. We do that every orientation. That was all her idea to make the girls feel more comfortable. And I must say, it does make all the girls laugh every time we do it. I just feel sad that with the new regulations, we will not be allowed to maintain the manner or style of teaching that we were accustomed to," she noted now in a more subdued tone.

"I am aware of that, Mother Superior," Annie broke in, "and it is exactly for that reason that I'm going to be transferring over to the state university next year," she informed them all in surprise. "I have really learned a lot while I have been here, and you can't imagine how much you have helped me feel better about myself," she soberly confessed. "And I am also ever so grateful to *all* the sisters here at Saint Margaret's," she testified, "and especially for the two of you, Sister Sara and Sister Ruth. I feel terrible that you have to compromise your values because of the changes in the Church since Vatican Two, but I just can't sit here and watch this degradation happen. And besides, if I am going to eventually have to find employment in the secular world anyway, I feel that by going to the state university it will help me better prepare for the future," she concluded in earnest.

"Well, when you find out that you are no happier out there than we are here, we'll still be here, just waiting away to hear about the lamentations of your soul," spoke up Jill with her old familiar smirk.

"Vell, I don't know if dot ist da vay I voud put it, but you vil alvays be in my remembrances, right next to my liddle poem. You vill alvays be my little lieb kuchen," Sister Ruth added.

"And I will never forget the very first day that you walked into the abbey with your father," Sister Sara enjoined. "It makes me happy that you have been able to find a least some of the peace that you have been searching for," she graciously imparted.

"I, too, will always have you in my prayers, Miss Russo," Sister Elizabeth affirmed. "And also, thank God that He has still left me with the task of enlightening Miss Jillian here as to what the true meaning of suffering really is," she added with one of her rare, thin smiles. "In any case, we all love you here at Saint Margaret's, and wish you Godspeed."

Chapter Twenty-Eight

"Home again, home again, jiggedy jog," Annie thought in amusement, sitting at the state college's admission desk while waiting to have her credits confirmed from Saint Margaret's. *"Boy, what a difference this is,"* she continued to think, reckoning she was now being processed like a hunk of American Cheese, instead being interviewed as if she was person.

Once Annie was finished with the business of registering, the next difference she noticed was that the majesty of an ornate church spire, or the Gothic architecture of a cloistered Abbey, was nowhere to be seen, nor were any of the Ionian, Doric, or Corinthian columns that had supported the artistic thinking of the classical masters, either; instead, the stone efficiency of Frank Lloyd Wright was seen everywhere.

And the smell was different too, as the flowered gardens and the exotic incensed buildings, which had heretofore provided her with the natural feeling of being alive, were not to be found, either. Everything smelled of Lysol. "They must be trying to sanitize our brains, ha, ha," Annie wrote Jill after her first week of being there. Jill did not think this was funny whatsoever, and promptly recited a Hail Mary for Annie's sake.

Coming home was different this time for Annie, for it was not just for the summer break. Annie had come back to stay and be a part of the family unit once again, surrendering her status of semi-independence. Capricia had graduated high school was now attending a technical school to learn how to operate a "minicomputer." It was what she wanted, and so Enrico paid for it. He had no idea of what Capricia was talking about when she first tried to explain why it would get her a good job, but since the glossy pamphlet that he had been shown looked expensive and professionally laid out, he figured the school to be legitimate and gave his daughter his blessing.

And since Annie was going to be staying at home while she was attending the state college for the next two years, Enrico additionally went and purchased a brand-new cherry red GTO convertible for her to drive there in, and presumably to come home in, as well. Upon noticing the car parked in the driveway on that very first Saturday morning Annie was officially accepted as "home," she couldn't help but question, standing by the kitchen window, "Whose car is that parked in the driveway, Mom? Does it belong to Cappy's boyfriend?"

"I don't think so. He already picked up your sister about an hour ago. They said they were going to some kind of company bar-b-que where he works," Jolanda replied with little concern, continuing to putz around the kitchen.

"Well, it's parked in back of her Chevy, so if I want to borrow her car, I can't get out. Do you know where Daddy is?" Annie asked.

"Oh, he's out in the breezeway with his paper and coffee. Why don't you just go out and see him?" Jolanda innocently suggested.

"Daddy, whose car is that in the driveway in back of Cappy's?" Annie inquired, while her father was intently trying to read the morning newspaper.

Then, without looking up, and with no discernable emotion, Enrico casually answered, "It's yours, honey, who else's would it be?"

"What? Mine! You mean it's mine?" Annie stammered in disbelief.

"Yup, that's what I mean, all right," Enrico responded, still reading his newspaper and ignoring her excitement.

"Oh, Daddy, I love you!" Annie exclaimed, yanking the newspaper from his possession and plunking herself upon his lap with her arm around his shoulder.

"Hey, watch it, you'll knock my coffee over," Enrico pointed out, trying to keep from being passionately assaulted.

"Don't worry, I won't knock it over," Annie maintained, kissing him on the cheek.

He had not seen her react in this fashion since the loss of Bobby, and it did his heart good, thinking that to see her like this was well worth the price of the car.

Enrico's business had almost doubled in size over that last two years alone. He had paved almost half of the five-acre parcel where his office and storage yard was located. He also constructed a large steel building to maintain and store his heavy equipment in, along with his other weather sensitive supplies, and the entrance to the property no longer faced a dirt road, either.

Congenially touting the financial advantages of having the county improve their properties at the cost of the public, he convinced the other commercial property owners adjacent to his own to request that the access road be paved, officially for safety reasons.

The county commissioner who was elected to represent the commercial district of the county, while over a most excellent dinner with his wife at D'Agostino's, then proposed that every single one of the other commissioners would gladly welcome the additional tax revenue to be garnered, for the good of the people, when the inevitable reassessment of the improved properties would be made. Enrico was absent during the property owners' presentation that was made in public directly before the commissioners, nonetheless the proposal for the project was unanimously approved by consent agenda.

Then, at the very next commissioner's meeting, Dora Paglaroli, after spending a three-day and two-night respite in Las Vegas from the rigors of her demanding civil job as the county's purchasing agent, opened and read aloud the "sealed bids" for the paving of the road. Since there were no objections to the contract being awarded to the Russo Paving Company, even though there was only a thousand-dollar bid difference on the million-dollar contract, Enrico's bid was declared "accepted" by all.

Finally, after the meeting, Enrico and the other four contractors who had also submitted bids reportedly met at the Starlight Lounge to soothe over any hard feelings that anyone still might have for not being awarded the contract. Then, in closing, after paying for the entire tab, Enrico graciously offered that the next time they all would be at odds, it would be his turn to be the ridiculously high bidder to be laughed at, now taking his position at the back of the queue.

~

It was definitely obvious to everyone that the mood of the entire country was changing. Nixon, as promised, was reducing the troop levels in Vietnam, so that by the end of the year they were brought down from almost a half million to only a little over a hundred fifty thousand. Clearly, the end the war was imminent.

For those who yet admired the bravery of the American soldier, the movie *Patton* had taken center stage. For those who were yet innocently in love with love, there was *Love Story, The Summer of '42*, and the tale of *Carnal Knowledge* to reach out to in their quest for a greater sophistication.

As for the entirety of the "*silent majority*" who were completely in a state of transition, they could not help form singing a joy to the world as they felt the earth move under their feet. And then, in putting their hand in the hand of the man who was one toke over the line, they drove old Dixie down, in the summer time, when the weather was high, and they said their good byes to the American pie on a train they called The City of New Orleans, never to return again.

The entire society broke down into a myriad of diverse factions which all claimed to be disadvantaged. Then, as a natural course of events, in one manner or another, they all attempted to solidify themselves as legitimate organizations who then claimed to be worthy of being supported by whichever financial institution or governmental department had the greatest wherewithal to fund them.

Not to be a member of one organization or another was to be a man without a country, alone by virtue of one's own insignificance. The stature of a person had become measured by his, or her, ability to rise within an accepted self-ordained organization in the promotion of the goals of the group as a whole; individuality was considered an anathema to the very organization itself. Certainly, there was always a face to the organization for the altogether purpose of representational identification, but the all over goals, —and especially purse strings, —were generally controlled by an unseen committee which, at its sole discretion, decided the parameters of its own identity.

The college "social" organizations were no different. There were quite a number of different sororities that offered a variety of identities from which one could associate their super egos with, and since Annie did not have Jill to pal around with anymore, she decided that after attending a Greek "rush" at the beginning of her first semester, she would give one of them a try.

Outside of the camaraderie of spirit that all of the sororities shared, Annie realized that each had also each developed and cultivated a special genre which particularly affiliated their organization with a defined social class. This was projected to be the individual essence of their club. There was the Athletic Sorority, the Science Sorority, the Literary Sorority, the High Brow Society Sorority, the Low Brow Society Sorority, and of course, The Barbie Sorority.

"If I join your Literary Sorority, can you guarantee me that I won't be shunned because I just can't help having that Barbie look?" Annie remarked sardonically to one of the sorority sisters who was stationed at their recruitment display for new pledges.

"If you think that you won't be shunned by the Barbies for having that Jonathan Swift attitude, you had better think again. You would be ostracized immediately. You do understand the verbiage, don't you?" the plain looking, brown haired girl with black horned rimmed glasses responded from behind her table, while Annie made no comment in return.

"I take it by your silence then that you do," the girl then continued. "Well, all of us here at the Literary Sorority appreciate, nay, we encourage wit, not the witless. Take one of those pamphlets on the corner of the table with you. It has our address on it. Our next meeting is on this Thursday night at eight o'clock. Be there, or we will publish a satirical piece about the pledgeless girl who plays with Barbie Dolls in the next edition of the school's newspaper, and we'll all have a good laugh," she taunted. "You see, that's what we literary types like to do, —honestly express ourselves in our writing. Do you have a problem with that, Pledge?" the recruiter provocatively questioned.

"Nope, I have no problem with that," Annie curtly assured the recruiter, to then pick up a pamphlet thinking, *Wait till they get a taste of my attitude. This ought to be interesting.*

~

Queen Elizabeth herself would have been proud to have stayed in the Literary Sorority's house, styled after the period of her reign. Three stories high with a four-story tower, white and massive, sufficed to describe the structure behind its classic white picket fence and expansive front porch. It was located on the same side street adjacent to the other campus sororities, and was considered to be part of what everyone at the university called "Sorority Row."

At exactly eight o'clock on that next Thursday evening, Annie showed up, front and center, promptly ringing the chime affixed to the right side of the Sorority House's front porch door.

"Well, I can see that you can tell time," a voice stated from inside the house. "I'm Paula, by the way, and I had a feeling that you would show up. Come on in," she invited.

"I'm Annie," she introduced herself plainly, beginning to inspect the place the minute she walked inside.

The staircase went straight up off the foyer past the twelve-foot ceiling up to the second floor. There was a wide hallway off to the right of the staircase and two large rooms opposite each other off to the sides of the entrance way. The kitchen Annie assumed to be down the hall and in back of the staircase, because both of the rooms to each of her sides were noticeably not.

"This sure is a big place," Annie additionally commented politely.

"Come on into the lounge," Paula invited, leading Annie past a mahogany secretary and into the room to the right of the door.

The room was tastefully decorated with a half-dozen upholstered couches, easy chairs and ottomans, all in a flowered selection of light and buoyant pastel colors. There were a number of ceramic matching lamps with cream colored silk shades that were placed upon end tables beside the sofas and chairs. A small selection of torchiere floor lamps, each with its own uniquely large and expansive globe, gave a comfortable lighting effect throughout the room, which centered a large eight-sided glass topped coffee table upon a bright and intricately patterned red, blue, and gold oriental rug. Potted plants were everywhere, either sprouting up from floor planters, or hanging pendulously from the ceiling in their hand-woven macramé baskets.

"How many girls stay here?" Annie inquired, seating herself in one of the overstuffed easy chairs.

"We have twelve bedrooms and sixteen girls live here. Obviously, some of them share a room. And we have a total of twenty-eight members presently, counting the off-campus ones," Paula answered efficiently, taking a seat on the couch closest to Annie.

"So, what is the advantage to join this sorority in the first place?" Annie asked.

"Friendship is a big one, I would say," Paula replied. "Scholastic help is another," she added factually. "And the parties aren't bad, either," she mentioned with a faintly provocative smile.

"Yeah, go on," said Annie.

"Sure, but first, you must also know that because we are an exclusive club, we don't just invite *anyone* to join," Paula stated in a more serious tone. "We have our secret vows to each other and to the sorority, and its objectives that are not of anyone's concern but our own. We have our own rules, regulations, and moral behavior that we all must abide by, or you can be demitted.

"Now, I can nominate you to become a member, but you will still have to go before the membership committee, at which time they will vote to determine your worthiness to join," she noted in finality.

"Do you think I would make a good member?" asked Annie specifically.

"If I didn't think that now, I wouldn't be wasting my time," Paula answered concisely.

"So, what do I do now?" Annie asked.

"Well, I guess can offer you some wine, that is, until the other sisters arrive, and then you are on your own. What do you say?" Paula questioned leadingly.

"Do you have any Chianti? Is what *I* say," Annie quipped back with an easy smile.

"No, but I do have some Lancers. It's not all that sweet, but it's light, and it tastes pretty good. It's kind of fancy," Paula added with a shrug, "But then again, we don't drink any of that mad dog twenty-twenty around here, either," she offhandedly remarked.

"Would I be expelled if I did?" chuckled Annie.

"The term is demitted, and the answer is probably yes," Paula retorted, rising up from the couch. "After all, we *do* have a reputation to keep, you know," she added, leaving directly for the kitchen.

~

It turned out to be a great fit. Annie had found an entire bevy of beautiful minds that were technically congruent with her own. Becoming a member, would now give her a better sense of understanding the secular world from perhaps a social point of view, but learning how to advance in it from a leadership perspective was something different. This she was also was eager to learn.

There no way she was ever going to be a follower, and she knew it. She was too socially independent, reasoning that if she ever needed to defend her integrity, she would rather do it from the top looking down than from the bottom looking up. It was the structure of leadership she needed, not its concept, —*and what better way to learn it then to experience first-hand how Robert's Rules of Order actually works, —even if it is only the sorority's rendition of them,* she accepted.

Still, Annie longed for her pal, Jill. The intellectualism she had found to keep her mind busy at the sorority was rewarding indeed, but she missed all the passionate arguments that she used to have with her good-buddy friend over the nature of one's soul. *At least we write, and I get to drive up and visit with her occasionally, that's something,* she frequently reflected.

And Annie had not forgotten Bobby, either. Even though the outrage which she initially felt over his senseless death had subsided, the thought of her love for him had not waned from her constitution one single iota. Now without Jill to banter with in the evenings, she only thought of Bobby more and more from the solitude of her old bedroom, trying her best to go to sleep.

She still often thought of that very first day that she had met Bobby on that Saturday morning when the sun, in all its brilliance, shone down upon him, and how, without a care in the world, she temerariously raced the "Whirling Dervish" about the parking lot of the school.

Sometimes, every now and then, she would go out of her way to drive by the old willow tree that was still standing on the far corner of her block. Graciously, it would seem to call out to her in quiet sympathy while its whispering branches would softly sway in the gentle breeze, beseeching her to once again embrace the passions of love, while weeping sadly for her loss.

Annie also frequently reminisced over the many times that she and Bobby had gone to visit Dr. Fizz, as well as her day of her surrender at the picturesque lakeside cabin, the elegant dinner they had at D'Agostino's, and the clear and crystalline winter's day that had coldheartedly reached out to forever claim her true love's destiny.

And these were only some of the memories that haunted her, both constantly and painfully. But now, at long last, after two agonizing years of mourning, the severity of her grief had finally begun to ease. A truly sacred love, a love that no one could put asunder, a love that would forever and always remain deep within in her heart, was still *something* to be thankful for, Annie ultimately accepted. However, to think that she would end up like Mary Hopkins singing "Those Were the Days," in total capitulation to the bleakest of futures and without any hope of happiness regained, was still a concern she could not totally eradicate from her mind.

The fatalism that had been enshrined within the Sisters of Saint Margaret's daily lives, as to their service unto will of God, Annie believed to be quite honorable, but nonetheless realized she was not cut from the same cloth. And although she had come to have a great respect for the fortitude in which the nuns did hold their beliefs, and would never forget the fond understanding of their ways, she still could not help herself from thinking that *her* story was going to be a different one, for she already had a taste of mortal ecstasy and could not deny its existence.

Determinedly, no longer was Annie going to live her life in a state of melancholia, seeking now to find a new social path, a happy path that would lift up her spirits and restore the natural vibrancy of her soul. *Just a little cheer is all I need,* she thought, *but this time, I intend to be in total control.*

~

The first advantage Annie saw by joining the sorority was that no longer did she have to drive home between her classes on the same day. She could remain right there on campus at the sorority house and not waste the time or her gas. Secondly, there was an academic advantage in joining as well. Files on all the professors were kept by the sorority, along with copies of their past tests, but they were forbidden to be taken from the sorority house. They were only to be accessed there. And since at least ninety percent of the exam questions were touted to be the exact ones which would reappear on the next test, and the correct answers were included as well, it was hard for anyone to resist perusing them.

This benefit alone was worth the price of admission, Annie had to concede, for as nefarious as it was, it meant that there was no possible excuse for anyone in the sorority to fail. *Man, this is a better scam than to get a degree using Cliff Notes,* Annie thought to herself, which were absolutely forbidden to be used at Saint Margaret's. *Heck, all you have to do is just memorize the answers and the hell with understanding anything,* she concluded. *And oh my God, if I told Jill about this, she'd go off on a tantrum for at least a week. To actually promote obtaining a degree as a task of recitalment, rather than receiving one as a distinguished mark of one's intellectual proficiency, I think, no, I know, would drive her nuts. Maybe after I graduate, then I'll tell her about this,* she prudently decided.

Annie was now starting to enjoy her leisure time, but on a much different plane than when she was attending Saint Margaret's. The sorority life, in all its regalia, was beginning to seduce her. She now often spent her nights "crashing" over at the sorority house in the guest room after engaging in an evening of adventuresome behavior.

It was at the end of Greek Week when all the sororities and fraternities traditionally opened their doors to each other in shared camaraderie. It was also considered to be the greatest party week of all on the entire campus. Unfettered from the usual restrictions, Annie's sorority sisters would take turns in guarding their own house while taking turns to visit the others, fraternity houses included, where the party was famed to be considerably more raucous.

A giggle here, a giggle there, a catty remark in refusing a dare, and so on and on it went as the never-ending supply of wine was excessively consumed. Then, one by one, the sisters disappeared up to Rose's room on the second floor, where her window opened out behind the massive chimney on the east side of the building. The boldest of all the girls, Rose was every bit the audacious redhead that she was rumored to be.

"Why did I just know you had a feather boa?" mentioned Annie, seeing it hanging from Rose's mirror, upon entering her room for the first time.

"You want to borrow it sometime, just let me know," Rose offered, walking over to a small oval table that was situated under a half-open window on the far side of her room.

"I'll keep that in mind," Annie responded with a slight grin.

"Come on over here, I'm not going to smoke it for you," Rose declared, while Annie began to respectfully negotiate herself past the numerous piles laundry that were in her way. "Oh, don't worry about all that stuff on the floor, it's dirty, anyway. Come on, you can sit right here," she directed, gesturing out to the pea green parlor chair positioned across from her at the table.

The room was carpeted in a dark royal blue, while all four walls were papered in a stripped mauve print. *Whoa, only a seriously unbalanced person could live in such a room?* Annie thought, once seated and further looking about the room. Mismatched prints in an unending graphic display were on display everywhere, depicting the very festival of life in brightest of terms. From the New Orleans Mardi Gras to the Moulin Rouge in Paris, to the Dia de Muertos celebration in Mexico, all were given equal representation.

But amidst all this frivolity, however, like everyone else, Annie still could not help feeling that she was being spied upon by an entire troupe of freakish clowns in pictures, puppets and figurines that had been positioned everywhere and in every conceivable manner. *You know,* she addressed herself, *as bizarre as this actually is, it all seems to coalesce together in a festive, albeit creepy, sort of way,* she reassessed, once finally adjusting to the initial shock of it all.

"So, I guess you are an art major?" Annie proposed in a curious tone.

"How'd you figure that?" Rose asked facetiously as she took the top off an old battered shoebox which she picked up off the floor.

"Oh, just a guess," Annie responded benignly. "I don't know of anyone but an art major who would have a room like this," she openly critiqued.

"So, you like it, huh?" rhetorically remarked Rose while finishing rolling a joint from the pot she had taken from the shoebox. "Here, take a hit. All the rest of us are ahead of you," she stated, relaxing back in her chair after handing Annie the joint and a Bic lighter to go with it.

"And for your edification, I am not simply an art major. I am a marketing major whose specialty is advertising. I only have a minor in art. In essence, that only makes me a fancy salesman, that's all," Rose casually offered. "Well, actually, don't let that fool you either, because I can sell snow to an Eskimo and my grade point shows it," she bragged with an unpretentious smirk.

"Oh, I believe you," Annie certified, taking a second hit on the joint.

"Hey, don't Bogart that joint, my friend," admonished Rose, reaching out for the half-smoked doobie.

"Wow, I'm impressed," remarked Annie, relaxing back as her buzz set in. "Yeah, just look at this place. It's a real trip," she acknowledged, resurveying the room. "You know, I'll bet you actually wear those tiger panties, don't you?" she then asked, pointing to one of the laundry piles with a grin.

"Doesn't every girl have a pair?" smiled Rose, taking another hit.

"I don't," Annie confessed.

"Well, maybe you should get some," suggested Rose, handing back what was left of the joint. "And, here's a fork for the roach," she offered. "Just put it between the tines backwards and it'll work perfectly," she instructed. "Now, there are two things that I have to clarify for you," she began while Annie was trying to engineer the roach and the fork together.

"The first one is, you never wear those leopard panties. The spots make you look fat. You wear the tiger panties. The stripes will accentuate your hips. Secondly, this room has a purpose for being trashy. Would you want to look under that pile of dirty underwear over there to see what's in an old shoebox?" Rose grilled her.

"No, not me," answered Annie in disgust.

"Well neither does anyone else," Rose certified. "You've read *The Purloined Letter* by Poe, I presume?" she then questioned.

"Oh yeah, that's the one where a letter was hidden in plain sight so that no one paid any attention to it," Annie answered.

"Yup, that's the one," accredited Rose.

"Oh, I see," said Annie, "so you not only hide the goods right in plain sight, but you go one step further and put it in the sickest place ever, too. Oh, that's a riot, ha, ha, ha," she laughed in amusement.

"Well, I think we're high enough," said Rose, "We need to go downstairs now, —after all, we don't want to miss the whole show now, do we?"

"I thought you were the show," snickered Annie as they started down the stairs.

"Oh no, it is you who is definitely the show of all shows, Annie," Rose disagreed.

"Nope, it's you," replied Annie.

"Nope, it's all you," the two of them kept on bantering back in forth, until holding on to each other for support and laughing whimsically until they finally reached the bottom of the staircase.

Life was becoming livable again for Annie, attempting to recapture the joy of her youth one last time before it was forever gone with the wind. Her sorority years were now furnishing her with a more cosmopolitan look at her future which the cloistered life at St. Margaret's could never have provided.

Annie was also beginning to appreciate the insight which could be gained by receiving an education from both the secular and the non-secular perspectives. She had left Saint Margaret's a cynic with no agenda, but now, although she was still a cynic, she had an agenda. Never again would she let herself lose control over her emotions. Never again would she lose control over anything, she flatly decided.

And thus, it was in Annie's quest in supporting that total control of her surroundings that she vapidly asked of Eugene on that first night in his apartment, "What is that bottle of Lancers you have in the refrigerator?"

Chapter Twenty-Nine

It was the best of times, it was the worst of times, Annie mused, but was it the absolute best opening line ever printed in a book, —or was the actual de facto phrase *"In the beginning"* superior by virtue of its simplicity and proven longevity? "Oh, whatever," she dismissed, "right now I feel pretty good," she said to herself, waking up the next morning in Eugene's apartment.

"Did I die and go to heaven?" Eugene muttered with his face still in his pillow as he was awakened by Annie rustling the sheets around her.

"Don't you remember?" Annie asked.

"I don't know if I do. Let me see if you are real or not," Eugene replied, boldly rolling over and tugging at the blanket bunched around her.

"Oh, no you don't," said Annie firmly. "I'm real enough, alright. Now you get up first and go into the other room, so I can get dressed. Go on, I don't have all day," she dictated.

"Okay, I'm going," Eugene said compliantly, while rolling off his side of his bed to retrieve the clothes he had cast upon the floor.

"And don't forget to close the door on your way out," Annie added. "I don't want you peeking."

"I think it's a little late for that," Eugene chuckled, to then close the door behind him.

By the time Eugene returned from his other bedroom, now fully dressed, Annie was already back in the living room, seated on the same bar stool as before.

"What are you going to be doing today?" asked Eugene, coming into the living room from the hallway.

"Well, the first thing I am going to do is go home and take a shower. Why?" Annie inquired, as if it wasn't any of his concern.

"Did you have a good time last night?" Eugene then asked, without answering her question.

"Yeah, I had a great time. And I want to thank you for everything, especially for that bottle of Lancers. It's some pretty good stuff. And your weed wasn't bad, either," Annie tepidly complimented.

"Yeah, Pete usually has some pretty good pot," Eugene noted agreeably. "But the reason that I asked you what you were doing later was because I was wondering if you wanted to go somewhere tonight?" he politely offered.

"Yeah, well, that's nice, but my Mom is making a big dinner and we are having some family over, so I'm all booked up for the rest of the weekend," Annie casually replied.

"So, you don't stay at the sorority house?" Eugene questioned, a little confused.

"No, only when they have an event. I'm a commuter. Rose stays at the sorority house, not me. I live in Colonial Heights," Annie clarified.

"Then, you live at home," Eugene stated in conformation.

"Yup, and that's where I am going now," Annie answered succinctly, getting up from the bar.

"Do you have a number where I can get a hold of you again?" Eugene asked as he followed behind her.

"Just leave a message at the sorority house. I'll get it," Annie replied.

"So, do you want to go out somewhere, sometime?" Eugene persisted.

"Oh, I might. What do you have in mind?" Annie mildly questioned.

"Oh, I don't know, maybe a movie or something?" Eugene suggested.

"I'll tell you what," capitulated Annie, "Wednesday, do you have any classes?"

"Yeah, it's one of my heaviest days. I have one at ten, one at two, and another at three," Eugene enumerated.

"Well, I could meet you at the snack counter in the student union about twelve, if you want. Until then, I'll think about the movie offer," Annie finalized, putting on her coat that Pete had laid over the arm of the couch.

"Yeah, I'm sure I can make it. I'll see you there then, okay?" he asked in affirmation.

"Okay, I'll be there," she ratified, while turning towards the door.

"Oh, one second, excuse me," said Eugene, tapping her on the shoulder. "Don't I get a kiss goodbye?" he pleaded like a little boy who was not given his dessert.

"Sure, you do," Annie responded without hesitation, abruptly turning to stand on her toes, toss her arms around his neck, and then passionately kiss him, square upon his mouth. Then, just as abruptly, she lightly bit his lower lip and broke the kiss off. "And don't forget to be there," she remarked unambiguously, poking him on the chest. Turning, she then deftly opened her door, and without looking back or even uttering another word, summarily got out of the car.

"I won't forget," Eugene loudly avowed, hoping she could still hear him.

I can't believe it. She is so hot! was all Eugene could think of after she left. *She's by far the prettiest girl I've ever had a date with. And she isn't stupid, either. What a trophy. I can't wait to tell Scott.*

~

"So, tell me about what happened after I left here the other night," solicited Scott as he went over to lounge on the couch in Eugene's living room on the following Monday evening. "You know how us medical families are brought up to question the patient," he goaded Eugene. "Did you perform coitus without interruptus on that poor needy girl?" he smirked sardonically.

Eugene sat down on one of the upholstered easy chairs opposite Scott across from the coffee table, mechanically took out a pack of Marlboros from his shirt pocket, turned it upside down, patted it smartly on the top of the table to pack down the tobacco, turned it over to peel off the top corner of the pack, and then tapped out a cigarette.

After tossing the pack down on to the table, Eugene casually put the cigarette to his lips and reached down to take out his Zippo lighter from his pocket. Then, as the familiar tintinnabulation of its distinctive ch'ing was heard and the subtle crackle of the dried tobacco had been stifled by the sound of the exhaled satisfaction, the ritual abruptly ended with the metallic clamping of the lighter's top. Finally, Eugene decisively snapped the iconic lighter back down atop the coffee table and casually reclined to think a moment before responding to Scott's question.

Regardless of Eugene's outward casual appearance, his mind was racing. *'Be careful what you say about a girl you go out with, because she just may end up being the one and you might regret it later,'* his mother had often told him. *And what about when I graduate this year, what will I do then, go into plastics? Of course I'll have to get a job, but then what am I going to do for fun? Scott's going off to become a law bag, and I'll be left here all by myself with no one to screw around with. I better be careful here,* he determined, for now he concluded that there indeed was a brave new world out there, and he had no intention of facing it alone.

"That, my good man, is as they say, going to remain between her and me," was Eugene's measured remark, now relaxing further back in his chair with a satisfied look on his countenance.

"So, you blew it. You didn't get any. Go on, admit it to your pal. I won't impugn your reputation to the other guys," Scott pledged in trying his best to intimidate him.

"Nope, I have no comment," smiled Eugene, "but I will tell you one thing, I had a most excellent time. And actually, I'm going to see her again on Wednesday, as a matter of fact," he revealed.

"Whoa, still trying to tame that thing, huh? Okay, so I give you some credit for not wanting to give up. She does seem like she'd be pretty hot. Big Red was a real smoker, Buddy. Let me tell you, don't let those nerdy sorority houses fool you, those girls are always hot," Scott categorically testified.

"Well, I'll take your word for it," Eugene responded with a thin smile.

For discretion is the better part of valor, Eugene thought in recalling his classical reading of Socrates, finding himself to be quite comfortable in not having boasted. He also realized that in not doing so, he actually boosted his self-esteem. Annie was now all he could think about until his next scheduled rendezvous.

~

Annie had been sprawled out on the couch in the bay window of the living room at the sorority house reading Ayn Rand's *The Fountainhead* on that next Monday afternoon when in walked her partner in crime, Rose.

"I see ya got back here okay," stated Rose walking directly over to Annie. "Did ya have a good time?" she paused, while Annie did not break her attention from her book. "I mean with that Gene guy, you know, after I left?" Rose kept on questioning.

"One second Rose, let me finish this chapter first," replied Annie, not breaking her concentration.

Completely unoffended, Rose simply sat down leisurely on the overstuffed chair next to the couch, leaned back, put her feet up on the coffee table and pretended in her mind to be reclining in a pile of down stuffed pillows at the Maharaja's palace. "I love this chair," she declared to the heavens above as she closed her eyes, stretched up her arms, drew in a deep breath, and audibly released it, graphically enunciating the value of her contentment.

"Okay, I'm done," declared Annie, suddenly putting the book down and turning her attention to Rose. "Well, I see that you made it back all by yourself, too, and without any of *my* help, I might add," Annie finally replied.

"Oh yeah, I got back just fine. How about you? And, so like I asked, did ya have a good time after I left?" Rose asked again, seeking to amuse her curiosity.

"Most definitely I had a good time, and by the way, my car *always* gets me home," Annie categorically proclaimed. "That's why my Dad bought it for me in the first place, so at least, once in a while, I would come home," she elaborated further. "Anyway, did you have a good time with the one *you* left with?" she reciprocated, "You were pretty blown away, you know," she also noted for posterity.

"Oh, you mean Scott? Oh yeah, I had a great time. He was quite useful. I even got a breakfast out of the deal. You know, he's sarcastic as hell, but that's just his nature. Once you get to know him, he's really not such a bad guy. And he does have manners. He's just self-impressed, that's all, and that's okay by me, but anyway, like I said, he was useful enough and I'm not complaining. You know what they say, 'If you can't be with the one you love, love the one you're with,' and all that. You get the picture," she elucidated.

"Yeah, I got it," Annie confirmed squarely.

"But what about that guy I left *you* with? You going to see him again? The only thing you told me was that you had a good time. Come on, you gotta give me more than that," Rose doggedly appealed.

"As a matter of fact, yeah," Annie disclosed. "I'm supposed to meet him over at the student union on Wednesday about twelve. He asked me if I would go out with him, you know, like on a date, and so I told him that I had to think about it first," she said clinically.

"Well, I don't know about you Catholic girls. Waiting for that right man is like *Waiting for Godot*. It's just an effort in futility, and personally, I'd rather be an effort in fertility, ha, ha, ha," Rose laughed.

"I already know that. Tell me something I don't know," responded Annie, reputedly holding the moral high ground. "For example," she continued, "are you going to be seeing Scott again?" she questioned in turn, raising her eyebrows in the anticipation of a most intriguing reply.

"I don't know. Like I said, he's enamored with himself. He gave me his number. If I need him again, all I have to do is just give him a call. Right now, I don't need him. Besides, I have a lot of other numbers I can call if I need anything, for all kinds of stuff. You never know," ended Rose, quite candidly.

"Well, that is one thing you are definitely right about, Rosie, you never know," agreed Annie.

~

Eugene arrived a quarter of an hour early on that next cold and bleak Wednesday afternoon, and was pushing his way past the line at the snack counter in the student union when he saw Annie already sitting at a deuce table by herself against the far wall with a soda already in front of her.

"Hey, how are you doing today?" greeted Eugene, taking a seat at the table.

"I'm doing good, and you?" Annie replied.

"I'm doing great. I got an A on most of my mid-terms and it looks like I'm going to graduate in the spring after all, heh, heh," Eugene remarked lightheartedly. "Did you get something to eat already?"

"No, I just got a coke," said Annie.

"Well, if you want to go to McDonald's, I'll drive," Eugene offered politely.

"Sure, if you can get me back here in less than an hour so I'm not late for my next class," Annie conditioned.

"Oh yeah, that's no problem. It won't take that long. Just get your coat on and we'll go right now," Eugene suggested, rising from his chair.

It was the standard cold and grey December day outside, which did not warm the cockles of anyone's heart when having to experience it. Nonetheless, totally innocuous to the weather, the both of them, having sufficiently bundled themselves up in their coats, summarily left the warmth of the student union to brave the inhospitable trip to where Eugene had parked his car.

"Let me get the door for you," proposed Eugene, taking a half step in front of her while retrieving his keys from his pocket. After opening her door and going around to the other side of the car, Eugene got in as quickly as he could and then immediately started up his second new Mustang.

"Man, we're lucky. The car is still somewhat warm," Eugene commented while he turned on the heater. "At least it hasn't snowed yet," he added.

"Not yet, but it still might tonight. It's cold enough to," responded Annie.

"So, you're going to graduate in the spring also?" Eugene asked, pulling the car out of the parking lot.

"Yeah, I sure am, and then I'll have my Bachelor's in English," Annie notably affirmed.

"Well, I'll have my Bachelor's in History then, too," Eugene offered. "I really don't know what it's good for, except teaching, so I got a minor in Education just in case. I mean, I'm going to have to get some type of job once I graduate, and I guess that being a teacher is as good as anything," he said frankly. "At least until I figure out what I really want to do. You know what I mean?" Eugene questioned.

"Oh yeah, I know what you mean," Annie acknowledged. "I have a minor in Art which, for your edification, includes Art History. And I don't know what it's good for, either, except I find it interesting. I guess I could get a job writing for one of those upscale art magazines, or something along those lines, perhaps. Maybe I could even get a job reviewing Botticelli paintings for Cosmo, ha, ha, ha," she cavalierly laughed.

"Actually, that's probably not a bad idea," remarked Eugene, pulling into the entrance ramp of the nearby McDonald's. "So, what do you want? I'm buying," he announced, while parking the car and leaving it running for the heat.

"Just get me a strawberry shake and a cheeseburger," ordered Annie.

"You want a shake in this weather?" asked Eugene with a bewildered look on his face.

"Sure, why not? I'm not drinking it outside. Besides, they're pretty good and that's what I want," she established conclusively.

"Okay, if that's what you want," he accepted. "Well, I'll be back in a minute," he prognosticated, leaving on his trek to the counter at take out window.

At least their Speedee Service System works pretty well, Eugene thought while waiting for his order outside in the freezing cold.

"Well, I made it back. Jesus, it's cold out there!" Eugene vehemently vented, after slamming his car door shut.

"Please don't use the Lord's name in vain in front of me," Annie minded him.

"Okay, I didn't know you were that sensitive," Eugene apologized, holding out the strawberry shake.

"Before I came here last year I transferred over from Saint Margaret's, up state. I studied there for two years. If they hadn't allowed in all of the secular students and teachers in for the sake of getting the government's money, I would still be there," Annie explained, taking the shake from his hand. "Why my father should be paying pay for a Catholic education when the college doesn't give you one is stupid. I'd just as soon have a car and go wherever I please instead," Annie stated plainly, putting her shake on top of the dashboard and taking the cheeseburger now being held out.

"So your parents had no problem in you leaving St. Margaret's?" Eugene questioned, handing Annie a straw for her shake to then retrieve his own cheeseburger from the take out bag.

"Not my father. He'd just as soon have me home," Annie conceded. "My mother was a little disappointed, though, because she was really happy that I went there in the first place, but you know, after I told her about the disrespectful attitude towards the Catholic religion that the secular teachers were allowed get away with, she got over it," Annie said dismissively. "Anyway, can we start back now? I can finish the rest of this on the way," she submitted

"Yeah, of course," Eugene replied agreeably, assiduously woofing down the last of his burger. Then, after finishing his soda in the same manner, he stuffed his empty cup and paper wrapper into the bag and put the car in reverse. "You want to go out somewhere this weekend?" he politely asked, once pulling out of the exit ramp.

"I don't know. What did you have in mind?" Annie responded.

"I don't know. Do you want to see a movie?" Eugene countered.

"I understand *Jeremiah Johnson* will be out on Friday. It has Robert Redford in it. I could see that," Annie suggested.

"Well, would you want to go and see it on Friday night or Saturday?" Eugene asked, deliberately giving her a choice.

"I guess Friday would be okay," Annie replied amiably.

"Where do you want me to pick you up, then?" Eugene asked.

"You can pick me up at the sorority house at seven if you want. Oh, and by the way, you can drop me off there right now if you please," Annie instructed.

"Sure, not a problem, Annie," Eugene dutifully replied.

"So, I guess I'll see you right here on Friday night, at seven, right?" Eugene questioned, pulling his car over in front of the sorority house.

"You got it right, Gene," verified Annie, reaching over for the door handle to get out of the car.

"Hey, wait just a minute, don't I get a kiss?" pandered Eugene.

"Sure, I don't see why not, lean over here," Annie explicitly motioned with her finger.

And as he did, Annie quickly kissed him on the cheek, retreated, turned back around to open the door, and then cleanly stepped out of the car. "I'll see you at seven," she affirmed, succinctly closing the car door behind her with a thud.

Captivated by Annie's gait as she sauntered down the walkway to the front porch of the Sorority house, Eugene intently watched her from the curbside until, without looking back, she completely disappeared from his sight. *What am I going to do? I hope I don't blow it. I don't think I'm ever going to find another one that even comes close to her. She is not only beautiful, but she's no dope, either. I guess I'll just see what happens,* he concluded, pulling away from the curb while trying to dismiss any further interceding thoughts which might begin to compromise his optimism.

Pitch black, cold and windless, was the night when Eugene re-parked his car precisely in front of the sorority house, exactly at the appointed time. Then, while pensively resting for a moment in trying to figure out what he should do next, out from the front door came Annie to subsequently get into his car.

"Are you ready?" asked Eugene as soon as the car door closed.

"I guess so. Which theatre are we going to?" Annie asked.

"I thought we'd go over to the one by the mall, if that's okay by you," Eugene responded politely.

"That's fine by me," agreed Annie, while Eugene put the car into gear and got underway.

"So, what do you think of my car?" Eugene questioned egotistically. "My dad buys me a new one every two years. He says his accountant told him that, 'considering what you get to trade it in and the wear and tear on it, that you now have to start paying for, and you'll need to buy a new set of tires too, you're much better off to trade it in.' My dad also said that, 'once you can afford to buy a new one, you should never trade down.' Anyway, that's least that's what I was told," he dismissively shrugged before supplementing, "Of course, I've always had a Mustang because I just think they're cool," he flaunted pretentiously.

"I like my GTO better," Annie stated indifferently, as to imply her automotive superiority.

"You've a GTO?" Eugene asked in complete surprise.

"Yeah, my dad bought me a new one last year. Of course, it's nothing like this. It's more like a race car, you know," Annie mentioned laconically. "I think they call it a 'muscle car' because it has a four speed Hurst and all those air scoops on the hood. My dad even put that stupid racing stripe over the top of it, too. And so, with its dark burgundy color, I guess it does looks like a race car," she admitted, "but your car is really nice, too," she offered benevolently, "and I really like its pastel powder blue color. It's seems to make the car so nice and comfortable. Did your mother pick it out for you?" she asked.

Unexpectedly, Eugene's mind was like a pinball machine on tilt. All he could think of was, *Warning! Warning! Danger Will Robinson!* as it seemed that he was the one who was lost in space.

"I said, did your mother pick it out for you?" Annie asked once again, while Eugene was still in shock of being upstaged.

"Oh, eh, no," Eugene finally replied, now pretending to be intently concerned with the traffic. "Actually, I picked it out," he said candidly, thinking *'Oh, what a tangled web we weave, when first we practice to deceive!'* to then prudently add, "because, well, —I like it," he admitted.

"Yeah, well, I like it too," Annie supported graciously. "It makes the car so nice and comfortable, like I said. And it's also kind of fun, you know?"

"Yeah, I just like the color, that's all. And it's like you said, it *is* kind of fun, especially in the summertime with the top down," Eugene amiably appended, not even mentioning that his first one was painted a candy apple red. "Well, here's the mall. I hope there isn't a line," he announced, effectively changing the subject.

"I hope not. I hate standing in line," Annie attested.

"Well, we're right on time, so even if there is a line, they should be open by now and the line should go pretty fast," Eugene noted, putting the car into park. "Come on, let's go before we freeze," he added, opening his car door.

Meeting Annie around the front of the car, Eugene took hold of her arm proceeded to escort her to the entrance of the theater. Then, fortuitously in having no line to wait in, ostensibly because of the cold, they were able to go right in and once seated, when Annie had given no objection to Eugene putting his arm around her, he thought back to his faux pas in his egotistical boasting about his car. Her allowance of this gesture of affection now made him quite happy, for he consequently assumed that it was indicative that his little experiment of trying to reveal her presumptive mercantilist nature had gone unnoticed.

But it did not. Annie simply found his devious behavior a harmless insecurity, but for right now, the one and only thing that was on her mind was, *Can Robert Redford really act without Paul Newman to carry him?*

Chapter Thirty

Slowing down upon seeing the sign that read, Mom's Pizzeria, after leaving the theatre and agreeing to get something to eat, Eugene offered, "I don't know if you have been here before, but the pizza is pretty good. Our frat orders it from here once in a while, but I've never been inside. Do you want to give it a try?"

"Sure, what else are we going to do, eat it in the car?" replied Annie offhandedly.

The restaurant was actually a small converted house which avoided being taken down when the highway was widened years before. It had a faux brick facade with an arched entrance in the front of the building which supported an indisputably large sign that patiently advertised it to be, in the brightest of red and green neon, "Mom's Pizzeria."

Both sides of the structure still had the original white clapboard siding and a small mismatched addition had been added onto the back for additional kitchen space. The asphalt pavement around it completely encircled the small restaurant. This gave the quaint eatery a more than ample area for parking, along with an easy access to both arrive and then subsequently leave its pleasantries behind. It was a popular local eating place for the intimacy that could be had in one of its small dining rooms. It was also famous for serving the greasiest pizza on the planet. "Greasy, but God is it good!" was their coveted reputation.

"What do you want on the pizza?" Eugene asked, after putting his menu aside.

"Everything," replied Annie.

"Anchovies too?" asked Eugene apprehensively.

"And olives," Annie instructed.

"Do you mind if I just have pepperoni on my half?" Eugene asked permissively.

"Gene, you can have it any way you want. You asked me what I wanted, and I told you. If you want tuna fish on your half, why don't you just order it? I'm not eating it for you," Annie said bluntly, leaning back in the booth and looking up in exasperation.

"Okay, have you figured out what you want now?" the returning waitress now asked with a pad in one hand and a pencil in the other. "First of all, what are you guys drinking?" she asked before they could answer.

"I'll have a Coke," ordered Annie succinctly.

"Me too, and I know what we're having now," Eugene said.

"Okay, I'm listenin'," said the waitress.

"Can I get a half and half pizza?" asked Eugene politely.

"Sure, waddle it be?" asked the waitress, her pencil at the ready.

"We'd like a medium, please" Eugene requested, "and on half of it I would like everything, including olives and anchovies, and on the second half... oh, and excuse me, do you have any tuna fish?" he asked, interrupting himself.

"Yeah, we make a tuna fish sub. You want one?" the waitress seriously answered.

"No, not really," Eugene replied with a slight grin.

"He wants it on his pizza," Annie interjected.

"You do? We can do that. We have some customers that order it that way. They say it's pretty good," answered the waitress directly to Eugene.

"No, I was just kidding. You have to excuse me, I'm just having fun," Eugene playfully smiled. "Pepperoni is all I want on my half," he now responded decisively.

"Is that everything, then?" the waitress asked in finality.

"Yes ma'am. That will be all, thank you," Eugene replied in a more courteous manner.

"Okay, you got it," the woman declared, moving on to place their order.

"So, what did you think of old Jeremiah Johnson?" Eugene now solicited.

"I thought it was great. It seemed fairly realistic. What do you think?" Annie asked in return.

"I liked it, too. The photography was really awesome. I've never been out there, but I bet it's beautiful," Eugene surmised.

"I thought that the portrayal of the Indian's lives and customs were quite interesting," critiqued Annie, while the waitress, without interrupting their conversation, put their sodas on the table, tossed down a couple of straws, and left.

"I thought the guy who played Bear Claw, you know, the other mountain man, was great. I mean he had real character. Without him, after all, the story wouldn't have any bearing, ha, ha," Eugene humorously remarked, taking a drink from his Coke. "After all, it probably was him who was telling the story in the first place," he proposed in a more practical tone.

"Well, I liked Robert Redford," Annie stated frankly. "It was his character development that drove the movie forward, and I thought that he did a great job. He reflected the change and suffering that people have to go through after having made the smallest of mistakes which have come to plague them for the rest of their lives. And sometimes, as in this case, it can be so severe that it drives them into becoming a totally different person that they never intended to be in the first place, just to survive," she postulated.

"I grant you all that," affirmed Eugene, "I think that your synopsis of the movie is correct, but I still, never the less, cannot give the bulk of the movie's success to Redford all by himself. He hardly had any dialogue. In fact, he hardly had any dialogue in Butch Cassidy and the Sundance Kid, either. I mean, why can't we cast him next as Helen Keller's long-lost twin brother in 'The Miracle Worker Revisited?' He'd be great for the part. He'd only have to utter one line, 'Wa Wa,' and the audience would love him," he smirked.

"Well, as far as I'm concerned," retorted Annie, "he doesn't have to say anything to get his point across, and that is precisely what makes him the great actor that he is. If you could be just as successful without opening your mouth, you would do so, too, —instead of just sticking your foot in it all the time," she fervently argued.

"So, we are in concert, then," Eugene evenly proposed. "It was a great film because the director did not clutter it up with a lot of useless dialogue," extrapolated Eugene, in trying to find some middle ground.

"Exactly, and it was precisely Redford's job to get the point of the movie across with his silent suggestive powers that gave the director the time, *in the first place*," Annie stressed, "to record the awesome panorama of the setting, which *you* said you loved. I think that you need to give credit where credit is due and stop being contrary only for the sake of it," Annie captiously proposed.

"Listen, I told you I thought it was a great film," Eugene recertified defensively. "I also think that he was perfect for the part. After seeing the movie, he has become Jeremiah Johnson forever in my mind. He's a great actor, okay? Now, here comes our pizza," Eugene pointed out, leaning back in his booth.

"Is there anything else I can get you?" the waitress asked after putting the pizza on the table between them.

"No, thank you, everything is fine," responded Annie, shortly dismissing the woman.

"So then, we both agree it was a great film, right?" Eugene offered in trying to pacify her.

"Yeah it was, and I am happy that you took me to see it. I'm also happy that you agree with my review," Annie grinned victoriously, yielding no ground whatsoever in the world of cinematic debate. "Now, let's see if this pizza is as good as it looks," she further challenged, handing her plate over to Eugene.

"You know, you're something else, Annie," Eugene said. "Maybe you *should* write for Cosmo. Your viewpoint of Botticelli's nudes I'm sure would make for an interesting article. Who knows? They're always looking for some artistically provocative arguments to drive up their sales," he seriously reasoned. "Well, anyway, here's your pizza with everything on it, and I must say, it sure does look good," he noted, offering Annie back her plate.

"Yeah, it sure does, and I'm hungry too," Annie admitted, picking up the slice to take a bite.

"So, what does your dad do for a living?' questioned Eugene in changing the subject while serving himself.

"Oh he's a paving contractor," Annie said directly.

"Well, that's a coincidence," Eugene replied. "My dad's a contractor, too. What counties does he cover?" Eugene questioned further. "The reason I ask is because maybe my dad might know him, since we build all over the state," he disclosed.

"He might, because he puts down roads wherever the state wants them, sometimes, from one side to the other," Annie answered. "What kind of construction does *your* father do?" she asked in return.

"Oh, he builds commercial and industrial buildings. Warehouses, factories, offices, you know, that sort of thing. He bids on some city buildings, as well. Sometimes, he will even bid on a county school," Eugene added. "Anyway, he's fairly big," he contended.

"So, how come you are not going to work for your dad after you graduate?" Annie questioned. "I mean, before you said that you just wanted to be a history professor. That doesn't pay anything compared to what your dad could pay you. Certainly, working for him, I would think, would be a lot better for you, don't you?" Annie questioned.

"You would think so, wouldn't you?" Eugene answered, reclining back in his seat with a slight sigh. "You see, my dad's got plenty of money. Sure, he gives me a new car every two years, but he also gives my sisters a new car every two years, too. That doesn't have anything whatsoever to do with his business," Eugene stated.

"Don't you have any brothers?" Annie further inquired, picking up another piece of pizza off the platter.

"No. I'm the only masculine child, as Luca Brasi would say," Eugene kidded, "and I'm also the youngest," he noted. "Listen, paying for my school and giving me the money to do whatever I want while I go to college is one thing, but paying me more than I could make in the outside world at another job is altogether something else. My father is a businessman, and my mother is right behind him. In both their opinions, I would have to 'start at the bottom,' just like he did, and that's a quote," he related seriously.

"Besides, I don't want to go into construction," Eugene continued. "In no way, am I even slightly mechanically inclined. I can't even change the oil in my car, and I don't want to. Now, as I see it, the hand-outs that they give me are not going to change, so why don't I do something that *I* like to do, —instead of what *they* think I should. I can teach history for a while, and maybe go for my Master's Degree, and then, just see what happens. Meanwhile, I could enjoy my own life, instead of having to live it according to *their* dreams," he vented as Annie continued to patiently listen.

"Now, my father is more pissed off that I don't go into construction than my mother is. My mother is somewhat happy because I will at least have a college education, and to her, it represents a higher degree of sophistication for the family's status. So, that's not all bad. And then maybe, just maybe, I could somehow become a famous historian like Shelby Foote, or write a book, or even receive some kind of award. Then, perhaps my father would come around a little and at least acknowledge me as a person in my own right. But pay me any more of a salary to work for him than I could get elsewhere? That damn sure isn't going to happen. And even my mother is with him on that one," he categorically stated.

"And still there is another thing," Eugene pressed on. "You see, I already worked for my dad in the summertime. I know what it's like. Everyone who works for my father would be squealing on me, —all the time, from what I ate for lunch, to how many times I took a leak. Then, if they didn't report to my father, they would report to my mother, and that's even worse, because she'd even nag me at home.

"No, there would be no life for Eugene, as Eugene would have it, if I went to work for my father. It would be my life as *they* want it to be. So, you can see that working for my dad would become torture beyond belief, and it would be on a daily basis, too. I'd rather bust suds in a restaurant for a living," he then said adamantly. "Now, does that answer your question, 'why I don't want to work for my father?'" he mimicked incisively.

"I didn't know that your home life was so crappy," Annie commented. "My father makes good money, too. And we're also all over the state. But my parents let me do whatever I want, as far as deciding my own future. They only want me to be happy, no matter what I do. For almost a year after I graduated, I worked for my father and actually liked being in the office. As long as I was there and had something to do, no one ever gave me a hard time, and no one ever reported on me to my father, either. It was me who reported to him on what everyone else did," she openly validated, while it was now Eugene's turn to listen and eat.

"And *my* mother has nothing to do with the business at all," Annie continued. "She takes care of the home. Of course, some of my cousins and one of my uncles *do* work for my dad, —so it's still like we're all family. But everyone knows their job and it doesn't have anything to do with what you do after work. That's your business. And if you want to better yourself and move on, there are no hard feelings. We believe that you should live to be happy, and not just try to make money for its own sake.

"My father can be the most empathetic guy in the world, but that has nothing to do with what he pays his people. The job you do, pays what it pays, and you know that going in. So, either you do it, or you don't. It's that simple with him. When I got paid, I got paid exactly what the office job pays, no more, and I was happy with that. And he never asked me a single time what I did with my own money," she stressed.

"But I can see that you're not really happy," Annie went on, "even with the money that your father does gives you. So, let me ask you. What's the point of having money, if you can't be free to do what you want with it? Is that your problem? I'll bet you have to justify every single cent you spend, and if it isn't spent on something that they approve of, you'll catch hell for it. Is that about right?" Annie asked in conclusion.

"You understand perfectly," Eugene concurred. "I just want to do, what *I* want to do. And I don't want to live as if the Great Depression is still here, like they do," he repined.

"Well, then don't. Become a history professor and be happy," Annie proposed straightforwardly.

"What about you? What are *you* going to do after you graduate?" Eugene inquired in turn.

"I don't know exactly. There are plenty of jobs out there. I could be a copy editor, or perhaps a general editor for the right publication. I could even write articles, do reviews as a freelance writer, or, just like you laughed about, maybe I could land a job with Cosmo. I took both a journalism class and a critical analysis of mass media class, —and got an A in both of them. I'm going to graduate Summa Cum Laude, too. So I don't think I'll be hurting for a job," Annie stated with confidence. "Besides, after I graduate, I'll still have plenty of time to look because I can always go back to work for my dad. But, then again, maybe I *will* get a job with Cosmo, —you never know," she subtly smiled.

"Oh, I didn't laugh about the Cosmo job, really, not at all," clarified Eugene. "In fact, I thought it would be a great opportunity. Besides, I think it would be pretty cool, as a matter of fact. Like you said, you never know. Virgil said that 'fortune sides with he who dares,' and so, my question for you is, do you dare to go over to my place after we leave here?" he slyly segued as the waitress was putting the bill on the table.

"No, I want to go back to the sorority house where my car is, so I can go home," she said plainly.

"I have some weed back at my place and we could get high," Eugene tempted, raising his eyebrows.

"No, I have to go home," Annie reinforced.

"Well, what about the last time you were over? Didn't you have a good time then?" he almost pouted, in trying to prey on her emotions.

"Of course I did. I told you that. That doesn't mean that I'm a pot head or a juice head, just because I got a little stoned and drank your wine. I just want to go home, and I don't care for your inferences," Annie snapped back in an unmistakably perturbed manner. "I'm not one of those party girls that pander after a good time looking for some guy with money," she stated clearly. "I'm sure your buddy Scott can always find you one of those. He makes a good upper class pimp, and I must say, he has style, too. Maybe I ought to go out with him, because I don't see much of a difference here. Rose, or 'Big Red,' as he calls her, had a good time with him and you know... that's it!" she then exclaimed with her index finger up, as a new thought was about to be revealed, "When we get back to the sorority house, I'll just see if Rose wants to go over to your apartment with you. I'm sure that she won't make you feel so dejected. It will be my gift to you for the pizza you bought tonight," she peevishly proposed.

"Oh no, I'm sorry," Eugene apologized regretfully, "I didn't mean it that way. I like you. I'm happy being with you. I can talk to you about things that I don't talk to anyone else about. I feel that you can understand me. I like going out with you, that's all," he explained in a panic.

"I even thought that you might want to see *Grease* with me. It's playing in the city, and we could take the train. I think it would be a lot of fun. I didn't mean to offend you. Of course I'll take you back to the sorority house," Eugene stated, pausing a moment to think of what he should say next, "Do you think that you could still go with me to see *Grease* next week? Would that make you happy?" he then asked repentantly, desperately hoping for clemency.

"Yeah, I'd like to see *Grease*," Annie said flatly, "and I'll go with you next weekend, but when I want to go home, I want to go home," she stated insistently. "And if I want to go over to your apartment with you for fun and games, then I will let you know," she ruled. "You see, I like you, Gene.

And I like going out with you, too, but I make my own decisions and I don't like being conned into them. Now, I am going to tell you one thing about me, and that is, you can harness a raging river and you can harness a wild horse, but it would be a big mistake for you to even begin to think that you can put a bridle on me. So, as long as you remember that, we'll get along just fine, okay?" Annie warned in no uncertain terms, conditionally accepting his apology.

"You know something, Annie? That's exactly why I like you. I don't want a yes person who does whatever I want because I pay for everything. I want someone who has their own thoughts and can understand mine, like you. And I really can't wait to see *Grease* with you, so I can listen to your review of it. You know, Annie, you are such a trip," Eugene stated in a complementary manner.

Then, sliding over and getting up from the booth, Eugene picked up the check, looked at it for a second, put some money on the top of it, and laid it back down on the table. "Well, if you're ready, I'll take you back to the sorority house now," he duly announced, hoping he had placated her sufficiently.

"Well, I'm ready too, so let's go," Annie replied affably, also getting up to leave.

~

By their third time together, the accustomed expectations of each other's roles, now having been more defined, produced a welcomed comfortability which all but yearned to replace the previous tenuous feelings of insecurity which had pervaded their last encounter. Being totally honest was yet somewhat elusive, but so was the matter of truth, while how to begin to define these concepts to each other's satisfaction had not yet even been broached. Subsequently, in philosophically bantering over these differences, as well as acknowledging the ones which they did concur upon, they now began to foster a genuine and mutual respect for each other, allowing each of them to retain their own individual personas while at the same time being perceived as a couple.

And like all young people of the day who had seen *Butch Cassidy and the Sundance Kid*, *The Graduate* and *Easy Rider,* both Annie and Eugene sought to interface their future with every unrestricted passion that their youth would allow in the total disregard of any accountability unto the status quo. First, however, before even considering delving into such a quest, their date to the theatre had to come first.

So, off they went that following weekend to see *Grease*, the iconic doo-wop dream of all time, while relevance was the word of the day as the production hit home with the two of them. It was the first Broadway musical production that either of them had attended, and it wowed them to the max. Each had seen a number of different musicals on the big screen, but neither had ever before witnessed a professional live performance.

It wasn't *Oklahoma* or *South Pacific*, of which they had no personal experience with, it was *Grease*, and that they were familiar with. Whether it had been in their hair or on a hamburger griddle, or it was simply something that was a necessary ingredient to make their cars run, it was all the same to them. It was a culture that they could identify with, and as such, it was real. Reviewing it directly after the show this time, however, was simply out of the question, for once Annie and Eugene had gotten outside the theatre, they were more concerned in avoiding the panhandlers in catching the train ride home than they were about intellectualizing over anything.

Finally, after claiming their not-so-comfortable seat on the train, Eugene decided that he would put off talking about the show to ask the "question of all questions," thinking, *Oh God, she's in such a great mood, I guess I'd better bring this up right now, and strike while the iron is hot.*

"So, have you ever been to Fort Lauderdale on spring break?" Eugene asked as benignly as possible. "I haven't, and I was thinking of going this year," he gratuitously added. "What do you think about it?" he posed to Annie directly.

"Oh really? Don't you think that I know what you up to?" Annie replied with a smirk.

"Well of course you do. I don't underestimate you," Eugene candidly admitted. "Considerate it a polite offer. You don't have to go. I just thought it might be an adventure you might want to go on, that's all," he proposed affably. "And you don't have to worry about the money, because I can pay for everything myself," he cordially attached.

"I can pay for everything myself, too, if I want to go, thank you very much," Annie answered smartly. "But, I will tell you one thing. I will think about it. And, to answer your question, no, —I haven't been there, either," she clarified. "Here," she then said, rummaging through her pocketbook and taking out a small spiral pad and pen. "Here's my phone number at home. You can call me next Sunday night after seven o'clock, and I'll give you your answer then. Not this Sunday," she stressed, "but next Sunday, okay?"

"Okay, then, next Sunday it is," Eugene agreed, taking the note from her hand while thinking, *Oh man, I finally got her home phone number. I guess I am really making progress.* He was ecstatic.

Annie, on the other hand, was simply amused over the obvious display of meticulous concern that Eugene used in folding the small piece paper up to specifically tuck it into the "secret place" in his wallet. She knew he would call.

"So, what did you think of the musical?" Eugene finally got around to asking, purposefully changing the subject as not to muddle up his newly completed contract.

"Well, as far as it being a musical production, it did a great job of engaging the audience," Annie began. "The dancing, or choreography as they call it, was fantastic, and the music was just as passionate as it could be, I'll give you that. But you know, although I thought it was a great performance, at the same time, it made me kind of sad," she then confessed sedately.

"How could a production like that possibly make you sad?" Eugene asked in concern.

"It's because I will never have those times again, that's why," Annie answered, now in a more somber tone.

"Well, of course you will. That's why I thought we could go to Fort Lauderdale on spring break, where we could have exactly those kinds of times. That's why I asked you to go," said Eugene compassionately.

"No. You don't understand. It will never be the same," Annie stated, not only definitively, but in such unexpected forlornness that it took Eugene completely by surprise.

"What do you mean?" Eugene asked sympathetically, having no clue as to Annie's bout with melancholia.

"I don't want to talk about it," Annie dismissed shortly.

"Okay, then we'll talk about something else," Eugene propitiously, and most wisely, retreated. "Well, how about, when am I going to see you again this week?" he pleasantly asked.

"You're not. I have my finals to study for," Annie answered shortly. "Like I said, you can call me at home next Sunday night after seven o'clock," she reiterated clearly.

"Okay, I'll call you then," Eugene obediently replied. "Look, I'm sorry if you feel bad. I didn't mean to make you feel bad," he then delicately apologized.

"You didn't make me feel bad. That's just the way it is. Like I said, I just don't want to talk about it. It's not you, okay?" Annie consoled, reaching over and gratuitously petting him on the forearm arm.

"Well, okay, I'll call you on Sunday night, then," Eugene confirmed. "I hope you feel better," he sincerely offered.

~

And call Eugene did, exactly as permitted, on that next Sunday evening. It was then that he could not believe his ears when Annie told him that she would indeed be going to Fort Lauderdale for the up and coming spring break. The exhilaration he felt was immeasurable. It was as if he had just won the million-dollar one armed bandit in Las Vegas.

Then, all of a sudden, as if the Internal Revenue Service had just seized his fortune, Annie informed him that she had already made her reservations at the Castaway Resort in Miami, and that her girlfriend Jill from St. Margaret's was coming along.

"Are you kidding me? Come on. Are you just teasing me?" asked Eugene in total disbelief.

"No, I'm not kidding. It's now a done deal," Annie definitively declared. "Why don't you come down with your friend Scott, and we can all have a good time?" she proposed with such a grin that Eugene could readily sense it from the other end of the phone.

"Well, I have to ask him first, but either way, I want you to know, I am definitely going," confirmed Eugene, pausing momentarily to ask another hopeful question. "Well, do you think that, at least, we can all go in one car?"

"No, I don't think my father would go for that at all, and he's the one that made the reservation. Also, so you know, if Jill wasn't going with me in the first place, I doubt that he would have made it at all," Annie said in the frankest of terms. "So, call your friend Scott, and the two of you can share a room in the same place as. Then we can all go out together once we get there," she light heartedly suggested. "Now, don't tell me your best goomba friend is going to desert you in the time of your greatest need, is he?" she deliberately taunted.

"You're right, Annie, he'd better not," asserted Eugene forcefully, considering her taunt to be a challenge.

And the die was cast.

Chapter Thirty-One

It was only forty-eight degrees on that cold adventurous morning when Annie and Scott took their cars onto the road, endeavoring to leave behind that dank and chilly rain which seemed to haunt them all the way down through the entire State of Virginia. It was as if the overcast blanket of grey and tumultuous clouds at every turn was doing its best to thwart them from ever escaping its thoroughly depressing shroud of incarceration.

After about an eleven-hour drive, Annie pulled her GTO into the Florence Holiday Inn in North Carolina, determined to be the half-way point to their destination. Since Enrico had booked Annie and Jill's room over the motel's Hollidex system, the two girls were checked in right away, but Eugene and Scott's check in took a little longer, as they had made no reservations at all.

It was already eight o'clock in the evening, and since the restaurant was only open for another hour, they all decided to just dump their bags off in their rooms and immediately meet back in the lobby. Then, by the time all four of them had gotten to the restaurant, there was only a single couple left dining, however, the lounge attached to it was totally packed as the local crooner was trying to empathetically convey the lament of *Me and Mrs. Jones* to anyone who would listen.

Post haste, Eugene led the way as they all took a seat to order the simplest items on the menu, for they were tired, hungry, and above all else, wanted to get an early start. The service was quite efficient, and after consuming two club sandwiches, a BLT, and a cheeseburger, all with fries and sodas to match, the two young gentlemen were then soundly introduced to the unabashed convictions, moral attitudes, and otherwise syllogistic logic of Jill Jillian.

"Where in the hell did Annie find her?" Scott expressed in complete and utter discombobulation as soon as he and Eugene had gotten back to their room.

"At Saint Margaret's Catholic School for Women, that's where," remarked Eugene in amusement. "Don't worry, you'll have all week to try to get into her pants," he added, while Scott abandoned the remark to seek some comfort in the bathroom.

Except for Annie declaring "You know, the first thing that I am going to do when we get to the Castaways is hit the beach," they both had little else to say, while she and Jill's only concern was preparing themselves for the next day.

Thereafter, it was neigh on five o'clock in the afternoon when, at long last, they all arrived at the resort. And, with the sun still up and shining brightly, it verily amazed them that the temperature had yet remained a healthy eighty degrees. After expeditiously checking in, Annie and Jill went directly to their room, abruptly dropped their luggage, and expeditiously set out for Annie to keep her promise, while Eugene and Scott were summarily left behind, still to check in.

Bounding past the pool area and over a hilly sand berm, which separated the motel area from the beach, Annie suddenly stopped dead in her tracks, took a pronounced look at the shoreline, and expressly certified unto God and out loud for everyone to hear, "Yes siree, Bob, that's the Atlantic Ocean, all right."

"Well, do you want to go down to the shore, or are you just going stand here?" asked Jill, who had finally caught up to Annie at the top of the dune.

"Yeah, let me get my sneakers off first," replied Annie, sitting down on the ground next to a clump of sea oats.

"Good idea champ. —You know, I might actually enjoy myself here," Jill offered, sitting down in suit to do the same. "By the way, where do you suppose the guys went to?" she asked in mild curiosity.

"I don't know, and I don't care. I'm going down to the water," declared Annie, standing up to throw her tied-together sneakers over her shoulder.

"We're right here," Eugene suddenly announced. And there he was, along with his buddy Scott, both in their swim trunks, tee shirts, ball caps, and having nothing on their feet at all. "You see, we came prepared," he stated with a smile.

"Well, I didn't want to wait, and right now I'm going down to the surf with Jill. You guys can tag along if you want," Annie succinctly informed him, with Jill finally standing up, brushing the sand off the back of her britches, and picking up her sneakers to join Annie down to the serf.

Closer to the shore line, although late in the afternoon, remained a few clusters of beach goers lying about on their colorful towels and folding canvas chairs which still dotted the area in a peaceful and serene manner. Patiently, these few folks had remained behind to enjoy the very last of the day in a valiant attempt to absorb the lingering warmth from the radiant sand below them, along with the light and breezy air from above, as to perchance encapsulate the experience within themselves forever.

For perhaps an hour, the four young students played in the ebbing surf, all taking notice of the high-water mark of smooth sand which had been left renewed by the gains of the flood tide earlier in the day. And while Annie intrepidly set off to dabble in the retreating water, randomly searching for some shells of interest along the shoreline, Eugene tagged along to keep her company. Jill followed in looking for a find as well, only keeping herself a couple of yards up from the surf, not wanting to get the bottom of her jeans wet.

Scott trailed along a few feet behind Jill, silently observing the three of them.

Playfully, this foray went on for about an hour until the evening sun began to set and all had decided it was time they should get something to eat.

"Why don't we just get in my car and drive down the street until we find a place?" Scott suggested.

"That's fine by me," agreed Annie

And that's what they did, until they had found a small hamburger eatery, cornered right down on the highway from their resort. Bright and clean looking, with signage reading "Royal Castle," and not appearing to be busy, either, it was decided by all that it should be given a try.

"I wonder if their hamburgers are anything like the ones at the White Castle," mentioned Eugene, as they all piled into one of the booths enjoining the counter service. "What does everyone want? I'm buying," he offered as he was the last to be seated next to Scott and across from the girls.

"I can pay for my own," announced Jill.

"No, you can't," spoke up Annie sitting next to her. "Gene offered to buy, so let him buy. Don't insult him. It's called being gracious, Jill. He's not trying to buy you, and when you're with me, you have to be gracious. I insist upon it," Annie redressed her with a grin.

"Okay, if you insist, Annie," Jill responded, flippantly unconcerned.

"So, again, what are we all going to have? I guess that's the menu on the wall behind the counter," Eugene pointed out, while one of the waitresses approached.

"I want a Coke," said Annie.

"Me, too," answered Jill.

"I'll have a Coke, too, Gene," added Scott.

"We'll have four Cokes," Eugene ordered from the exceedingly tanned and curly headed girl who had just gotten to there to take their order.

"Do you know what else you want?" the girl questioned pleasantly, taking out a pencil and pad from her apron.

"Are your hamburgers like those little square ones that the White Castle serves?" asked Eugene politely.

"What's a White Castle?" questioned the waitress, witless of its existence, to the laughter of all at the table. "What's so funny?" the bewildered young girl asked further.

"It's another hamburger place like this one that is known for its greasy little hamburgers that everyone says gives them a stomach ache, but they can't resist eating a ton of them because they taste great. There's nothing like them. They're on little square rolls with chopped onions, and they steam the bun so they're nice and soft. You can really eat a crapload of them when you have the munchies. You understand now?" Scott enunciated, clearly and directly.

"Oh, that sounds just like us," the girl cheerfully replied. "So how many do you want?" she then pleasantly asked.

"I want three with cheese, and a fry," ordered Annie.

"I'll have the same," said Jill.

"I want five and an order of fries too," requested Scott, while everyone looked over mutely and wide eyed in his direction. "I'm hungry," he responded, gesturing out with his hands in an earnest display to be held blameless as to his formidable appetite.

"Make that another four and another fry for me," ordered Eugene, also looking around the table advancing, "So let's just all pig out," For everyone intended to do exactly that.

"So, you go to Saint Margaret's, is that right Jill?" Scott addressed her directly.

"Yeah, that's right. I've been there all four years," she stated.

"So, what's your major?" Scott further questioned.

"What is this, The Grill Jill Hour?" Jill countered in an adversarial manner.

"Jill," censured Annie softly, "He didn't ask if you were a Home Ec. Major, like some chauvinistic pig. I believe he was simply trying to make pleasant conversation," she clarified. "After all, we're all friends here, isn't that right, Scott? At least I thought we were. Aren't we Scott? Aren't we all friends here? I thought we were friends, Scott," Annie mimicked in a low and even voice intended to emulate the Hal 9000 computer.

"Sure, that's all I meant. I was just trying to be pleasant Hal… I mean, Annie," Scott smiled as he gave recognition to Annie's performance. "But that's okay, she doesn't have to answer," he added. "I'm sorry I asked," he offered benignly.

"No, I'm sorry, I was rude," apologized Jill. "Let's just forget about it," she said dismissively, "Anyway, I'm an English Major, with a minor in journalism. What's your major?" she then light-heartedly asked Scott, to the amazement of all.

"Here's your order," announced the waitress from behind the partitioned end of the booth, arbitrarily breaching their conversation while putting down the Cokes one by one. "And here is the rest of your stuff, too," she added, handing over a bright red tray with all of the food stacked upon it in little boxes. "I hope it's as good as that White Castle place has. My name is Judy, and if you need anything else, just give me a holler," she said, leaving just as abruptly as she had arrived.

"I am also an English Major, Jill, but my minor is in Psychology. So, together, I guess we are all literary geniuses of some variety," Scott smiled warmly, finally replying to Jill's question.

"That we are," interjected Eugene. "Now all we need is a name," he announced, reached for a burger.

"How about The Critical Critters Society? That sounds kind of secret," Annie proposed effervescently.

"You know, that sounds pretty good," officiated Eugene, looking around the table for support.

"I think it's too cute, it's not serious enough," declared Jill. "It sounds like all we exist for is to review children's books and stories about unicorns, and I can't stand unicorns. Now, with all due respect, I can understand why Annie here would say such a thing, after all, she considers Cinderella to be a literary masterpiece, —whereas I do not," she satirically differentiated, giving Annie no quarter. "How about 'The Critical Commentators Society? That way we could give our agreed upon opinions about anything we want, and not be taken as a joke," she suggested.

"Thanks a lot, pal," remarked Annie.

"Well, I think it has merit," spoke up Scott. "Critics are never liked, regardless. So why should you even bother with the cute?" he parenthesized with his hands, "I'm voting for Jill's title. I don't have one. What do you think, Gene?" he asked, putting Eugene in a most unwanted position.

"I think they both have some good merits," Eugene began. "One is on the folksy imaginative side, which people seem to like, while the other one is on the practical side, or shall I say, the business end of its purpose. Both seem to have a value. I don't know which would be best. What do you think, Annie?" solicited Eugene, trying his best to dance the dance of a social diplomat.

"I was only kidding when I said that. Oh, give me a break. You people really don't think that I seriously meant that?" Annie chastised everyone defensively. "If we called it what I suggested, then the only publication we could criticize would be *Sixteen Magazine*, or even worse, that stupid *Honey Magazine*. It was a joke, you morons. How would you like to be assigned to write a critical review of *Boy's Life*, Gene? Or you, Scott? Gee, do you think you could do it? How insulting," she chastised, and so irascibly that the entire table went dead silent and stopped eating, garnering their full and unadulterated attention.

"Ha, ha!, Annie laughed out loud, "I'm still just kidding," she laughed. "What's the matter? You fellow critics of 'The Critical Commentator's Society' can't take being criticized? — That's hilarious," she continued to chuckle while picking up the last hamburger on the tray.

"All I can say is that, 'Such welcome and unwelcome things at once tis' hard to reconcile,'" Scott quoted, finishing the last of his fare.

"So, your last name is Macduff. Is that right, Scott?" Jill challenged, continuing the fray.

"No, as a matter of fact, it's Campbell. We were on the winning side," Scott imparted proudly.

"I'm impressed, he knows wherefrom he speaks," Jill bantered back, providing a provocative smile of engagement directed towards Eugene.

"This is too much for me," responded Eugene. "We're supposed to be beach people now, and all *I* want to know is, —exactly what are we going to be doing tomorrow?" he questioned in trying to put an end to the literary sparring.

"We all get into Scott's car, and then we drive up to the beach at Ft. Lauderdale. That's what we do, Gene," replied Annie.

"At what time?" Eugene implored.

"At eight o'clock," Jill spoke up unambiguously, to the obvious chagrin of Scott who, saying nothing, rolled up his eyes and looked away with an obvious sigh.

~

"You know, that Scott doesn't seem to be all that bad," Jill offered, the minute that she and Annie had gotten back to the privacy of their room. "He just thinks that all women are weak and that he's the big strong guy," she expressed, beginning to get ready for bed.

"Except for his own mother, I'll bet," Annie submitted. "He uses girls. And he likes them just like his car, slow and comfortable," she quipped.

"That's okay, I'm neither, and I don't care what his insecurities are," responded Jill aloofly. "He does seem to be educated though, and if called out, he can even be polite. I've seen that. I merely find him interesting, that's all," she pretended to dispassionately note for the record.

"Oh, my goodness, Jill isn't a man hater after all!" declared Annie in feigned shock. "Maybe Scott will actually be the one to end all her suffering. Tune in for the six o'clock news," laughed Annie, as Jill threw a pillow at her head.

~

"So, now what do you think of Jill, ole buddy?" Eugene prodded, once they had gotten back to their room as Scott was securing the door.

"She's different, I'll give you that. And she's got an education, I'll give you that, too," Scott answered in a factual tone, chaining the door while Eugene nonchalantly flopped down on the nearest bed.

"No, I mean, do you think she's a babe? You know a 'hottie,' a 'good looker.' Does she turn you on? You know, is she bonerific?" Eugene smiled like the cat that had just eaten the mouse, turning on his side to see Scott's reaction.

"Well, first of all, I've taken out some pretty tall girls before, but she tops them all," Scott stated factually, starting to unpack and arrange his things. "She's almost as tall as I am, and if she wore spikes, she'd be taller. Anyway, as tall as she is, she's still got the cutest and most impish face of a pixie I ever saw, especially with that tousled short black hair. And also, you've got to admit, that skinny thing still has got some hips," he noted. "So, if you are so damned interested, the answer to your question is yeah, I think she's a 'hottie,' if that's what you want to know," he definitively answered, while emptying his suitcase on the other bed.

"Well, like I said before, you have all week to get into her pants," grinned Eugene, continuing his best to needle him.

"And don't forget, pal, you also have all week to get into Annie's pants too," Scott retorted.

"Oh, I can sincerely tell you, ole buddy, that just ain'ta gonna happen, Eugene cartoonishly emphasized.

"Oh yeah? Aren't you man enough to at least try? —Or maybe you're saving yourself, you know, for that right girl," laughed Scott.

"Aw, you don't have a clue ole' buddy. That's not the reason it just 'ain'ta gonna happen,'" Eugene asserted.

"Oh yeah, then what is it, then?" Scott challenged

"It's because Jill is here, that's why," answered Eugene self-assuredly. "You remember Jill, the girl with the pixie face? You know, the girl who goes to a Catholic women's college named after a person they refer to as 'St. Margaret the Virgin?' That Jill, and she's right here with Annie," he reminded him with a most satirical smile.

"You've got to be kidding me. Are you trying to tell me that Jill's still a virgin? ha, ha, ha, ha," Scott chuckled.

"I'd bet my car on it, Scott. Any time. You want to take that bet? You're a gambling man," offered Eugene with the unwavering conviction of a self-righteous man.

"Well, what about Annie? Are you going to tell me that she's a virgin, too? That you dumped going out with all our party girls, who will screw just about anybody, to go out with one who won't even let you play with that thing? Somehow, I don't believe that," stated Scott with an equal amount of conviction.

"We're not talking about Annie, here, we're talking about Jill," Eugene said evasively. "All I meant was, I doubt that even I don't stand a chance as long as Jill is here, that's all. But the bet still stands," Eugene audaciously proposed again.

"I'm not taking any bet with you," replied Scott flatly, finishing putting his clothes in one of the dressers. "Aren't you going to put any of *your* stuff away?" he questioned.

"Nah, I'll just live out of my suitcase," Eugene remarked, completely without concern. "Turn the TV on while you're over there, would you please?" he asked politely, propping himself up on a pillow.

~

Already bright and sunny the next morning, the girls' door to their motel room was already open for business by the time their two gentlemen callers had arrived to pick them up. Sun glasses, flowered tops, sandals, and wrap-around skirts made up the elected uniform of the day for the two female sojourners, and after picking up their ample bags of ancillary secret equipment, they promptly locked the door securely behind them and left, —escorts at the ready.

It didn't take but minutes for Scott to get his big black Buick underway, driving straight up A-1A until he had reached Las Olas Boulevard. Turning right he crossed over to Atlantic Avenue and continued to slowly travel north in looking for a parking space as close to the ocean as he could find. Finally turning left on to one of side streets, only about a block in, he found a vacant spot that was large enough to park his car in. The young adventurers then picked up their oversized colorful beach towels, their Coppertone sun tan oil, and their sundry tote bags of beach paraphernalia, proceeding intrepidly to find a suitable place to set up camp for the day.

"I can't believe the road runs right by the beach like this," Annie exclaimed, trudging out onto the sand.

"How about right here?" Eugene suggested at last. "It's about half way to the beach and the street, just in case we need to get something to eat or use a bathroom."

"It's fine by me," said Scott.

"Annie, Jill, okay with you?" asked Eugene respectfully.

"It's as good a place as any, I guess," Annie accepted, shrugging her shoulders. "What about you, Jill?"

"I'm okay with it," Jill affirmed.

"Okay then, let's lay out our towels and set up," Eugene directed.

After the towels were laid down with Annie's and Eugene's in the center, Jill's next to the outside of Annie's, and Scott's next to the opposite side of Eugene's, they all began to take off their sneakers and sandals and put their tote bags on the west end of their towels to be used as pillows in directly addressing the morning's already risen sun. Eugene and Scott, having finished with their task ahead of the girls, sat down patiently on their towels and began to amuse themselves by unashamedly studying the girls, still puttering about with the whole business of displaying their presence to the world.

"What are *you* looking at?" Jill indignantly questioned Scott.

"You," was Scott's one-word answer.

"Why are you looking at me? I'm sure you've seen other girls before. I'm no different," Jill prudently maintained.

"Of course you are. Everyone is different. In fact, I find you to be most different than 'other girls,' Scott distinctly replied.

"Oh yeah? Like I have a tail, or maybe a double set of teeth like a shark?" Jill answered back smartly, unwrapping the skirt from around her.

"I was talking about Jill the person, —your attitude, the way you look at things, the way you analyze things. That's what I find different. And so, believe it or not, I find you very interesting," Scott explained as candidly possible, in a cordial attempt to justify his open observations as being solely being the object of a compliment.

"So, you were looking at my mind when I was undressing? That's it?" Jill rhetorically commented, as she openly modeled herself to him with her arms out stretched. "So, you pity me for having this uninteresting body, then? Is that it? I would advise you to think twice about your answer before you make another stupid comment, Scott," she warned as she arched back her shoulders to accentuate the heretofore unnoticed fullness of her breasts.

"You see, that's exactly what I mean. Your analysis is faultless again, Jill," Scott responded with a smile. "And you know, I *was* going to say something else, but now, I believe you are one hundred percent right. It really would be stupid of me to go on, especially now, when there is absolutely nothing more to say.

"Yup, I'm just going to lie down here for a while and get a tan, not saying another word," Scott persisted. "Uh huh, that's exactly what I'm going to do," he confirmed again in complete resignation, stretching himself out on his towel and pulling his baseball cap down over his eyes. "Yes, sir, buddy, just lay here and think about getting a good old tan, that's exactly what I'm a going do," he continued to mutter, following his final remark with a small sardonic smile which could be seen from below the brim of his hat.

"Did you catch all that, Gene?" giggled Annie, while Jill's presence continued to command the scene.

"Eh, nope," Eugene shortly replied. "I think I'll just catch some rays, too," he wisely imparted, following Scott's example to say nothing more.

"Good, then, that's settled," announced Annie. "Well, while you two lie here and collect your rays, or catch them, or do whatever you want to with them, me and Jill are going down for a swim," she officially announced.

"Don't worry, we'll be back," Jill gratuitously annotated, taking her leave to traipse down to the water's edge with Annie.

"I told you not to argue with her. I told you she goes to that school full of Jesuits and that all they do. You know that," complained Eugene, still lying on his back with his hat over his face.

"Are you kidding me? I think she's a riot. I think she's perfect, just the way she is," Scott smiled again beneath his hat.

Chapter Thirty-Two

Having paid no attention to anything that was going on around them as they were setting up their temporary rendezvous point, both Annie and Jill now noticed that something was just downright strange. There were no other people there. Sure, there were a few isolated couples setting up camp for the day, a couple of folks walking their dogs, and a lone itinerant man with a metal detector sweeping the beach for someone's treasure lost in a moment of frivolity, but where was everyone else? There were supposed to be throngs of people there, they thought.

"Where the heck are all the people?" Annie questioned out loud, scanning up and down the beach while she and Jill marched down to the water's edge.

"I guess they're all probably hung over," theorized Jill. And she wasn't far from the truth.

Once they both had gotten into the water and waded out from the shoreline to what they considered to be a goodly distance, again they were completely amazed. The ocean did not drop off nearly as fast as it did up North and it just seemed weird.

After plodding in a good forty feet, the water was still only up to their knees, and then it took them another three to five minutes more to reach a depth that was deep enough to swim in. They also noticed that the waves were much smaller and considerably more gentile. This was nothing like what they were used to. It was, however, simply perfect for splashing about in the uninterrupted venue of incidental twaddle, to which they frivolously now engaged in.

After about an hour had passed, the girls were then joined by Eugene and Scott, who had eventually decided that their self-administered punishment had been long enough for simply being themselves. Together, they all now splashed about in the surf for perhaps another hour until deciding to go back and check to see if their belongings were still intact, which they were. It was then the girls began to anoint themselves with suntan lotion from head to toe as their two young suitors took it upon themselves to go back to the street area to fetch everyone something to drink, while the population on the beach began to steadily grow.

It had almost reached eleven thirty in the morning when Eugene and Scott wandered into the Elbow Room Bar through its patio side of the building off the beach area and immediately discovered what mysteriously had happened to all the people who were supposed to have been on the beach. They were in the bar.

"Damn, this place is already half-full, and it isn't even noon yet," Scott commented to Eugene, as soon as they had gotten through the doorway.

"Yeah, and it doesn't seem that anyone in here is over twenty-one, either," Eugene observed as well.

"Well, I guess the drinking age here is eighteen," Scott said assumptively, while the two of them briefly waited for their eyes to adjust to the darkness of the lounge. Finally, after they had gotten somewhat accustomed to the relative darkness, they proceeded onward to determine exactly where the service counter was.

"How much are four Cokes to go?" asked Scott to the petite barmaid, who was wearing a flowered halter top and a pair of the tightest white hot-pants imaginable.

"Where are you from?" the barmaid responded before answering Scott's question.

"I'm from the Northeast, why?" Scott responded in kind.

"And you're here for spring break, right?" the girl said intuitively.

"Yeah, does it show?" answered Scott, with an amused smile.

"Sure, it does," the girl confirmed. "You see, the locals here don't get out of bed before eleven, and obviously you've already been on the beach because the both of you still got sand stuck all over you. But that's okay. Everyone else in here is on spring break, too. This is where everyone comes right after they get down here, sooner or later," she asserted fatalistically.

"The busiest time is at night, though," she apprised them further. "We usually have a band playing here of some kind, but the place gets packed, anyway, even if we don't," she said dismissively. "Once the sun goes down that's when we really get busy, cause everyone comes in off the beach. That's when they all try to get zonked to the eyeballs, and it goes on like that until we close. Anyhoo, we call it the 'Carnival of Characters, —if you wana to stop by," she summed up. "Now, do you still want your four Cokes, or do you two want a real drink?" she enticingly solicited, waving about an empty Tom Collins glass and pausing just long enough to add with a come-hither smile. "And by the way, my name is Sheila," she finally officially greeted.

"Oh, no thanks," replied Scott politely.

"But we're still going to need those four Cokes anyway," Eugene interrupted.

"Yeah, we have two other people waiting for us, so we have to get back," Scott added.

"Well, you can go down a couple of storefronts and get what you want a lot cheaper at the food mart. It's right out the front door to the right," Sheila informed them gratuitously. "We only have these little plastic cups, and I'd have to charge you for them," she demonstratively held up, displaying one in her hand. "And believe me, it's a lot cheaper in a can, right down a couple stores to the right," she reiterated, vaguely pointing away. "Why don't you just bring your friends back here later, and then we can all have a good time? That's what it's all about, —having a good time, not ripping you off a dollar for just a tiny little coke in a plastic cup. We like our customers and we want them to come back," she stated candidly.

"Why, thanks a lot," said Eugene appreciatively. "Maybe we will," he entertained.

"Yeah, maybe so," supported Scott, turning away from the service bar to look for the front door that lead to the street.

Then, quite unexpectedly, and precisely before the two newbies had almost made it out the door, Sheila called out loudly to everyone else who was there, "and what do we say to our guests down here when they have to leave? All together now!" she commanded, cajoling entire room to yell out in unison, "*Y'all come back now, ya hear!*" as everyone raucously laughed.

"I can just imagine what that place is like at night," said Eugene, as he and Scott passed by the bar again on their way back to the beach with the four cans of cold soda in hand.

"I don't know, but I bet it's a lot wilder than the party nights at your apartment featuring 'Big Dick and Little Peter with the Hole in the Wall Gamblers, Scott humorously footnoted.

"Yeah, but I guess since we're graduating, we're not going to be seeing any more of those," Eugene commented with a slight degree of relief.

"And that's a big 10-4 for me, too, buddy," confirmed Scott. —But seriously, maybe we can all go there one night. I'll even buy," he offered.

"What are you buying now, Scott?" questioned Annie, overhearing the end of their conversation as he and Eugene were approaching their beach site.

"Yeah, what are you buying now, Scott?" chimed in Jill, while the two of them sat up, shielding their eyes from the sun.

"Here's your Cokes," announced Eugene, handing Annie hers, while Scott handed one down to Jill.

"Thank you," said Annie, with Jill following suit.

"Scott was just saying that one night this week we could all go over to that bar over there," explained Eugene, pointing back over from where he and Scott had just been. "Supposedly it's where all the spring breakers go, or so they said," he qualified. "Scott was offering to pick up the whole tab, that's all. Of course, that's if the two of you want to go. It's totally up to you," he amiably proposed.

"I don't mind going, What about you Jill? Are you interested?" asked Annie.

"I'll go if everyone else is going," Jill responded without objection.

"Well, I don't know about anyone else, but I need to get out of the sun now. If I don't, I'll burn to a crisp," Annie then announced, getting up and brushing off some of the unwanted sand yet sticking to her. "And by the way, thanks again for getting us the sodas, you two. I really needed one," she added appreciatively.

"Me, too. I've also had enough," joined in Jill, beginning to collect her things. "Besides, we have a pool back at the motel," she reminded everyone.

"Yeah, I'm done too," added Eugene in concert. "And besides I'm hungry," he whined. "We didn't stop and get anything to eat this morning," he stated in looking for some sympathy.

"I saw a hot dog place down the street called Lum's. We could go there," offered Scott.

"That's fine by me," said Eugene eagerly.

"I could eat a hot dog, but I'm paying for it myself this time," Annie conditioned, deliberately averting any further social concerns.

"And that's the only way I'll go, too," supported Jill. "Believe me, I am just as happy paying for myself," she pleasantly attested.

"Okay, so we all pay for ourselves. I can dig it," accepted Eugene. "Now can we just get going, because like I said, I'm hungry," he repeated.

Picking up their accoutrements of beaching, the foursome then headed off to Scott's car, collectively attempting to brave their way through the streets of unending slow-moving traffic. And as everyone had almost had achieved their destination without another spoken word, no longer could Annie hold back her thoughts any longer, reconciling to herself, *I just can't let this pass.*

"So, Jill, did I actually hear you say that you were *happy* back there? You know, in buying your own hot dog?" Annie instigated.

"I can't say that I'm suffering, if that's what you mean," answered Jill. "And since I don't have to suffer the pain of being obligated to anyone by paying for my own food, yes, I couldn't be happier," she responded cheerfully, and so much so that Annie was baffled into silence. "You know, you ought to go to Mass more often, Annie," she then suggested blithely. "And, oh, by the way, when was your last confession?" she added, surprising Annie with the subtly of her tact.

"Let's not go there, okay?" Annie responded.

"Okay, but you brought the whole subject up, not me," Jill clarified, ending the conversation.

"So, we're off to that Lum's hot dog place, is that right?" asked Scott in the affirmative, purposely changing the tone of the conversation, and being the first to approach the car.

"Yup," responded Annie.

"Yeah, that's good for me," said Jill.

"Let's just get there, I'm hungry," decried Eugene again, as everyone piled back into the car and drove off to eat "Hot Dogs Steamed in Beer," as touted in bright red letters on its signage.

~

It was four o'clock in the afternoon when they all returned to the resort, passing right through the colossal Japanese Torii that was vigilantly guarding its main entrance with all the repute of a Shogun's palace, when concertedly they all decided to stop by the lobby to pick up some of the tourist brochures, which were free for the taking. Then, with all their bundles still about them, along with a fist full of the colorful pamphlets in hand, Annie and Jill lumbered back to their room while the agreement was for everyone to meet back in the coffee shop in about an hour, as Eugene and Scott went back to their room as well.

The spacious rooms were decorated in a modern natural wood motif and were cheerfully appointed with sets of brightly flowered drapes and matching comforters. The rest of the complex had been constructed to simulate a classic Japanese village, styled in tropical Hawaiian setting

Its terracotta red and pagoda shaped roofs dramatically vaunting over the buildings' towering gables of glass were a thing to behold. Bucolically ensconced by the resort's plentitudinous palm trees, the entirety of the whole resort reflected the unequivocal embodiment of paradise and serenity itself. In the current world of romance, it was without peers. From the moment of passage under the sanctity of its guardianship, one could verily hear the words

"All ye who enter here, surrender unto me your loneliness," as love was certified omnipotent.

It was after they all had showered, changed, and went through the picturesque brochures in their respective rooms that they all met again in the lobby by the entrance to the coffee shop, as agreed. Then, as no one wanted to be inside, they all decided instead to abandon the coffee shop idea and go and sit poolside, from whence they could overlook the ocean while diligently making their plans.

"It sure is beautiful out here," pronounced Annie, taking a seat at one of the umbrellaed poolside tables which overlooked the multitudes of lackadaisical sunbathers who were spread out on the camel colored carpet beneath them.

"Yeah, just look at that sky. I can't see a cloud anywhere," observed Eugene pleasantly, his hand at his brow in shading his eyes while scrupulously surveying the horizon.

"I just wish it could be like this all the time," remarked Annie further, also glancing over towards the shoreline.

"On such a clear day like this, it almost makes you feel like you could see forever," Scott philosophized, enjoining the conversation.

"Oh, give me a break," chuckled Jill sitting down at the table. "I saw the movie. You've got to do better than that Scott. I just hope you don't start quoting lessons from *The Twilight Zone* as if they were your own observations," she mocked with a smile.

"Well, exactly where do you think you get your ideas from?" responded Scott defensively, also taking a seat along with Eugene. "*Your* ideas only come from a synthesis of other books that you have read, just like anyone else's. So, the real question is, do you or do you not have the brains to retain what you have read? And then of course, be able to apply it, —that's all," he stated as fact.

"You're supposed to be an English major. So can you recite the opening lines to the *Canterbury Tales*?" Scott continued in challenging Jill's veracity. "Isn't it something that all English majors are required to know as the very foundation of your craft?" he propounded directly.

"Can you?" reciprocated Jill in boldly defying Scott's declaration in return, falling for the bait.

"Whan that Aprille with his shoures soote
The droghte of Marche hath perced to the roote.
And bathed every veyne in swich licour,
Of which vertu engendred is the flour;
Whan Zephirus eek with his swete breeth
Inspired hath in every holt and heath,"

Scott recited flawlessly in keeping his rectitude intact.

"Well, I am genuinely impressed," Jill affably conceded, leaning back in her chair.

"Okay, you two," interjected Eugene. "It think we've had enough English lessons for today. Can we now just figure out what we are going to do here for the rest of the week?"

"Yeah, we need your input," supported Annie. "What do you guys want to do?" she put to them flatly.

"I'd like to see the Parrot Jungle," Jill said immediately.

"And I would like to go to the Crandon Park Zoo and see the white tiger," added Annie, just as decisively. "And you, Gene? What do you want to do? This whole thing was your idea," she reminded him.

"If you really want to know," Eugene lightly responded, "I would just like to take you out one night, alone, Annie. Other than that, I'm happy to go anywhere," he stated candidly. "What about you Scott?" he asked in not waiting for Annie's response.

"I already offered to buy a night out for everyone at the Elbow Room Lounge," Scott reaffirmed. "I figured it's a happenin' place," he commented in the vernacular of the day. "You know, a place to experience. That's all. I wouldn't mind cruisin' on over to The University of Miami and checkin' *it* out, either, —but what everyone else wants to do is also fine by me," he amiably stated.

"Okay, then, I'll make the decision," assertively declared Annie, appropriating her control over the situation. "First of all, I want to see the rest of this place and take a swim in the pool. There is also an indoor Japanese pool somewhere here that looks kind of cool that I saw on this post card I got from the lobby, and we could try that, too. Then, afterwards, we could all eat in the Shinto Temple Room tonight and move over to the Wreak Bar afterwards. I think that would be good," she advocated. "They got some guy playing here by the name of Wayne Cochran, and the people at the front desk said that he's pretty good," she proposed without any objections.

"Anyway, tomorrow we could either see the Parrot Jungle or go to the zoo, I don't care which. And on Wednesday night, I'll go anywhere you want to take me Gene. Now, if everyone is happy with that, then I'm happy," Annie ended, fully satisfied with her plan of attack.

"I picked up a map at the front desk, and it shows where all of those places are," Eugene said, now spreading it out on the table.

"According to this map, the zoo is on Key Biscayne. And here it looks like there is a beach next to it, too," Scott physically pointed out.

"Yup, that's right," agreed Eugene. "So, we could all go to the beach there tomorrow and visit the zoo at the same. Then, after we get back here, we catch a shower, get something to eat, and finally make it over to the Elbow Room. How about that?" he proposed.

"I'm good with that," said Scott agreeably.

"And then the next day, we could go to the Parrot Jungle. Is that okay with you Jill?" Annie submitted.

"Sure, that's fine by me," responded Jill.

"Hey, and look at that! The University of Miami is right by the Parrot Jungle, so we can all go their afterwards," excitedly proposed Eugene. "Then, in the evening, me and Annie can go out, —and no offense, leave you two guys to fend for yourselves, heh, heh, heh," he chuckled maniacally, looking precisely across the table at both Scott and Jill.

"It's fine by me," said Scott.

"Yeah, it's okay by me, too," spoke up Annie. "And it still gives me and Jill the rest of the week to get more sun and go shopping. "What do you think, Jill? You haven't said much," she asked in turn.

"That's because there isn't much to say," Jill agreeably explained. "It all sounds interesting, and I get to go to the Parrot Jungle. What more could a good Catholic girl ask for... except maybe a museum or two?" she theatrically mumbled with her hand held lightly over her mouth while looking askance.

"I don't mind that at all," said Scott without hesitation. "Jill, when we go to the university you can ask them yourself where all the good museums are, and then we can go from there, —if that's what you want," he graciously suggested.

"And, as far as the rest of it is concerned, I'm fine," Scott continued. "I'm already having a great time. I'm only sorry that I didn't think of coming here first," he confessed. "I guess we all have that knucklehead Gene here to thank for that, and believe me, I hate having to thank him for anything. I much prefer having him thanking me, to tell you the truth," he smirked. "But regardless," he continued in a more candid tone, "thanks a lot for picking this place out, Gene. It sure is a winner," he complimented in conclusion.

"You gotta be kidding me!" irascibly declared Annie. "It was Gene's idea to come here on spring break, all right, I'll grant you that, but it was my father who booked my room at this place. God knows where Gene wanted us to stay. You know, you guys can sit around and praise each other on your great accomplishments all day long, but you're not fooling us one bit. Are they, Jill?" she puissantly questioned

"Oh, I think they mean well, Annie," Jill began, pausing a moment to contemplate her next words, while everyone else sat dead silent by her totally unexpected proclamation. "Yes, I do believe that they mean well," she then charitably judged. "However... I *do* think they need to work on their presentations, though" she edited in a more authoritative tone.

"And you, Scott," Jill addressed him specifically, "You might be able to recite Chaucer, all right, but your all over delivery was just horrid," she righteously admonished as if she were a chastising nun.

Oh, my God, where did that come from? Annie thought about Jill's harshness, while Eugene was completely taken aback. Scott, too, had become absolutely petrified, and for the first time ever witnessed, had no retort at all.

And then it happened. Jill could not keep it in any longer, and burst out laughing like she had never laughed before. And while the other three could not believe nor understand the whole situation, they just shook their heads in total obfuscation.

"I don't get it, Jill, what's so funny?" Annie asked.

"What's so funny? What's so funny?" Jill repeated after she had stopped laughing. "I'll tell you what's so funny. I realize that I don't have any of your personalities, and that

I'm looked at by everyone as if I'm a wet noodle," she smiled superciliously, "but I realize now that I have something that *none* of you have," she professed, leaning back in her chair with a self-assured grin, not saying another word.

"Okay. What is it, then?" Annie anxiously inquired.

"An acting career, that's what!" Jill laughed heartily again.

"Oh, brother," Eugene commented, shaking his head and looking away.

"Heh, heh, heh," chuckled Scott. "I guess you got me there, Jill. I thought you were really pissed off at me for some reason or another," he admitted good naturedly.

"Yeah, so did I," Annie confessed as well.

"You know something, I think I'm actually having fun for a change, and I really do need to say, 'thank you,' Gene, for coming up with the whole idea, regardless," Jill offered respectfully.

"All hails accepted," responded Eugene, feigning to be Caesar Augustus.

"And actually, I have to thank you again for bringing Scott along, too," Jill further acknowledged. "For without having him to ridicule, I think I would still be having a miserable time," she wryly smiled, causing once again the table to fall silent. "I'm sorry, I was just trying to make fun again," she quickly recanted, once more causing a sigh of relief to be heard.

"You know, Scott, I really hope you weren't offended. — I really do," Jill now said in earnest. "Because you really *have* been a gentleman and I do appreciate it. And the truth is, I really don't know anyone who can recite the opening lines to *The Canterbury Tales* like you did. That really and truly *did* impress me. And again, I am sorry if I hurt your feelings, I didn't mean to," she shamefully said.

And then, having apologized with such honesty, even Scott was humbled.

"Well, I don't know what to say, except, thank you for the compliment," Scott empathetically responded.

For the first time in her life, Jill was beginning to understand how to be social. *Perhaps I can actually have some friends who care about me,* she thought. *I can't believe they were all really concerned about what I wanted to do, or that they even honestly considered my opinions about anything. No one ever gave two hoots about my feelings before. And Scott even put up with my antics. So I wonder, maybe my life doesn't have to be so bleak after all? Maybe, just maybe, it could at least be somewhat interesting. I guess that wouldn't be so bad,"* she proposed before falling asleep that evening, comforted by her new affiliation with the concept of hope.

~

Content with their plans for the next few days, the four adventurers went on to discover the sights, sounds, and the very heartbeat of South Florida. Beginning with the sandy and serene shores of Crandon Park, with its tropical coconut laden palm trees, and the adjacent admission free zoo, they explored away. They also took a cruise down the Miracle Mile in Coral Gables, "just for the halibut," as Eugene had petitioned. Then, after enjoying Jill's request to visit the Parrot Jungle, with its awesome subtropical and fructiferous foliage, they left for a visit to The University of Miami. Thereafter, they even had the time to tour the Biltmore Hotel and James Deering's palatial estate which he had christened The Vizcaya. It had become a truly a grand adventure that day for all, one never to be forgotten.

Most importantly, however, the greatest thing that they all had discovered was that they were no longer going to be "students" anymore. This was their last hurrah. Poignantly, this became quite clear when they no longer derived the same enjoyment from going to the Elbow Room that they would have had only a year earlier.

Dismally, this venture now turned to be nothing more than a contrived nostalgic event in the making, a plastic fabrication of spontaneity, and was unmistakably not the "happenin'" that Scott had expected it to be. The fact was, they were just not "into it" anymore, and although there were some sad regrets expressed over the passage of this revelation, Jill, naturally, had none.

Together they were all entering their Summer of '42, and were beginning to realize the truth in Herman Raucher's observation that *"Life was made up of small comings and goings; and for everything we take with us, there is something that we leave behind."* The raucous behavior, the frivolity of irresponsibility, and the obtuse application of the impractical philosophical social theories that they had all so readily embraced in the past, were now giving way to the organizational approach of trying to arrange a predetermined outcome from their endeavors.

They were on the doorstep of understanding that to have respect for one's own dignity is the underpinning of all that is important. The occasional brusque behavior, the puerile view of no accountability, and the sometimes arrogant belief that such a thing called "equality" could be engineered by arbitrary enforcing a dictatorial regulation, —just had to go. Their own individual personas were at stake now, and there was no theoretical dictate, no religious belief, or anything having to do with the government at all that could shield them from their own innate insecurities of becoming an adult.

Now, having graciously to accept and additionally adopt in practice, a social or intellectual tenant that heretofore had been decried and obstinately touted as being false, is no insignificant task to tackle, in and of itself; but to further embrace such a task, and yet keep your dignity in the ugly face of self-deprecation, is even a greater achievement.

And with this in mind, Annie and her friends had no trouble with their imminent fate to meet their future, having no problem in accepting the past to only be considered "knowledge gained," something to build upon and not whatsoever a repudiation of their previously held beliefs. It was simply the yin and yang of life they acceded to understand now, and nothing more.

Chapter Thirty-Three

"So, do you want to go out and have dinner with me tonight?" Scott asked Jill, pulling his Buick back into the Castaway's parking lot on that late midweek afternoon. "Since Annie and Gene are going out by themselves, that leaves us by ourselves, and so I'm asking, would like to go out and have dinner with me tonight?" he rephrased, while Jill had paused a moment.

"Like on a date?" Jill asked in clarification.

"Yes, like on a date," Scott asserted distinctly. "You know, like I make a reservation for the two of us, by ourselves, eating across the table from each other, engaging in some pleasant small talk while simply trying to enjoy each other's company for the evening. Yes, I guess you can consider that a date," he responded.

"And, another thing I might as well bring up," he continued, "I pay for it, and I am not going to be embarrassed by haggling over it either. That's what a gentleman does, and that's how it's supposed to be," he stipulated factually. "Now all you have to do is graciously accept or deny the invitation," he said dispassionately, while he finished putting the car into park and then faced her directly.

Then before she could reply, he looked straight into her eyes and further added, "You know, I asked you to go with me because I want you to go, but if you don't want to go, just say so graciously, and everything will be just fine, okay?" he stated as respectfully as he could.

Now as all this was said, both Annie and Eugene had not uttered so much as a single word from the back seat of the car, nor in any way did they attempt to leave, either. To them, it was as if they were awaiting the climax of a great movie scene in a drive-in theatre as Annie thought, *just go for it Jill, you'll probably have a great time! At least it will be an adventure to remember,* while Eugene was busy musing, *Well, how about that! I'll be darned, I didn't think ole Scott had it in him, to treat a girl with decency.*

"No, I'll go," Jill answered sheepishly, to everyone's surprise. "What time should I be ready, then?" she added with no particular inflection.

"About eight o'clock would be good," Scott established, turning completely around to confer with his buddy in the back seat, "Is that about right, Gene?"

"That's about what I planned," confirmed Eugene.

"Then it's all set," declared Scott. "Me and Gene will pick you girls up at about eight o'clock, and then we go our separate ways. Is everyone good with that?" he questioned.

"Eight o'clock is fine by me. It gives me a good three hours to get ready, and believe me, I need it," responded Annie with a small degree of levity.

"I guess it's fine by me, too," agreed Jill.

"Yup, fine by me, too," said Eugene.

Then, with the evening's plans confirmed, the two pairs retired to their rooms to get themselves prepared.

"Did you bring that black velvet dress with the cowl neck that you sometimes wear to Mass?" asked Annie, as soon as they had gotten back in their room.

"Yeah. It's about the only nice dress I own, so I brought it just in case. I don't have the money that all of you have, so I don't have a whole lot of nice stuff," confessed Jill.

"Don't worry about it," advised Annie as she trotted off to take a shower. "Just get it out and the shoes that you're going wear, and I'll help you get fixed up," she instructed before closing the bathroom door behind her.

Once they had both showered and put on some clean shorts and tops, Annie began their transformations. Pausing for a second to think, the first thing that she did was take out her spaghetti strapped above the knee frock of fuchsia colored chiffon, and laid it down flat across her bed. She then took out a pair of medium heeled pumps, adorned with a single ankle strap, and placed them aside her dress to see how well they all matched. Now, taking out a small luggage case from the closet, she plunked it on the main dresser in front of its large mirror and flipped open its top to take out an ornate silver and turquoise choker and a set of matching pendant earrings, placing them all together on the pillow above her dress.

Jill also had laid out her black velvet dress and was starting to brush off its ever-present lint when abruptly Annie stopped what she was doing in noticing the flat soled shoes that Jill had placed beside it.

"Whoa ho, wait just a minute," Annie cautioned. "You're not actually going to wear those Mary Janes, are you?" she questioned, dramatically taken aback with her hand on her chest.

"Well, that's all I have," Jill answered defensively. "I've always wore flats because I'm so tall. My mother told me that the reason that I didn't have any boyfriends was because my height intimidated them, so I've always worn them," she meekly explained.

"We'll, your mother is an egghead, and what does she know, anyway? I'm the Fashion Queen around here, and if I'm going to do this, you darn well aren't going to wear those ridiculous looking things," Annie decisively ruled.

"Well, like I said, they're all I have," Jill despondently replied.

"Listen, we still have over two hours to go. So, we'll just go down to that shopping center with that big blue tower we passed on the way here and I'll buy you a different pair. But like I said, no way in heck are you wearing those," Annie adamantly declared.

"Okay, whatever you say, you're the boss this time. So, let's just go," Jill capitulated, going over to her dresser to pick up her purse.

Then, driving off to the Burdines Department Store at the Dadeland Mall to secure Jill a fashionably acceptable new pair of shoes, she trepidatiously couldn't help but think, *Oh, Mary and Jesus, what am I getting myself into.*

~

"I can't believe you bought those for me!" laughed Jill after returning to their room. "I'll be as tall as him with those things on," she twittered.

"That's the whole point, silly goose," Annie said. "You see, everyone is different, and you should be proud of your height. I'd kill to have your legs… and by the way, so would all the guys too, heh, heh," she kidded. "So, get used to it," she added, going over to her jewelry box on her dresser.

"You're not in high school anymore, and you're not in a convent, either," Annie all but reprimanded. "No siree, no hiding you're candle under a basket any more for you, for tonight, you're gonna shine, and I'm gonna light the candle," she grinned, turning around from her dresser while holding out a black obsidian lavaliere.

"What's that, a necklace?" asked Jill, sitting on the edge of her bed.

"Yup, sure is, and I have its matching earrings, too," Annie confirmed. "You see, you forget, I roomed with you for two years," Annie reminded her. "I already know what clothes you have. I only bet that you would bring that black dress with you, that's all, —especially since it is the only formal dress I've ever seen you wear," she stated frankly.

"Here, it's yours for tonight. Now let's finish getting ready," she directed.

"Do you know where Gene is taking you?" Jill asked out of curiosity, after accepting the necklace and going back to brush the lint off her dress.

"Yeah, to some dinner show that has flamenco dancers with castanets, maracas, and all that kind of stuff. He found the place from some yellow page ad. I saw it. It ought to be fun," Annie replied chipperly.

"Did he say where Scott was taking me?" asked Jill, stopping to intently hear Annie's answer.

"Oh yeah, I got it out of him, all right," Annie revealed smartly, while putting on her makeup.

"Well, where is he taking me?" Jill impatiently asked.

"Come over here while I put on your makeup and I will tell you," commanded Annie.

"I don't wear makeup," Jill plainly answered.

"Well, tonight you are," responded Annie definitively. "Don't worry, I'm not going to make you look like a prostitute, I'm only going to bring out your natural highlights. Even Sister Ruth wore foundation powder, so come over here," she directed, taping impatiently on the dresser with the end of one of her makeup brushes.

"Okay, I'm here," said Jill, after walking over to Annie obediently. "So, tell me now, where is Scott taking me?" she once again asked.

"Here, sit on the end of my bed while I work on your face and I will tell you," Annie instructed. "Well, at first Gene wanted to take me to a place called Los Violinos, where they have live violin players strolling all over the place and you can dance, but I told him I've already been to one of those places. Then, he came up with the flamenco place, and like I said, I haven't seen them yet, so I told him that's where I wanted to go, and he said okay. I guess it's you who is going to the violin place with Scott. You should have a great time," she optimistically predicted. "Unless of course you've already been to one of those places, too?" Annie thoughtfully questioned, while pausing a moment from applying Jill's rouge.

"Oh, no. I've never been to any of those kinds of places before," Jill wistfully admitted. "This will be my first actual date. You know, me, just me, without being in some kind of a group," she annotated.

"Well, I only meant that maybe your parents might have taken you out to a nice place once in a while, that's all," Annie innocently explained.

"No, not my parents," Jill said adamantly. "'You mean spend money on a good time now, when we are trying to save for our retirement? That would be totally irresponsible. Every educated person should know that. That is exactly why we are paying for *your* education, so you don't make stupid mistakes like that. If we squandered our money on stupid things like going out to eat all the time, we'd only end up in the poor house. You don't wish that on us, do you?' And that's how it all would end," she mocked, more in a factual tone than anything else.

"So, tell me, what's the point of living, then? Just to retire and die?" Annie responded rhetorically. "How sad for them. But you know, you don't have to worry. There is a bright side to all this, because you will always have one thing that they will never have, and do you know what that is?" she specifically questioned.

"A lot of make up on my face?" Jill answered blankly.

"Nooo, wrong again, Jill. Like you said before, you have an acting career," Annie laughed. "You know, I could just picture your father sitting in his easy chair giving you that lecture. You were great, but not as great as you're gonna be tonight," she resolutely declared. "Well, I'm done now, and you look just fantabulous!" she decreed. "So let's get the rest of our things on and check one last time, just to see if anything was missed," she suggested.

Then no sooner than they had finished putting on their dresses and strapped their shoes around their ankles, there came the knock of inevitability upon their door.

"Go away! And don't come back for another fifteen minutes," Annie called out briskly, then shushing Jill with a grin while putting her index finger to her lips.

"Okay, we'll be back in fifteen minutes, then," came the answer from the other side of the door. The two girls waited in silence for a second or two, and once feeling assured that their dates had hence respectfully retreated for the time being, Annie escorted Jill back over to her dresser's mirror, one final time, to critique their allover appearances.

"You see how that patent leather belt matches both your shoes and jewelry, and accentuates your waist and hips?" Annie noted.

"Yeah, I sure do," Jill replied. "I also see how when you pulled it tight, my hemline went up a good three inches.

"Yeah, it sure did," Annie smiled wryly. "Oops, I guess I forgot all about those long legs of yours. Oh well, I don't think Scott will notice, do you?" she mischievously smirked.

"Of course he will. You know he will, you devious little harpy," replied Jill, feigning to be perturbed. "And you know something else? If you didn't look as good as you do right now, all made up like the Queen of Sheba, we'd already be having a pillow fight to the death for what you have done to me," she chided.

"Well, I'll have to take a rain check on that, you long cool woman in a black dress," remarked Annie in turn, only to continue with her fashion appraisal. "Now, can you see how even just a little dark blue eye shadow brings out the color in your eyes? And how the blush on your cheeks brings out the life in that little kid face of yours?" she rhetorically noted. "Not to mention those little rose colored lips of yours saying, 'Oh, kiss me, kiss me do, Scott,' ha, ha, ha! I can just see it now," she teased.

"Yeah, sure," replied Jill distantly, not hearing a single word that Annie was saying, for she was now wholly entranced with her new image in the mirror. Then, moments later, after the trance had all but worn off, she faint heartedly asked as if she was Dorothy arriving in Oz, "Where in the world did you learn all this stuff, Annie?"

"Someday I'll have to introduce you to Barbara," Annie said, now being interrupted by the returning knock at the door.

Dressed for evening in suit and tie, their escorts stood, vigilantly awaiting the formal soiree to begin. And then, appearing to be elegance incarnate, into the night the two couples left on their separate ways together, one desiring to enhance their already flowering relationship, and the other searching to discover a new relationship which predestinedly had eluded them both.

While Annie and Eugene were enjoying the Steak Diane for two, Scott had ordered the Veal Oscar for himself and the Coquille St. Jacques for Jill. Then, when Eugene and Annie were being entertained by a troupe of bolero, tango, and flamenco dancers, Scott cajoled Jill onto the dance floor for a waltz to Ludwig van Beethoven's "Concierto de Violin." Finally, while Annie allowed Eugene to drive her car back over the Rickenbacker Causeway for an intimate moment on the beach at Crandon Park, Scott had returned with Jill to the resort where, they too, went for a walk upon the beach.

"I know you are aware that I roomed with Annie for two years, and because I know her very well, I figure that you know from Gene that I have never been out on a date before," Jill informed Scott, while meandering along the beach to the gentle lapping of the waves upon its shoreline.

"Yeah, it was mentioned," Scott replied indifferently. "I think that the whole social importance of quote, 'having a date,' is highly overrated. I think that people should do what they want to do, and not because it's socially acceptable, or just the thing to do, but because they choose to do it, or in your case, maybe not to.

"What anyone does, I believe, is totally of their own making, and whatever decisions they make are theirs," he continued. After all, we all have to live with our own decisions, so what is the point of listening to other people's social comments? That's what I have to say," he candidly offered.

"Well, the truth is, Scott, I never really had any of those decisions to make. No one even ever asked me out to make them," Jill frankly admitted.

"Now, I don't believe that," challenged Scott, halting her forward movement by taking her arm in hand and turning her to face him straight on. "No, you always had choices, Jill," he said. "You could have proclaimed yourself as a free love child if you wanted to, and believe me, no young guy turns it down. So you didn't conform, so what, so you're different. That is why I like you, don't you understand that?" he posed compassionately, looking fetchingly into her eyes. "You know you are a beautiful girl, don't you?" he then said.

Suddenly, Jill had become completely overwhelmed. And stunned with the gravity of an admonition that she had never expected to hear, she just stood there, dazed before him, blank as a new tablet that was yearning for its first inscription to be impressed upon it. And impress her he did, as he put his left hand behind her back, leaned forward, and gently placed that fatal kiss of rapture precisely on her lips.

Oh God help my soul, she prayed as her knees gave way beneath her.

Then, when Scott had tightened his grip around her waist, and she had fallen listless within his arms, instantly he knew, she was the one. His tawdry days of loneliness had finally come to end, as now he prayed in kind, *I hope my past will be forgiven.*

For the next few days, the four of them were on top of the world as the sun shone bright, the Frisbees flew high, and their spirits flew even higher above the sands of time. "Live on, live on," Mother Nature had called out to them in their final days of innocence. "Live on, live on!" she cheered, before the crushing days of self-reliance and responsibility were to be thrust upon them. And in hearing this, they did their best to comply.

And so pell-mell they all went into hell
With righteous good intentions
We watched them leave and wished them well
As products of our own invention

And so as well, like farmers in the dell
We stay behind, our fates have been decided
We watch them leave, still feeling compelled
To have their needs provided

And so, we wait a spell, to listen to the bell
That rings, anticipating their return
We watched them leave and bid farewell
To the very soul of our concerns

To plant a seed and watch it grow
Is the greatest joy that one can know

And when the train left the station you could hear the whistle blow five hundred miles as it wrenched out its cry and said its goodbyes to the innocence of youth. Onward the Christian soldiers went. Onward they went to find their destiny. Onward they went to catch the waving banner of their souls, still fluttering elusively before them in the wind.

www.ingramcontent.com/pod-product-compliance
Lightning Source LLC
Chambersburg PA
CBHW020245030726
47499CB00001B/62